Rem

C000067503

By Randi Darren

Dedicated:
To those who know me

Books by William D. Arand-

The Selfless Hero Trilogy:
Otherlife Dreams
Otherlife Nightmares
Otherlife Awakenings
Omnibus Edition(All Three)

Super Sales on Super Heroes Trilogy:
Super Sales on Super Heroes 1
Super Sales on Super Heroes 2
Super Sales on Super Heroes 3
Omnibus Edition(All Three)

Dungeon Deposed Trilogy:
Dungeon Deposed
Dungeon Deposed 2
Dungeon Deposed 3
Omnibus Edition(All Three)

Swing Shift Trilogy:
Swing Shift
Swing Shift 2
Swing Shift 3 (To be release 2020)

Books by Randi Darren-

Wild Wastes Trilogy:
Wild Wastes
Wild Wastes: Eastern Expansion
Wild Wastes: Southern Storm
Omnibus Edition(All Three)

Fostering Faust Trilogy:
Fostering Faust
Fostering Faust 2
Fostering Faust 3
Omnibus Edition(All Three)

Remnant Trilogy:

Remnant
Remnant 3 (To be released 2020)

Incubus Inc. Trilogy:

Incubus Inc
Incubus Inc 2 (To be released 2019)
Incubus Inc 3 (To be released 2020)

Books in the VeilVerse-

Cultivating Chaos: By William D. Arand
Asgard Awakening: By Blaise Corvin

One

Steve sighed and shook his head, staring out at the vast, empty plain before him.

"The fuck did I agree to this?" he muttered. "I should have just… stayed on the farm and taken Gwen up on her offer.

"I could be playing 'make the Siren sing,' but noooo, I decided I wanted to take my stupid ass out to work some more."

"Because it's what we should do."

Turning to look at the speaker, Steve found Ina standing nearby.

Dressed out in light-leather armor and without a weapon, she looked mildly out of place.

Mostly because she was extremely easy on the eyes and had a figure that didn't belong on a farm. She had short blond hair the color of wheat and blue eyes that, for whatever reason, hit the right spots in Steve's head.

Standing next to her were Jaina and Kassandra.

"It's true. Very, very true," Jaina said. "As much, much land as we can take."

The small Kobold woman was an interesting-looking creature. Her bust was on par with Ina's, but she was considerably smaller in stature. It made her look oddly top heavy. Especially given that she often ran on all fours.

She was covered in almost invisibly short brown fur from head to toe, with black accents here and there. The only different-colored spot was her belly, which was a large white oval.

Her nose and ears were very beastlike. She was somewhat removed from humanity as far as her species went.

Yet her very blue eyes held the spark of life and intelligence. She was no different than Steve. At least, to Steve she wasn't any different.

Kassandra the Lamia rose above both the other two women.

Dark-blond hair peeked out from under her bronze helmet. Her bright-green reptilian eyes moved across the horizon in front of them.

Ina was definitely pretty, but Kassandra was stunning.

With all her armor, there wasn't much to be seen of her shape, but Steve knew she wasn't unfortunate.

From her armored hip plates and down, her scaled snake tail wound itself around and under her.

"Well? You gonna chime in?" Steve asked.

"No," Kassandra said, looking down at him. A smile flitted across her face. "Because I like this idea. It's us four alone out in the wilderness again. I enjoyed our time together. We worked well with one another."

"Shelly's joining us in a day or two," Jaina said.

"I don't mind her; she's fine," Kassandra said. "She's a fighter even though she doesn't look it. I don't think for a minute she wouldn't pick up a weapon and defend herself or others."

Steve blew out a huff and looked back out in front of him.

Nikki had digested everything he'd told her about what he'd seen at the wall. What he'd learned of, and from, the citadel commander.

That even the grass and trees were becoming sick with the Creep.

Her thought in the end for all of that was that they were better off enclosing as much land as they could for the future.

Because once the soil itself was tainted, it would be all the more difficult to turn it to their purposes later.

"Nikki was right," Ina said confidently. "While I'll miss the comforts of our home, we need to be able to provide for our children. And that means more land. Land for the farm.

"Land for Nia and her eventual brothers and sisters."

Clicking his tongue at that, Steve brought his shovel down into the grass with a thump.

"Yeah," he said. "I just don't like it. Feel like with this much more space to incorporate, we're asking for more bandit problems. Like those idiots who stole Nikki."

"No, no," Jaina said. "In taking this land, it's to prevent stuff like that. Or, or, to prevent other cities from bothering us. So we don't have a repeat of Filch and what happened to Xivin."

Steve didn't get Jaina's logic, but then she wasn't Human.

Ina walked by with her hands on top of her head. She looked thoughtful.

"I suppose. Though with what happened at the wall, does it lift the temporary quarantine? In the end, the whole wall came down and blocked the way through. Right? You said it looked like it was going into our neighbor's lands."

Steve grunted as he began to methodically work his shovel to prepare the land they were standing on right now. They'd need to be able to survive at a temporary outpost here as they worked.

That meant getting some defenses and a place to sleep first.

"Steve?" Ina asked, turning to face him.

He closed his eyes for a second, not wanting to think about the wall. All he could think of was the citadel commander who had sabotaged a peer. It had left a strange anger in Steve which he didn't really understand.

Not to mention, Lucia had almost died there protecting him.

"Yeah," he said. "Looks like I knocked it down just right. We'll see. Doesn't change that the Creep is still here in Lamals. Was there last night. So were the monsters."

"Pity that little girl didn't survive her witch ceremony last night," Jaina said. "She was cute. Cute, cute for a little Human girl."

It was a never-ending train of subjects Steve didn't want to talk about, it seemed. They'd found a little girl at the walls this morning, and Steve had tried to resurrect her in the same way he had Jaina and Ina.

"Not everyone seems to be strong enough to survive dying and coming back to life," he said.

"Alright. Come on, Jaina. Let's go see if we can start raising up some rock," Ina said. "Maybe all that practice will finally pay off."

Ina turned and began walking away toward the west.

"Oh, yes, yes. That'd be good, wouldn't it?" Jaina said, moving after Ina.

"I'd say so," Ina said. "Now, let's try with you lifting, and I'll see about forming it into a wall."

"Okay!" Jaina said as she fell in line with Ina.

"They work well together," Kassandra said. "Think they can do it?"

"Can, can't—doesn't matter," Steve said as he moved over and dug another spot out with his shovel. "Regardless, we'll still be here for a while. Don't like being away from home. Hate it."

"Think of it this way," Kassandra said, drawing closer to him. "Once we build this outpost, we'll have lots of room for our family. It even runs right over the road, so we can include a gate and gate house. We'll be able to protect ourselves, the road to Filch, and everyone we care about."

"I don't care about Filch," Steve muttered.

"Yes, you do. You care about Shelly and Xivin, don't you?" Kassandra asked. "In protecting Filch, you protect them and what they care about."

Growling, Steve stood up from his work and glared at Kassandra. He really didn't want to be told what he cared about right now.

She smiled at him and leaned in close, coming down to his height.

"Punish me a little tonight?" she asked, her tone warm and smooth.

Ugh. She's baiting me.

"Little snake." Steve grinned at her and held up a hand. "Keep pushing my buttons and I'll punish you a bit more than you want."

"Maybe I want that," Kassandra said, inching ever closer to him. "And besides, you're just angry because you know I'm right but you hate being forced into things. And you feel like Nikki forced you into this. At least a little bit."

Steve glowered at her. He didn't know how to respond.

Instead, he grabbed her breast plate, pulled her close, and kissed her.

Several seconds passed before he released her and patted her on the shoulder.

"You're right," he admitted. "But by the time I see her next, I'll have forgiven her. I may be just an angry brute, but I'm not stupid.

"Besides, everyone agreed with Nikki. Hard to say no at that point."

Kassandra was watching him with something akin to a predatory stare.

It reminded him of Chessa.

Feeling an ache in his chest, Steve turned back to his work.

He missed Chessa and regretted her death, but he didn't feel it as keenly as Jaina had. Nor did he feel her loss as he imagined he should.

There were times he felt like something was wrong with him for not feeling her loss more deeply.

But he couldn't pinpoint it. Nor could he attribute it to anything other than himself. Especially since Jaina and the others had expressed sincere grief.

Then again, they were over it in a day or three. I still feel it, and they seemed to have moved on completely.

I wonder if this is part of that strange mind-control thing again. In fact... I wonder if it's changed.

"Little snake, I want to put hundreds of kids in you, till you drown in them. Till our children literally crush you with their weight," Steve said as he worked his shovel through the dirt. "You good with that? Can I try right now?"

"Of course. I have to have children to make sure I provide more soldiers to fight the Creep. That's my duty," Kassandra said immediately, and in that same dead tone.

"Even if it was thousands of eggs? If I wanted you pregnant forever after?" Steve asked, deciding to press.

"Yes, please. I have to have children to make sure I provide more soldiers to fight the Creep. That's my duty. Especially now that you're my man. I'm a failure because I haven't become pregnant," she said.

Now that's odd. No one's ever mentioned anything like that before.

Had the same tone, too.

Need to be careful.

Maybe there's something else in there for them if they don't have children.

"Oh? You shouldn't feel like a failure. It isn't as if you're guaranteed to get pregnant from having sex. It's kinda random, ya know?" Steve said.

Pausing in his work, Steve lifted his head up to meet Kassandra's eyes directly.

"I'm... I..." Kassandra's voice fell off, unable to break away from his gaze.

"My little snake, you're not a failure. If you say that again, I'll be cross," Steve said.

"I understand," Kassandra said, though there was a strange undercurrent in her voice. "I'm not a failure."

"No. You're not. Now watch over me. I need to get this field done so we have something to eat."

***

Dropping onto the top of a water barrel, Steve let out a sigh. He'd been digging for most of the day. The field was planted, and he'd immediately followed it with a very small moat.

Right now, it was really just a deep trench. It'd serve well enough for the time being. That was a temporary solution with a timer on it.

If the zombies showed up in any number, they could possibly make a pile of their bodies and climb up.

It was one of the reasons Shelly, once named Rachele, was coming in a day or two. She'd be bringing a wagon full of water barrels and taking the wagon they'd brought with them back.

Looking to the west, he could see a wall of stone. It wasn't very large, but it was there.

Which means it's possible for the Creep Witches to replace the logs with actual stone for a longer-term solution.

"I'm going to have to send them back to the farm to start working on replacing the palisade," Steve said.

"They won't care for that," Kassandra said.

"Nope. Not really a concern, though. They'll do it because that's what needs to be done," Steve said.

"I think they'll argue your safety is paramount," Kassandra countered. "Which Nikki would agree with."

Steve frowned, his brows drawing together. He caught the underlying implication there.

Sending them back would simply prompt Nikki to send someone else in their place.

Probably... Lucia and Misty? Misty's busy working on getting the moat around Filch finalized, and Lucia's been making bows and arrows nonstop.

"You're right," Steve mumbled. Ina and Jaina were walking back toward Steve even now. They looked worn, but not exhausted.

"Will we be sleeping under the stars tonight?" Kassandra asked.

Steve looked at the sun and found it was already past noon. He figured they had six hours of daylight left.

"Yeah," he said. "I can probably knock down a bunch of trees in that grove to the east and start getting them ready. Won't have a cabin today, though. Maybe tomorrow. After I build one, the second one should be much easier. That could just be my ego talking, but—"

"There's someone coming," Kassandra said, interrupting him. "A number of someones."

Standing up immediately, Steve started walking toward the wagon. He didn't care who it was—he wasn't about to welcome anyone on his land, in his territory, or in his presence without his weapon in hand.

"It's… two groups of someones," Kassandra said. "They're coming from different angles, but both are heading this way. I don't think they're aware of each other."

"How is that even possible?" Steve groused. "We've seen no one. At all. We told no one we were coming here."

"I think you're forgetting just how wild and varied life is. The many species that exist," Kassandra said. "It's very possible there were those watching us that we did not see. Could not see."

"I wanna argue, but clearly I can't since they're coming this way. Kinda lends credence to your point," Steve said.

"Yes. They're too far to get a hard count but… there are at least forty of them in total between both sides," Kassandra said.

"Great," Steve muttered. Turning to where Ina and Jaina were leisurely walking his way, he lifted his hand and waved at them. "Need them to hurry up and get over here to drink some water and rest. They're gonna be earning their keep, I think. One on one, I can murder people. A group? Need my Creep Witches."

"You underestimate yourself," Kassandra murmured.

Jaina must have picked up on Steve's need because she made a quick hand gesture at Ina. Then she dropped to all fours and started running toward Steve in her animalistic way.

Ina started moving at a jog, though she wasn't built for such a thing. She'd fight and battle with others, but there was no mistaking her distaste for running or moving quickly.

After coming to a grass-tearing sliding stop, Jaina bounced up on two feet.

"What is it, husband?" she asked.

"People coming this way, and I really need you and Ina here, resting and recuperating," Steve said. "Start drinking water and grab a snack."

"Others?" Jaina head turned around in a full circle while her ears swiveled this way and that.

Kassandra held up a hand and pointed to one point, then another.

Steve couldn't see what they were looking at, to be honest. His eyesight was very Human.

Jaina nodded as she peered off in the direction Kassandra had indicated. Then she looked a bit further to the northeast, her tail rather still behind her. "I see both groups. They're carrying weapons."

Growling, Steve picked up his axe and grabbed his shield. He buckled the shield on and gave his axe a quick spin with his wrist.

When he'd first donned it as a weapon, it had felt uncomfortable.

Unwieldy.

Now it felt normal, like an extension of his arm. Mismatched balance and ugly form.

Just like him.

"Hate running," Ina said, coming to a walk nearby. "Hate it so much. Makes everything hurt."

"Enemies," Jaina said, still looking out into the distance.

"Oh," Ina said. Then she sighed and nodded her head. She moved over to the open water barrel, grabbed the mug that was dangling from the edge, and began drinking deeply. After finishing off the contents in one go, she blew out a breath. "Get the sand?"

"Yes, yes. I will." Jaina broke her eyes from the distant people and moved off to the wagon.

"Sand?" Steve asked, coming to stand next to Kassandra.

"The black sand left over from the zombies," Ina said. "We've been experimenting with it. It makes spells more powerful. Goes really quick, though."

"Huh. Alright," Steve said, thinking.

"Misty started collecting it this morning. She said there was quite a bit of it at the bottom of her waters," Ina explained. "I may not be built for… physical things and war, but I'm doing my best with all of this."

"You're doing amazingly, Ina." Steve gave her a small smile.

The young woman with the confidence issue was quite dead, it seemed.

In her place was a very strong woman with a bright mind.

"When we're done with these people, we're having sex. And then again later, probably," Ina stated. "And you're not going to say no."

She was incredibly sexually active, beyond the definition of forward. Ina consistently and often took Steve, whether he was in the mood or she had to work him up to it.

Steve stood there without responding to her in any way.

He'd found that sometimes, if he ignored her, she'd forget. Or her sex drive might reverse itself if given some time.

Responding at all gave her something to latch on to and work with.

"I think they just saw each other," Jaina said, walking up and holding a small pouch out to Ina. "They're moving toward one another now and are no longer concerned with us at all."

"I think I like that even less," Steve muttered. "Let's… see if we can't get closer to see what's going on before it happens. If they want to make this easy and group up so you two can smoke 'em with a wave of fire, great."

"I will lead the way," Kassandra said, moving out in front. "Move out to the side, Jaina. Wait for my whistle to engage. You will be our flanker. Do as Steve suggested and wipe them out with a flame wave."

"Yes, yes. I'm going," Jaina said.

She dropped down to all fours, then brushed up against Steve and rubbed herself bodily against him before she ran off, keeping low to the ground.

Way too much like a dog. Way too much.

Two

Moving at a fast walk, Steve wasn't really sure how he felt about all this. He wanted these people away from his family and the land he viewed as theirs.

If he had to kill every single one of them to do that, he would.

Without regret.

This was a dog-eat-dog world, and there wasn't anything anyone could say to convince him otherwise. Especially since he'd already lost people he cared about.

Leathers and feathers, baby, it's Mad Ma... Mad... God damnit, Shitty Steve.

This is becoming tiresome.

Kassandra and Ina were matching him pace for pace on his left, Ina between him and the Lamia. She was the most likely to meet a bad end if someone got close enough to her, but she was also the most dangerous to the enemy if they didn't close on her.

Steve knew he was no whirlwind of violence with sword and pistol.

He was a brute with an axe whose imagination didn't go very far at all. He wasn't a deep thinker, a strategist, or a politician.

Carrying out orders in a brutal, intelligent, direct manner was what he did.

Out ahead of him, he could finally see the two groups. They were little more than smears of dark brown moving towards one another, but at least he could finally recognize that they weren't part of the horizon.

"What's in that lovely soldier's mind of yours, my little snake?" Steve asked.

"We get close enough to see what's going on and proceed no further," Kassandra explained. "If we see an opportunity to attack both sides, then we do it.

"They'll have items on them we could easily benefit from having."

"I like it," Steve said. The plan fit his mercenary mentality.

The conversation fell off a cliff with that statement, and no one said anything further.

By the time Steve could finally discern people and what they were doing, he found they were in the process of killing each other.

They all looked to be wearing the same type of clothes, both in fabric and quality.

And the weapons they were using looked as if they'd been tools not long ago. Strange swords that probably hadn't been forged by a weaponsmith. Sickles that had no business being in a fight. And axes much like Steve's were being swung like they were two-headed battle axes.

"They look like peasants," Kassandra murmured. "Not one of them has any training. In fact, I think they've forgotten entirely about us."

"Let's capture them," Steve said. "We could use some Creep bait or Creep Witches. Or we let them get turned and burn them down for black dust. You said it was useful, Ina?"

"Very useful," Ina confirmed.

"Alright. I'm going to go find Jaina and work with her from that side. Our goal is to capture them if possible," Kassandra said, then moved off. She was swift, low to the ground, and gone.

"Is this normal?" Steve asked.

"What?" Ina responded, sounding confused.

"Never mind." Steve realized his question was actually rather stupid.

Of course, this isn't normal. This was a functioning country not long ago. Death may have always come easy and cheap here, but it wasn't always a full-out murder pit of awful.

But… if that's true… why did everyone resort to absolute anarchy so quickly and easily?

In fact… even Nikki is absolutely ruthless when she decides it's worthwhile. Though she'll tend towards forgiveness and optimism if she can.

Gwen is the softest heart, but I think she'd butcher someone if it came down to it.

And that doesn't even include when Nia comes into the equation. Heaven protect anyone who crosses Gwen when it comes to Nia.

"I'm going to put up walls of flame around them," Ina said. "That should box them in and force them to face us. It might just be enough to intimidate them into surrendering."

Steve nodded as he watched a pretty woman smash an axe down into a beautiful woman's head. Blood splashed all over her well-endowed chest.

It is... absolutely strange to watch really pretty people murder one another.

Wouldn't this mean most of these women had mothers who paid to have them beautified in a city?

That means they had a little wealth, right?

This whole world is so strange.

"I think it's about time. The survivors on both sides seem to be eyeing the people on the ground. The wounded would work just as well as the living for us," Ina said.

"Right," Steve said, then started forward at a trot. Brining his axe up onto his shoulder, he ran straight for the biggest woman he could see.

Before he reached his target, a wall of purple flame rose up from the ground and surrounded the group of people from two sides.

Everyone who had just been brawling was startled out of their mad scrum. Heads turned to find Steve running at them.

As if Ina were a prophet, many women simply threw their weapons down and then held up their hands.

Steve didn't stop. He kept running straight at his target. She was a rather large, broad-shouldered woman. The closer he got, the bigger she seemed.

"Surrender!" he screamed at the top of his lungs.

His shout was echoed by Jaina and Kassandra as they rushed forward from a different angle off to his right.

A few more women threw their weapons down after realizing they were being engaged by an unknown force.

The big one didn't, though. She looked grimly at Steve, her hands clutching her axe.

Much like every other woman he saw in this messed up world, she was pretty. With light-brown eyes and dark-brown hair.

Her big frame let her sport an impressive bust as well.

"Put it down, big girl, or I'm gonna crack your head open," Steve said, coming to a stop six feet away from her.

She was the only one with a weapon now.

"No, I'm leaving," she said.

"You're not. You're going to be my prisoner. Or a corpse," Steve said.

"What kind of—"

Steve was done talking. He started forward toward the woman. She'd had her chance to surrender, and he wasn't about to bother with her further.

Grunting, the woman brought her axe around in a wide swing. Her arm length gave her an impressive reach. She could easily keep Steve at bay with it.

Except he didn't care one whit about her attack.

No matter how strong she was, she was nothing compared to the Basilisk and the Troll he'd killed.

Deciding to sacrifice his shield—since he had several more and could easily make more—Steve used it to swat at the axe.

With a crash and a splintering noise, the shield broke at the midpoint. It had absorbed the woman's full attack.

"I surrender, I surr—"

The woman's voice was cut off as Steve brought his axe down into the top of her head.

Which promptly exploded into a pulpy mess that spewed blood, bone, and brains in every direction.

"Should have surrendered before you attacked me," Steve said, spitting out some of the woman's blood that had trickled down into his mouth. "Anyone else wanna try their hand at me?"

The surviving nine women shook their heads as they stood there with their hands up.

"Then get the fuck over there." Steve pointed to Kassandra and Jaina with his axe. "Hand over any weapons on your person, get on your knees, and let them tie you up. Or I just fucking make your head axe-plode. Your choice."

The twitching and blood-fountaining corpse at his feet decided this was a great moment to let loose a particularly strong stream of blood. It shot high up in the air in a red arc.

Women who'd been lying down scrambled to their feet, and those who were already up hustled over. They all practically tripped over themselves to get to Jaina and Kassandra.

"Alright, let's figure out who's wounded on the ground, who we can keep, and who's worm food," Steve said as he worked at stripping the woman he'd just killed of her clothes and possessions.

He pulled at one of her boots, hopeful they might fit him. His own boots were starting to look rather worn, and hers seemed in much better condition.

***

Having made a wagon, Steve was able to carry a good number of logs back with him each trip.

That alone was making him feel like he would get this done much quicker than he'd originally thought.

Moving across the temporary stone bridge Jaina had put in just for him, Steve kept trudging along.

Up ahead, Kassandra was still grilling their prisoners for information. Jaina was busily using Steve's hoe on the fields he'd dug up, and Ina was digging out the remainder of the trench around the area they'd be living in.

They could use any of his tools, provided he gave it to them and they had the strength and will to use it.

Looking at his log pile, Steve turned his wagon as it cleared the bridge and made his way over.

He moved the logs from his wagon to the pile, then started pulling the wagon around to head back out to get more trees.

"Steve, I need a minute of your time," Kassandra said from where she stood.

Fourteen heads turned to face him at the same time. His prisoners had nowhere else to be stored right now. There were four more nearby with wounds that prevented them from moving.

The rest of the dead and dying had been dumped into the ditch.

Hopefully, they'd return as zombies and could be doused.

"Right," Steve grumbled. Not stopping, he pulled his wagon out and over the bridge. Only then did he turn back around and come over to Kassandra. He didn't want to forget what he was doing next, and leaving the wagon there would be a great reminder.

"Okay, I'm here. What's up?" Steve asked. He turned to look down at the upturned faces of his prisoners.

They ranged the entire gamut of possibility. From black hair to blond, brown eyes to green, and every body type from full figured and overflowing to athletic and toned.

And a number looked very non-Human.

"There's a series of villages not far from here, out to the west, northwest, and north. There are perhaps nine of them. These two groups are from opposing villages," Kassandra said. "They're not from the biggest villages, either. Perhaps middle-sized is the best I can figure."

"Alright, any of them explain how they found us?" Steve asked. "Am I giving someone a reward?"

Kassandra opened her mouth to reply, but was interrupted.

"I found you!" one of the women immediately said. "I was scouting around, and I found your wagon trail! I came back and told Missy, and we came immediately!"

"Great. She gets a prize of some sort," Steve said, indicating the woman who'd spoken. He didn't bother to really look at her or pay her any attention. "And the other group?"

Steve got no answer as he looked around from woman to woman, and then the wounded ones.

"No one knows?" he asked.

"We were… just following their group," offered one of the women who'd been in the more numerous party. "We didn't notice your little setup until their group started speeding up. Then we moved to engage them. We just wanted their stuff."

"Uh huh," Steve said. "Think we should send one of the girls back to cover the tracks?"

"Yes," Kassandra said with a nod. "I wanted to do that, but I didn't feel right ordering Ina or Jaina around."

Steve nodded at that.

This world had a matriarchy at the top, and it all rolled up to whoever the "lead wife" was, as far as he could tell.

Nikki was a fairly benevolent leader who didn't force anything on anyone else.

Still doesn't make sense.

Sending all the men to the front as soon as they have enough children doesn't… add up.

Does it?

I feel like there's something inherently wrong with everything.

"Right." Steve looked out at where Jaina was. "Jaina!"

The small Kobold turned to face him from where she was working.

Steve waved his hand at her to come over.

Jaina came over with a smile, the hoe she'd been using resting on her shoulders.

"Yes, husband?" she asked.

"Need you to double back the way we came and obscure the wagon trail we left behind us," Steve said. "After that, could you go clean up the battlefield and the trails those two groups made?"

"Of course!" Jaina said with a beaming smile. "Yes, yes. I can do that very, very well."

"Great. Make sure you're back before sunset. If you're back before the sun touches the horizon, I'll give you a really good belly rub."

"Yes, yes!" Jaina said, then handed the hoe to Kassandra. She stepped in close to Steve and kissed him briefly, and then she was off in a flash. Running on all fours and sending grass up behind her.

"You spoil her," Kassandra murmured.

"She deserves to be spoiled," Steve said with a shake of his head. "She's had a hard life so far."

Steve had a deep suspicion that Jaina wasn't altogether right in the head given what'd happened to her. That she was emotionally fragile or broken.

"There, that's that then," Steve said. "Anything else?"

"I think one of the wounded isn't going to survive the night," Kassandra said.

"Okay. Dump her in the trench once she's dead. If sunset comes and she hasn't died yet... make it quick for her and then dump her." Steve shrugged. These people were nothing but resources to him. "Make sure it doesn't destroy her body. Suffocate her or something."

"I understand. I'll make sure it happens. What do we do with them?" Kassandra indicated the bound women who were all kneeling next to them. "Should I make their deaths quick as well?"

There was a sudden gaggle of pleas, offers, and begging from all the women.

"Shut up!" Steve shouted at them, and they immediately quieted.

"No. Don't kill them," Steve said, glaring at them. "They all criminals?"

"Yes. Every single one of them is a murderer," Kassandra said.

"Any of them married?" Steve asked.

"No. Apparently they send out the single women to fight to prove themselves," Kassandra said.

"I'll bed you!" called a beautiful woman with pitch-black hair, bright green eyes, and an amazing body. She was dressed in black leather and had incredibly pale skin. Pale to the point of looking sickly. "I'll do anything you want me to!"

Suddenly all of the women were offering the same thing.

Steve held up a hand, very close to losing his patience and killing someone. These weren't people to him. They were criminals, resources—things to be used and discarded.

Respect for life had no place here.

"I have enough wives—"

"You can use me as you wish, and I won't be your wife!" said the same green-eyed, dark-haired beauty.

Once more, everyone started agreeing with her, though they weren't as loud this time. They apparently weren't as eager for that end, but they were willing.

"I have enough wives. That means I have more than enough women," Steve said. "For now, you live. You'll work my farm and do as I tell you. Anything beyond that is a question mark.

"If you do anything that even makes me think you're going to be a problem, I'll just kill you. You're criminals. By the laws of Lamals, you should be executed outright."

Actually, that's strange. I don't have a murderer tag. I've killed people.

In fact, what does that even look like?

Looking at the green-eyed woman who was trying to save herself, Steve tried to get some insight into her.

Nancy Abellis
Wight
Father: deceased
Mother: living
Murderer- killed someone illegally
Depraved Predator- lives on the suffering of others
Merciful- has spared others for no reason

"I know," Nancy said, apparently having caught Steve checking her information. "I only feed passively, though. I mean it! I don't... I don't cause suffering. There's enough going around that I don't have to do anything to anyone."

"You spared people?" Steve closed the window without bothering to hide that he'd been looking.

"They... they were harmless. There was no reason to kill them," Nancy said. "I'd already killed their leader and they were just... they had nothing. I let them go."

"What? You said you got that for letting travelers go through," said another woman.

"I lied—what of it? There was no reason to kill them, and I lied to protect myself after letting them go." Nancy lifted her chin up. Apparently she wasn't going to back down from the idea that she wasn't in the wrong.

"Right. Don't care." Steve waved a hand at all of them. "Get Ina to make some massive stone weights. Put 'em on a chain gang. They can work the fields together and be their own anchor. I'm going to go cut down more trees."

"I'll be good for you," Nancy called after him. "I can get people to do what you want if I use my abilities! I could make everyone else here work without having to use chains!

"Make me the prison warder!"

Steve stopped at that. If he could use Nancy in the way she suggested, it'd work out rather well.

"Fine," Steve said without turning around. "Shackle Nancy down separately from the rest. We'll see how she does with them shackled for a while. Once the walls go up, we'll let her try being the warder."

"Need trees."

Grabbing his wagon, Steve set off for the wooded area. He needed to get back to work.

Need to tell Ina.

He turned the wagon and headed over to where Ina had been working last. Spotting her, he pushed his wagon up to the side where she was digging away.

"Hey there," he said as he came to a stop.

"Oh, hello. Look at that, you're just the right height. How about you sit down on the edge right there and see if I can't get you warmed up for me?" Ina said, reaching up to pat the edge of the trench.

Steve smirked at that, and then he instead leaned down into the trench and kissed Ina.

"Later," he said as he pulled away. "Kassandra is going to ask you to make some things for our prisoners. I gave her the idea."

"Mm. Okay," Ina said, then grabbed him by the head and jerked him into the trench. "Never mind about sitting on the edge, we're going to do it right here in the trench. Don't mind the dirt; I was going to take a bath anyway in one of the barrels before you dumped it in. You can take one with me."

Ina was already working at his belt buckle as he lay there.

He'd forgotten the cardinal rule with Ina.

Don't respond to her when she talks about sex.

Three

Scratching at his cheek, Steve stared down at the knee-deep water below him. It wasn't deep enough to have made Creep Witches, unfortunately.

They'd simply become corpses and remained there.

It was unfortunate, but in the same breath, he wouldn't have had a way to control them if he'd made them Creep Witches.

At least he'd learned something.

To make a Creep Witch, they have to be completely submerged.

Steve nodded, then stood up and stretched out his back.

Last night had been different. He'd ended up spending it with Jaina after she'd gotten back. Kassandra had been bashful and declined his offer. Apparently, it was too much for her that there were so many unwed women nearby.

It wasn't too much for Jaina.

Ever since their frank discussion outside of Filch, she'd never turned him away, not for any reason.

Even if it was in front of a dozen other people, she'd welcomed him eagerly to couple with her.

Pushing his fists into his back, he got a satisfying crack, and then he bent at the waist in the other direction.

"That was a good one," Steve muttered. Grabbing his wagon, he left the corpses and slowly melting Creeps in the water. He had more trees to fell. Both for the cabin and the eventual palisade.

"Jaina and Ina will be working on the western wall. Adding stone again," Kassandra said as she slid up to him. It was always interesting to watch her propel herself along.

"Pity I can't hook you up to a wagon. I bet you could pull a lot more than I can," Steve said.

"I... sincerely doubt that. You're incredibly strong, Steve," Kassandra said. "Though I do plan on joining you today. Our pet project will be starting, after all. It'll be a good opportunity to see what she does."

"You're not afraid of her running? Or trying to help the others run?" Steve dragged his wagon along behind him as he walked to the trees.

"No. Jaina buried a spell wall a little way out from the camp," Kassandra said. "If any of them cross it, they'll… ah, she said 'big, big boom,' so I assume they'll explode."

"Hmm. Alright," Steve said. "Think they'll try?"

"No, I think Nancy is looking for a safe place to land," Kassandra said. "Though I think they might try to overpower her, or one might break free on their own. She'll need to be able to handle herself if she wants to be a taskmaster. I'm not sure on her motives. She's… different."

Steve felt a mite squeamish at what he was doing to the people he'd taken prisoner.

"By law, they'll be put to death in any city they visit forever going forward," Kassandra. "Murder isn't a forgivable crime. While mating and having children with a Human is definitely a problem, it doesn't merit an instantaneous death sentence. Murder does.

"You could always execute them and dump their bodies without anyone caring. You'd actually receive prestige for it. I'm sure you already did for killing the big one, in fact. Putting them to work rather than killing them is a mercy."

Steve only grunted at that. He wasn't about to debate the laws of the land with an inhabitant. As far as he could tell, he didn't belong here. Everything always felt strange and slightly off beat to him.

"I'd like to go hunting for their villages later. It sounds as if their entire population is flagged appropriately for prestige gains. If we were to round them all up, we'd have a good chance to become nationally acclaimed by executing them," Kassandra said. "So long as we did it as a group, we'd all get credit. It'd be very good for us."

"You want to… go bounty hunting?" Steve asked, trudging along. It was an odd idea, but he wasn't against it. If they were singled out for death, who was he to say no to a reward for doing the work?

"I do. Even as deeply as we've fallen into religious anathema, we've done nothing that would garner us a death sentence," Kassandra said. "As much as everyone would make out Lamals to be a puppet nation for the priests, we do have our own laws."

"Mm. Definitely something to consider," Steve admitted. It had an appeal to him he couldn't deny. "What exactly would prestige do for us?"

"Well, with enough of it, you could claim hero status. You could easily petition for anything from the nation. Become a mayor, counselor, ambassador — any position someone can hold without being born to it," Kassandra explained.

"Like a citadel commander?" Steve asked.

"That'd be one open position, certainly," Kassandra said. "Especially with a hero title. It would be hard for anyone to disregard that."

I like this idea much more now. If we had enough prestige, we could challenge Linne Lynn for the citadel. And from there… from there I could wage a war for humanity.

For everyone in the pig pens. Male and female alike.

Taking it a step further… couldn't I change some policies? Couldn't I make this place better?

Nikki made it sound like this nation was one step away from being destroyed by their neighbors. Could I go outside for assistance? Could I stage a coup?

Would I want to?

"My little snake, I want to ask you a question. One that you can't discuss with anyone else," Steve said.

Kassandra turned her eyes his way, looking at him with undisguised curiosity.

"Can you swear that?" Steve asked, giving her a sidelong glance.

"Of course. I'm your little snake, and I swear to tell no one of what you're about to speak," Kassandra said.

"You remember that I named Linne, right?" Steve asked.

"Yes. She violated an oath to you and was threatening you accordingly. You named her as is your right as a citizen," Kassandra said.

"I can name anyone anything at any time," Steve said. He'd been testing it out on corpses, Creeps, and critters. Anything he could see and was close enough to, he could title or name.

"You can… you can what?" Kassandra asked.

"I can title or name anything I want. Here, watch." Steve turned to look at Kassandra fully. He put his entire attention on her. "I name you Little Snake the Punished."

Kassandra practically flinched away from something in front of her.

"My... my name is now Little Snake the Punished. Kassandra is... it's just a nickname," she said, her eyes scanning back and forth across the screen only she could see.

"I remove my formal naming," Steve commanded, doing the same thing as earlier.

"It's gone," Kassandra whispered.

"Yeah. In other words, if I wanted to name you Head Bedwarmer, that'd be your name and that'd be the end of it," Steve said. "It isn't just because Linne violated her oath. And I don't know what that means, really."

"Only citadel commanders really have that... right," Kassandra said softly. "A few others do, but it's fairly uncommon. But... Nikki said you couldn't do it. She said you tried."

"I did try. I didn't do it right, I guess," Steve said. "Because now... now I can do it. It's as easy as swinging an axe to me now."

"Name... name me Head Wife," Kassandra said.

"I name you Head Wife," Steve repeated with a flippant hand gesture.

"I'm your head wife," Kassandra said, her tone almost listless. "I don't... name me Queen of Lamals."

"I remove your status as Head Wife and name you Queen of Lamals," Steve said, still walking along. He wasn't far off from the trees now and would be getting to work shortly.

"That didn't work," Kassandra murmured.

"Mm-hmm. Seems I need to have some type of claim or personal right to do what I'm doing," Steve said. "I wasn't able to name myself King either, if it makes you feel better. I name you Lead Bedwarmer and Personal Snake."

"I'm... I'm exactly that now," Kassandra said, her voice growing soft.

"I formally remove your status and return you to normal," Steve said, reversing what he'd just done.

"Were... you able to name yourself a citadel commander?" Kassandra asked.

"No," Steve said, letting go of his wagon. He picked up his axe and looked down at the head of it. He'd tried several things. "But for all I know, I tried to name myself incorrectly. Maybe there's a specific title or attachment I need. No idea. And no help to be found either, obviously."

"I suppose that's true," Kassandra said. Turning around, she rose up high off the ground and looked back the way they'd come. "Nancy seems to be getting everyone into their teams. Doesn't seem like anyone is fighting her."

"And you don't think they can see us from this distance?" Steve pulled his axe back. Then he whipped it forward with a smooth swish.

With a *thunk*, the back of the tree exploded into a shower of woodchips. The tree began toppling over immediately.

"A few might be able to, but it's unlikely. None of them are actually… made… for combat," Kassandra said. "They're farm girls. Their species are all the types that live in the fringe cities, villages, and towns. Not really in the bigger locations.

"Someone like Nancy wouldn't really be welcome in a big city."

"Awfully great looking for someone who wouldn't be welcome in a big city," Steve said. "I thought mothers went to big cities to have their girls prettied up. Like you."

"Yes, well, I would wager Nancy is a bit more like Gwendolin," Kassandra said. "Naturally pretty, with some hedge-wizard or witch work done out in the middle of nowhere. They're a very similar species, you realize. They just differ slightly in how they survive."

"What d'ya mean?" Steve asked as he walked alongside the downed tree. He lifted his axe, then brought it down and cut the tree into a manageable section he could get on his wagon.

"Gwendolin is a parasite race. She eats food and drinks water like anyone else, but to her… the attention of a man is something she craves. Much as I crave warmth and heat. We all have our little things that make us not very Human.

"Nancy is similar to Gwendolin, and feeds off despair and suffering."

"Like how Nikki can't help herself and starts *baah*ing sometimes in bed?" Steve asked, bringing his axe down again.

"I… yes. That works, too," she said.

"Goodie. Let's see if we can't find a nearby village," Steve said, making a choice. "Might be interesting to see if we can raid it of everyone with a murderer tag."

"Yes. I think we could manage that. I'll head back for now and see what I can arrange," Kassandra agreed. "That and check in on Nancy. See how she's doing in her task."

***

"They're down there," Jaina whispered softly in his ear.

In the end, Jaina had been chosen to go with him to see what they could. Kassandra remained in the camp with Ina to watch over things. There was no telling when another village patrol might stumble across their outpost, after all.

Ina by herself could probably wreck half the group before they even got close enough to shout at her.

"Many, many of them," Jaina said, her lips brushing his earlobe.

Steve grit his teeth. He couldn't see as well as Jaina could. He was starting to really hate the limitations of his race here.

Only thing we're good for is breeding, damnit.

Thankfully, Steve's foes seemed rather confident with their camp and defense. They'd lit torches at various points around their settlement. They also had a decent wall with a barricade of outward-facing spikes all along it.

There was no moat, though, and nothing to keep out the Creep.

Then again, we haven't seen much of it since we knocked the wall down into that gap.

Creeps, those bitten, and a bit of the Creep itself, but nothing like it used to be.

In fact, now that I think about it, is that why I couldn't turn those women who'd died into Creep Witches?

There wasn't enough Creep to convert them?

"Everyone I've checked is a murderer or a murderer and a robber," Jaina said as she began to rub her face into Steve's neck. "They're all valid targets."

Jaina never failed to get affectionate if they were alone or somewhere quiet. She'd never turn away his affections, but it was obvious she preferred privacy.

"Should we take one? Kill them and get the nice, nice rewards, just to see?" Jaina asked.

"Probably. Not a terrible idea," Steve said. He wanted to see if what Kassandra had said was true. He'd tried to look backward as he'd done before, but too many things had happened since then. There'd been no record to find.

"Got anyone in mind?" Steve asked.

"Yes, yes. There's a murderer just outside the gates in a tower. We've already seen their guards move in rotations. They changed their duties twice already," Jaina said. They'd been hiding here for the better part of the afternoon and evening, watching. "She should be changing out soon. We can grab her then and make her end fast. Once she's dead, we can run quick, quick away."

Steve nodded at that. It was a solid plan. Certainly better than what he'd come up with.

Jaina suddenly nipped at his neck, her teeth sliding over his skin. There was even some light pressure followed immediately by several licks. Then she stood up in a low crouch.

Been getting more and more bitey. Must be a Kobold thing.

Getting to his feet, Steve grabbed Jaina at the base of her tail. It was something easy to hold on to, and she swore up and down it didn't bother her in the least.

If Steve had to guess, she actually rather liked it.

Moving forward, the Kobold began leading him through the brush and dense undergrowth. What little light Steve had been able to see by was gone immediately.

To Steve, the world was as dark as if someone had put his head into the ground.

Much to his joy, Jaina kept them on something he could vaguely discern might be a path. His feet didn't seem to slip out from under him as they would if he were walking on roots and rocks.

In all honesty, he had no way of truly knowing since he couldn't even see his hand in front of his face.

Let alone Jaina.

Almost as quickly as they'd entered the forest of ultimate darkness and spiders waiting to crawl into their hair, it seemed they came to the edge of it.

Moving to the side, Jaina grabbed him and stuffed him down into a low crouch. Right into a bush that practically ate him.

She didn't move away, though; she got down in front of him on all fours. She eased her head out of the brush and peered around at their surroundings.

Looking around, Steve couldn't really see much of what was going on. He got the distinct impression the guard tower was directly out ahead of them. Looming above them in the darkness, just waiting for someone to walk out and be spotted.

That or it was security theater.

Wait, what? Security... theater?

Shaking his head lightly, Steve wanted to punch Shitty Steve for his lack of memories. Repeatedly.

Until Shitty Steve was Steve the Stain.

Taking in a breath, Steve looked down at Jaina's rear end.

He smirked to himself and pushed down on her with the hand holding her tail. Jaina was an honest girl and responded with sincerity.

As if some internal switch had been flicked at the pressure of his hand on her, Jaina's rear end shot upward and her shoulders hit the dirt. Putting her in a very natural and obvious pose to receive a mate.

One of her hands came back into view and gently swatted at his wrist, her body going back into the crouch it'd been in earlier.

Poor thing. She's more animal than Human, isn't she?

Then her hand quickly patted his wrist. Interpreting that as the signal to let go of her tail, he did so.

Jaina was off in a flash, scurrying off into the darkness ahead of him.

There was a squeak in the dark, out ahead of him.

Jaina came back with a much larger woman tossed over her shoulder. She was bound in purple magic ties from the Creep Witch's magic.

"Go. Time to go, go," Jaina said, pushing her rear end into Steve's hand. "Grab my tail."

Grabbing it, he had only a second to get moving before she was hurrying along.

Taking them right back into the woods of blackness and snakes probably waiting to bite them as they walked along, Jaina kept them moving.

"Here is good," she panted after a few minutes of moving quite fast. "I will rest. She's bound and gagged. She's not a struggler. Check her panel and then take her life. After that, check your own status. Then we'll go."

Tossing the struggling woman to one side, Jaina flopped down on the grass and lay there, panting hard.

"Good work, Jaina. You're a... you're a good girl," Steve said, feeling incredibly awkward.

"Yes. Yes, I am. Thank you, Steve. Thank you." Jaina sounded incredibly pleased with herself at that.

Looking at the woman struggling on the ground, Steve tried to see into her for more information.

Heather Bissell
Human
Father: living
Mother: living
Murderer- killed someone illegally
Purist- married her own kind
Traitorous- slept with a man outside her marriage
Divorced- no longer married to her spouse

Unable to see her face, and thankful for that, Steve shrugged his shoulders.

This had been the plan. This was someone marked for death if they ever encountered a soldier, officer of the law, or anyone who wanted prestige for the bounty.

Steve pulled out the bronze knife at his hip, then grabbed the woman by her short hair and rammed the blade home into her throat.

Working the blade to one side and then the other, he tried to make the kill as quick and clean as possible.

Just the same way you take care of the rabbits.
Right?
Same way Nikki does.
Or Jaina, the deer.
Just like that... it's humane, it's quick.

Steve grimaced. He wasn't afraid of violence or hurting others. He'd killed people.

This was a person specifically marked to die. If he didn't take her life, it was very likely someone else would for the same reason.

It was just strange to him to butcher the woman as if she were little more than cattle.

Steve checked her status and found that she was indeed already quite dead. It'd only taken seconds.

Though her body was still quivering and making strange gasping noises.

Something not right here… Then again, what is right here?

Looking at his own status, Steve called up where he was hoping to find a new notification.

Log:

Bounty collected.

Coin to be collected (12s) at a government-sponsored fine, tax, and levy station.

Steve has gained prestige for enforcing a cardinal law of the Lamals.

Steve has gained the title "Bounty Hunter" for his continued actions.

"That worked," he muttered.

"Good," Jaina said, still panting. Then she whined and got up to her feet. "Check her pockets. Then we go. We must be swift, swift."

Nodding his head, Steve checked the dead woman's pockets for anything.

"Be sure to check her undergarments for purses," Jaina said as she stretched herself out.

Steve did so.

And found several coins.

Four

With a grunt, Steve nodded after he shifted the A-frame of the cabin's roof into place.

It was nowhere near as big as the one back home.

Not at all.

This would be little more than a bedroom in comparison. Enough to house him, Jaina, Ina, and Kassandra, and that was it.

All his prisoners were going to be sleeping under a lean-to that was already lashed to the front of the cabin.

Nancy had been given the benefit of sleeping in the entryway of the cabin for her work. She would have a much more solid roof over her as she slept, and a solid wooden floor.

So far, the woman had earned her keep and then some. She'd kept her one-time compatriots and enemies in check and working smoothly while she maintained order.

There was no dissension in the ranks and no grumbling of any sort.

Looking out, Steve was pleased to see Nancy was indeed helping to tend the field as she oversaw everyone else.

Seems like she's got a knack for it.

Steve dragged a wrist across his brow, feeling accomplished. All he had left to do was bring up the thatching he'd already tied together and lay it across the roof. That wouldn't take him much more than an hour.

He'd be done today and sleeping behind walls.

Thinking about walls, he looked out at the moat around them. It was the same depth as the one that went around his home, but it didn't have the same volume of water.

And that depth wouldn't stay. It would eventually seep away and evaporate.

He was going to have to connect it with the main moat soon if he wanted this area to be as safe.

But in the same breath, I need to get the palisade walls up. Those murderers are all still out there. And the prisoners said it wasn't just two villages, but more like... what... nine? Ten?

Mm.

Not something I can ignore.

Suppose I need to get the prisoners working on the wall with me now that the cabin is up. Moat can wait.

Except… Shelly's late.
Should have been here two days ago.

Scratching at his shoulder, he looked out to the south. He didn't like that Shelly was late. It made him nervous. Very nervous. He wanted to rush back home and see what was going on.

But Nikki had sent him out this way to take care of this. To handle it for her and secure their future, as she'd put it.

"Not about to disappoint her either," Steve grumbled as his eyes slid across the horizon.

In the far distance, although it looked like little more than a speck to him, Steve felt like he saw something.

"Jaina," he called aloud, looking where he'd last seen the Kobold.

She was happily gutting and skinning animals she caught in the area around their campsite.

"Yes, husband?" she asked, not looking up as she finished pulling her knife all the way down to the neck of the deer she was dressing.

"Is that Shelly?" Steve pointed in the direction he was looking.

Looking up from her work, Jaina turned her head toward him. Then she looked where he was pointing.

"Oh. Yes, yes. I think it is. It's definitely a wagon, but it's too far for me to see the details," Jaina said. Then she went back to her work. It looked like she was getting ready to start pulling out entrails.

They'd use those later to lure predators into traps.

Jaina was rapidly becoming a very accomplished hunter.

"Kassandra and Ina should be back before the wagon gets here," she said, again without looking up.

The pair had gone off to cut down trees with Steve's axe while he finished up with the cabin. He wasn't about to tell them no, and if anything, he appreciated it.

It frustrated him sometimes to think he was the only one who could do anything with his tools.

"I think…" Steve said after a pause. "I think I'm going to go greet whoever it is and see what took them so long."

"Oh, yes. That's not a bad idea." Jaina used her knife to cut something out of the animal. "Have a nice, nice walk, husband. I'll watch over our home and prisoners."

Nodding at that, Steve hopped down from the roof and landed with a soft pat.

Nancy looked up from where she was pulling out a carrot. It wasn't quite as big as the ones back home, but it was definitely larger than average.

The problem was that they'd been forced to ration the water they were using. Without a constant source of watering-can water, it was clear the effects were quite a bit less.

"I'll be back," Steve said when he met Nancy's eyes. "Wagon coming in with supplies. Should make things easier."

"Oh. Alright," said his taskmaster.

"Should have one of my wives on it. Curious why it took them so long to get up here." Steve brushed his hands off on his pants.

"Ah, yes. That would be a worry in my mind as well," Nancy said. "May I introduce myself to them?"

"I don't see why not," Steve said. Nancy had been nothing if not kind and polite to him so far. He'd seen her enforcing obedience with her workers. She was swift, economical, and without cruelty, but she was unbending.

All in all, he was impressed with her when he really put some thought into it.

After nodding his head at Nancy, Steve turned and started heading off in the direction of the wagon.

"Break time," Nancy said behind him. "Get some lunch, rest, and clean up. We'll be on log clean-up after this."

The soft padding of feet behind him made Steve turn around.

Nancy was coming his way, moving a bit quicker than normal to catch up with him.

Unable to help himself, he watched the way she moved for several seconds before he turned forward again.

Too pretty.

As pretty as Gwen and built the same way.

Wait, why's she coming with me again?

"Ah, thank you for letting me join you," Nancy said, falling in step with him. She was holding the solid stone ball and chain that was normally around her ankles in both arms. It looked really heavy, but she didn't seem to let it bother her.

Frowning, Steve stopped and turned to look at Jaina. If he took Nancy with him, she'd explode from the inside out.

And he didn't want to deal with her ball and chain right now.

Feeling annoyed, he realized he'd need to go ask Jaina to take care of this for him.

As if feeling his eyes on her, Jaina looked up from her field dressing.

Her eyebrows moved up on her forehead. Then she shrugged her shoulders and flicked a finger at Nancy.

There was a dull whine, and the anklet fell away from her.

"Oh. Oh, alright. Okay," Nancy said, looking at her leg. "I… okay. Okay."

She set the heavy stone ball on the ground and lifted up her foot to rotate her ankle around.

"Uhm, thank you for the trust," she said, folding her hands together behind her back.

"Shut up," Steve growled out. He didn't want to deal with her right now. Part of him still wanted to pop her head open for the prestige alone.

But she'd earned her keep so far, and doing anything untoward to her would violate one of the only principles he had.

"Okay, yes, I'm sorry. I'll be silent," Nancy said, moving with him as he started to walk toward the wagon again.

***

Long before he reached the wagon, Steve realized it wasn't Shelly.

It was Gwendolin. She was riding the cart as easily as if it were the simplest thing in the world for her. Like it wasn't a problem and was as natural as walking.

They were maybe a minute out from reaching one another, he figured.

"She's a Siren," Steve said, breaking the silence.

Nancy had been as good as her word. She'd been absolutely silent for the entire walk so far.

"I see," Nancy said. "She's very beautiful. Even for a Siren. Very pretty."

"Yes. Yes, she is," Steve said. "Her name's Gwendolin, but I just call her Gwen. Her daughter's name is Nia."

"Yes, that would make sense," Nancy said. "Her child?"

"Yes, her child," Steve said softly. "Though I'd kill for Nia."

Must have read my status lines. Probably looked through it all.

"The uhm... the accolade for marrying a Wight is 'Animator' by the way," Nancy said.

"Huh. It is?" Steve asked.

"Yes. I'm Undead, technically. I won't age. I'll look like this forever. And it's very hard to kill me," Nancy said. "It's why I was chosen to be a team leader so often. I've been stabbed, gutted, and poisoned."

"Oh. Interesting," Steve said.

"I could have children just like anyone else, though. I'm not... not that different from a Siren. Or... or from a few of your other wives," Nancy said.

Steve glanced at the beautiful Wight and then turned back to the wagon. He knew what she was getting at, and he didn't really care.

All he cared about right now was that she was serving his purpose. Any talk of her doing anything other than keeping track of the prisoners or being executed for her bounty was pointless.

Up ahead, Steve could see Gwendolin and her wagon very clearly now.

She looked out of place dressed in riding clothes.

Possibly because she was stunning. Beautiful to the point that it made Steve's thoughts wander at times.

Her long black hair was gathered loosely behind her head and likely reached down to her rear end. Where she'd worn no adornments in her hair previously, she now had small blue ribbons throughout it.

The clothes, ribbons, and hair made her pale skin glow in the sun.

Those big, bright green eyes were locked on him. Where he'd seen a weathered and optimistic soul previously, he now only saw a woman with joy in her heart and a positive outlook.

The features of her face, from her nose and lips to her jaw and ears, looked practically constructed to be part of the amazing whole that was her beauty.

Partially concealed by her clothes, and part of the reason she looked out of place in them, was a figure that had clearly been put together by a magical hand.

Gwendolin was a dream made real with wide hips, a narrow waist, and an expansive bosom.

And the smile she unleashed on Steve made his heart skip several times.

It was a smile only for him.

"Hello, Steve," Gwen said as soon as they were close enough to hold a conversation. "I missed you."

Grinning stupidly, Steve jumped onto the side of the wagon and wrapped Gwendolin up in a hug before kissing her soundly.

"Ah... I got it. Just... hand them—there we go," Nancy said from somewhere beyond Gwendolin.

Pulling at the Siren, Steve practically dragged her out of her seat. He held her tightly against him as he kissed her like a starving man finding food.

A short time later, he finally released her and looked into her face.

For a reason he couldn't explain, Gwendolin had slid through his heart and latched there tightly. Right next to Nikki.

Perhaps it was the fact that she cared for her daughter so deeply that she'd forsaken herself of ever finding a man.

Or that she'd given so much to protect her daughter that she had become completely secondary. One of the initial reasons she'd even agreed to leave with Steve was for Nia.

In this world, this land, it seemed abnormal for her to have done such a thing. And it endeared her to him.

"Goodness, Steve," Gwendolin said, looking up at him. "Isn't it the Siren who's supposed to take the other's breath away?"

"I missed you," Steve said, pressing his forehead to hers.

"I... yes. As I said, I missed you, too." Gwendolin's eyes scrunched up a bit as she grinned at him from an inch away. "Uhm, should you introduce me?"

"I'm Nancy," Nancy said. "I have a murderer accolade. Steve took me as a prisoner rather than executing me. I'm a Wight. I'm working to become a mistress or bed-woman for him, though I'm also his prison warder for the others."

"It's a pleasure to meet you, Gwendolin."

"Ah, yes. A pleasure," Gwendolin said, unable to pull away from Steve. After giving him a light kiss, she did turn her head toward Nancy. "I'm so sorry. He's our beloved brute, and it's just what he is. His head wife is Nikki; she's a Faun. I'll relay your intention back to her."

Steve looked at the back of the wagon. It was far larger than any wagon he remembered them having.

Packed in close and tight were a good many water barrels. There were also plenty of supplies, and a bedroll had been laid out.

Grabbing Gwendolin a bit tighter around the hips, Steve pulled her up and over the rim of the wagon bed.

"Eep! It was nice meeting you," Gwendolin said as Steve dragged her over the lip and out of sight.

"I look forward to speaking with you more at length," Nancy said, vanishing from Steve's view.

Steve laid Gwendolin down on the bedroll, then set his head on her shoulder and snuggled in close.

Nikki was where he went for comfort, but Gwendolin had rapidly become secondary in that regard. She'd started to seek him out to make sure he was well at times.

Which only further pushed her into his awareness.

"Oh, Steve," murmured the Siren, running a hand through his hair. "Were you worried?"

"Yeah." Steve pressed his face against the Siren's neck.

"Nothing's wrong," Gwendolin said, getting both of her arms around Steve. "Shelly had to go to Filch. Someone from Commander Lynn arrived and asked to speak with the governor. We thought she'd be back in a day, but it took longer. So I came instead."

"Oh, good," Steve said, closing his eyes.

"I brought the watering can with me. We were able to move the barrel you put it in just like you thought, even though we couldn't move the watering can itself," Gwendolin said.

"Ferrah sent something to test out that you'd mentioned as well, and—"

Steve bit gently into Gwendolin's throat, his hands coming down to rest on her hips.

"Oh. Ah... mm," Gwendolin said. Her head tilted to one side, exposing her neck to Steve entirely. "I... could we? Could we... do it... right here? Right now?"

That was a surprising request to Steve.

He thought for sure she'd tell him no or to wait for a real bed. Certainly not in a wagon with Nancy less than two feet away.

"And uhm, can you do that thing we talked about? I want one," Gwendolin said, leaning her head back and lifting her shoulder, forcing Steve to meet her eyes. "I want one as soon as possible. Before Nia gets older."

"You do?" Steve asked. He knew exactly what she was asking. She wanted him to impregnate her.

Here, on this world, he'd found that being pregnant was an honored status. One that widows like her supposedly couldn't achieve.

It was doubly honored if you were the first in a marriage to become pregnant.

"Yes," Gwendolin said, smiling at him. She looked up at the edge of the wagon and then back to Steve. "I know Jaina would agree as well."

Ah. So... she does want me to impregnate both widows first.
Alright. I think... I think I could do that.

Gwendolin reached down to his pants and almost instantly got them loosened, then pushed them down towards his knees.

"You're positive?" Steve asked.

"I... Steve," Gwendolin said, pausing to deliberately glance toward the front of the wagon where Nancy was sitting.

Frowning, Steve sat up and moved to the wagon's lip.

He reached out, wrapped a hand around Nancy's throat, and pulled her backward till she was looking up at him, bending her partially over the rim of the wagon bed.

"Nancy," Steve growled, giving her throat a soft squeeze.

She nodded her head and stared up at him with wide eyes.

"Whatever you hear, you're to repeat it to no one," Steve whispered into her ear. He didn't want Gwendolin to hear anything of this either, for that matter. "No matter what you hear. Do you understand? To no one. Not even my other wives."

"Yes," whispered the Wight. "I swear it."

"Good. You want to be my mistress? Then start acting like it. You'll be my secret keeper from everyone, and you'll do the things I want you to and like it," Steve continued, his lips almost inside her ear canal. "Do you agree?"

"I understand. I agree," Nancy murmured, nodding her head quickly. "Your mistress and secret keeper. I understand. I can do that. Yes. If you swear to keep me alive, healthy, and taken care of."

Steve considered her offer. She'd been useful so far. Very useful. She'd bent to his will and done what he asked and offered everything up to him.

"Done. I swear it," he whispered in her ear. "Now swear in return."

"I swear it," Nancy said, one of her hands coming up to rest on his around her throat. "I swear to be your mistress and secret keeper."

Letting out a breath, Steve released her and moved back down to Gwendolin. She had a very confused look on her face.

"She won't talk," Steve said. "Are you sure? Pregnancy for you and Jaina?"

Gwendolin took in a slow breath and then let it out. "Yes. I'm sure."

Then she opened her arms to him, her tunic falling open as well. He noticed in that instant that her pants were all the way down past her ankles and coiled next to a box.

Apparently while he'd been chatting with Nancy, Gwendolin had taken care of her own clothes.

She was impossibly beautiful.

"Come show your wife your love," Gwendolin purred at him, then immediately began humming her personal Steve song.

He pushed down on his pants and nearly jumped atop Gwendolin, he moved so quickly.

Laughing softly, she shimmied around to get her legs spread out and around his hips.

"I'm not going anywhere," she murmured, humming her song whenever she wasn't speaking. "Slow down and take me gently."

He gave her a nod, then leaned down and kissed her hungrily. His tongue immediately slipped into her mouth as his hands pressed into her hips.

Gwendolin received him without hesitation, practically moaning her song as her tongue slid along his own.

Her thighs trailed up along his hips, her ankles and feet brushing against his calves. She was pulling at him subtly.

Before he could do anything to insert himself into her, she'd already taken his tip with her left hand and was guiding him up and in.

Moving with the motion she'd started, Steve slid into the Siren.

Gwendolin laid her hand on his rear end and pulled at him with her fingers as he filled her.

She broke her song partially with a groan, and her body flexed and went tight under him. Pushing down on her hips, Steve kept going till he felt there was nothing left to fit in. He was at the hilt, and he could feel her insides pulsing around his shaft.

Breaking the kiss, Gwendolin laid her head against the bedroll and let out a rush of air.

"You're a lot bigger than I expected. I didn't really believe everyone," she murmured. She shifted around under him, tilting her hips slightly until she seemed to get comfortable. Then she lifted her hands up and laid them around the back of his neck. "Come, husband. Lay claim to me, fill me, and give me our first child. Give Nia a sibling."

As her words died away, she began to hum his song again, her eyes wide and bright, her smile huge.

Encouraged, flattered, and feeling beyond sexually needy, Steve pulled out of her and then rolled forward. He worked to curve his hips up and over her so he could grind at her clit at the same time.

Gwendolin moaned as he moved atop her, then shifted a little more and lay still beneath him. Her eyes slowly narrowed till they were only halfway open. It was obvious she was watching him and enjoying his response to her song.

Leaning his head down, unable to look at her amazing face, Steve began to lightly bite at her neck and shoulders. At the same time, he rocked back and forth, gliding in and out of the lovely Siren.

As she hummed and moaned in tune with his thrusts, Gwendolin seemed lost in her own little musically enhanced, sexual world.

Steve was going easy on her, enjoying the simple act of making love to her. His hips ground down into her with each thrust, and he wasn't trying to pound away at her.

Pushing down with his hands on her hips as he moved upward was the extent of the force he was using on her.

"Steve," Gwendolin said in a throaty whisper. "I love you."

Unable to help himself, he bit down on her shoulder at her words, and his fingers tightened on her hips.

"It feels so wonderful—you're amazing," she said, her melody resuming its cadence immediately after she finished speaking.

Steve shivered at her words. With the way she was stroking his ego and emotions, he felt like he was being bathed in the warmth of her heart. Her song pulled at him.

"Don't forget to give me our first child," Gwendolin murmured, kissing the side of his head and ear. "Give us our firstborn."

Letting out a soft pant as he picked up speed, Steve continued to pin and love Gwendolin into her bedroll. There was no force in any of it, however.

He was making sure to try and hit all her needs at the same time.

Where Ina and Kassandra often wanted to be split in half, it was obvious Gwendolin was far more like Shelly.

"Steve, tell me it's going to happen," she whispered. "I want to hear it. I'll be the firstborn-wife."

"You're going to be pregnant," Steve mumbled, letting go of her shoulder with his teeth. "You'll be the firstborn-wife."

"Yes," Gwendolin whispered.

Taking the opportunity he'd presented her by lifting his head to respond, Gwendolin immediately kissed him, her tongue pushing into his mouth. Her right hand was combing through the back of his hair as her left hand slid down towards his rear end again.

Steve pumped into her over and over, losing himself in it. In the madness of making love to such a beautiful and willing woman, one whose constant humming drove his heart, mind, and soul into a maddening frenzy.

And to impregnate her right now.

You've requested to enable procreation. Please confirm that you wish to disable your procreation limitation.

Yes! Yes, please. Give Gwendolin a child.

Procreation enabled.

Grunting, Steve began to thrust a bit harder into Gwendolin as he hit his peak. His shaft expanded, and he felt himself spilling seed into her depths. Unable to breathe, and feeling a bit dizzy, he forcefully broke the kiss with Gwendolin.

Singing aloud now, the Siren was pulling at him, moaning, and shuddering under him.

Impregnate Gwendolin Bril?

"Yes," Steve panted, "Impregnate Gwendolin Bril."

He ground into her and pushed as deep as he could while continuing to climax.

"Gods, yes," Gwendolin groaned, rolling her whole body with each of his thrusts. "Impregnate Gwendolin Bril."

Conception achieved.

Steve has gained notoriety for breaking the laws of the Lamals.

Steve has gained the Number One Fan accolade.

Steve has gained the Father accolade.

Panting, Steve finally came to an end and laid his forehead down on Gwendolin's shoulder.

She laughed softly under her breath as she ran her hands all over his back and shoulders.

"It happened," she said in a laughing pant. "I'm pregnant. I got my Humanist accolade and the Firstborn Mother accolade."

"Congratulations," Nancy said from up front.

"Thank you," Gwendolin said, apparently not caring in the least about Nancy. She started laughing again, her arms tightening around Steve's shoulders. Then she pressed her lips to his ear and hummed several notes of his song. "Let's do it again. Maybe you can give me twins. A Firstborn Mother with Twins would be an amazing accolade to have."

Five

Pulling the lid off a water barrel, Gwendolin looked inside.

"Oh, it's only half full," she said, then turned to Steve with a smile.

While it had been several hours since their first time in the wagon, two hours since their second and third time, it still felt surreal to Steve.

Gwendolin was pregnant beyond a doubt, and she was acting very affectionate with him. More than she had previously, certainly.

She'd cared for him and shown him that care, but now it was downright almost smothering.

Reaching in, Steve fetched out the watering can and carried it over to the moat. He jammed it in at an angle and then gave it a once-over. It was draining appropriately.

He shrugged and turned the whole thing upside down. After watching it for a few seconds, he thought it was emptying faster like this, but he had no way to be sure.

"Ferrah sent these... things," Gwendolin said from behind him. "She said you had talked to her about it?"

Looking up at the Siren, Steve found she was holding what seemed like a copper pipe in the shape of a J and a stopper.

"Great," Steve said, taking it from her.

He'd had a weird thought when he'd been trying to figure out ways to make the water come out faster.

Mostly it was weird because he swore he had a memory of this from somewhere, but he couldn't relate it back to anything.

It was just one more thing to heap upon the many curses for Shitty Steve.

He took the stopper and fit it into the spout of the watering can. Water ceased to flow, and it seemed to be perfectly sealed.

With a nod of his head, Steve pushed the copper pipe into the watering can. The long side of the pipe slid into the body of the can itself.

He felt and heard when it hit the bottom of the watering can. Ferrah had designed it specifically to rest there. The hook of the pipe came out and went upwards and away.

Giving the watering can a shake, Steve felt like he was supposed to do something else, but he wasn't sure.

He frowned, then leaned down and then blew as hard as he could into the pipe.

The result was immediate.

Water began pouring out of the watering can at an increased rate.

Not sure... if this is how it's supposed to work, if this world is messed up, or what, but I'll take what I can get.

He left the watering can there, and as it emptied endlessly, he felt better.

It was definitely flowing much faster now, and it seemed to be able to continue with whatever he'd done.

Then again, an endless watering can isn't exactly realistic, is it? Hah.

"Well," Gwendolin murmured. "That'll be helpful. If it fills everything as quickly as I think it will, does that mean we should take even more land?"

Steve frowned, thinking on that.

He knew that was the exact question Nikki would pose to him. She had plans within plans to provide for her family, and future generations.

That included taking as much land as possible and holding it as their own.

But isn't that thinking more for when the Creep was here? We haven't seen much of it lately.

Maybe this is over and we won't have to worry about it much. Maybe we can just... give up this outpost and go back to the farm and settle in there.

Have a normal life.

Standing up, Steve brushed his hands off on his hips.

If that's the truth, doesn't that mean I need to round up and execute all those murderers as quickly as possible? We'll need to catch them, bring them back to the farm, and execute them.

Earn prestige for everyone so the government leaves us alone. I'm on a time-limit with the criminals.

He nodded his head as he firmed up a plan.

"I meant to ask," Steve said, looking up. "How's Lucia? You wouldn't be here unless… she was worse beyond saving or better enough that you could leave."

"Oh! Oh, I'm so sorry," Gwendolin said, touching his chest with a hand. "She's fine. Absolutely fine. I find that my ability to help others has grown substantially. She's well and good. Though rather angry at you. She was expecting to find you when she woke up, I think."

"Err, yeah. That sounds about right for her, I suppose," Steve said with a grin.

"Indeed. Expect her to show up and possibly beat you.

"Oh, there's Jaina. I'm going to go chat with her. I think I have a new subject to talk to her about. One that I think will raise her spirits without me giving anything away," Gwendolin said. Walking up to his side, she laid a kiss on his lips that practically made him ask for a fourth round before she moved off.

Steve glanced at the watering can and found it unchanged. Emptying into the moat.

I'll have to dig it into the expansion line for the eventual goal of the outpost, then finish out the final size quickly. That'll keep me non-stop busy for a while.

Maybe tie it into the water heading to Filch itself.

Turning to his side, he found Nancy standing there. She had her hands behind her back, seemingly waiting for him to give her direction.

"Get your women together. We're going to go ditch digging," Steve said. "Meet me in the far boundary. Tell everyone not to cross to the other side of it no matter what. Not on any circumstance."

"Yes, of course," Nancy said, and immediately moved away from him.

Clicking his tongue, Steve walked over to the small cabin, grabbed his shovel, and started digging straight toward the expansion line. He had no desire to waste any of his can water.

He worked quickly and was able to finish digging to the extension before Nancy rejoined him with her women in tow. They were all holding shovels and looking bored.

They'd been fed better than they had back in their villages, treated kindly for murderers, clothed, and given water as often as they wished.

By all accounts, they were more farmhands at this point than anything else.

On top of that, someone had removed their stone balls and chains.

Wonder if that was Jaina or Ina. Kassandra couldn't do it.

"We're digging along the far boundary," Steve said, looking up from where he'd stopped working. "Pay heed to the markers and don't cross them. If you cross them, you'll die. It's very simple.

"Questions?"

"No," Nancy said.

"Get 'em going and then come back, Nancy," Steve said. Bending to his task, he started digging straight out from the expansion line toward the boundary.

Nancy didn't leave, though. She turned, motioning to her women and then the boundary.

"I'll catch up with you," she said to them.

As one, the group moved off without a word. They apparently had no resentment toward Nancy.

It didn't really make sense to Steve.

Standing up, he watched the women leave and leaned on his shovel handle.

"You didn't kill them," Nancy said. "Or me. Nor are you… abusing… them. Far as they can determine, you're treating them more like farmhands."

"They are farmhands," Steve said, looking at Nancy. "Farmhands I'll kill if they do anything I don't like. But… as long as they earn their keep, they have nothing to fear."

"And that's why they're not trying to make problems. To be fair, there's more food here than where we came from," Nancy said. "And your wives are actually quite pleasant. It speaks well to your character."

"Says my mistress and secret keeper," Steve said with a scoff.

"Yes, says the woman you could strangle to death and get a bounty for it," Nancy admitted. "A woman who willingly and eagerly threw herself at your feet to avoid her fate. I know what you think of me, and you're not wrong. Not really."

"You're that willing, huh?" Steve asked, peering at Nancy. He wasn't really sure what he thought of her, to be honest. She was a worker to him and not much else. He had no grand designs on her. No plans to use her or discard her.

"Yes. I'm that willing. I sold all those women out in a flash, and I'd do it again. I'd sell your wives out to you if the opportunity presented itself. I'll do whatever's necessary to ingratiate myself to you," Nancy said. "As a murderer, I have no hope or long-term longevity other than your good graces."

Steve didn't quite believe that.

"I'd do what you wanted," Nancy promised, apparently noticing his skepticism. "I just… I just want to live."

"How many people did you kill?" Steve asked.

"Twenty or so. I'm not sure anymore," Nancy said.

"Innocents and fighters both?"

"Yes. Both. Sometimes for coin, sometimes for nothing."

"You did spare a few, though."

"Teenage girls," Nancy replied and shrugged her shoulders. "Little better than children."

"If I told you to go kill all your women out there?" Steve hooked a thumb at the people who were now digging a trench.

"I'd kill them," Nancy offered, holding up her hands. "If that's what would make you happy, I'd do it. I'd kill your wives if you asked. I'll lie in your bed all day or work till my fingers bleed. I just want to live and be comfortable."

Snorting at that, Steve thought hard on what he wanted.

"Alright," Steve said. "You're my mistress and secret keeper, right?"

"Yes, I am," Nancy said.

"How big was your village?"

"Not very. Maybe a hundred or so were left. We were the largest party we'd sent out in a long time," Nancy said.

"Go get them and bring them back to me," Steve said. "Get them to march into this field. My witches will handle the rest. I want them. All of them."

"Do that, and I'll formally take you as my mistress and taskmaster. Give you some people to work under you."

"I… you want me to bring them here," Nancy said.

"Yeah. That's what I want," Steve confirmed. "You said you'd do what I want? There you go. And by the way, I'm going to have one of my witches put a spell in you. One that'll blow up in a few days. So you'll be on a time limit.

"That or you shut up, get to back to work. I'll keep you safe and you'll protect my single secret, but we'll never discuss the mistress thing again."

Taking in a shuddering breath, Nancy seemed to be considering her options.

"Okay," she said suddenly. "Okay. I'll... go get my village and bring it back. You'll make me your mistress and your secret keeper. You'll tell me all your secrets so I can ensure I take care of them. You'll protect me from everyone else for that. I'll warm your bed and you'll treat me as a wife without the title."

"Mm-hmm," Steve said after a second. Her deal wasn't terrible.

"I want... I want to bind our oath by blood," Nancy said. "I know a little bit of black magic. Not much... nothing that elaborate. But enough that if either of us breaks our deal, one of us would suffer for it. Me with death and you with... maybe... maybe losing an arm?"

Hmm. That's... odd. She deliberately weighed it against herself. She must truly believe that her position has no power at all.

"Fine," Steve said. "Get to it then. Get back here with your village and we'll get that black magic of yours in place."

***

Nancy was stumbling off toward the west. The magic Jaina had put in her had definitely stolen some of her own energy to see it done.

"Think it'll work?" Kassandra asked.

"Don't know. Doesn't matter either," Steve said. "She'll get it done, or not. If she fails, Jaina gets credit for her death. If she succeeds, we march her village back home and just... have an execution festival, I guess."

"Yes, yes," Jaina said, bouncing in place. "Yes, yes. It'll work out either way. No matter what we do."

"Poor thing," Gwendolin lamented, shaking her head with a sigh. "Then again, she chose her fate. It isn't as if she wouldn't simply be put to the sword if someone wanted her bounty. She's lucky it was you and not someone else."

"Hmph," Steve said, running a hand along his jaw. He saw all the murderers in this area as a means to an end. A way to protect his farm and his family. He'd scour this whole land free of those bounties, if that was what it took.

"Should we send one of the others to the other village?" Kassandra asked. "It wouldn't hurt to send out another with the same task and mission. Would it?

"If we could get both villages that would be a very substantial boon."

Not a terrible idea.

"Could you put another spell-bomb in someone?" Steve asked, looking at Jaina.

Jaina turned to Ina for direction.

"Of course we could," Ina said, taking the lead. "Not a problem. You just tell us what you want, and we'll take care of it."

Steve turned and looked at the distant forms of the women digging the ditch.

"Go find a volunteer, Kass," Steve said finally. "Make sure it's someone who understands what they're getting out of it."

"Of course," Kassandra said and immediately started slithering away.

"Husband," Jaina said in an excited tone. "Could… could we go try for pups? If you were able to put them in Gwen, it's very possible I could have pups. Right?"

Ina chuckled to herself, putting one hand on her hip.

"Now I'm glad I never let you finish in me," Ina said. "Apparently all those silly ninnies were afraid for nothing."

"Later, Jaina," Steve said. "Lot of work to do today. That watering can is moving fast. I kinda want to get most of the ditch dug.

"Besides, you and Ina need to get working on a spell that'll let us capture a hundred or more people at the same time. For all you know… Nancy could show up in a few hours with everyone."

"I… do you think so?" Ina asked, looking confused.

"I think she's very driven," Steve said neutrally. He didn't actually think she'd be coming back, but he'd rather put a positive spin on it. "I think if anyone could do it, she'd be the one. I'm of the belief she'll show up with the village or not at all.

"That means having the ditch ready so we can start laying walls in. I plan on working her village and only getting rid of troublemakers at first. We have lots of work to do."

Ina turned to Jaina, and they started to talk about magical constructs.

Realizing they'd be engaged in that for a while, Steve walked away from them.

Gwendolin caught up to him immediately, pacing along beside him.

"I think I'll just keep you company, Steve. My number-one fan," Gwendolin said with a smile.

Apparently she'd looked over his accolades and noticed her own contribution.

"And if you don't mind, I'll sing for you. I think my song might have changed a bit for you since you heard it in the wagon. Everyone always says it changes once you bed your husband, but I never expected it to be like this." Gwendolin's cheeks turned a faint red.

Hmm. That's... true. Isn't it? Everyone changed after I had sex with them.

Even Xivin changed. From cautious about being hurt during sex to simply demanding I bed her while I was in the city with her.

Or is that tied with the robotic "must have children" brainwashing?

"Can't wait to hear it, but if I like it too much, you might end up in the grass," Steve said.

"I think that'd be enjoyable," Gwendolin said with a smile. "Just because I made you wait, doesn't mean I didn't want it. Or that I'm shy."

Delightful.

***

Sighing, Steve threw down his shovel. He was tired of digging.

It was well beyond nightfall, and he was still out here digging and throwing dirt. And the stupid part was the watering-can water was slowly catching up to him. Every time he took a break, it gained ground.

"Fuck. It's working almost too well. Need to stuff it up in a water tower somewhere on the farm and call it done. Everything will be dug outward from there going forward," Steve grumbled.

"You're doing much better this time," said a masculine voice from nowhere.

"Huh?" Steve said, looking around himself. "Who's there? Where are you?"

"It's me. You're doing much better this time," said the same voice, in a near exact match of the same words.

"And who are you, 'me'? I've never met you. And why can't I see you?" Steve asked. Picking up his shovel, he held it like a weapon.

"I see. You traded away your memories for tools with the master tender," said the voice after a slight pause. "An interesting exchange. One I didn't predict.

"Perhaps that's why you're doing better this time. Something to consider. Though now I should go check on the master tender."

Steve felt like there was something ominous in that statement. He was glad he wasn't this master tender and had nothing to do with them.

"How'd you know about my memories and tools? Do you know who I am?" Steve asked.

"Yes. You're Steven Bril, and you're currently in your final examination," said the voice.

"Final examination... what am I being tested for?"

"You traded away your memories. The information you're requesting was part of that," said the voice.

"Ok... can I trade you something for some answers?" Steve asked, slowly turning around in place.

"No. You have nothing I wish for," said the voice. "I was merely checking in to let you know you're succeeding. Though I now see that this conversation is pointless. You have no way of knowing what you're testing for or how to improve.

"We'll see how it turns out at the end."

"Wait, tell me more. Give me an idea here. I'm sure I can do better," Steve said. "Better than good. I bet I can be great."

"No," said the voice simply.

"What about—"

"No. Good luck," said the voice.

"Wait!" Steve said.

There was no response from the voice. As far as Steve could tell, they were gone.

Okay… so… there's someone watching me.

Testing me.

The notes Shitty Steve left behind weren't just for shits and giggles. And maybe… maybe Shitty Steve set me up as best as he could, given conditions I don't know about.

And if that's true… does that mean the voice is responsible for the brainwashing?

For the fact that the need to breed is stronger than survival instinct?

Steve frowned and shook his head; thinking.

What else are they controlling then? Are they the reason the birth rate is so skewed?

Wouldn't natural genetics redistribute a population over time? There's no reason men would continue to have a low birth rate.

Could they be behind men being sent to the front after they've finished breeding?

No. No… that's a country-specific thing.

Nikki said that Lamals would be destroyed for its views if it wasn't for the manpower it produced. That means men might be treated better or different in another country.

In fact, she mentioned that, didn't she?

Fuck.

Grunting, Steve got back to work.

If whoever was watching him said he was doing well, he'd continue with what he was doing.

Expand, take land, earn bounties, wipe out murderers, and destroy Creep.

That's what I've been doing. We'll keep doing that.

Keep doing all those things.

Yes. That's what we'll do.

Six

For the last day and a half, Steve had done little else but dig. Relentlessly, ever southward, backbreaking digging.

Gwendolin had gone back with the wagon the other day with a promise that someone else would come back soon with the watering can.

Steve had insisted on it going back with her. There was no way he would ever dare leave it away from the farm too long. His plan was to link to the waterway that ran to Filch. Once he did that, the outpost would be fed all on its own.

When he'd finally managed to reach it hours ago, water had started filling in the expanded trench-way to the outpost immediately after he'd connected to it.

And only with water that was runoff from the farm, no less. He never wanted to risk his farm. That one location was home to everything he gave a crap about.

Looking where he knew the cabin was, he could just barely make out the details for it. The long trek back to the outpost after he'd finished his dig had felt never-ending.

"Husband, welcome back!" said Jaina, rapidly approaching him from the west and slightly behind him. She seemed to delight in surprising him. Coming up at him from his blind spots or whenever he couldn't sense her.

"Thanks. All good here?" Steve asked, not stopping.

"Yes, yes. Everything is good." Jaina came up out of her four-legged running sprint and moved into a casual walk next to him. "Ina and I have been working at adding rock walls while the farmhands dig."

"Good work. Think it's worth trying to put up a palisade, or is it just easier to do it all in stone?" Steve asked.

The loving and kind Kobold looked thoughtful.

"I think stone would be best, husband. It's very, very strong. Witch-stone is what we're calling it," Jaina said. "I've been making arrowheads out of it for practice. I think Lucia will like them."

"Oh? Interesting," Steve said.

"Can we have sex? Right here?" Jaina asked out of nowhere.

Ever since she'd been shown the proof that Gwendolin, a widow, was pregnant, Jaina had been unceasing in her quest for sex and a litter.

It was a constant, all-day thing.

Steve had been reluctant. Part of him really didn't want more children. He was happy with just impregnating Gwendolin for now. If he had his way, he'd make Jaina wait a few months.

"I mean, we could. You sure you won't get depressed again?" Steve asked. Jaina was taking it hard after each time they had sex without getting her pregnant.

"Yes, yes. It's fine. I realized it doesn't matter. Gwen is pregnant. She was a widow and had a child before you met her," Jaina said. "I only need to be patient and have lots of sex with you. Soon enough, I'll get my litter. The priestesses lied."

"That… makes sense," Steve said cautiously. It was honestly what he wanted to hear from her. If Gwendolin was pregnant, anyone could be. Time and repetition were all that was needed to ensure that.

"Lots and lots of sex," Jaina said. "Good thing I like sex."

"Heh, good thing I like se—"

A giant purple square went screeching up into the sky.

It was truly massive. Massive, dense, and angry looking.

Angry sounding as well.

A loud, nasty crackling noise drowned everything else out.

Jaina didn't wait for him. She went off at maximum speed on all fours. Burning across the grass toward the square.

Must be Ina.

What could it be, though? That's a fucking huge —

Blinking, Steve had a thought. A thought that, if true, was frightening in a way.

Nancy?

Holding tight to his axe and shovel, Steve started sprinting as fast as he could. He needed to get to that square as soon as he could.

He wasn't expecting Nancy to have come back. Truth be told, he wasn't half as confident in her as he'd made it seem outwardly.

Unfortunately, he couldn't see very much of what was going on. The big purple magical construct itself made it almost impossible. With the density of the magic and the power it was putting out, it was almost like a wall.

Even as he ran on and got closer, he still couldn't see very much.

It wasn't until he was practically on top of it that he could finally see what was going on.

Inside of the big magical square were a very large number of people. More than Steve could readily or willingly count. They were, one and all, looking around. Each and every one looked bewildered, confused, and angry.

Off to one side was Ina, Jaina, Kassandra, and surprisingly, Nancy.

She had a black eye and a fat lip, but otherwise looked intact.

Behind her and to the side were three women, a man, and seven children.

She's not married, though. Must be the rest of her family.

Steve came to a stop in front of the group and looked at the square again.

"I take it this is your village, Nancy?" he asked.

"Yes," Nancy said. "It's... everyone, really. Or almost everyone. A small group of people were left behind to guard the village, along with all of the men."

"They do that to you, by the way?" Steve asked, not looking at her. He was curious who'd given her the beating.

"Yeah." Nancy's tone dropped. "They didn't believe me that I'd escaped and the others hadn't. It took some convincing, but I made it happen."

"How in the world did you get everyone out here?" Kassandra asked, her arms folded in front of her.

"I told them there was a village here, full of food and water," Nancy said. "Told them we'd have to send everyone here if we wanted to secure it before the other village could take it. This is everyone who could walk and carry food back."

Looking into that mass of people, Steve saw quite a few children in there. Quite a few.

This isn't what I was thinking it would be.

Not at all.

This is... this isn't what I was expecting. I made a mistake, didn't I?

"Even the young girls are murderers," Kassandra said softly, her eyes moving from person to person. "But not all of them. There's quite a few in there who aren't. Innocents."

Great. That's just what I needed.

Great, grand, peachy, lovely.

Fuck me.

"Yeah," Steve grumbled. "I'm just going to be honest here and admit I fucked up. I didn't think it was really a village."

"I said it was a village," Nancy said.

"Yeah, I get that—I mean that's... ugh," Steve groused. "You said it was a village, and all I heard in my head was 'bandit camp' and thought nothing more. I fucked up, okay? I fucked up."

Everyone was staring at the people as they walked around, angrily beat on the purple walls, or shouted soundlessly at Steve and company.

"What do we do?" Kassandra asked. "We could go through and put all the murderers to death. Offer the innocents a chance to leave or work on the farm."

"I... don't want to kill children," Ina said. "Even if they're murderers. I don't want to. I don't think I can do that, Steve. I'm sorry.

"You know I'd damn well do almost anything for you. Or let you do anything to me. But I can't. I just can't."

"Me either. No, no," Jaina said.

The two Witches were off to one side, looking disheartened.

Yeah... or me.

Fuck, I fucked this one up.

Fuck.

"How many people do you think we'll need defending the walls up here, my little snake?" Steve asked.

"Hmm? A thousand, if you wanted all the walls watched. Thousand more for rotation and defense," Kassandra said.

"And there's no... magical... easy-to-implement overpowered way to ensure obedience," Steve said.

"No, not with these numbers. There's bits of magic that can bind a few people, but not like this," Kassandra said. "That seems almost too fantastical to even comprehend."

"If we convinced them all to fight for me, live here, and die here, how could we keep them on the line, so to speak?" Steve asked.

"I don't know," Kassandra said. "With the army it—you know what, that doesn't make sense either. I can't even tell you why I was so determined to follow orders. That I never considered having children and just... lived for the army.

"I don't know."

Steve frowned, wanting to change the subject away from that. He had an inkling that the army might be brainwashed in the same way as those with the need to breed.

That there might be something going on around the world, and something else at a national level.

On top of that, there was a clear distinction between the citadel soldiers and the country's army. The citadel soldiers seemed far more like normal women with needs and vices.

Kassandra had said many times that she was a model soldier and everyone was just like her. That the army was something special unto itself.

Even citadel city soldiers were different than the army.

And there was something telling Steve not to take any of this head-on right now.

"Nancy, you think they'd take an offer like that?" Steve asked.

"No. They'd kill you the first night," Nancy said.

"Right," Steve said, having expected that answer exactly. "Then we... imprison the murderers and begin executing them. Offer the innocents a job or to leave, and carry on. The murderers who're young can just... remain in prison, I guess."

"That doesn't feel like a good answer," Ina said.

"No, it doesn't," Steve agreed.

"What if I set up areas where they're allowed to be?" Ina asked.

"I wouldn't even know how that would work," Steve said. "What if they decide to rebel? To take up arms? Destroy the crops? The walls?"

"Collars," Jaina said, shifting her weight around. "Let's put collars on them. They're murderers; their lives aren't theirs. They should all be executed. Hung to death till dead. Dead, dead."

"Collars with stones and magic. Spells that would prevent them from going very far from the outpost, from hurting any of us or going against orders, yes," Ina said, picking up where Jaina had left off. "We could easily do that. So far, the magic we've been utilizing is all combat-oriented or triggered. I'm sure we could figure out how to put latent combat spells into a collar."

"Yes, yes," Jaina said, nodding her head. "Very doable. Better than killing them all. We could make it so the collars leech off them to say powered. Tie it back in, so you can't break the collar without killing them."

"Oh, I like that," Ina said with a nod.

"Get working on it," Steve said. "I'd like something I can test out by the end of the day. Will this... hold?"

He pointed at the square.

"Oh, definitely," Ina said, turning to him with a beautiful smile. "We can even pass them items like water or food as needed. Won't even be an issue. Hardly an inconvenience."

"Good... get working on it then, and thank you. Both of you. This'd be much harder without you," Steve said. He felt weird thanking them, but he knew he should.

"Of course, husband!" Jaina said. Then she turned to Ina. "Oh! I was thinking—you don't like him finishing in you, and I want his seed. Can I join you later? He can finish in me rather than you."

"That'd work out rather well, wouldn't it?" Ina said, turning back to Jaina. "Deal. But let's get to work first."

Rolling his eyes at that, Steve started heading back to the cabin.

"Come on Nancy. Bring your friends. They can wait outside the cabin," Steve said. "We need to talk."

***

Sitting down at the small table in the cabin, Steve gestured to the seat across from him. Nancy sat down in it.

She was moving normally, but Steve got the impression she'd been beaten far more severely than she let on.

"You did it," Steve said, looking at the Wight. From what he could tell, she was tired, sore, and hurting, but generally healthy. Her cheeks were also slightly flushed, and her complexion looked much better.

In fact, she was practically healing before his eyes.

Then he realized what was happening.

She's feeding off them. She gets what she wants, remains free, and enjoys an unending food source.

"You did it," Steve repeated, holding his hands out neutrally. "I'm surprised. I honestly didn't expect you to come back."

"Did... you not want me to come back?" Nancy asked.

"No. I'm pleased you came back, I just didn't expect it. You surprised me. Good job, Nancy." Steve laid his hands down on the table between them. "Good job."

"Thank you. I... wanted to make it happen. I want to be your mistress and secret keeper," Nancy said, her fingers curling into her palms.

"Really? That's it?" Steve asked, his eyes sliding to the door behind her.

Nancy pressed her lips together tightly, refusing to turn around.

"As your mistress, I would expect my family to be taken care of. My sisters, nieces, and nephew. Murderers or not," Nancy said.

"Fine," Steve said. "Fine. I can do that. I'll send them back to the farm, out of harm's way."

And away from you.

Nancy blinked her one good eye twice, the other swollen shut still, then nodded her head. "Agreed. May I contract us now? It's black magic... you'll be marked. The priestesses would try to have you executed immediately if they saw you."

"Have you looked at my status?" Steve asked with a chuckle. "I clearly don't ascribe to the religious views of Lamals. It's very likely they'd try to have me executed anyways."

"Okay. It's not a pretty binding. I think we should use our feet. Probably the soles," Nancy said.

"What exactly do you mean by 'not a pretty binding'?" Steve asked.

"It's going to look like an inky blot. Almost like you were sick," Nancy said.

"Uh huh… and just what exactly is this going to do again?"

"It'll bind me to you, and you to me. If I betray you, I die. If you betray me, you lose your big toes," Nancy said. Steve raised an eyebrow at that.

He'd noted her deliberate imbalance last time. This time it seemed even more skewed to his side.

"I'm not stupid enough to think this is a binding of equals. I'll be a mistress. I'll likely never have children, I'll be a decoration for your bed when you wish it, and probably… I'll probably be told to do many awful things. But it's better than being a prisoner, or being executed."

Running his tongue along his molars, Steve thought on it. He really didn't need her.

He'd made a promise, though. He'd given her his word.

"Alright, bind us, Nancy the Wight, my Mistress and Secret Keeper," Steve said, making sure to really state those titles. "And let's be clear here. If you tell my secrets to anyone, even my wives, that'd be a betrayal and I'd expect you to die immediately."

"I understand. I can do that," Nancy said.

"Alright, bind us then. As soon as you're done, I'll mark you." Steve leaned back in his chair.

"Okay, yes. I'll do it." Nancy nodded. Then she held her hands up, palms upward, and clearly focused on them.

Black flecks began to form on her hands. Settling into the center of her palms.

Slowly, they continued to fill with pieces of absolute blackness. An ink-like color that seemed to devour light without any reflection.

Minutes later and one was the size of a large orange, the other a marble.

"Okay," Nancy said in a wheeze, sweat dripping down her face and neck. "That's done. I'm not very good at black magic. I'm sorry it took so long for such a simple thing."

"It's fine," Steve said. "What do you expect me to do exactly?"

"Take this one," Nancy said, moving her right hand out in front of her. It contained the small marble-like ball of darkness. "Just put it under your foot and then crush it."

Picking it up between thumb and forefinger, Steve inspected the marble.

You've been given a black-magic contract.

The contract binds Steven Bril to Nancy Abellis for all time.

The majority contract holder is Steven Bril.

The lesser contract holder is Nancy Abellis.

The lesser contract holder shall obey, abide, and adhere to all rules given by the majority contract holder.

The penalties of the contract are based on the perception of the majority contract holder.

All penalties will be judged and assessed accordingly by the majority contract holder, Steven Bril.

Major sub-clauses exist:

Should Nancy Abellis betray Steven Bril, she will instantly cease to live.

Should Steven Bril betray Nancy Abellis, he will lose both his left hallux and right hallux.

Please confirm that you wish to accept this black-magic contract.

Hallux?

That's a new one.

Big toe would have been fine.

Fine. Yes, but I don't wish for anyone to know of this contract. Nor for it to have a physical manifestation.

Contract accepted under condition of anonymity.

Contract is now active.

"Ah!" Nancy squeaked, the black magic in her hand vanishing. "Where... what... It's active. I saw the message, but I didn't—"

"Yes," Steve said, interrupting her. "And welcome to my first secret. I'm not normal. I can modify many things I wish to. I have enchanted tools. I can impregnate whomever I wish to impregnate. I can give people titles, names, and monikers. I'm incredibly strong, to the point that I worry I might hurt someone accidentally. I have no memories of anything before this year. I've heard a voice speak to me from nowhere, and apparently I'm in some sort of test that I already failed once."

Nancy was staring at him wide eyed right now, and her eye that had been swollen shut was rapidly returning to normal.

The despair in the surrounding area seemed to be nourishing her to an absurd degree.

"Okay," she said.

"Good. I name you Secret Keeper, but no one else will be able to see the title. I also name you my Mistress, which anyone can see," Steve said. "In addition to that, I strike the Murderer title from you. In giving yourself to me, I rule that you're no longer a free person, and are property."

Nancy gasped and leaned back in her chair, her eye moving to the space in front of her.

Nancy Abellis
Wight
Father: Deceased
Mother: Living
Property of Steven Bril
Mistress- personal mistress of Steven Bril
Sellout- willingly became the property of another
Prostitute- willingly sold herself for gains
Depraved Predator- lives on the suffering of others
Merciful- has spared others for no reason
Secret Keeper*- the one who knows all *This title is
hidden.

Black-magic contractor*- vile magic enthusiast *This title is hidden.

"What... what are you?" Nancy asked, looking at Steve.

"No idea," Steve said honestly and stood up. "And I'd tell you if I did, since you're mine, my Wight. Go take care of your family and send them off to the farm. They can literally just follow the waterway.

"Then get yourself ready. We're going to need more taskmasters, and I'm going to make you find them and sort them out for me."

He walked over to Nancy and laid a hand on her shoulder.

"Work hard, Mistress," Steve said, then gave her shoulder a reassuring pat.

Seven

Leaning on his axe, Steve watched as Jaina and Ina systematically brought someone over to the edge of the purple square and collared them.

Only after confirming they were a murderer, however.

If they encountered someone who was innocent of crime, they were given food and water, then told to do as they pleased. They could stay, leave, or do whatever they wished.

Which meant there were a lot of children all standing around near the farm fields with nothing to do.

Kassandra had been directing them over that way as soon as it was clear there was going to be plenty of them.

As soon as murderers were collared, they were brought through the square and then sent to the fields. Sometimes they'd go to the children, collect theirs, and then move on.

Kinda glad we're not killing them out of hand after all.

Being a villain doesn't make someone incapable of good.

It just means they made shitty decisions and ended up in a downward spiral.

Or maybe it means they had no other choice but to make shitty decisions. I'd become a murderer if it meant saving my loved ones.

Or I'd do worse.

I'm no better than they are.

Sighing, Steve regretted his plan and not for the first time.

In the same breath, he also didn't regret it. He was going to get a massive influx of workers who could all assist with protecting what was his. The fact that they'd work for food, water, and the ability to continue on living was a bonus.

"Kill me," said a woman standing at the edge of the square.

Ina turned and looked at Steve.

Steve shrugged. He didn't have any reason to deny her the request.

"She a murderer?" he asked.

"Yeah," Ina said, looking back at the woman.

"Then kill her for me, in the name of our farm," he said. "Try to kill her without any bloodshed. We can probably use her clothes. Just need to make sure we get them off her before she shits herself."

- 67 -

Jaina flicked her hand out in front of her and then closed it.

The woman crumpled to the ground, clutching at her chest. That only lasted for a few seconds before she went completely still.

Bounty collected.

Coin to be collected (36s) at a government-sponsored fine, tax, and levy station.

Steve has gained prestige for enforcing a cardinal law of the Lamals.

Reaching into the square, Jaina grabbed the now-dead woman by her foot and hauled her out to one side.

"You. Take her clothes off," Ina said, addressing the woman Jaina had just collared. "You can keep one item for yourself if you do it before she soils them."

Immediately, the woman dove on the dead one and began working at her pants.

Smart. The pants are what would get soiled. Doesn't matter if the corpse does its thing when the pants aren't there.

Turning back to the square, Steve sighed.

"You, come forward." Ina pointed at a young woman.

Steve judged her to be about thirteen.

"Murderer, thief, and liar," Ina said aloud. "Anything I need to know?"

"No," said the young girl, looking down at the grass.

"Serve or die," Ina said.

"Serve," said the girl.

"Step over to Jaina," Ina said, gesturing to the side. Then she looked into the square again. "You, step forward."

The young girl moved over to stand in front of Jaina.

"Hi, hi," Jaina said with a smile. "I'm Jaina. My husband is Steve. He's who you owe your life to. He's nice. Very, very nice."

Jaina formed a stone necklace, the slave collar, right there on the spot.

"Do you have a favorite color?" she asked, smiling at the girl.

"I like purple," said the girl.

Jaina dragged her thumb over the stone in the center of the slave collar, and it immediately became a bright purple.

"Like this?" Jaina asked, holding it up. All in all, it wasn't bad looking. It was an ornate collar, almost like a thick necklace with a bright jewel at its center.

The girl nodded and then leaned forward, tilting her head toward Jaina.

Jaina snapped the collar in place, then touched it to activate it and pulled the girl through the square.

"Is your family still in there?" Jaina asked.

"No. I'm alone. I have no family," said the girl.

"Okay, that's fine. Go stand with the other children. We'll find you someone to care for you," Jaina patted her on the shoulder. "I promise."

"I don't need anyone," muttered the girl.

"Okay. Then go stand with the women," Jaina said with a smile and a shrug of her shoulders. "Your choice, your choice."

Shambling off, the young girl picked up the provisions being given to everyone and went to join the women.

They were all working at putting together shelters from the various logs, sticks, and foliage Steve had been stockpiling.

It had set him back to build massive bunkhouses for them, but it was better to have them and protect them, than do the work by himself without them.

One of Nancy's family members intercepted the girl and guided her to a different group. They were all much younger and seemed to walk the line between adult and child.

"Good," Steve said softly, looking at Nancy beside him.

The swelling around her black eye was long gone now. The black eye remained, but it was fading quickly.

"I've told my taskmasters to make sure they take care of everyone," Nancy said. "They're resources and living people at the same time, not animals or things to be broken."

Steve didn't care one way or the other, as long as they were cared for. To him, everyone was a resource unless they were part of his family. He neither wished them dead nor alive.

Nancy made more sense to him now, though, with how she was handling herself. But not completely. She was certainly not quite a resource anymore, but not family either. The Wight was creating a strange middle ground in Steve's thinking.

"Another to die," Ina said, looking over at Steve.

Steve shrugged at that. "I mean, go for it? Don't need my permission. Just make sure you get her clothes and that she actually has an execution pinned to her."

Ina looked back at the woman as Jaina made the same grabbing motion she had earlier. The woman crumpled over to one side, clutching at her heart.

Bounty collected.

Coin to be collected (40s) at a government-sponsored fine, tax, and levy station.

Steve has gained prestige for enforcing a cardinal law of the Lamals.

Steve sighed, hoping this would be over soon.

He had work to do.

Need to go check out the village and see what's left. Then go check on the other one we sent that other girl to.

***

Steve scratched at his hip and yawned.

The work parties, all wearing collars, were busily looting all of their own possessions.

One of the innocents they'd let free had apparently run back to the village to warn everyone there of what'd happened. They'd looted everything they wanted and hit the road.

It was a complete ghost town.

Not even the animals had remained. To Steve, it looked as if quite a few had been butchered on the spot and harvested, the remains left to rot.

Or so the forty-some-odd dead animals, that'd clearly been killed and cleaned in a hurry, seemed to suggest. They lay around the fields, flies buzzing around them in hordes, stinking of spoiled meat and foulness.

Clearly they'd been dead for the entire three days it'd been since they'd killed, freed, or collared everyone from this village.

"A waste," Kassandra muttered. "They could have just as easily joined us. It's already quite well spread around the camp that Nancy no longer has her murderer title."

"They wouldn't have known that when they took off," Steve argued. "Besides. They were innocent. They can go wherever they want. It isn't like we had a bigger claim to this village than they did."

"Foolish," Kassandra said, shaking her head. "All they had to do was serve you. Innocent or not."

"Not really looking for servants. I'm not a king, or a governor, or anything like that. I want my farm and my lands," Steve said. "Beyond that, maybe an army to kick over people I don't like. I'm fine with that."

Kassandra looked like she wanted to disagree, but she said nothing further on the subject.

"I'm going to go inspect the warehouse," the Lamia said and then began slithering away.

"She's very devoted," Nancy said once she was out of earshot.

"Mm-hmm," Steve said.

"Do you want me to learn everyone else's secrets and report them back to you?" Nancy asked suddenly.

"Sure," Steve said with a shrug. He didn't care one way or the other. With any luck, it'd get Nancy out of his hair. She'd been acting like a giant barnacle since she'd come back. If she wasn't within three feet of him, it was because he was taking a shit or he'd somehow lost her.

Fuck it. No reason not to use her as she's asking. Then I can just blame it on her.

Besides, it'd be fun to find out more about the girls.

Nikki always has seemed rather mysterious, in a way.

"Just don't do anything stupid or get caught. You'd be an awful secret keeper if it was obvious you were spying on them," Steve said, making up his mind.

"Got it," Nancy said. "I can do that. Will you take me to bed tonight?"

"No." Steve shook his head. "I've got plans with Ina and Jaina. Remember?"

"I do, but I'm still going to ask," Nancy professed.

He looked over at the rather beautiful Wight, who was definitely built for the comforts of home and a bed, and gave her a quick once-over.

She was dressed far more like Jaina and Kassandra today. At several points, Steve had also noticed her doing simple exercises, eating what Kassandra and Jaina did, and questioning Kassandra for information on weapon usage.

"How's that going, by the way?" Steve said, not looking away from her. "Trying to become my mistress, bodyguard, and bed toy, that is."

"Ah… I'm already your mistress, I'm getting advice on being your bodyguard, and the bed toy… well, no one will speak with me about that," Nancy observed. "They just change the subject, and you keep telling me no.

"I've already put on some muscle, and I feel like I can run much farther than I could when I came back."

"Didn't ask you to become those things," Steve said, finally looking away from her.

"I know, but I want to be the other things," Nancy said. "I can keep my family in luxury if I am, and you'll be less likely to kill me out of hand.

"I don't believe for a minute you haven't considered simply eliminating me."

It was true.

He'd considered casually killing her several times. The price to do so wasn't that bad, after all, and he wouldn't lose anything for it.

"I think you're far more cold… more… evil… than anyone thinks," Nancy said. "I think you'd strangle me as casually as take me to bed. Or both. Bed me, then strangle me. I think you're only keeping it contained because you see no reason to let it out."

Hmm.

Curious. She seems to know me better than even Nikki.

"And that doesn't bother you?" Steve asked.

"No. I think I'll be more useful to you alive then dead, and I've been proving that," Nancy noted. "You'll keep me alive, bed me, and then consider me useful. See that I'm pulling my weight. Then I'll be safe, and my family will be safe."

Clicking his tongue, Steve considered reaching over and strangling Nancy right now. She was annoying him, and he didn't like what she was saying.

"Don't, please don't," Nancy said as if reading his mind. "I'm only telling you what you asked. I'm useful. Very useful."

"Hmm. Alright, Miss Useful—you and I are going to go find that other village. The woman we sent to bring them in never came back, which means it's time to check on them," Steve said, looking at Nancy again. "If they catch us, I want you to remain behind so I can get away."

Nancy nodded her head at that.

"Stay behind so you can escape if I get us caught. I understand," Nancy said, turning on her heel. She immediately began marching away.

"Small detour to make, Miss Strangle-Me. I need to tell Kassandra where I'm going," Steve said.

He wasn't quite sure why Nancy was so quick to do such things. So eager to give all of herself to him.

But he wasn't going to question it either.

He was growing fond of the idea of having a henchwoman.

***

"Well, that explains where she went," Steve muttered.

Out ahead of them, tied to a stake in front of the city, was the woman they'd sent to talk her village into coming to the farm.

She was quite dead and looked to have been eviscerated.

The whole place looked like a giant shanty town surrounded by part of a wooden wall and barricades. It had the look of something that had been thrown together, held up with hope and mud, and was constantly being repaired.

"You couldn't keep a cow out of this place," Steve muttered.

"Yes," Nancy agreed. They were laid out flat on the ground near the village, doing their best to pretend they were nothing more than clods of grass. "It's never been a good place."

The village was quite well prepared for people to try and attack them, despite looking like a wreck.

It would just be a fight amongst the houses themselves rather than at a wall.

Steve wasn't a strategist, but he couldn't see a valid way to get a hold of the inhabitants of the village without a lot of people on both sides ending up dead.

And he wanted them all for himself. Either to kill them or put them to work.

Murderers seem to be easy money.

With every woman that had chosen death from the square, Steve had gained coins and bounty prestige.

"Anything you can tell me about them?" he asked.

"Very warlike," Nancy answered, shifting around in the grass. "Very aggressive. They'll take men captive and bring them back if they can. Kill them if they can't. Lots of children in there. And most everyone is pregnant. Even the young ones. They... all husband swap."

Steve wasn't sure what that meant, but he got the impression it wasn't good.

Best he could figure was it meant men were more like communal property than husbands.

Could be good, could be bad. Depends on how good looking they are, I guess.

Well, that's my thought at least. Maybe they wouldn't want to be hip deep in eager women all day.

Sounds nice to me, though.

"Uh huh," Steve said. "How do we capture them all?"

Nancy shrugged.

"I was able to convince my village through greed. I'm not sure what would convince the Felistins. They're very... stubborn and violent," she said.

"Hmm. Okay. So... trickery, subterfuge, or something like that," Steve elaborated. "None of which I seem very suited for."

"I'll handle all that for you," Nancy offered. "I'll pick up the slack where you fall off. I'll be your support and foundation with those things."

"Think so, huh?" Steve asked with a chuckle. "And you think you're qualified for that?"

"I'm very bright. Very intelligent. I learn quickly. I taught myself the rudiments of black magic. Invest in me, I'll make everything else happen for you," Nancy said, staring at him with wide eyes.

There was a certain madness to her that'd he'd come to recognize. She wanted to punish herself and be punished.

All the while becoming more.

He didn't quite get it, but Nancy wasn't quite right in the head.

"Fine," Steve said. "Can you read?"

"No," Nancy said.

"We'll start there then, I suppose." Steve looked back toward the village. "What's the name of this shit hole again?"

"Felistin," Nancy said. "It was fou—"

"I don't care," Steve hissed, interrupting her. "I don't. I really don't care."

"Okay," Nancy said.

"Anywhere we can bed down for the night?" Steve asked. "Probably should have asked you how far away it was before we left. I really don't want to be stumbling the entire way home through the night, just to arrive before dawn."

"There's a scouting rest point my village used not far from here. We didn't use it often, so it shouldn't be known," Nancy said. "And those who would know about it are wearing collars."

Steve nodded and sighed.

"Alright, Mistress and Secret Keeper, tell me why I shouldn't strangle you right now and leave your corpse here," Steve said. "Tell me how you're going to take Felistin. Why are you useful?"

He didn't actually want to strangle her, but he wasn't going to hide his thoughts from her. She'd already accurately guessed his mentality, so there was no reason to put on the Human mask Nikki had convinced him to wear.

Which meant he didn't need to hide the fact that he didn't see her as useful yet.

"Uhm," Nancy pontificated intelligently, looking at the city. "You just want them captured, right?"

"Mm-hmm," Steve said.

"Can I do it however I want to? Even if it made it so the church could try to execute us without a trial?" Nancy asked.

"Pretty sure they hate me already, or would if they knew about me, so why not?" Steve said.

"I'll poison them. All of them," Nancy said. "All we have to do is dig down deep enough with a well. Then I poison it with black magic. Magic that would seep through the ground and into their wells.

"A black magic poison that would incapacitate everyone within a day but not show any symptoms until then."

"Hmm," Steve said, thinking.

It was a reasonable plan. He had no idea how deep you'd have to dig to do such a thing, though.

Could do it quickly enough with the shovel. Wouldn't even be an issue, would it?

Something to consider. I think I want to head back and talk to Nikki about all this first.

Then decide from there.

"Alright. Come on, Mistress," Steve said. "Take us to that scout camp. Going to bed down there for the night."

Damnit. Going to miss out on having Ina and Jaina, too. That's fun. Always fun.

They make sure it's fun.

There was something extremely gratifying and strange about having Ina and then finishing in Jaina.

Each woman pretending as if the other didn't exist during the whole thing, but both getting what they wanted.

While Steve got to have both of them.

"Of course, this way," Nancy said, as she started to crawl away from the village.

Eight

"Right here," Nancy called.

Grunting, Steve moved over to one side and dropped the massive load of large branches and two chunks of logs he'd been carrying.

Moving to one side, he went to start pulling his boots off. He dropped them and sat down, leaning against the cave wall.

"Again, I'm sorry. I really didn't think it'd be inhabited," Nancy said.

"Yeah, well, it was. And I'm not about to go in there and kill a bunch of people who didn't do anything wrong," Steve said. "Maybe if they were murderers."

Steve wasn't really that annoyed at Nancy. He was mostly angry that the people they'd found at the scout camp had indeed been innocents.

They'd done no wrong to anyone. Which made Steve feel like he couldn't really bother them.

They didn't deserve his wrath.

"I never suggested you should," Nancy countered, bending down over a small pile of sticks.

Their light was rapidly failing now. Nancy had been quick witted enough to suggest a cave she knew of. One with a jumpable gap that would prevent the Creep and its monsters from getting to them.

Unfortunately, it also had some problems. There wasn't much in the way of luxuries, the ground was rocky, and there were no supplies.

At best, they'd have a fire to keep warm.

"Though I'm glad you didn't even consider it," Nancy murmured, a soft repetitive click drawing his eyes to what she was doing.

Much like Nikki had done numerous times, Nancy was starting a fire for them.

"Shouldn't you be like… living for the despair of others? Isn't it what you eat?" Steve asked.

"Yes, I live on the despair of others," Nancy confirmed. "But no, I don't. I have a trick or two my mother taught me to keep me pleasantly Human. Otherwise, I'd probably have started doing exactly what you think I'd be doing."

"Tricks?" Steve asked. He was curious. "Tell me your secrets, Mistress. Yours are mine, mine are yours."

"I can feed off my own suffering," Nancy answered without any hesitation. "The fact that I'm yours, that I have no free will, that I did it to myself, that I'm branded as a prostitute and property where anyone can see it, and that I'll never be a wife—it's all horrifying to me.

"It makes my heart quiver, and I feel like I want to throw up all the time.

"And it's amazing. It's… delicious."

Nancy let out a soft whimper that sounded eerily like a moan at the same time.

"It tastes so wonderful," Nancy said, still working at the fire. "My misery is so intense, and it's the best tasting thing I've ever had. I want to suffer so much more. I want you to make it so I weep at night when I'm alone, curled at the foot of your bed like an animal. Maybe naked with just a thin ratty blanket."

Nancy paused in what she was doing and bent over slightly, a hiccupping sob breaking through her breathing, immediately followed by a deep moan that was clearly sexual.

"It'll taste absolutely incredible, I'm sure, when you do that to me. No blanket." Nancy clicked the fire-starters together again. "No blanket. No clothes. Maybe force me into your bed, ravage me, then kick me out of it when you're done with me. Only to have one of your wives join you in the bed."

"So you're crazy then?" Steve asked, scratching at his stomach.

Suddenly her responses to his threats, actions, and everything else made a lot more sense to him.

It'd never bothered her because she'd been getting off on it to a degree.

"I'm not crazy, no. I just… I feed off myself. And the worse I am, the better I taste. The more I thought about it, the more being your toy sounded absolutely soul wrenching to me. I almost threw up right there, when I offered myself up," Nancy said. "And it was so… so… succulent."

"Crazy," Steve said, nodding his head. "That's fine. Nothing wrong with crazy, so long as you can get it to work for you in the right way. You're not going to go stupid and try to hurt me, are you?"

"No, but I want you to hurt me. Make me despair to live," Nancy gushed. "Maybe hit me a little? Work up to a full beating? Break a finger or two? Brand me? I heal really well. I don't scar at all. Not even a blemish."

"Uh, no." Steve felt a sudden hard stop on the conversation pop up in his head. "Sorry. Not really into causing pain."

"Will you at least bed me or make me take you in my mouth?" Nancy asked, finally getting several sparks to catch in the tinder. "Ah, there we go."

She leaned in quickly and started to blow into her small glowing bundle.

Well… I'm kinda horny.
Could use it.
But it horrifies her?
But she wants it.
What the actual fuck.

"You want me to bed you," Steve clarified, watching as the amazingly attractive Wight transferred her glowing bundle to a bunch of small sticks.

"Yes, repeatedly. Preferably with my wrists tied as you slap me around," Nancy said.

"Ah… no. I'm not… no." Steve shook his head at that. He was very much opposed to hurting her.

Deathly so.

The small games he played with Ina were nothing in the end, little more than some dark psychological roleplay.

Kassandra was a little different, but it still wasn't like this.

What Nancy wanted felt like crossing a line. One he wasn't willing to commit to at the moment.

"Then yes, I want you to bed me. Can you at least tie me up? That'd be pretty nice. Nice and tight till my wrists ache," Nancy said. "Maybe after you force yourself down my throat?"

Steve shook his head, not really knowing what to say.

Nancy finished adding in branches and sticks to the crackling fire.

"Just the idea of you doing that, does it for me…" Nancy's voice trailed off in a soft moan. "Please? Do that? Tie me up, use me, and leave me naked when you're done like a broken doll?"

Steve felt like he could do some of the last bit, at least. That felt like just normal rough sex. Like what he had with Ina and Kassandra.

Especially Kassandra.

What Nancy had asked for before was just beyond his ability, but it wasn't exactly too strange either, when he thought about it. He knew very well there were those who wanted to be humiliated. Those who wanted to feel pain.

There were many forms of masochism.

The problem was, he just wasn't a sadist.

"Alright," Steve said, deciding to roll with it. "Strip for me."

Nancy made a soft whining noise and then rose up next to the fire.

Slowly, hesitatingly, she started to peel her clothes off. Her skin was so pale, it practically glowed in the firelight. Her black hair partially covered her face, but every now and then, he caught her green eyes watching him. They were haunted and excited at the same time.

Isn't there a saying? Don't stick your dick in cr… don't stick your… eh… whatever.

In no time at all, Nancy was nude before him. One of her hands fluttered over her privates while her other arm lay across her breasts. Her head was tilted to one side, her hair entirely obscuring her face.

"Move your hands," Steve said.

With a very soft whimper, Nancy moved her hands and twitching fingers away. Then she moaned.

"Let me see your face," Steve said.

Nancy lifted her hands and pulled her hair back behind her.

Her eyes looked insanely excited, and she had a massive grin on her face. In the same breath, she looked like she was on the verge of laughing maniacally.

"Keep going," Nancy said in a low voice, her grin becoming odd as her lips trembled. "Do more to me. Are you sure I can't talk you into hitting me? I want you to hit me."

"No violence," Steve said simply. "Don't bring it up again. Ever."

"No violence," Nancy repeated. She looked angry at that, but then nodded her head, and her creepy smile came back. "Is... rough is okay, though?"

"Rough is okay," Steve admitted.

"Good. Great. Tie me up and force it down my throat, then," Nancy purred at him.

I can do that. Kassandra has me do that sometimes.

Getting to his feet, Steve began to unbuckle his belt. He pulled it free, then shook his pants down and stepped out of them.

"Turn around, Nancy," Steve said in a commanding voice. "And I'm ordering you to tell me what you actually want. No games. If you lie to me, it's a betrayal."

He wanted to be absolutely sure this was what she wanted.

"I want you to beat me," Nancy said in a choked whisper. "To brand me. To cut me. To scar me up with your name and let everyone see it. I want you to slap me while ravaging me. To destroy me and make me suffer. Brand my face repeatedly.

"I want to suffer so much. I've never tasted anything like this. I need more. So much more. Force a child on me and never marry me. Make me raise your other children, but never let them call me Mother."

Completely crazy. But it's what she wants.

No violence though. None of that.

Cinching his belt around her wrists just as he did with Kassandra, he grabbed her by a shoulder and forced her down to her knees.

Nancy grunted as she hit the cave floor and knelt there.

"Yes, more," she whispered. "More."

Sliding his fingers through Nancy's hair, he slowly bent her head around until she ended up facing him. He kept pulling until she'd turned herself around completely.

She was panting, staring up at him with wide eyes and that broken smile on her face.

"Yes, in my throat. Deep," she murmured, and her eyes slid down to his fully erect member in front of her. "Force it deep down in my throat. Make me choke."

Steve couldn't deny that her incessant dirty talk was pushing his desire upward. It was strange and erotic at the same time.

Taking a good hold on Nancy's hair, he moved his left hand up to cup her face and guided his tip toward her lips.

Opening her mouth wider than Steve thought was possible, Nancy looked incredibly sexy. Then she slid her tongue out and wriggled it up and down as she looked up at him.

He crammed himself into her mouth, immediately going straight to the hilt and pushing himself down her throat.

Nancy's response was to close her mouth tight around him. Her eyes watered, and she gagged hard on him. But she didn't pull away. He could actually feel her trying to push him deeper. Till her chin was crushing his nuts.

Pushing her head away, Steve watched her as she watched him. The madness in her eyes was only growing by the second.

He paused when he got to the tip, hesitating.

"Down my throat," Nancy said around his tip. "I want it. Hard. Rough. Don't worry about me. Just do it. Can't hurt me. I'll heal."

Giving in, Steve pulled Nancy's head down and stuffing himself to the hilt back down her throat.

Moaning at the action, Nancy just gazed up at him. Her throat contracted, and then she gagged roughly on him, her body shuddering. Tears formed at the corners of her eyes as she continued to gag, the reaction clearly involuntary as she struggled to keep him there.

So messed up.

Holding tight to her hair, Steve began to pump back and forth through her mouth exactly as he wished to without regard for her.

Just what Nancy wanted.

Moaning, groaning, and gagging between, she quivered the whole time.

Nancy took it and tried to get more from him, pushing her face into him. Staring up at him without ever looking away.

Her tongue writhed, her lips were tight, and he could feel her sucking at him even as he thrust back and forth.

Sooner than he thought he would, Steve was pretty ready to simply burst.

"I'm right on the edge—you want it down your throat?" he asked. Then he decided to push her in the way he thought she wanted. "Or do you want me to drop a load of seed in you and try to get you pregnant?"

Nancy gagged the hardest he'd seen as she started to moan at his words, her whole body shaking. Jerking herself out of his grasp, she turned around, angled herself forward, and ended up with her face on the cave floor.

Her rear end was sticking straight up at him, and her back was arched. Giving him a perfect view of her dripping privates.

She coughed the entire time, and it was obvious she wasn't able to speak. Instead she shook her rear end at him. Inviting him.

So broken.

Grabbing Nancy by the hips, Steve immediately pushed himself completely into her slit.

If he had any doubts about what she wanted, they were dispelled in that instant. She was as wet as could be. To the point that it felt like he'd forced some of her wetness out due to the overwhelming amount of it.

Leaning over her, Steve began to ram himself down and into her. He reached down and pressed his hands into her shoulders, holding her still as he plowed her into the cave floor.

Nancy finally stopped coughing and instead began to sob and wail. Each one was punctuated by a twisted, deep moan.

"In me," she said after she took in a big hiccupping breath. "Risk a pregnancy on me. I want it. Give it to me. I want your seed."

Then she immediately started sobbing and moaning again. Her wails made a strange counterpoint to it all.

"Say it!" Nancy called out sucking in a deep breath. "Tell me you're gonna do it!"

Fuck, that's right, she knows I have some control over it.

Grunting as he pounded away at Nancy, Steve contemplated how to make this work. He leaned back, grabbed her hips, and pulled on her sides.

"Impregnate Nancy Abellis, my mistress," Steve said in a growl.

Impregnate Nancy Abellis?

No!

Nancy wailed loudly in what was practically a howl.

Steve came then, pumping hard into Nancy as he coated her insides.

"Yes!" Nancy wailed in a sob.

Pushing hard up against her, Steve felt himself filling her up. Far more than he'd been expecting.

Pulling at her as he finished up and grunting with each thrust, Steve finally came to an end.

With a wet squelch, he pulled himself out of Nancy. A sea of fluid spilled out of her and dribbled all down her thighs.

Steve has gained notoriety for breaking the laws of the Lamals.

Steve has gained the Took a Mistress accolade.

Steve has gained the Schadenfreude accolade.

Damn, she really had me going.

And what's with that accolade? Is that because I bedded her outside of a marriage?

She said it would be Animator if it was a marriage.

Maybe her being a Wight is way more abnormal than I thought. I need to talk to Nikki.

Whimpering, Nancy let her rear fall to the cave stone floor.

"Make me clean you up," she said in a sob. "Tell me to do it."

Shrugging his shoulders, Steve sat down against the cave wall. "Come clean me up, Mistress."

Sobbing softly, Nancy came over on her knees and inhaled him eagerly.

And started moaning around his girth. Bobbing her head up and down, fast and hard, while sucking at him.

Her green eyes immediately slid up to watch him again.

What in the fuck?

But that was a lot of fun.

***

Walking back toward the outpost, Steve felt a little odd about everything.

Nancy had reverted back to her somewhat quiet and stoic self. Acting like the perfect henchwoman again.

The previous night's activities had not been spoken of. Steve imagined it would come up eventually; he just wasn't sure when.

He could see the moat and partial stone walls up ahead.

"I'm not pregnant," Nancy said suddenly.

Apparently, this was the moment.

"Nope. It apparently isn't a guarantee," Steve said, deciding to lie to Nancy about this one facet. It'd keep her twisted up. If her entire deal was her own agony, that was how he'd keep her "fed" so to speak.

"That's why Jaina isn't pregnant," Nancy said.

"Mm-hmm," Steve said.

As they walked along, only the sound of their feet hitting the grass could be heard.

"You're not... treating me differently," Nancy remarked after the silence grew longer.

"Am I supposed to?" Steve asked.

"No. I thought... you would, though. I know that wasn't normal," Nancy said. "I'm not... I'm not crazy. I know what happened was crazy, but I'm not crazy."

You're crazy.

"Okay," Steve said.

"You don't mind it?" Nancy asked.

"It was pretty crazy," Steve admitted with a chuckle. "But it was fun in a dark way, too."

"And that I use black magic doesn't concern you?" Nancy said.

"Nope. You're my mistress. Your black magic is mine," Steve emphasized.

Nancy nodded at that, folding her arms across her stomach.

"Will you... please... use me like that again? Soon?" Nancy asked. "Now? Tonight?"

"Sure, I imagine we can find some time for that," Steve said.

"Will you slap m—"

"No. I won't. No violence. Remember?" Steve said.

"Light slaps? Just... a little? A couple?" Nancy asked, her tone taking on that strange edge again. "It'd just be rough, not really violence. I want it."

"Hush," Steve muttered.

Nancy immediately fell silent.

"I want to plan out an attack on that village. I want to take them tonight or tomorrow. Do you understand?" Steve asked.

"As your dark-magic mistress, I shall make sure it happens," Nancy said. "If I make it happen tonight, will you slap me? Just a little?"

"Nancy, I'm getting tired of this," Steve warned.

"Maybe you should slap me for not listening," she said.

"Or maybe I should make love to you next time instead, on a feather bed, with big fluffy blankets while telling you I love you," Steve hissed.

"That'd work, too. I don't think I'd like it as much, but I'm open to try," Nancy said with a shrug. "I'd really prefer a good, hard slap though. Maybe three of them. Or a brand of your name. Right on my cheek. Maybe my forehead. It'd heal in a day or two."

"Shut up," Steve said, shaking his head. "Go get me that village. Tell no one about the black magic. Tell them you're using poison. Take some of the women with you as henchwomen for yourself."

"Yes, Steve," Nancy said.

Without any more strangeness, Steve managed to get back to the outpost.

All around were women from the village. Working in groups with their taskmasters to accomplish their goals.

There were no chains, no whips, no batons, and no signs of even threatened violence.

Everyone was moving quickly and efficiently, though there was still clearly an air of partial resentment.

Not that he blamed them. They didn't want to be there. They were wearing magical collars that kept them in check, and their alternative was execution.

A death they'd earned, of course. Steve was being merciful for letting them live and treating them above and beyond well, so he didn't feel much in the way of guilt over it.

"Welcome home," Ina said, as Steve made it to the cabin. She was messing with what looked like a collar. "Any news?"

"A little." Steve walked over to the beautiful Creep Witch.

Reaching down, he lightly ran his fingers through her hair, then kissed her temple.

After dealing with Nancy, Ina was great with her very strong, very forward, and very honest view of their relationship.

"I love you, Ina. You know that?" Steve asked, standing next to her.

Visibly swallowing, Ina peered up at him. Then she gave him a slow and beautiful smile.

"I love you, too, Steve," she said in a soft voice. "Uhm… can… we go into the cabin? I think… I think I just changed my mind. I'd really like you to… to put a child… in me.

"Can we go try?"

Chuckling at that, Steve nodded his head. "Sure. But after, we need to talk about that village. I have a plan."

Nine

"I'm uncomfortable trusting her," Kassandra said, staring at Nancy.

The Wight stared back at the Lamia without any emotion. Much as she always did with everyone but Steve.

"Her name is Nancy," Jaina said, shifting her weight around where she squatted. "And I trust her because my husband does."

Kassandra sighed at that, then looked away. "This world doesn't allow for easy or swift trust."

"I don't trust her either," Ina said, lounging in one of the few chairs in the cabin. "But I also didn't trust you or Jaina at first."

"I trust none of you but Steve," Nancy said firmly. She didn't change her posture, shift, or move in any way, but to Steve she looked rather imposing with that statement.

Slowly, all four women turned to look at Steve as he sat in the corner.

"What?" he asked. "If I didn't trust you, I wouldn't be bedding you. We're all one criminal family, aren't we? You all have a Humanist accolade for a reason."

Each pretty face frowned at that, then started looking at one another.

"Figure out how we make that plan work to take that village. I want it," Steve said. "Sooner rather than later. Because there's a bunch of other villages to take, too. If we're going to do this, we need to do it right."

"You're not going to help us?" Ina asked.

"No. I'm going to go back home for a short while. I want to bathe in the lake, see Nia and everyone else. See what's going on, then come back," Steve said. He'd been thinking about it for a while, and he really did want to go back home for a quick check-in.

He wasn't exactly an introvert, but he didn't feel right not being at home at the moment.

Shitty Steve had put him there for a reason, and so far, Steve had no reason to doubt him.

Other than trading away his memories, he'd done right by Steve.

"I understand," Kassandra said. "I'll make sure to have a workable plan by the time you return."

"Good. Anyone need anything while I'm over there?" Steve asked. "And just to confirm, we haven't seen much of the Creep since I busted the wall, right?

"I haven't seen much of it personally, at least. A little here and there, but less and less every night."

"There was none last night," Kassandra said. "Not a wisp of it."

Jaina and Ina seemed thoughtful, then looked at one another.

"I haven't felt any. Have you?" Ina asked.

"No, no. None at all," Jaina responded.

Ina was still regarded as the leader of the Creep Witches. Every one of them, including Jaina, deferred to her.

Turning her head to Steve, Ina shook her head. "We can usually sense it when it's near. I hadn't really thought about it, but I haven't felt anything from it in days."

Steve nodded as that single statement solidified his final thoughts.

Kill all the murderers we don't need, gain prestige, protect ourselves. Just because the Creep is gone, doesn't mean this hell-hole country will magically become safe again.

No. This is going to continue. It'll probably get worse unless they let the country back into the alliance.

If they do, we move.

If they don't, we gain authority by killing everyone with a price on their head. Then we go for the citadel or something similar.

And that's all there is to it.

Now we just need to run it all by Nikki and see what she says.

***

Trooping toward the bridge and towers of his farm, Steve felt better already. He'd seen it a long way away, and it had made his spirit rise with every step.

Standing in the towers were a number of women he recognized, but didn't know. There were more people than ever all over his farm, and he had no idea who they all were.

- 89 -

At least we're still under a hundred people. This isn't a village or a city — it's a farm.

Falling free of its hinges, the drawbridge began lowering down toward the ground.

Nikki, Misty, Shelly, Ferrah, and Lucia stood there in the gap.

Speeding toward him at full speed was Nia, and halfway between her and the other women was Gwendolin. Gwendolin had clearly started to chase after Nia before giving up.

Chirping, singing, and stumbling all over herself, the little girl came onward. Gwendolin's daughter, the miniature version of her.

The moment Steve heard Nia's "Steve song," he felt like the weight of the world was gone.

It gave him a feeling of invulnerability and enduring strength, like he was a massive rock in the ocean. Like he gave ground for no one and nothing.

Then Nia slammed into him and hugged him for all she was worth.

"Welcome home, Steve!" Nia said happily. "It's a good afternoon because you're home!"

Grinning, Steve pulled her up and cradled her against his side. She fit there perfectly, and she didn't seem to mind.

Wrapping her arms around his neck, she gave him a fierce hug, and her shoulder jammed right into his throat.

Chuckling, he turned his head slightly to one side so he could keep breathing. He looked back at his welcoming committee, happy to see they were all there.

No one was missing.

His mind skittered away from thoughts of Chessa, Rachel, and Raelin. Their deaths were something he'd tried to put behind him as quickly as possible, without feeling them.

He didn't have the time or luxury for such foolishness. There was simply too much to get done for the living.

Like making sure Nia was well.

"Well, thank you. I'm glad to be home. I'm only here for a short while, though. I just came to talk to your mother and aunts." Steve reached up to tap Nia's nose.

"Mama's pregnant," Nia said. "I'm going to have a brother or a sister!"

"I know. I'm going to be their daddy. Whether it's a brother or a sister to you, I have no idea." Steve nodded. He was walking towards Gwendolin as he talked to the small girl.

"Oh! I see. Yes. You can be my daddy, too," Nia said, nodding her heard in the same way as Steve.

"Is that so? Well, I'd like to be your daddy, but I think pretty Mama has to say that's okay," Steve said as he stopped in front of Gwendolin

The Siren was standing there, her hands clutched together in one another. He didn't doubt she'd heard what Nia had said.

There was a clear tremble in her lip.

"Mama, can Steve be my daddy, too?" Nia said, looking at Gwendolin.

"I… if that's what you want, of course," Gwendolin said with a tremor in her voice.

"Yes! I do," Nia said. Then she promptly hugged Steve around the throat again, partially strangling him.

He knew it was probably going to be a change in his life, but he'd wanted to provide for Nia since the start.

He'd have to work doubly hard to make sure she remembered her actual father as well, while making room for himself to be her new daddy.

After all, without that man, Nia wouldn't be here at all. Steve would need to respect his memory.

"You got lucky, Shelf-ren. It happened after you got what you wanted," Steve said with a grin at Gwendolin. "No need for you to hold those toys up after all."

Wrinkling her nose at that, and smiling, Gwendolin smacked him gently on the arm. Then she took his elbow and guided him into the farm.

Steve's eyes immediately went from person to person in front of him. Checking them.

Ferrah the Dwarf looked the same as she always had, though significantly cleaner.

Her hair was a thick red braid behind her, except it no longer looked like she'd done it three weeks ago and forgotten about it. Her face was free of the normal soot and dirt he usually found her with.

She was dressed in her leather apron like usual, which only made her stout frame stouter. Though he knew she had more to her beneath it than the imagination might suppose.

Holy fuck, she doesn't look like a wheelbarrow after a hard day's work.

Next to her was Lucia the Fae. Her wings were fluttering, and her bright blond hair was pulled back from her face with little wooden clips. Her black eyes were locked on Steve, and she had a full-lipped pout on her face.

Moving down the line, he found Misty. The last time he'd seen her, he'd wondered if she was getting close to six-foot-six. Now he didn't have to wonder.

The beautiful and athletically fit Nereid was huge. Wearing little better than a tank top and a loin cloth, she looked like some sort of Amazonian warrior. Her blue hair was wet, and it made the small black horns on her head glisten. Her green eyes were locked on him.

Side by side at the end were Shelly and Nikki.

The former was one of the most hauntingly pretty, if not achingly beautiful, women he'd ever seen. Shelly had been built hair by hair, toe by toe, to catch a man. Her light-brown hair looked like spun silk, and her green eyes were so brilliant, they sparked.

Last in line, and first in his heart, was Nikki.

A Faun of limited beauty, with black curly hair, slotted brown eyes, dark horns, and furry legs.

Her smile was like a sunrise, and it chased away all the doubts in his heart and head.

Gwendolin guided him to Ferrah and released him over to the Dwarf. She picked up Nia in her arms at the same time.

Steve immediately gave Ferrah a hug, holding her tightly. He wasn't going to impose on her, but he was delighted that she'd showed up to greet him.

"Don't forget the kiss," Ferrah said in a gruff voice, hugging him in return.

Gleeful at that proposition, Steve immediately gave Ferrah a firm, if brief, kiss.

Then he worked his way down the line, giving each a hug and kiss, although Lucia demanded that he kiss her cheek instead.

Which he, of course, gave in to.

When he reached Nikki, he took her by the hand and immediately led her away from everyone else. He had a lot to talk to her about, and he just wanted to be alone with her.

"Steve, you really shouldn't," Nikki murmured, letting him escort her away even as the other women stared after both of them.

"Why? Give me a good reason. You were here first," Steve said, forcefully sliding his arm through hers. "You were the woman I spent my first night in this world with. We cuddled for warmth under a lean-to with not a coin or scrap of food between us.

"They all look to you for guidance—why shouldn't I steal you away for my own needs?"

Nikki sighed, then leaned her head to the side and laid it on his shoulder.

"I love you, my brute," Nikki said. "Lay your worries at my hooves, and I'll tend to you and them at the same time."

"That's… just what I wanted. Well, let's start with the murderers," Steve said, trying to figure out where to get the story moving from.

Two hours later, and just before dinner would be served, Steve felt like he'd wrung everything out of his mind for her.

From the villages to the cabin and the outpost, to Nancy, and to the innocents, children, and the voice that had spoken to him.

"Well," Nikki said, her fingers slowly curling through Steve's hair.

Opening his eyes, Steve looked up at the Faun above him. She was staring out at the lake, looking thoughtful.

"That's certainly a lot more going on than I expected," Nikki said softly. "Gwendolin told me some of it, but I don't think she really understood it all."

"No. Probably not. She was, uh… her brain turned off after she got pregnant," Steve said.

Laughing at that, Nikki nodded.

"Yes, it really did. She's better now, though. Much more like herself. When she got back, it caused a bit of a stir on the farm," Nikki said. "Many people who'd been harboring fears and worries were suddenly assured.

"Not to mention that the woman you got pregnant was a widow. One with a child from her previous husband. I can only begin to imagine what kind of stories that'll generate for us. Both good and bad.

"Wait, is anyone else pregnant?"

"No," Steve said.

"Oh, that's good. I think if both widows were pregnant and no one else, I'd be rather nervous," Nikki said. "That would be almost as bad as having no pregnancies."

He wanted to tell Nikki that he could control it.

Wanted to desperately. But he didn't. There was something holding him back from doing it. Something he couldn't explain.

It wasn't that he didn't trust her; it was that he didn't trust himself. That he hadn't already told her.

There really wasn't a way to walk into that conversation without making everything worse around it.

"Do you want to be pregnant?" Steve asked instead.

Nikki frowned at that, her hand pausing in his hair.

"I do," she said after several seconds. "Not simply for my duty, but because... because I want a little one. One I can show the world to. To experience the world through their eyes. Guide them and set a place for them in the world and... and just be a mom.

"I do want to be pregnant. I do. Even if it's still a little scary at times. Just the idea of it is scary."

"In other words, if I bedded you tonight and you got pregnant, you'd be happy?" Steve asked.

"Very," Nikki said, looking down at him now. She gave him her square-toothed smile, her slotted eyes twinkling. "But don't take that as me saying you're a failure if it doesn't happen, Steve. My brute. If it happens, it happens. If it doesn't, it doesn't.

"I'm very content to be with you. But it'd be fun to have a little brute of a daughter running around. Hopefully, she'll have your ridiculous strength."

"That'd be weird," Steve said with a grin, peering up at the Faun. "So... about the other stuff. What d'ya think?"

"Mm. It's not really what I had in mind," Nikki said, tapping a thumb against Steve's brow. "I wanted more land because I want places for our children to go. They won't want to stay on the farm.

"Having the outpost up there gives them one more spot to go other than Filch. Whether they're my babies or, say… Shelly's. Misty's. Or Gwen's unborn baby. They're still our children. My children. And I'll care for them just as my own mother did for me."

"What was your mother's name?" Steve asked suddenly.

Smiling wider at him, Nikki tilted her head to one side.

"My poor brute, you're going soft on me," Nikki said, one of her fingers running along his eyebrow. "Her name was Annette, though her friends and family called her Ann."

"Still your brute. I just love you. Would burn the world for you," Steve said.

"Oh, I wouldn't want that." Nikki stuck her tongue between her teeth. "The world is perfectly fine the way it is. I'd rather you better the world in my name."

"Well, apparently that'll start with me killing hundreds of murderers," Steve said.

"Or putting them to work. I do think that's a valid solution. It'll give them a chance to redeem themselves and live a life," Nikki said. "For all you know, they could be the sweetest and nicest women you ever met. Just put in some ugly choices they had to make."

"I know. I know. I think we've killed like… five, so far," Steve said. "Everyone else is working."

"Good. I'd like to think we're giving them a chance to fix their lives," Nikki said. "Let them figure themselves out and work towards it."

"Speaking of figuring themselves out," Steve said. "Nancy Abellis. Nancy the Wight. Nancy the Mistress. I'm not really sure what to make of her."

"Yes… I gathered that," Nikki said, peering into his face. "I'm afraid this is another one of those little blocks in your head."

"It is?" Steve said, feeling confused by that statement.

"Wights are definitely considered a parasite race, but they're not that rare," Nikki said softly, her fingers curling along his jaw. "They feed passively, and honestly they don't have to do much other than live around other people.

"As for her… self… soothing, that's really just a preference, I imagine. I'd more likely equate it to masturbation with a fantasy in mind.

"She doesn't seem that strange to me. Just with different needs."

Frowning, Steve wondered whether by leaving out certain parts of how he'd dealt with Nancy and her titles, maybe he'd undersold her oddities.

"Truly, she's not that concerning to me," Nikki said. "If anything, it'll be good for you. She'll be a positive outlet to explore your own emotions and feelings with, to a degree. One who won't judge you, because you've already seen the darkness in her."

Steve didn't agree with that, but he wasn't going to argue with her. Nikki tended to be right about stuff like this. He could disagree as much as he liked, but she'd still be right in the end.

"Truly," Nikki said. "Give her what you feel comfortable with and no more. Other than that... I think she'll work hard for you and will do well for us up there.

"Though I'm a little concerned about these collars you had Ina and Jaina make. I fear that perhaps they'll be used for terrible purposes down the road."

Didn't think about that. She's not wrong, though.

Need to make sure we keep a tight hold on all the collars.

"You're right, of course. My beautiful and kind Faun," Steve said. "I'll make sure none of them get away from us."

"Good. Oh, I made a decision on your behalf. I need a leatherworker to join the farm. My hands can't handle it, and I'm busy with all our clothes," Nikki said.

"Okay, sure. Just... pay 'em or whatever and make it happen," Steve said. He really didn't care about hiring people. There were roles they'd need to fill, and that would be that.

"Okay, thank you, dear. I appreciate it. I know it isn't really something you'd wish for, so... thank you.

"Lastly... the voice," Nikki murmured, lifting her gaze up to the area around them. "I don't know what to say about that at all. At the very least... you know the message you left yourself is honest now, and that someone is watching you.

"All we can do is keep on keeping on."

"I guess," Steve said. That was the one he felt the least secure about. He wanted to know more, but it simply had never responded to him again.

And it didn't sound like it was going to.

"It's all we can do. Unless there's something you haven't said?" Nikki asked, peering back down at him again.

"No. That's everything that happened," Steve said.

"Good! There isn't much to be said for things here. It's all rather mundane. Though we did have a close encounter with Linne in Filch. Nothing bad, though.

"Outside of that, other than that I'm very much done with leather-working, all is good.

"Now, how about we go to our bed and see if you're just lucky this month?" Nikki said. Then she leaned down and kissed him warmly, one of her hands cupping his cheek. "Because we both know that after, Nia is going to try and steal your time away, while your other women do the same."

Okay. Definitely... going to let Nikki have a child soon.

She'd be a wonderful mother. Not giving her what she wants would be an incredible loss for the entirety of existence.

Ten

Steve had spent the night in his own bed with Nikki, Misty, and Shelly, but only after he made sure each one got some time with him. From there they'd had dinner, and then the four of them had had one big slumber party. It had been a sweaty mass of arms and legs, all wrapped up in each other.

Nothing had happened on a sexual level, they'd just all slept together.

It'd been far too warm, sticky, and a little uncomfortable for Steve.

But he was apparently the only one who felt that way.

The girls seemed quite happy with the arrangement and had all remarked over breakfast on how they'd have to do that more often.

After saying goodbye to everyone and spending a little more time with Nia, he'd set off. There was work to be done, and he needed to be there to do it.

With his tools in hand, he worked at following the water way all the way back to the outpost.

"You've done quite a bit of work," Lucia said, walking along beside him. She'd decided to come with him.

Her argument was rather simple. She could do her work anywhere, but she could only help protect Steve from wherever he was.

Nikki didn't even consider arguing with that logic; it was far too clean and clear.

"Trying," Steve said. Up ahead he could see the outpost cabin and the farm. "Nikki wants this land for our children. So I'm going to get it."

It didn't take more than a glance into the trench to realize it was filling well. It was already at hip depth. The lake behind the cabin had not dipped at all in depth, nor had the waterway heading to Filch.

The modification to the watering can seemed to have been what they'd needed.

Which means I really need to get on that water tower. As soon as I can.

I could always put one on the outpost, too.

"Oh? You're so certain I'll take to child-bearing so quickly?" Lucia said with a teasing tone. "Your accuracy isn't very high, my sweet lovable brute."

I'll show you accuracy. Knock you up in the first go-round just to make a point out of you.

"I'm sure with such a beautiful Fae and her most assuredly impressive womb, I'd succeed on the first time," Steve growled.

"Most likely," Lucia said, tossing her hair back over her shoulder. "It's a royal womb and deserving of its significance. Any child born unto me is royalty. Even with your low accuracy, I have no doubt I would be successful."

Prideful thing. Always prideful.

"And as my man—a most deserving man, and I'll take no arguments from you—a man whom… whom I truly do care for… I expect your seed itself is quite special." Lucia's fingertips touched his arm for a split second.

And yet… quite determined to make me feel worthy of her.

"Whenever you're ready, Princess Lucia," Steve said with a chuckle. He might even do exactly that and put a kid in her.

"Soon. Very soon," said the Fae. "Ah, is that the Wight?"

Turning his head slightly, Steve found Nancy standing at the corner of the cabin. She was very clearly waiting for him, her hands held behind her back.

"Yep. Nancy. My mistress," Steve said.

"Good. All men of your caliber should have mistresses," Lucia said. "I'll be sure to begin her instruction today. She'll need to learn how to serve in all the ways befitting your eventual station."

"My eventual station?" Steve asked.

"As my husband. Your station is that of my husband. And I'll make sure you receive all the proper trappings for such a thing," Lucia promised. "Don't worry, I've dealt with species like her previously. You won't even notice a change in her demeanor."

Steve wasn't really sold on that, but he wasn't about to argue with Lucia. She'd nearly died for him. Battled for his safety at the cost of her own. To the point of having been bitten to pieces.

Her attitude, her personality, her entire being was beyond reproach in Steve's eyes. Lucia was on her own pedestal and had earned it. If she told him she wanted a pregnancy, he'd give her one.

"I love you, Lucia," Steve said suddenly. "Realized it when I carried you out of that horde we were in."

"Oh. I... I see," Lucia murmured. "I'm flattered to know it."

Steve smirked at that. He wasn't sure Lucia would ever be able to talk about her feelings.

Nancy had begun walking toward them now, a small smile on her face.

"Welcome back," she said, stopping directly in front of Steve. Then she turned her head toward Lucia.

"This is Lucia," Steve explained. "She's my Fae, bowyer, and fletcher."

"Ah," Nancy said. "I'm Nancy, his taken mistress."

Taken?

Lucia cleared her throat and smiled at Nancy.

"Steve spoke of you," Lucia said.

"I'm glad to hear that," Nancy commented, turning back to Steve. "What can I do to help you today? Do you need food? Water? Company?"

"Uh, no. I'm fine," Steve said.

"I understand. The plan then? Kassandra, Jaina, Ina, and I have prepared for the assault on that village. We've also made plans to collect all the other villages and towns."

"You did?" Steve asked.

"Of course," Nancy said, smiling widely at him. "As your taken mistress, it's my absolute duty to ensure everything you desire is taken care of to the utmost of my ability."

There's that taken thing again.

"I mean... actually, no. I don't need to hear the plan. Kass thinks it'll work?" Steve asked.

"She does indeed. We can accomplish the first attack tonight and move from there," Nancy elaborated. "Shall I prepare and then initiate it?"

"Ah... in a little bit. I want to settle for a moment and see what's going on," Steve said.

"I understand," Nancy said, her stoic face neutral other than her smile. "The walls are being extended accordingly. I've seen to guiding Jaina and Ina in the rock wall placement. We're putting up towers and the section facing the villages and towns first.

"I had a very large cellar dug out, and much of the produce is being stored there in containers. I spent some logs to have those made, but I felt they were worthwhile."

She's been busy.

"Good work, Nancy. I appreciate all that," Steve said.

"Of course. I also had layouts made for large bunkhouses," Nancy said, holding up a hand and gesturing to the far side of the cabin. "They're merely dirt-mounded outlines at the moment, but once you approve them, I'll have work begin immediately.

"Last, but not least, I must report we had twenty women make an escape attempt. Twelve of them perished when they crossed the line. I had the other eight executed to make a point of the situation."

"So many," Steve murmured, moving in the indicated direction.

"They clearly didn't understand your magnanimous gesture," Nancy countered. "They're all worthy of a death sentence, and you've commuted it with the possibility of living and being provided for. We're better off without them.

"I can report that since the executions, morale has been high and everyone is working together quite well."

"That seems backward," Lucia said.

"And yet, it's true," Nancy said, leading Steve and Lucia around to the front of the cabin. "I speak with them often, as I was once one of them. I also have informants who report back to me what they know. All is as it should be. The prisoners are calm and cared for."

And that's what this is. A prison labor camp. Everyone here is under a death sentence and would be executed for their bounty alone.

"It doesn't hurt that the Creep hasn't been seen in a long while. Everyone is expecting things to start moving back towards how they used to be," Nancy said. "Their only chance to survive the government coming back is to make themselves essential somewhere.

"A farm that provides food would definitely be essential. Considering that most of them became murderers because there was no food. Every farm I know of failed after the Creep came. You're the only one able to grow anything, anywhere."

"Good," Lucia said, folding her hands together in front of her. "My husband is a man of worth, and they'd all do well to lower their heads to him."

"Agreed," Nancy said. "They're learning."

Steve felt weird about all this. A strange feeling kept circling around him, and he wasn't sure how to deal with it.

It felt like there were those in his group who wanted to push him up, and then there were those who simply wanted to be safe.

Lucia, Kassandra, Jaina, Shelly, Xivin, and Nancy all were pushing hard for him to keep becoming stronger. To take ground, build defenses, train up more fighters, and empower himself.

Nikki, Misty, Ferrah, Gwendolin, and Ina liked the idea of being safe and secure. Their viewpoint was that if this could be accomplished, it would be all they needed.

And Steve was somewhere in the middle. He didn't think he'd feel safe and secure unless he moved up, took more, and made it so others couldn't push him around.

As they walked into the fields, prisoners on every side bowed their heads to Steve, bending at the waist to him in the middle of their work.

Steve said nothing about it and let Nancy show him the changes.

***

"You trust her too readily," Lucia murmured, squatting low in the brush next to Steve.

"I have my reasons," Steve replied. He wasn't about to explain everything to Lucia.

Nancy was his creature and his alone. There was no reason to reveal her to anyone else as anything other than his mistress.

In the short time he'd had her, she'd been extremely useful.

Loving my henchwoman. Loving her lots.

"Hmph. I'm sure I can perform her duties and tasks just as easily," Lucia grumped.

"I'm sure you could, too. But you're already busy with your own work," Steve said. "So the simple reality is, I needed another person to assist me. Nancy is that."

"I don't disagree with you, but you just trust her too much," Lucia repeated.

"She's not so bad," Kassandra said from behind the two of them. "We had a good conversation and I understand her much better."

"Me too, me too," Jaina said.

Ina and half the prisoners had remained on the farm. The other half were all here with Steve.

Waiting.

They would be the ones to load everyone up and carry them back to the farm. Then the half on the farm would switch out and go loot the town, or continue picking people up.

"She wants what's best for Steve," Kassandra said. "While I disagree with her methods and her actions, I think working with her will be fine."

"Really?" Lucia asked, turning her head towards the other two women.

"Yes, yes. She knows that Steve must go higher. He must be a master of many, to make a large pack," Jaina said.

Lucia frowned, looking thoughtful but annoyed as well.

Everyone fell silent as they sat there, waiting. Steve had dug the hole and then retreated, leaving it to Nancy. There wasn't anything for him to do until she gave a signal, came back, or died.

Time crept by like a slug on a path littered with salt.

"Someone's coming," Jaina said very softly.

"It's her," Kassandra replied several seconds later.

A minute later, Nancy stumbled out of the woods. She was white faced, sweating, and panting hard.

"I put the poison in two hours ago. Should be happening any moment." She stopped in front of Steve. "It's done, Steve. Though I think I got a little on my hands. I'm feeling rather weak and tired."

"Hard to work with poison," Kassandra said, setting a hand on Nancy's back. "Come lie down. Your part is done."

"Yes, yes, go lie down," Jaina agreed, pawing at the ground nervously.

"Alright, our turn then," Steve said, then looked at Lucia and Jaina. They would be going with him to watch the village. They'd be the ones to signal the attack when it was time, and Kassandra would lead it.

Jaina darted in close to him, bit him roughly on the neck, and licked the spot several times. Then she kissed his jaw and moved away several steps.

Getting more and more bitey and licky. More so now that Gwendolin caught a pregnancy.

Without waiting, Jaina turned and bounded off into the woods, vanishing into the foliage.

"She's just excited," Lucia explained. "With a widow being pregnant, it isn't a hope anymore, or a problem. Her chances are guaranteed with enough effort.

"Kobolds are very physical creatures with their expression of affection. She just loves you very much and can't hold it in."

"Oh? Are Fae?" Steve said, getting to his feet and following after the Kobold.

"We can be. Want me to give you a Fae love bite?" Lucia asked.

"Kinda. Wanna give it a go right now?"

"Bend down here and I'll show you, just don't regret the invitation," Lucia said.

Steve contemplated doing that, but decided against it. He needed to get moving. For whatever reason, he really enjoyed flirting with Lucia. It was a game of give and take with her. She won more often than not, but now and again he got her to back down.

Moving after the Kobold, Lucia seemed to be able to follow her without too much of an issue. Which was a good thing since Steve was more or less blind in the woods.

I really kinda hate being Human. Would love to trade some of this strength for some other abilities.

"Stop," Lucia commanded, a hand pressing into Steve's chest.

Just ahead of them, he swore he could see something. And he could hear someone now that he was trying to listen.

He couldn't quite identify it, but he was fairly certain someone was there.

There was a sudden grunt, followed by a whoosh of air.

The hand on his chest pulled him forward suddenly, then stopped him after ten steps forward.

Laid out in front of him were Jaina and another woman.

Jaina's mouth was wrapped around the woman's throat. Her hands pushed down on the woman's head and stomach, keeping her pinned.

"Keep her down," Lucia whispered as she got down on one knee. Pulling the woman's rope belt out of her pants, Lucia rapidly tied the woman up with her hands behind her back. "Done."

Jaina released the woman's throat and then spat several times.

"Be silent, or be dead," Lucia said, pointing a hand at the woman. "Understand?"

"Yes, I understand," said the woman. Steve had no idea what she looked like, let alone what she was wearing. Everything was mostly shadows and blurry images to him.

"Tear her throat out of if she makes a noise louder than breathing," Lucia said. "Why were you out here?"

"Spying," said the woman. "Spying on this village."

"Oh?" Lucia mused. "Wonderful. Come on."

Lucia started pulling on Steve again, dragging him onward for another ten or so steps. Then they stopped, and she pulled him down into a bush.

They were looking out at the walled village.

Steve couldn't see a thing, though. The torches were out, there was no light coming from inside the village, and as far as he could tell, everyone was asleep.

"I think… it already happened," Lucia said. "Maybe even sooner than Nancy thought. There's no guards. No one on the walls. Nothing."

Standing up and feeling frustrated, Steve marched out of the bush.

"Steve!" Lucia hissed.

He kept walking without bothering to respond. Straight up to the gatehouse. There was no moat, just a wooden wall and gatehouse.

Lifting his axe off his shoulder, Steve brought it around in a wild swing.

With a shower of splinters and shattered wood, the entryway was blasted to nothing. There was a creaking noise as part of the gatehouse shifted ominously, then went sideways. With a boom and a rattle, everything was cleared away.

Staring into the village from where he was, Steve saw a number of people lying in the street, some off to the sides, some even sitting upright.

Everyone was unconscious and unmoving.

They looked dead.

Steve marched into the village up to the first person and reached down. He pushed his hand against the woman's chest and held it there. Slowly, he felt her chest rise and then fall.

Good.

Standing up, he turned around and looked back the way he'd come.

"Send 'em up! We're all ready up here for pick up!" he shouted back toward Lucia.

Eleven

Watching the efficiency of his prisoners, Steve couldn't really fault them. They were earning their keep.

Within minutes of arriving, they'd formed a human conveyor belt of hands passing unconscious people backward toward the outpost. Then it became items and possessions.

Then furniture.

Finally, even the walls and parts of the buildings themselves were being torn down and handed backward.

His people looked exhausted, but they were still working despite having been moving for almost an entire day.

"Remind me to give them two days of rest after this," Steve muttered. "The new people can work their shifts."

"I'll do so. Do I get two days off as well?" Nancy asked.

"No. I'm going to work you till you beg me to work you till your body gives out," Steve said. He knew what she wanted.

Knew what she wanted to hear, too.

"Thank you. I look forward to it. Do be sure to take me to bed and use me thoroughly each night for your own pleasure and leisure. Maybe risk a pregnancy on me one night," Nancy added, standing next to Steve. "Maybe a slap or two? I deserve to have my needs tended to. I did very well in this task you gave me."

Kassandra, Jaina, and Lucia were overseeing the human chain, as well as the village that was being taken apart.

Nancy never left his side unless he ordered it. She wouldn't use the restroom unless he did. Nor would she eat or drink unless he did.

She was a shadow that wouldn't go away for very long.

"No violence," Steve said. No matter how many times he told her not to ask, she still asked.

"Just one? A good solid slap?" Nancy asked.

"No. No violence," Steve said.

Nancy sighed and nodded, her arms folded behind her back.

"Maybe next time," she amended. "Personally, I might have thought capturing three hundred murderers would get me what I wanted."

"The problem is it isn't what I want," Steve said.

"Mm. Maybe when you fall in love with me, you'll give me what I want," Nancy said.

Steve shook his head and didn't reply. Nancy was too pushy for him at times.

"Oh, Susan is signaling that everything she thinks is worth anything is gone," Nancy said.

And on the other hand, she's a really damn good henchwoman. A fantastic henchwoman. Nearly perfect henchwoman.

I can tolerate all the rest for how she just… does what I want in every other facet.

Doesn't even argue with me. Just gets it done.

Nancy held up a hand and then made a gesture to Susan.

"We're all done, Steve," Nancy said, turning to him. "Everyone will be heading back now. The Creep Witches said they'd have the square put up and everyone dumped off in there for collaring."

"Good work, Mistress," Steve said.

"Of course," Nancy replied demurely. "And I've been thinking on that voice you heard. You realize… you could probably force it to respond to you. If you threatened to kill yourself and intended to follow through, it's likely it would make itself known.

"It's not much of a weakness, but it might work. Exploit their interest in you."

Huh. I… that might work.

That or threaten to go live in a cave. As long as I did the opposite of what it wanted.

Maybe?

It might not care at all.

Might tell me to kill myself.

Something to consider.

"Shall we go?" Nancy asked. "Or would you like to take a short detour into the village, find something hard that'll ruin my back and knees, and absolutely destroy me?"

Perfect henchwoman.

***

Steve was leaning back in the grass, watching the collaring continue for all his new prisoners.

For whatever reason, this entire village was full of murderers. There hadn't been a single innocent so far. Even the children, little more than pre-teen girls more often than not, had all gotten their hands bloody at some point.

Even the men.

Very few chose to die rather than be put to work.

Nancy stood beside him in her ever-present position. Jaina and Ina were doing the collaring work while Kassandra stood guard.

"It's very strange to be the hand of justice," Lucia murmured from beside him. She was seated in the grass, watching the proceedings.

"It'll help us become bigger. Not to mention, these aren't even the biggest villages," Steve suggested.

"They're not. Two others are considerably bigger. Stronger, too," Nancy said. "They're more akin to perhaps… half the size of Filch? Each one of them."

"We'll have to deal with those later," Steve said. "For now, our goal is the same. Walls, walls, walls. I'm not convinced the Creep is done or gone, but it isn't much of a problem right now."

"Hmm. Yes," Lucia agreed with a sigh. She lifted a hand and set it on the side of her face. "If the country goes back to normal, I'll have to go home for a time."

"What?" Steve asked, looking at Lucia.

"As a maiden of the court and the royal family, it's my duty to report a change in my status," Lucia said. "That includes taking a man."

"Wait, you really are part of the royal family?" Steve asked. He'd only been teasing her about such a thing. He thought it'd all been a joke about how she carried herself. He didn't question that she was nobility, but her being of royal blood wasn't something he'd really believed.

She did make that comment about the royal womb. But I thought she was just being her.

"Indeed. I'm a very minor princess. Twentieth in line for the throne or some such. Nowhere near anything of relevance. But it's still something I must attend to. If I'm to start giving birth to princes and princesses in a land like Lamals, then I'll have to make sure the royal guard knows of it."

"Royal guard," Steve said, watching Lucia now to see if she was messing with him.

"Indeed. I don't personally warrant that many. Only fifty or so. Our children will probably each receive just as many," Lucia said with a sigh. "I'm sure they're all extremely cross with me for sneaking out the way I did.

"Mother will surely have an aneurysm when she finds out I married without her permission. Father won't mind. He's always been fascinated by Humans. He never did talk mother into having a Human woman join their marriage, though. Your species just doesn't live very long."

Lucia grinned at that, as if the idea of bothering her mother was actually a good thing.

"And... yours does?" Steve asked, not really keeping up with the full conversation.

"Six or seven hundred years, give or take a few centuries. It'll be hard to live on after you pass, but being your wife and having children with you will be worth it. At least, I personally think so," Lucia said.

I'm not Human, though. Not really. There's that... asterisk... next to my species.

Still don't know what that means.

Do I live as long as a Human? Longer? Shorter?

Hmm.

I wond —

"Incoming!" Kassandra shouted at the top of her lungs.

Shaking free of his thoughts, Steve jumped to his feet and turned his eyes to where Kassandra was looking.

In the distance, across the plain, he could see a massive group of people heading his way.

Looks like a damn army.

Not knowing what it was, Steve was left to guesses.

"Nancy, think that might be one of our city-size friends?" Steve asked.

"Could be. Can't tell," Nancy said.

Steve marched over to Kassandra, not really sure how to handle this. He wasn't a soldier, and he had no idea if they could even handle a group that large in their current state.

"No, we can't hold," she said the moment he was close enough. "We don't have the defenses for something that large."

"Uh… kay. What're our options then?" Steve asked. Behind him, he could hear Lucia and Nancy practically standing on his heels.

"Run," Kassandra said simply. "Run back home. Leave everything here."

"Fuck that," Steve growled. "They'd turn this into a fortification and just end up using it against us. No. Running isn't a valid option."

"Then we die," Kassandra said. "We can't fight that in a head-on conflict. There is no tricky plan, no strategic dodge, no silly storybook maneuver. If we fight, we lose. If we stay, we fight. If we run, we lose the outpost."

"What if… what if we put up a Creep magic square over the fields we're working and the cabin?" Ina said. She and Jaina had stopped working on the collars for the time being. "Could easily keep them out in the same way we're keeping those in."

Ina gestured at the murderers as she spoke.

"Could… work," Kassandra said.

"Yes, yes. If we do it that way, we could shoot arrows through the barrier. Or use spears," Jaina said.

"I'm going to go gather everything I can for supplies," Lucia said. Taking a running leap, she zipped forward, and her wings fluttered rapidly behind her as she sailed away.

"Okay," Steve said. Then he threw a thumb at the people in the current Creep square, as Ina had called it. "And can we maintain them in their square, too?"

"Shouldn't be an issue. We can merge the spells. Cost wouldn't be that different," Ina said with a wave of her hand. "Jaina and I are the two strongest Creep Witches anyways."

"You are?" Steve asked. That was a curious statement.

"Very, very much," Jaina said with a prideful grin, showing off her teeth. "We can take on every other Creep Witch at the same time and win. Ina and I are so, so, deadly."

Ina smirked at that and put a hand on her hip.

"Well?" she asked.

"Do it. Right on the cabin and the fields," Steve said. "We don't have to kill them, just keep them out and pick them off one by one. We'll convert our prisoners at the same time, and then we can lower the second Creep square."

"Got it." Ina turned to look at Jaina. "You hold this one, I'll make the other and tie it in."

"Yes, yes," said the Kobold. "I'll continue collaring the beasts while you do that."

Beasts, hmm?

I suppose to Jaina they might be beasts. Those who broke too many pack laws.

Ina started heading for the cabin while Jaina turned to those in the square.

"Everyone get up! Up, up!" Jaina called. "We're going for walkies. You haven't earned your collars yet, so you have to stay in the square. Touch the square and die!"

Slowly, everyone began marching determinedly for the center of the outpost. Where the cabin and crops all were.

Should probably… dig a well. Can't rely on the water source remaining untainted.

Damn. Let's hope we can end this quick.

Glancing over his shoulder, Steve looked back toward the rather large mass of likely murderers heading his way.

Quicker than he expected, everyone was rounded up, settled down, and put to work.

Steve dug a massive pit that would serve as their well and cut into the moat water. The more he could fill the pit with it, the better off they'd be. He'd have to fill the passageway back in as soon as the enemy got close enough, though. He couldn't risk giving them the opportunity to get everyone sick by polluting their water.

Others spent their time barreling as much water as they could from the moat, while a very large team of people worked desperately to knock down as many trees as possible and drag them all back to the encampment.

There was no telling how long they'd be stuck this way. But Steve wasn't about to let it be said he didn't prepare for it. Or at least do as much as he could.

And just like that, there wasn't anything left they could do. Not because there was nothing to do, but because the enemy was here.

Standing outside of the large square Ina had thrown up was an army of women. All were armed with weapons, and almost all of them were wearing some type of leather armor.

It was clear they weren't soldiers, though, as a casual inspection see showed they all had skills.

As well as families.

Both were things that soldiers simply didn't have.

One woman, who was either braver or dumber than the rest, stuck her hand up against the massive glowing wall.

She instantly went rigid and collapsed sideways. The magic of the wall glowed brighter after that.

"Feed spell works," Jaina said, looking at Ina.

"Yes… your feed spell works," Ina replied. Steve couldn't tell, but it sounded like she wasn't very happy about that.

"I wonder if it took her soul. Or just her life," Jaina said, moving close to the wall and peering down at the dead woman. "Very, very dead."

"Yes, well, suppose we'll never find out," Ina said.

Makes sense. Ripping the soul out of someone sounds rather terrible.

"You," said a woman, pointing at Jaina. "Are you the one in charge?"

"No, no," Jaina said. Then her hand flashed out of the square and she grabbed the dead woman. Before anyone could respond, she'd pulled the corpse through the wall. "Oh, nicey, nice. A necklace. I like it."

Jaina began to happily strip the body right then and there, pulling the armor off.

"He is," Kassandra said, pointing at Steve. "He's in charge."

"Thanks, Kass," Steve muttered. "Remind me to make you howl later."

"I will," Nancy offered.

Taking the cue Kassandra had forced on him, Steve stepped up to the glowing wall.

"Can I help you?" he asked.

"You will take down this wall, give us your prisoners and your food, and then become slaves," said the woman.

"That's cute. But my answer is… no. Now get off my land," Steve said. Stepping up to the edge of the wall, he gauged that he was within reach with his axe. He could probably put it through the woman's head faster than she could react.

"You're handsome," said the woman, giving him a feral grin. "When it's all said and done, I think I'll keep you for myself. After I let my girls take you for a ride. Now, how about you just make the wall go away, and I promise it'll be fun for you. Rather than painful."

"Leave," Steve said. "This is my land, and you're not welcome. Last warning."

"No. I think not. You can't keep this magic up forever," the woman said, gesturing at the wall.

"Okay. Got it," Steve said. Before the woman could respond further, he'd whipped the axe around off his shoulder. It blasted through the woman's head, splattering her in every direction around her. All around the women surrounding her.

Steve lashed out with his axe again, killing two more women before they could get away from him.

Then Lucia began firing as fast as she could. Arrows ripping through the air and downing women left and right.

Jaina and Ina didn't join in, instead holding their magic in reserve to keep the walls up.

Steve picked up a rock nearby and flung it with all the force he could.

It detonated through a woman's arm and exploded through a second woman's head, and he realized he'd greatly underestimated how much power he could put into a throw.

Steve ran to the back of the cabin where he kept stones he'd found in the field, determined to kill a few more.

By the time he got back, though, the enemy had fallen out of Lucia's range.

A group of women wearing collars moved out from the safety of the square and started looting the dead.

In almost no time at all, the dead were stripped and their corpses piled into a mound. Including the one Jaina had grabbed.

"That was entertaining," Kassandra said. "I wonder if they'll try again."

"Probably," Lucia groused with a huff. "They sound like little better than jumped-up peasants. They've been battling their own kind, and with numbers, and now they have an inflated sense of self."

Turning to one side, Lucia gave Jaina a wide smile.

"Jaina dear, could you make me a very simple tower to fire out of? Doesn't have to be complicated. Just something I can work with," Lucia asked.

"Oh, yes, yes. Not a problem," Jaina said, smiling back at Lucia. "Will you teach me the bow?"

"Of course. I even have a short bow I was working on that you could train with," Lucia said.

All over the outpost, the prisoner work teams got back to their jobs. Farming, digging, or working logs.

"I can probably expand the square further out once we clear the rest," Ina said, pointing to the number of collarless prisoners. "Not out to the moat and walls, though."

"Don't bother then. Keep it small and tight. Something Lucia can watch from any side but still gives us room to work in," Steve said.

"Not a problem," Ina said, then sighed and leaned up against Steve. Her arm looped around his waist. "Think after we clear this group, finish the outpost, and settle in, it'll be over for a while?"

No.

"Maybe," Steve said. "Really comes down to what our enemies do."

"True." Ina shook her head. "I'll fight. I'll defend what's ours. But I feel like we'd be better off isolating ourselves. Just... hunker down and let everything else do whatever it wants."

No. That wouldn't protect us.

That'd just keep what we have.

No, we need to take a citadel commander's title for our own. Or higher.

This can't continue, and I'm not going to let it.

We'll start here and crush Lamals. End the pens, and maybe... maybe see what's going on behind all the brainwashing.

No one would willingly send their husband or father out to fight. Not with their numbers so low.

There must be more to it.

"They're coming back," Kassandra reported. "Don't shoot till they're up against the wall again. We can get more kills that way."

Steve nodded. It was good advice.

"'Will you walk into my parlor?' said the spider to the fly," Steve muttered.

Twelve

Steve methodically worked at the massive bunkhouse as efficiently as he could.

He needed a place to shelter and protect all his prisoners from the elements. A place for them to end their day and rest for the next.

In addition to that, he'd already built an infirmary for them. If they got sick, tired, or wounded, they needed a place they could recover in peace without being bothered as people came and went.

They were murderers. The worst of the worst, one and all.

But they were his.

And he was going to make sure he kept them alive, healthy, and working. Because a dead prisoner wasn't useful to anyone.

A happy prisoner—one who was well fed, cared for, and given a reason to put work in—was an extremely useful commodity.

Certainly a great deal better than killing them outright.

I wonder if the Lamals government does the same thing. Do they enlist murderers into the army and fling them out to the front?

Probably not a terrible idea if they're always short on soldiers.

Or is the military too much of a trust issue? They may not be able to use murderers simply because it's such a high-needs job.

Something to consider, I suppose.

Especially since it's unlikely they have the collars.

Standing up, Steve swung his axe up on his shoulder. He'd taken to working in his loin cloth once more. The clothes he'd arrived in this world wearing had long since become little better than rags. Though he was fairly certain Nikki had stolen his windbreaker and put it somewhere safe.

He wasn't about to ruin the clothes Nikki had made for him if he didn't have to.

"They're a terrible little rabble of worth-nothings," Kassandra hissed.

"I mean… yeah?" Steve said with a laugh. "They're murderers without skills from a village that could probably barely sustain itself before the Creep happened. Far as I can tell, most of the farms and food-producing communities got sick or were wiped out.

"What else were they supposed to do?"

"I… what? You identify with them?" Kassandra asked.

"Don't you? I mean, did you ever stop and wonder where you'd be if the Creep hadn't brought you down right now?" Steve asked. "If you were sent to Filch, you'd probably be doing patrols and not sure of your loyalty. Filch and its last human mayor or the kingdom. If you went to the capital, for all we know, you'd be killing citizens in a food riot.

"And you're telling me you can't identify with people doing what they have to?"

Kassandra's pretty face clouded up in annoyance.

"You're… right, Steve," she said, deflating partially. "You're right."

"Don't fret over it, my beautiful little snake," Steve said, then walked over to her to lay a hand on her scaled side. "I share your thoughts; I just understand where they're coming from. I'm sure a farming community would look at what we've done so far with a critical eye for all the ways we're failing."

Kassandra looked away and to the side. She apparently wasn't willing to respond to that.

"Hey, subject change—scales? Got any for me? You keep stringing me along," Steve said, running his hand back and forth along her muscular snake tail.

"I do, actually," Kassandra said, turning toward him with a small smile. "I was saving them. I want to see if I can't make a mail shirt out of them. Lamia scales are rather strong, you know. Stronger than bronze or iron."

"Oh? That'd be interesting," Steve said.

"I think I can make a punch for them if I use that new iron Ferrah is working with," Kassandra said. "Should I put one on a necklace for you?"

It was a strange question for anyone to ask, he imagined. Doubly so for someone like Kassandra.

Can I hang part of my skin around your neck on a necklace?

"I'd like that, please." Steve gave her a firm thump with his hand. It took a whole lot more force than that to move Kassandra in any way. He'd learned that from wrestling her during their sex-play. She often wanted to be forced, roughed up, and hurt just a little.

Nowhere near Nancy's level, but she still enjoyed the play of it.

Sighing, Steve looked out at the crowd of gathered misfit women. They were all in one spot, waiting for the magic Jaina and Ina had kept going to fail.

It'd been several days at this point, and the well water was noticeably starting to dry up.

"Alright, I'm done with this horse shit," Steve said.

"I... what?" Kassandra asked.

"Nancy," Steve said, looking for his henchwoman. She was never far.

"Yes, Steve?" she asked, looking up from where she sat. She was going over a very basic reading primer he'd put together for her. If she was going to serve him, she needed to be able to do it in every way.

"Get me a white flag and have someone stand over there waving it back and forth wildly. I want those idiots over there to come talk to us," Steve said. "Tell everyone not to attack, too. I'm done waiting for them to leave. Going to just fucking end this now."

"I understand," Nancy said, getting to her feet. She was off in a hurry, moving quickly at almost a run.

She never waited around once he'd given an order, and sometimes she would take off at a sprint if she felt it was needed.

No one paid Nancy much mind at this point. She was Steve's shadow and clearly working for his benefit. Wherever she went or whatever she did, it was simply viewed as an extension of Steve's will.

What no one seemed to realize was that Nancy was only working for his benefit. Anything anyone said to her was almost always relayed back to Steve.

Wife, prisoner, or otherwise.

Steve was careful to not betray her. As long as she was his creature, he'd reap benefits from people telling her things.

"What're you going to do?" Kassandra asked.

"Take 'em prisoner, get 'em to run, or kill 'em," Steve said. "I was a nice guy for more than long enough. They could have left, and that'd have been the end of it. Done with that. Done with this.

If they leave, I'm going to wipe out their village. If they stay, I'll kill 'em. If they surrender, they can wear a collar."

Holding his axe, Steve marched off towards where Ina and Jaina would be. They typically took turns holding the magical shell they had up. A few hours at a time each.

Right now, he was fairly certain it was Jaina.

"That'd be agreeable," Kassandra said. "It's… frustrating to listen to you entertaining at night."

Steve raised an eyebrow at that and looked at Kassandra.

"I want to, desperately, but… I just can't. Not in front of the others," Kassandra confessed. "With so many people practically on the other side of the wall."

Steve had spent the last several nights alternating between Ina and Jaina. Kassandra and Nancy had both declined, apparently not as willing to perform as the Creep Witches.

Both of whom were rather loud and boisterous about it.

Then again, Steve had the impression Nancy wanted him to force her to do it anyways. She just hadn't said anything to him about it yet.

Reaching the cabin, Steve found Jaina perched on the roof. She was staring out at the group of murdering bandits just outside of Lucia's range.

She was beautiful, exotic, strange, and her mother had spent way too much on her figure.

Boobie-dog indeed.

"Jaina," Steve said, coming to a stop below her.

"Husband," Jaina said, grinning down at him and showing him her impressive teeth.

"Get your cute furry butt down here," Steve said. "I need —"

Jaina leapt down from the building and slammed into him. She immediately started rubbing herself all over him, her hands going up under his loin cloth and grabbing hold of his shaft.

"Yes, yes, right here, right now," she said in a low rumble against his neck. "Mount me — show them all who's your wife. I'm Jaina Bril."

Then she bit him, her teeth sinking partially into his shoulder. Her eyes looked up at him, daring him to do anything other than what she'd said.

It didn't feel like she was breaking the skin, but he was pretty sure she wasn't far off.

Grinning at the feisty Kobold, Steve wrapped a hand around the back of her neck and took a firm grip on her.

Much in the way he'd done with Chessa. He'd learned from her directly that non-humans had very non-Human needs.

Perhaps he wasn't meeting one with Jaina.

In a way... I do miss Chessa.

Just not in the way I probably should.

Then again, I'm not Human myself.

Squeezing gently, he stopped once he felt Jaina go still, her jaw relaxing.

"Jaina," Steve said with a hint of iron in his voice. "That's not what I want."

Grunting, Jaina let go of his shoulder and began to rapidly lick the area she'd just bitten. Her tongue rolled over the skin repeatedly.

"Sorry, sorry," Jaina said, then kissed the spot and began nuzzling and kissing up along his shoulder and neck. "Sorry, sorry, Alpha. I love you. I need a belly rub and to be mated with. This magic is tiring and making me irritable."

Figures.

Patting Jaina lightly on the back, Steve got to his feet and held the Kobold physically against himself. He couldn't imagine having more than one of her kind. She was becoming quite the handful.

"Alright, we're going to talk to our temporary neighbors," Steve said. "I want you to wake up Ina. We're going to flash-fry them all if they don't get the fuck off my land."

"Okay," Jaina said, pressing her face against his shoulder. "I'm sorry. Sorry, sorry."

"I know, it's okay. Go get Ina," Steve said, putting the Kobold down.

Jaina fled immediately, her tail tucked between her thighs. She didn't seem upset or concerned, just put in her place.

Which apparently, was what she'd wanted.

Kassandra watched the whole interaction with interest, then looked at Steve.

"It's a wonder you can handle so many non-Human women without frustration," she commented.

"It's not so bad," Steve said with a shrug of his shoulders. "Just have to care enough, I guess."

"All done, Steve," Nancy said, coming up on him from the other side. "I told Lucia not to fire on anyone."

Steve grunted and then looked out toward the bandits.

A woman with a collar was frantically waving a white shirt back and forth as if her very life depended on it.

"Your family doing alright?" Steve asked.

"Yes, Steve. Thank you for asking," Nancy said. "They're adjusting very well and are quite pleased with their treatment. They're deciding what to do next at the current time."

"Good," Steve said, looking back at the cabin.

Jaina came back out dragging Ina along by her wrist.

The beautiful Creep Witch was rubbing at her eyes with her free hand, her hair a wild bush of blond strands sticking in every direction.

"Steve? What is it?" Ina asked as she was dragged along. "Jaina wouldn't say anything."

"Didn't tell her anything. We're going to end this right here and now," Steve explained. "Because I'm fucking done with this. Come on."

Steve marched off to where the prisoner was waving the white flag and slammed his axe head into the ground. The woman with the flag was momentarily startled, but then went back to waving back and forth.

Soon enough, a cautious group of women came ever closer to the outpost from the opposing camp. They looked very wary and clearly wanted nothing to do with Steve or his people.

They shouted at Steve and his group several times, but he couldn't understand what they were saying, so he didn't respond.

That didn't stop them from repeating the tactic over and over until they were close enough, however.

Eventually, they got into a range where a shout could be understood.

"What do you want?" shouted the woman in the front.

Steve decided to ignore it again.

He didn't feel like shouting this conversation.

The woman clearly got the picture that she'd have to come within talking distance. Looking annoyed, nervous, and angry all at the same time, she stopped twenty feet away.

"Okay, I'm here. What? What do you want?" demanded the woman.

"Do you speak for the group?" Steve asked, indicating the group of murderers.

"No, I'm just the one they sent out because they don't give a shit about me dying," groused the woman. The group that had come with her were still quite a ways away and making no move to get closer.

Right.

"What village are you all from?" Steve asked.

Puffing up slightly, the woman lifted her chin up.

"Carook," she said.

"I'm going to give you three options. Leave, surrender, or die," Steve said. "If you leave, I'm going to find your village and decimate it. I'll decapitate anyone who questions me and my axe. I'll stand in your square with my axe in hand and conquer your lands.

"If you surrender, I'll treat you all as prisoners and put you to work. You'll have a roof over your head, a chance to live your life, and food in your belly. As well as the promise that I'll treat you fairly, even if I don't pay you."

"I—"

"And if you stay," Steve said, cutting her off, "but you don't surrender, I'll kill every single one of you. Innocent, murderer, child, I don't care.

"Now go, give your leaders my ultimatum. Because that's what it is. I'll wait here for an answer. If no answer comes within twenty minutes after you get back to your group, I'll kill everyone.

"Do you understand?"

"I understand," said the woman. Turning, she fled quickly back the way she'd come.

"Nancy, do you know where Carook is?" Steve asked.

"Yes, I do," Nancy said.

"Good," he said. "Could we take it the same way we did the last one?"

"Probably. It isn't as if word got out of what we did, after all," Nancy said.

"Wonderful," Steve said, then turned to Jaina and Ina. "I want you two to put together a spell that will simply roll over them and wipe them out completely. A wave of Creep flame. Use all the black sand you brought with you, if you need to. I know where we can get more."

"I—Steve, I don't…" Ina paused and sighed, pressing a hand to her head.

"We can do it," Jaina said. "Clean and swift."

Ina turned to Jaina with a concerned glance, then nodded her head as she turned back to Steve.

"We can do it, husband," Ina said.

"Good. That's what we're going to do if they don't surrender," Steve said. "Because I'm done with this. I'm charging you to kill them all in the name of our farm. I'll take responsibility for any innocents killed."

Ina looked uncomfortable and unhappy, but willing to do what he'd asked of her.

Jaina on the other hand had eyes that were determined and beyond willing to carry out his orders.

"Mark the time, Nancy," Steve said.

"Fools," Lucia muttered. "They don't know they're tangling with a husband of the Fae's royal bloodline. If only they understood their folly, they'd immediately turn themselves over to be possessions like good little peasants."

No one said anything to that.

Though the woman with the white flag seemed rather nervous in this company.

Looking at her carefully, Steve found she was at the same level of beauty as Kassandra and Gwendolin. With an equally impressive build.

With strawberry-blond hair and dark blue eyes, she was an amazing specimen.

After eyeing her from head to toe for several seconds, he broke his gaze away.

She wasn't one of his women, which made her off limits.
Why was I even checking her out?
I've got more than enough women to my name. I don't need any more.

Standing there, Steve waited.

As patiently as he could manage.

"That's time," Nancy said finally. "And yes, it really is. I counted it out in my head."

"Thank you," Steve said. Then he turned to Jaina and Ina. "Kill them for me."

"Yes, yes," Jaina said, stepping out in front of Ina. Pushing her hands out in front of her, she ripped the massive magic square that'd been covering them away. More Creep magic was added to it, converted, and the whole thing became a vibrating and quivering purple flame in her hands.

Ina laid her hand on Jaina's shoulder, her other hand clutching a sack tied to her belt at the side, and the angry spell tripled in size.

Ina's playing second fiddle in this one.

Interesting.

The spell grew larger and larger as Jaina began to move it away from their group.

Glancing around, he found everyone watching the spell take form.

Everyone except Nancy. Her eyes were reflecting the spell in a dark and glittering way as she watched Ina and Jaina.

Turning his eyes back to the spell, Steve watched as Jaina grunted and then shoved her hands forward.

With a shriek, the purple morass became a flaming wave and shot forward across the plain.

Cracking, roaring, and spewing fire in every direction, it was like something out of a bard's tall tale.

Then, the whole thing landed on the enemy bandits. Landed on them and kept rolling forward.

Jaina grunted and jerked her hand to one side, and the purple ribbon of death sputtered before winking out.

Bounty collected.

Coin to be collected (241g 12s 05c) at a government-sponsored fine, tax, and levy station.

Steve has gained prestige for enforcing a cardinal law of the Lamals.

Steve has gained the Bringer of Justice accolade.

Steve has gained the title "Blade of the Law" for his continued actions.

"Let's go loot their village and see if there's anyone left to kill or claim," Steve said. He didn't want to waste resources if he could help it.

Every little bit helped.

Jaina looked at the bag at Ina's side and tapped its limp form with a finger. It didn't move very much at all.

"That used all of our sand," Jaina said. "All gone."

In other words, that's not something we can repeat often.

If ever again.

Thirteen

Grunting, Steve brought his axe around and put it straight through the tree in front of him.

Hmm. Used to be that I would hit the tree and it'd explode.

Now the damn thing just goes through it.

With a weird hiss, the tree slid off its own stump and went sideways. It hit the ground with a heavy boom and fell still.

Sighing, Steve walked over to the closest tree to him.

"Village is clear, Steve," Nancy said.

Looking behind him, he found the Wight standing nearby. Her hands were behind her back in her standard "henchwoman waiting for orders" pose he'd come to associate with her. She was wearing a dark dress that contrasted in a lovely way with her eyes and skin tone.

"Yeah? Took everything of value?" Steve asked, looking back at the tree.

"And then some. We dismantled part of the village of anything that would be useful. Nails, lashings, leather ties, anything," Nancy confirmed. "All that's left is used wood.

"Kassandra and Jaina are sorting through the haul and selecting what goes back home and what stays here."

Steve nodded at that. It made sense.

This was an outpost, and while it would need items, he did want to favor his wives back home first and foremost.

"I sensed hesitancy in Ina to carry out your will," Nancy stated. "I've been talking to her and those around her."

"Oh?" Steve asked. He was a bit more curious than he wanted to be. He'd noticed Ina's reception of his orders as well.

"She was afraid there were innocents in the group. Those she felt didn't deserve to be killed," Nancy said.

"Mm," Steve said, looking down at the ground. He couldn't deny the possibility that there were innocents in that group. He'd given them the chance to flee, told them what would happen.

Then had it done.

"She's weak," Nancy said. "Undeserving of your greatness. Jaina, Kassandra, and Lucia understand your superiority. Ina should be sent back to the farm. She can remain there with the other bleeding hearts and soft-headed ones."

Steve chuckled at that. He wasn't about to call Ina weak. She was rather strong, in his opinion.

But he couldn't deny she'd faltered in her duty to him.

When he needed her most to carry out his orders, would she?

What if she balked? Or disobeyed?

What would I do then?

It's not like I have control over them.

"I'll talk to her," Steve said.

"If you think that's wise," Nancy said.

Frowning, Steve turned to look at Nancy.

"Why wouldn't it be wise to talk to her?" Steve asked.

"I see no reason it wouldn't be. I'm merely stating that if you think it's wise, then it's the best course of action," Nancy said with a shrug of her pretty shoulders. "I have no alternative to offer."

"Oh. Sounded like you disapproved," Steve said.

"No. I wouldn't dare or deign to tell you what to do. You're Steve," Nancy said, shaking her head. "Your will and word are my wish and command. You'll bring this world to its knees. I plan to be there at your side when you do so.

"Or on my knees before you as you bring the world to heel. Whichever you prefer."

Chuckling, Steve looked back to his work. Nancy always threw herself into his thoughts as a toy to be used and dismissed at his whim and pleasure.

It was starting to get to his ego a little.

The thought that maybe he did deserve far more than he was taking.

And if I take it all, no one can harm us.

No one can hurt any of my wives.

I've already lost three, I'll not lose more.

I swear it.

"Good work, Nancy," Steve said. "Make sure you get your family back to the farm or Filch. Those two places are quite secure."

"They've left as of yesterday morning. For Filch. They felt they could probably do better there in the end, as they're not skilled to work a farm.

"Some remained to assist me in my work, though they're very few in number," Nancy said.

Lifting up his axe, Steve brought it around with a grunt. It passed through the large tree as if it were nothing. Neatly parting it once more.

"Do any villages still stand against us?" Steve asked, watching the tree fall to one side.

"They did this morning, but they won't by this afternoon," Nancy claimed. "Since we cleared out the enemy force two days ago, their village yesterday, and finished collaring all the prisoners, we had some resources available.

"I organized them, tasked Kassandra to lead one group, Jaina the other, and sent them off to conquer five smaller villages between them."

Not really knowing how to respond to that, Steve stared at the next tree he'd be bringing down.

Nancy had acted without his permission, but she'd done exactly what he would have wanted.

"If I hadn't been completely sure it was what you wanted, I wouldn't have done it," Nancy commented. "I may want you to beat me and ravage me as I lie there bleeding beneath you, but I don't seek to ruin your plans, Steve. I knew it was what you wanted, so I took care of it."

"And how are you so sure you know what I want?" Steve asked, finally looking at Nancy. His anger felt cold, but he was a little annoyed with her.

"Because I know you," Nancy said with a shrug. "I know you, Steve, and what you want. My only goal is to make you happy and reach your goals.

"And if I work hard enough and truly make you happy, maybe you'll brand me repeatedly on my face. Or at the very least give me a few good slaps. I'd love a really good open-handed slap.

"Hard enough to make my eyes sting. So my lip bleeds and I can taste it. Run my tongue over it. So my head rings and it feels like my knees might go out."

Sighing, Steve ran a hand through his hair and looked back at the tree.

Nancy is Nancy. She just wants me to kick the crap out of her.

I'm better off fearing ulterior motives from Nikki or Lucia rather than Nancy.

"When the prisoners get back, assemble them for me," Steve said. "I want to see what they bring back and reward them accordingly."

"Of course, Steve," Nancy said.

***

Looking out over the heads of his people, Steve felt his lips curl upward.

They'd gone out, fought, looted, killed, and a few had even died for him.

For which he'd received the bounties. They were his property after all. If they died in his service, he was entitled to what they were owed.

"Good work!" Steve said loudly. "If you captured or killed four or more people, I'm officially removing your murderer status and making you my property instead.

"If you believe you killed or captured four, go stand over there."

Steve lifted a hand and pointed to a field off to one side.

"Just so you know, though, I'm going to make you swear on your collar to the truth of your statement. If you're lying, you'll die," Steve said. "Be sure of your number before you go over there."

That was all he had to say, and he didn't want to say anything more.

They were the scum of the earth. Murderers one and all. If any law-abiding citizen caught them, they'd be killed for no reason.

But they were his scum of the earth and his bounties.

He'd reward some people this time with their murderer tags being removed. The next group would have to work twice as hard to earn it.

Rapidly, the field gained twenty women. All standing there looking at Steve with eager eyes.

Not that he could blame them.

The moment they lost the murderer tag, their life expectancy would shoot up. He would no longer be able to kill them out of hand.

Even if they were property.

Walking up to the first woman, a beautiful redhead, Steve set his hand on her collar and looked into her bright blue eyes.

"Take hold of your collar now," Steve said, then waited for her to do so. "How many did you kill or capture in my name? Swear it on your life as you hold your collar."

"I killed seven in your name and captured two," the woman said. "I swear it on my life."

Steve waited to see if she'd keel over dead.

Nothing happened. She stood there, staring back at him.

"Then I strike your murderer title from you. You're now only my property, and no longer marked for death," Steve said. "Good work. You can join the innocents and farm hands in their bunkhouse."

Letting go of the collar, Steve walked to the next woman in the line.

A stunning brunette with brown eyes and a wide smile on her lips.

Taking hold of her collar, Steve met her eyes. She immediately laid her hand over his at the same time.

"I killed fourteen in your name, and captured eight," she purred at him, taking a step closer. "I swear it on my life."

"Fourteen and eight?" Steve asked. "That's impressive. Does anyone claim a higher number?"

Looking around, Steve scanned the crowd.

A small woman with black hair and hazel eyes lifted a hand.

"Come up here." Steve pointed to his side and then turned back to the brunette.

"I strike your murderer title from you," he said. "You're now only my property, and no longer marked for death. Good work. You can join the innocents and farm hands in their bunkhouse."

Stepping away from her, Steve moved up to the much smaller woman and took her collar into his hand.

The woman immediately took his hand and her collar in both of hers, holding tightly to them. She stared up at him with eyes that made him feel like she wasn't quite right in the head.

"I killed twenty-six in your name, Steve," she said. "I captured ten."

"Goodness," Steve said with a grin. "You're rather devoted, aren't you?"

"Yes, I am," said the woman, staring up at him. "I'm very good at killing. I use a mace."

"Well. I strike your murderer title from you and name you my enforcer," Steve said. "You'll work for Nancy for me, as my property. Do you understand?"

"I understand," said the woman, not letting go of his hand.

Steve worked his way through the group and released them all. None had nearly the same number as his new enforcer. Nowhere near, in fact.

When it finally came to a close, he turned to Kassandra and Jaina.

"No issues?" he asked, walking over to the two women.

"No, no. They did what I told them to after I killed the first one who didn't listen," Jaina said.

"I killed one. Another tried to run and died when the collar ended her," Kassandra said. "After that, it wasn't a question of them following."

"Good. Glad the collars are working," Steve said. "Anything to report on the haul?"

"No," Jaina said quickly. "We took everything we could. Everything, everything. Nothing was left behind. We're now the apex and alpha predators here. Everyone else is prey."

"Yes, though unfortunately we have no prey left," Kassandra said with a sigh. "Those were the last bandit villages nearby. We'll have to go pretty far afield if we want to find more."

"You did release the innocents, right?" Steve asked.

"Yes. I offered them jobs and a place to stay. They all declined. Didn't believe me," Jaina said.

"The same was true for me, of course," Kassandra said. "It's unlikely they'd believe anything we said."

"Excellent. You both did very well," Steve professed.

"Indeed," Lucia agreed. She'd joined him at some point but had been rather quiet. "It was an excellent maneuver. We've gained loot, resources, and provided a safe working envelope for ourselves.

"This would all be worthy of a Fae general, let alone the little homestead family that we are."

Kassandra and Jaina both seemed to puff up a bit at that.

"Well, seeing as that's taken care of, I'm afraid Steve and I need to discuss something," Lucia apologized, slipping her arm through Steve's. Then she looked at Nancy. "Come along, you'll need to assist me."

Unsure what they needed to talk about, Steve kept his peace as the three of them trooped into the cabin.

"Alright," Lucia murmured after having closed the door behind her. "Nancy, my husband is going to avail himself of you, and then he's going to put his seed into my royal womb. You're acting as my surrogate until I learn what I'm supposed to do. I've been instructed as any good princess would be, but I've never seen any of it and have no experience."

"I don't—"

"You're his mistress, are you not?" Lucia said, walking over to Nancy and setting a hand on her back.

"I am," Nancy agreed.

"That means you rank beneath me," Lucia said. "You're mine to do with as I will when it comes to my husband.

"My goal is to make him an outstanding person of greatness, and you'll assist me in that. Now—"

Lucia gave Nancy's rear end a light pat.

"Be a dear and get down on your knees. Steve will use your mouth for a short period while I watch. As I mentioned, my mother instructed me often, but I have no practical knowledge," Lucia said as she began to undress herself. "You'll serve for my purposes of figuring out the truth of her lessons."

Nancy looked terrified, sick, and absolutely completely into the situation. She looked eager.

She loves being humiliated and torn apart. Of course, she'd enjoy this.

Nancy got down on her knees right there, then looked at Steve and opened her mouth wide, her tongue sliding out.

"Perfect. What a lovely little thing you are," Lucia purred, setting her clothes to one side. She was as beautiful naked as he'd always imagined her to be. "Come on over here, Steve, and use the mistress as befits her rank and station."

Shrugging, Steve walked over, undid his belt, and let his pants hit the floor.

Grabbing Nancy's head with his right hand and her right shoulder with his left, he stuffed himself into her mouth.

She liked it when he dominated her. Who was he to complain?

Moaning around him, Nancy looked up as his shaft vanished between her lips.

"Oh, it can't be that easy. Mother made it sound harder," Lucia said, kneeling down and watching closely. "Close your mouth more tightly."

Nancy glanced at Lucia and immediately did as she was told.

"Suck harder on him, and ease your chin up but the back of your head down. Make it so he can go down your throat when he pushes forward," Lucia said, tapping Nancy's chin.

The Wight did as instructed, gazing up at Steve.

He imagined she was loving every second of this.

Taking a good hold of Nancy's head, Steve began to thrust in and out of her mouth, his tip and shaft pushing down her throat each time. He made her neck bulge outward when he wedged his hilt up to her lips.

"Oh, yes. That looks much better," Lucia said, watching Nancy being used. "I suppose it really is that easy after all."

Nancy was grunting and moaning as Steve more or less ravaged her mouth.

Lucia merely watched for an entire minute as Nancy's mouth was used.

"Good, now, this way Steve. Time for you to experience royalty," Lucia said, pulling Nancy's head to one side. He slipped free from Nancy's mouth and went straight into Lucia's.

The demure Fae did everything opposite to what she'd made Nancy do.

She prevented him from going down her throat, angled him in such a way that he couldn't thrust into her very well, and refused to let his hands settle on her. Swatting them away when he tried.

Lucia instead began to slowly, leisurely move her head back and forth. Her mouth pulled at him wonderfully as her tongue rolled all around his tip and caressed him.

He felt her left hand come up between his legs and lightly fondle and caress his jewels. Her fingernails pulled gently against the skin.

It was a night and day difference between the two of them, but Lucia worked him masterfully whereas Nancy let herself be destroyed.

"Hmm, that was much simpler than I thought it would be," Lucia said, letting his tip fall away from her lips. "Alright, Mistress. I want you to bend over on hands and knees. Just lift your dress up, no need to strip."

Nancy looked away and nodded slightly. Getting onto her hands and knees, she got comfortable on the ground. Then she reached back with one hand and hiked up her dress, revealing her very naked rear end to Steve and Lucia.

"Goodness, you really are a beautiful Wight," Lucia said, running a hand over Nancy's bottom. "I think you'll be a perfect mistress for me and Steve.

"Alright, husband. I want you to slip it right in here and enjoy."

Lucia had reached up to lightly splay Nancy's thin lips apart as she spoke, giving him a very pink and moist view.

Steve did as he was told and immediately sank himself to the hilt inside of Nancy.

With a deep moan, Nancy shifted her hips and tilted her rear end up toward him.

"Ah, yes. That's very good positioning," Lucia said, stroking Nancy's hips. She was staring at the point where Steve was buried in Nancy.

Going straight for maximum force, Steve began pounding away at the Wight. Driving her forward with each and every heavy thrust.

Just the way she liked and wanted it.

Squirming, groaning, and pushing back as she could, Nancy was clearly in her own happy world.

"You're moving away too much. He needs to be caught by your hips, not blow through them," Lucia said and then reached over to pat Nancy on the shoulders. "Put your shoulders down and brace against the ground while tilting your hips up. Put your belly to the ground."

Nancy did what she was told, and Steve immediately found he could really pummel her in this position.

Cracking down into her with everything he could muster, he felt it when Nancy orgasmed hard, wailing into the ground. Getting absolutely destroyed.

Lucia concerned herself only with watching Steve's manhood slam through Nancy. Inches away from her face.

"Good, good," Lucia said, patting Nancy on the bottom as she leaned back. "Okay, husband. Time for you to have and fill the royal womb."

Lucia reached down and pushed Nancy's knees away from her chest, causing her to go flat on the ground and making Steve slide right out of her.

Then Lucia lay down on the ground and placed her hands on her own thighs.

"Come, lie atop me. You'll go slow and easy, and love me," Lucia said. "My royal self deserves the utmost when it comes to attention. I expect an orgasm before you seed me. And don't you fret, husband of mine. While I'm needy, I'm also going to be very attentive to you in return. More than you'll ever get from anyone else."

Somewhat lost in the desire to get off, but still hearing her, Steve lay down atop Lucia and instantly inserted his tip into her.

"Ah, yes. Now… enter slowly and claim me," Lucia said, her hands resting on his hips.

Steve started to move forward, going slow, just as she'd stated.

"Mm, that's wonderful, husband," Lucia said, shifting around beneath him. He felt her ankles lightly rest on his hips. With the way she angled herself, her legs didn't get in his way either.

Bottoming out inside her, Steve looked to her face for direction.

Lucia smiled at him, then leaned her head up and kissed him with some heat for several seconds. Laying her head back down, she caressed his face with one hand.

"Okay, have me, husband. Slowly, deeply, firmly. No force though," she said.

Pulling his hips back, Steve began to work himself in and out of the small Fae princess.

Lucia closed her eyes and lay there as she worked her hips with his movements. Her hands caressed him, as her ankles and feet offered him the way to get the deepest into her.

She was so active a partner that Steve almost didn't want to let it stop. He just wanted to ride her for the enjoyment of it.

It was an amazing experience.

After a minute or two, she opened her eyes.

Lucia's gaze lifted up to his own with a smile on her lips. She watched him even as she rolled her body and squeezed at him with her channel in time with his thrusts.

"Am I good?" she asked in a purring question.

"Amazing," Steve got out, wanting to keep going.

"Am I great?" Lucia asked, her voice getting a bit deeper.

"Best I've ever had," Steve said, and he meant it. Lucia was working him in a way he couldn't describe.

Lucia's eyes fluttered closed several times as he felt her depths flex and squeeze at him. He was pretty sure she'd hit her climax. He wasn't sure if it was from his comments or what he was doing, but he was glad he'd gotten her off.

Letting out a slow, shuddering breath as Steve continued to have her, Lucia opened her eyes wide now.

"Husband, that was wonderful," she said as he pushed into her again. "You may seed me now. Do give me a prince, alright? There are enough princesses in the royal family."

Warning: Lucia has issued a royal command as your wife to impregnate her.

If accepted, she will become pregnant.

Steve said nothing and instead focused on enjoying the Fae.

"Yes, that feels perfect," Lucia moaned, her fingers curling around the back of his neck. "Do it now, Steve. Now. Give me your seed."

Impregnate Lucia Bril?

No!

Steve hit his climax at that moment and pushed down into Lucia. He filled her up with each thrust. Pushing down on her hips, he risked it and thrust a bit harder into the small Fae.

Lucia moaned softly with each impact, apparently not taking offense to the increase in force.

After several more hard thrusts, Steve was empty and spent, pushing himself up into her one last time.

Royal command accepted.

Declination of impregnation overridden.

Royal conception achieved.

"That was heavenly," Lucia said, her left hand sliding through his hair while her right pet his shoulders. "And you even got me pregnant after all. We Fae women can be hard to pin down with a child sometimes. Well done, husband."

Steve has gained notoriety for breaking the laws of the Lamals.

Steve has gained prestige for wedding a princess of the Fae courts.

Steve has gained prestige for impregnating a princess of the Fae courts.

Steve has gained the Fairy Tale accolade.

Steve has gained the Royal Consort accolade.

Fuck.

Groaning, Steve laid his head down on Lucia's shoulder.

Maybe it was worth it.

That was amazing.

"Let's do that again tonight," Lucia said, still petting and holding Steve. "Though I think you'll finish in our mistress tonight. If I'm feeling especially kind, I'll bless her with a kiss myself. And by the way, do you admit you're my property now, Nancy?"

"I'm your property, Mistress, second only to Steve. And yes, please," Nancy murmured from the side. She'd lain there and watched, saying nothing. "Have me again tonight and bless me."

"Wonderful," Lucia said, humming happily as she ran her hands up and down Steve's back.

Steve didn't really care right now. He was really just enjoying what Lucia was doing to him.

And that her hips were still wide open, and she was squeezing at him with her channel.

Suddenly, Steve wondered if he could go again in a minute or two.

He certainly wanted to try.

Fourteen

Steve was impressed.

His prisoners were knocking down trees faster than he could. Even if he were to run from tree to tree and swing as fast as he could.

There was just so many prisoners that they were doing far more than he could by himself with his single tool.

Makes sense, I guess. Crush it with numbers. No different than throwing money at a problem.

Just resources instead.

Kassandra and Ina had gone back to the farm two days previous to update everyone there on the situation.

Since the first night with Lucia, though, Kassandra and Ina had changed.

The Fae woman had quickly taken over Steve's bedroom and had somehow coerced Ina and Kassandra to follow her lead.

Nancy was, of course, always on hand regardless of the situation. Fully acting the part of his mistress.

Another reason Kassandra and Ina had been sent back home was to see how things were going and bring back information.

That and prepare things.

The moat surrounding the cabin and lining where the walls would go was nearly full now.

To the point that they could start shipping supplies on the water.

That'd be far easier than sending things overland. Not to mention that Misty had set it up so a current was now happening. He didn't understand that part of it, but it was working.

One side of the moat brought in fresh water from the farm, and the other side took it out down along the waterway toward Filch.

"It would seem that… you're no longer needed for the manual labor," Nancy murmured from beside him.

Lucia had certainly tamed Nancy when it came to the bedroom. That was the extent of it, however.

It was considerably less control than Lucia thought she had.

Nancy had told him in no uncertain terms that she was his, first and foremost. She'd betray Lucia in a heartbeat if Nancy thought it'd benefit Steve. The only place she'd let Lucia rule was the bed, and that was because it suited Nancy's purposes.

In fact, she'd already been relaying everything Lucia told her back to Steve.

One such exchange had given him the chance to prepare for the "What shall we name him or her?" question Lucia was going to launch at him at some point.

"Yeah," Steve said, leaning on his axe. "Guess I'm on building duty. Only one more bunkhouse to go really."

"Yes. The stone walls are coming along much more slowly," Nancy said. "Though it's nice they're coming along at all. Those tend to take years to build. Not two… Creep Witches."

Nancy had never truly been comforted by the fact that Jaina and Ina were something that hadn't existed previously.

That their titles literally contained the word "Creep," and that their magic seemed to use the Creep as a fuel source when available.

Or so Steve interpreted it. He could be misreading Nancy entirely.

"Mm," Steve hummed. "Though it makes me curious to see what's going on back home. I wonder what all those Creep Witches have been up to. Nikki said they'd been working in the south, around the lake, to put in a stone wall all the way around."

"Do you think they'll finish quicker than we will?" Nancy asked.

"Probably. More of them. Just a simple matter of numbers," Steve said. "Like our tree-cutters. I'm very strong. Can do a lot. But I'm only one man."

"You have me," Nancy said immediately. "I would wield your axe for you all day while you stripped the logs if you wished. Or vice versa."

"One man and his mistress. What can't we do together?" Steve prophesied. "And no. What we're doing is… it's correct. Letting them do the work we took them for is right. It's just annoying. It was something I could measure myself by. What I did to earn my keep that day."

"I understand," Nancy said. "I often feel the same way."

"You're earning your keep and then some, Nancy," Steve disagreed. "I'll tell you if you're not."

"Thank you, Steve," Nancy purred. "I'm glad to hear that. Could I ask what it is I'm doing that you're appreciating? And maybe if I've earned a reward?"

"Just everything you've been doing, honestly," Steve said. "You're a wonderful mistress. Or henchwoman, if you prefer."

"Mistress is preferable. Taken mistress if we're being technical," Nancy said immediately. Then her head slowly turned to one side. She was facing the southwest now. "Though... that doesn't look right."

Following her gaze, Steve could see a partial dust cloud rising up in the distance.

He had no idea what that meant.

It was too far to see what was going on, given the natural rolling of the plains in that direction and the distance alone.

"Is it a storm or something?" Steve asked.

"I don't know," Nancy said, shaking her head. "Should we call everyone in and prepare?"

"No, we'll just send Jaina," Steve said. "Have someone find her and get her moving. Just to see what's going on and then get back here."

"Jaina?" Nancy asked. "Actually... I haven't seen her at all since we came out to inspect the tree line work."

Looking toward the cabin and the fields, Steve realized he hadn't seen Jaina either. She'd been in the fields before, but she wasn't there now.

Grunting, Steve decided to check the cabin. If she was anywhere else, it would be there.

Halfway there, though, he realized Jaina wouldn't be in the cabin.

Mostly because she was heading straight for him. She was coming from the direction of the dust cloud.

"I'm going to bet my little boobie-dog saw it before we did and went to go look," Steve said.

"Boobie... dog?" Nancy asked.

"That's right. And I do love my boobie-dog," Steve said.

"Does that make me a boobie-wight?" Nancy said, glancing down at her own extremely well-endowed form. "Or some other woefully unfortunate title?"

"No, you're my mistress and bed pillow. I can tell you my inner ugly thoughts about others," Steve said. "Or did you want a woefully unfortunate title?"

"A little," Nancy admitted.

So easy to read.

"How unfortunate are we talking here?" Steve asked.

"I'd... uhm... disparaging? Hurtful? Insulting?" Nancy elaborated. "Something that'd make me feel shame? Especially around others?"

Steve didn't have anything he wanted to call her, so he couldn't come up with anything on the spot.

"Like... cum-dumpster, personal whore, fuck doll, slut bucket, cock wrap, baby farm, g—"

"Okay, got it," Steve said. He really had no desire to call her any of those things.

Sighing, he ran a hand through his hair. Nancy was definitely too much for him at times.

He'd thought he'd been adventurous when it came to sex, but Nancy was in an entirely different league.

Different planet.

"Please?" Nancy asked.

For crying out lo—ugh. Fine.

If that's what she wants, we can... we can accommodate her needs. She accommodates mine, after all.

Or at least, some of her needs.

A little.

"Hush, my pretty little sex toy," Steve said. That was the best he could do right now. "Jaina's got very good ears, and she'll be able to hear us soon."

Jaina got closer and closer, but didn't slow down. Not in the least. It wasn't until she was practically atop him that she put her hands and feet down on the grass. Grass sprayed up around her as she did it.

Then she smacked into the front of him, wrapping herself bodily around him.

"Husband! Soldiers are coming. Many, many soldiers. All in the colors of Lamals," Jaina said, staring up at him with wide eyes.

"How many is many, many?" Steve asked.

"Less than the number of prisoners we have, more than the number of people back home," Jaina said.

"Okay, so less than a thousand but more than a hundred," Steve said. "A lot more than what we have at home?"

"Yes," Jaina said. Her eyes were wide and slightly fearful. He could only imagine what was going through her head. She was illegally wed after having been made a widow. Soldiers from Lamals wouldn't have meant anything good in her life so far.

"Do they look like soldiers from the citadel? The wall?" Steve asked.

"No. They look fresh, clean, and with perfect uniforms," Jaina said. "Clean, very clean. Marching perfectly."

"Hmm. Maybe from the capital," Steve mused. "Alright, we'll assume they're not here for us until they head our way. Then we'll deal with them as we have to."

"I'm sorry," Jaina said. "You're not supposed to wed widows. I could be the reason they try to kill you."

Jaina whined once, her tail hanging low between her legs.

"Oh, stop it." Steve scratched at her stiff ears. "Come on, I'll bed you right here and now just to make sure you understand it's what I want."

"Yes, yes," Jaina said, smiling at him. "I love you, husband. My alpha."

Jaina then let go of him and flopped onto her back, squirming on the grass for several seconds in a way that seemed very Kobold. After that, she started pushing her pants down.

"Come, husband," she said once she'd gotten her pants down to her ankles. Then she yanked her tunic up, exposing her chest.

"Show off your wife, Jaina Bril, to anyone who would watch," growled the Kobold, holding her arms out to him.

She was always quick to go.

And he was happy to oblige.

***

"It would seem they are indeed here for us," Nancy murmured.

Steve had counted as the enemy force came ever onward in the south. They were around five hundred and ninety, give or take, if he'd screwed up his count. Which was likely, given it was hard to count bobbing heads when they weren't all the same height.

The group didn't turn toward the cabin until the last thirty seconds or so. There was no mistaking their destination now.

Based on the way they were moving originally, however, Steve got the impression they were heading for the farm rather than this location.

Better us here than there. More soldiers to defend with here.

Gotta love prisoners.

"Think you can put up a square around us?" Steve asked.

"Yes, yes," Jaina immediately said from her squat at his side. "I'm stronger than Ina now. I grew much stronger from killing all those beasts."

So... killing people can empower you.

Good to know.

If it comes time to execute some of the prisoners, I'll have Jaina take care of it.

Lucia clicked her tongue and then sighed.

"The one in the front looks like a parade guard. Her armor is practically shining from the amount of buffing she's given it," said the Fae princess. "Even the royal guard isn't as prissy as that."

"Definitely looks like a silk soldier," Steve said.

"Silk soldier?" Nancy asked.

"Uh," Steve said, not sure where he'd gotten the term from. "Like they've never seen a day of fighting, but've been in the military their whole life."

"Oh," Nancy said.

With a hard clack, the entire enemy force came to a perfect stop.

"They march well," Lucia murmured. "If only armies were measured on walking around while being shiny."

Jaina growled softly as ten or so soldiers broke away from the group. They began marching straight for Steve, though their weapons remained at ease or in sheaths.

Reaching down with his right hand, he began to lightly pet and caress the top of Jaina's head. Her growl slowly died away at the attention he was giving her.

Most of the guard came to a stop around thirty feet away.

Only the lead soldier in the ever-so-bright armor continued until about ten feet away.

Then she pulled her helmet off.

It was a woman who looked very similar to the more bestial races he'd met so far.

With cat-like ears in a very Human-looking face, she had pale blond hair, ears of a darker brown, and bright yellow eyes that were almost gold. She was pretty, as all women seemed to be in this world, though far closer to Shelly in that almost too-pretty subset.

Additionally, there was a certain alien beauty to her cheeks and eyes, and in her jaw and mouth.

It reminded him of Chessa in a way.

"Greetings homesteader," said the soldier. He couldn't tell, but it seemed like the woman was speaking directly to Lucia at his side.

"Greetings in return," Steve said back.

The woman was momentarily silent, her head tilting fractionally toward Steve now.

The swipe of her hand was disguised in her shifting her helmet to the other hand. She'd done it so well that he'd almost missed it.

Except he'd been looking for it. He'd wanted to know if she would inspect him.

"I'm named Geneva. Geneva Gosti," said the woman. "I'm a captain of the royal guard, ambassador to the citadel cities, and royal envoy."

"I'm Steve. I own this outpost and the farm to the south," he said. "I'm also wed to the mayor of Filch.

"The surviving one, that is. The original mayor died, and so did two of her daughters. The only one who remains is S-Rachele."

"I see," said Geneva. Adjusting the helmet at her side, she seemed to be considering her words and what to say.

"Can we help you?" Steve inquired, deciding to make it easier on the woman. So far, she hadn't been rude or abrasive. As far as he could tell, she was just a soldier.

Gimme some insight into this walking set of polished armor, Shitty Steve.

Geneva Gosti
Lionan
Father: living
Mother: living
Royal Captain- captain of the royal guard
Ambassador- speaks on behalf of the queen of Lamals
Envoy- designated to treat with other nations for the queen of Lamals
Noble Line- part of the nobility of Lamals
Royal Branch Family- a branch member of the royal family

Steve didn't bother to close the window. He'd rather leave it up than admit he was peeking at her.

"I think maybe you can at that," Geneva said. "You have quite the fortification going up behind you."

Steve glanced over his shoulder, using the opportunity to swipe Geneva's window away at the same time.

From here, it was obviously a fortification. Not an outpost, but an actual fortification. A big one.

Looking back to the Beastkin, Steve shrugged.

"The country was being overrun by the Creep, zombies, murderers, and bandits. I've lost three wives to it already," Steve said. "We weren't getting any help from the citadel city, and there was no word from the capital. So... here we are.

"I now have something akin to... what's the count?" Steve asked, looking at Nancy.

"Close to a thousand," Nancy said immediately.

"A thousand murderers all working for me. Magically compelled to do so," Steve explained. "They make fairly decent soldiers, and they're very well motivated to do their best for me."

Everything that'd just gone back and forth was a threat, in a way. That Geneva was out of her league here. If he decided to attack, she'd take ungodly losses even if she won the fight.

That wasn't his goal, though. He needed to dial it back a bit.

"We do what we must to protect our homes and our people," Steve said. "We had an entire force of murderers show up the other day trying to rob us of our hard-won food stores."

"Yes, that certainly… makes sense when you put it like that," Geneva said, nodding her head slowly. "That would explain your… interesting status."

What if I dialed it a bit further back?

What if I made this an easy and obvious choice for her, if she truly wants to succeed? Made her see that what I can offer through my titles, farm, and presence is more than she can get without me.

If I could bed her and make her mine, that'd be ideal.

Wouldn't that bring a lot more power to my name?

Could I take on Linne if Geneva were mine?

She's well esteemed in the Lamals court. Having her under my thumb and under me would be a resource all on its own.

"Yeah, it's real colorful," Steve said with a grin. "Speaking of colorful—you're a rather beautiful woman, Geneva. Your eyes are simply amazing. The hue almost seems to shift when you move your head around."

Geneva's cheeks colored a soft red at that. Her ears slowly swiveled toward Steve and nowhere else.

Clearing her throat, Geneva couldn't hide the fact that her fingers were tapping along the hilt of her sword.

Maybe that was too forward.

"I've been dispatched to bring this part of Lamals back to order. To that end, I've been conferred with the title of military governor. This pertains to all the lands of Filch up to and including the citadel city it supports," Geneva reported. "In addition, this includes two cities above Filch, two below, and every village and town in those areas and between. My central base will be in Filch itself, as it was the largest city prior to the Creep invasion."

"Uh huh," Steve said, not really sure how to take that. It sounded a lot like she was here to try and make his life hell.

He could be wrong, but he didn't think he was. Most people from the government seemed to be rather worthless to him so far.

"And what is it you want from me, exactly?" Steve said.

"First of all, I'd very much like for you to provide me and my soldiers with a place to lay our heads, and perhaps food," Geneva said.

"Feel free to sleep anywhere around here, except for the fields," Steve said. "The water is pure and good to drink, so don't foul it up by having all those tin cans back there shitting in it. Have them dig a latrine.

"As for food, sure. So long as someone is paying. You paying for your soldiers, or are they paying for themselves?"

"I'm afraid I wouldn't have the coin to cover all their meals in addition to my own," Geneva said. "We've found that the cost of food is far different out here, and I don't have the coin to back up those purchases. I've been mis-provisioned. From what you've said, it sounds like I'm not going to have any luck at Filch either."

Oh? That's an admission and an invitation of sorts.
Isn't it?

"I could be convinced to sell the food at pre-Creep rates, or maybe even provide it free of charge," Steve said, staring hard into Geneva's face. This would give him a very good idea of how far he could push this little prim-and-proper polished soldier.

"Ah—" Geneva said, her mouth locked in an open position. She clearly understood his underlying statement, but it seemed she didn't know how to take it. "I… and how does Filch procure their food?"

"The mayor's my wife. I did mention that," Steve said with a shrug. "It wouldn't do to make problems for her, would it? Though the citadel commander will end up having to pay six times the going rate for food. I dislike her."

Bed her, wed her, turn her to your own ends.
She already knows I'm bedding a Fae princess.
It wouldn't be as if I'm beneath her in station.

"Would you care to join me in my cabin to discuss such an arrangement?" Steve asked. "If you like, you could always go back to your soldiers and decide what to do from there. We're really just looking to protect our own and don't want trouble from anyone."

Geneva blinked several times, looking a lot like a small animal caught in a snare.

"I suppose I must," she said, squaring her shoulders.

"I wouldn't say that," Lucia said with a smile on her face. "Though I can promise you the rewards are certainly better than if you choose not to take this course of action."

Geneva put a smile on her face, turned to her guards behind her, and then gestured around them.

"Break camp, settle in," she said loudly. They were too far to have heard any of the conversation, thankfully. "I'm going to negotiate for food with the homesteader. Dig latrines, post pickets, guards, and patrols. Keep everything on a tight watch and leash. Don't pollute the water source; it's drinkable."

Turning back to Steve, Geneva gave him a feral smile that was quite similar to Chessa's when he'd first met her.

Aggressive, combative, and curious.

"Well then, shall we go... talk?" she asked, clearly understanding what was in store for her.

Fifteen

"Before we go any further," Geneva said as the door closed behind her. "I cannot give you my maidenhood.

"I understand exactly what you were requesting. I agree to it and will lie with you. But not tonight. And not anytime until my forces are safely away at Filch.

"If I were to give myself to you before then, I know very well that my soldiers would lose what little respect they have for me. I'm not a fool. I know exactly what I appear to be to them, and I cannot change that opinion anytime soon.

"Being taken to bed would remove any chance I ever had of changing their view of me."

Huh. She's not wrong... but... if she knew what she looked like to her soldiers, why would she willingly walk into it?

Must be more there.

"You should get on your back and receive him," Nancy said. She was standing by the door. "That is what you agreed to, so do it."

"Yes, yes. Receive my husband willingly," Jaina growled.

"Now, now," Lucia said, laying a hand on Nancy's shoulder. "I do understand her point. She's actually quite right in her entire view of the situation. We just need to figure out a way to bind her that preserves her honor at the same time."

"I'll simply pledge myself to Steve in marriage," Geneva said with a shrug of her shoulders. "It's a rather common promissory oath to give amongst the nobility. Violating it is tantamount to giving oneself over to the queen for judgment."

"That'd be fine," Lucia said with a wave of her free hand, the other still resting on Nancy's back. "Though we should speak more on what we're expecting here."

Jaina was crouched down in the other corner of the room, glaring at Geneva.

"I want her as my wife, and I want to use her to build our power base," Steve said, looking at Lucia. "With her backing, we'll have a much better chance against the citadel. Or the queen, if it comes to that. Isn't that true, Geneva?"

"It... actually, it certainly is true," Geneva said, looking back at Steve. "My family isn't the strongest, perhaps the third, but we do well for ourselves. We'd certainly make a play for the crown if we had a better than average chance to win it.

"I may not speak for my family, as I'm not the head of it, but I could easily challenge for leadership on my return after we consummate our marriage. Although... what's your final goal?"

In other words, she's not officially an adult until she's in a marriage.

"Dunno," Steve said. "I've been thinking the current citadel commander failed. I'd be a better commander."

Geneva watched him without a word or a move. She didn't even blink.

Something else there. Can a man not be a citadel commander?

"That works," Geneva said. "It would also benefit my family if it happened. On top of you having a Fae princess and the mayor as wives."

"Splendid," Lucia said. "And what is it you want, Geneva?"

"Food and water for my troops, a guarantee that you'll support me in my task, and that you'll provide assistance to that end," Geneva said. "The better I can accomplish this task, the better my reward when I return. Coming back with a husband of worth will only make that reward all the better. I'll be able to request much more. My long-term goal is to take over my family."

"That's... yeah, agreed," Steve said.

This was all much better than trying to pussyfoot around Geneva while working with her and likely against her at the same time. Steve was looking for ways to increase his power base, and this would definitely be one.

All the better that it wouldn't cost him much other than bedding an attractive woman.

"Done. With those understandings in mind, and providing that they are followed, I pledge myself to you in marriage as per the customs of Lamals," Geneva said.

You've been given a nobility contract for a wedding vow.
The contract binds Steven Bril to Geneva Gosti for all time.

There is no majority contract holder.
There is no lesser contract holder.

Both parties shall obey, abide, and adhere to all rules given by each other during contracting.

The penalties of the contract are based on the perception the queen of Lamals.

All penalties will be judged and assessed accordingly by the queen of Lamals.

Please confirm that you wish to accept this nobility contract.

Yes, but I don't wish for anyone to know of this contract. Nor for it to have a physical manifestation.

Contract accepted by both parties under condition of anonymity.

Contract is now active.

"I... didn't expect that. Though I'm glad for it being invisible. Well, that's that," Geneva said with a wide smile for Steve. "Let's get my girls taken care of. They're rather beat, and I honestly can't wait to bask in their thanks for getting them full bellies.

"Oh, and have you been getting any Creep attacks?"

"No, not since the Creep pulled back and left," Steve said.

"Speaking of that, what happened?" Geneva asked. "One day the Creep simply stopped coming back."

"I knocked down part of the wall and filled the gap with rubble," Steve said. "By the way... it looks like Linne Lynn, the citadel commander, betrayed her neighbor. Something happened, something blew up, and the neighboring citadel city fell.

"Creep was pouring in through there until I filled it up."

"I... Lynn did this?" Geneva asked.

"That's the only thing we can figure," Steve said with a shrug. "Looked like they'd opened the doors for her to come in and then were hacked down right there. Some type of magic blew up, and that was all they wrote. She seemed quite... angry... at the idea of a Human citadel commander. She didn't like me much."

"Yes, her distaste for Humanity is well known," Geneva said, her brows coming together. "I never would have figured her to betray the wall, though. She's a traitor then. And should be my first visit."

"If you want to die a virgin, sure," Steve said. "She'll probably just kill you. She tried to enslave me as a sexual captive. I killed three of her champions and threatened her with titles."

"Titles?" Geneva asked. Nothing else he'd said seemed to spark her interest. Which was odd in a way.

Steve glanced over to Lucia, wanting to know what she thought.

"She's already sworn to you," Lucia said, interpreting his look. "She'd have to learn eventually. Better now. Besides… it isn't a bad thing."

"I have the right to give someone a title if it's valid," Steve said, looking back at Geneva. "I name you Future Wife of Steve. And thus it is so."

He didn't need to check; he knew it would happen.

"Lynn will just kill you," Steve continued. "She has no honor and obviously doesn't care. She caused the entire Creep problem. I remove your Future Wife of Steve title."

"Yes," Geneva murmured. "Yes… I understand. You're right. She really would just kill me. I'll take your suggestion to heart.

"What… would you suggest then?"

"Go to Filch," Lucia suggested. "Set up shop there. The assistant mayor, Xivin, also Steve's wife, is operating there at this time. It'll give you the opportunity to see what's going on in the area while you plan the rest of your moves.

"You did say you had other cities in your purview?"

"Yes, I do," Geneva confirmed. "Four cities other than Filch. Bexis, Faraday, Hilast, and Rennis."

"Then you have your direction," Lucia said with a bright smile. "You'll take a small contingent of your troops, along with Steve, myself, and perhaps Xivin. That'd be more than enough to stake your claim all throughout."

Geneva looked like she was digesting far too much too quickly.

"I'll… take that under advisement," she said finally, shaking her head. "I'm going to go get my girls settled in."

"I'll have food brought over immediately. Just have everyone drink from the moat; it's perfectly clean," Steve said. "It never has and never will hold even a trace of the Creep."

"Good," Geneva said, then turned and moved to the door.

Nancy held it open for the woman but didn't follow her out.

When it closed behind her, Jaina moved to the door and stuck her nose against the frame.

Sniffling softly, the Kobold stuck there for a short period.

"She's gone," Jaina said, lifting her head and turning back to the others.

"Thoughts on our new wife?" Lucia asked, looking at Nancy and Jaina.

Nancy said nothing. Instead, she folded her hands behind her back and fell silent.

"She's okay," Jaina said, moving over to Steve on all fours and rubbing up against him. "Seems nice. We'll see. Smelled of honesty. Smelled like Chessa."

"Considering her species, that's not terribly surprising," Lucia muttered, looking at Steve. "I don't have a problem with her, personally. The nobility of Lamals has ever been the… barest… edge… of nobility, but still nobility.

"I do wonder about what she said regarding their perception of her, however. I wonder what her family dynamic is if she willingly puts herself out in front looking the military fool."

Steve didn't know what to think of that. He shrugged his shoulders.

"Anyone you underestimate is someone who has the drop on you," Steve said.

"Mm. Yes," Lucia said, then sighed. "Though I'm afraid we're going to have to make a detour to the farm. Nikki will have to know about this."

Nikki.

Yeah. She'll say it's the best thing for the farm, I imagine.
Thankfully, that shouldn't be a bad conversation.

"You're right," Steve said. "So… head to the farm today, then to Filch after?"

"Probably," Lucia said. "We'll have to move some people around to cover here while we're away. Then again… with that little army arriving, having wiped out the murderers, and the Creep not having returned… this place might just be safe enough that we can leave it alone."

"Ill to speak in such a way," Jaina said, shaking her head. "Calls bad omens forward."

Yeah. Don't jinx it.

***

Fuck, I jinxed it.

"I don't like it," Nikki said again. Her hand was idly curling through Steve's hair. They were sitting out at the lakeside, with his head in her lap and her hooves dangling in the water.

"What part don't you like exactly?" Steve asked.

"Any of it, honestly," Nikki mumbled with a soft sigh. "Or maybe I'm just being a little prickly. I feel like pushing Geneva into our marriage just moves us ever forward in this forced confrontation with Lynn. And furthermore, the nobility of Lamals. It sounds like she has plans."

"That's pretty much inevitable, really," Steve said. "Linne is our enemy."

"No, it really isn't, and no, she isn't. Unless we make her one. We could easily maneuver this one around without ever having to openly oppose her," Nikki said. "We'd just duck our heads a bit, let her do as she would in the citadel city, and manage our own situation.

"Separated and happy on each side."

"I don't really believe that'd be what happens," Steve disagreed. "She's too evil to not get herself involved. She'd force us to pick a side the moment Geneva tried to exert her authority over her. Geneva seems more likely to have let it lie there, but not Linne."

"You really think she'd oppose the royal will?" Nikki asked.

"Considering we're almost certain she's the reason the Creep was a problem, I can't see a time and place she wouldn't," Steve said. "I mean, come on. She tried to have me turned into a sex slave with little to no care whatsoever.

"And don't get me started on her belief and treatment of Humans, let alone Human men."

"Yes… Lamals really is… a nasty little blot on a map," Nikki murmured. "Maybe we should consider escaping the country entirely. We could probably head south."

"We'd never get out of the quarantine," Steve said immediately. "And there's no telling when it'll break, regardless of what's happening with the Creep.

"You yourself said it was quite possible the other nations were attempting to use this as a way to batter Lamals into a corner."

"I did, I admit it," Nikki said. "I just… don't like any of this. It really does feel like we're inserting ourselves into a fight we don't have to take. I don't want to do this, and I don't feel like you're listening to me."

"I promise, I'm only doing what I think is best for the farm. I don't have aspirations to power," Steve promised. "I mean, I hear you, but… I think this is best. I'm listening to you, but I disagree with your desired course of action."

"Okay. Fine," Nikki said, the space between them growing as she shifted her position around. "I still really don't like it, though. It's not what I think we should do at all.

"And as much as I want to stay and talk to you, I believe you have others you should greet and say goodbye to. I think Lucia has the right of it. You'll need to travel with Geneva for a time."

"You think Xivin, Lucia, Nancy, and Geneva would be the best group for this?" Steve asked, levering himself into a sitting position. He wanted to move closer to her, to talk more about this, but it felt like she was trying to get rid of him.

"I do. No one else would be as useful as them," Nikki said. "Kassandra, Jaina, and Ina are best suited to holding the outpost for the time being while you're away. I'm no good anywhere but here. Misty doesn't want to go too far from her water source anymore. Ferrah is… Ferrah.

"Though… I suppose you could take Gwendolin, if you wanted. She might not be a terrible option as she's be the closest to a healer we have. I just… didn't even think about it because of Nia."

"Yeah… taking her from Nia would be somewhat… problematic, wouldn't it?" Steve asked.

"I'd say talk to her, give her the opportunity, let her decide," Nikki said. Then she nodded her head, seeming to consider the whole situation. "Alright. I'd say you've made your choice. If anything, you should leave as soon as possible. Likely you'll need to be in Filch by tomorrow. Before Geneva gets there. I imagine."

"Yeah… I guess that'd be the answer, wouldn't it?" Steve said. He really felt like she'd just dismissed everything and didn't want to deal with him anymore. That because he wasn't doing what she wanted, she was going to end the conversation.

"Exactly," Nikki said. Her tone didn't quite match the feeling she was trying to put out. Then she reached over and patted him on the back. "Get going. I'll see you when you get back."

Nikki walked off, leaving him sitting there.

It was still early enough that he could track down Shelly and talk to her about what was going on. Get her approval and ask to take her with him back to Filch.

Maybe ask Misty to go with her just so Shelly's not alone.

He felt like Nikki was more upset than she was letting on. The fact that she'd left without suggesting lovemaking later tonight added to that belief.

She'd never passed on such an idea before, and she'd always been the one to suggest it.

I fucked up, I guess.

Getting up, he decided to talk to everyone he needed to talk to before the sun went down.

If he hurried, he might be able to get out to Filch even before the sun hit the horizon. Then maybe he could talk to Nikki again and see if they could patch things up before he left.

Especially since traveling along the river with Misty in tow would be incredibly swift.

"You've completed the first task," said a voice out of nowhere. "While it's pointless to tell you, as you won't understand, I must abide by the rules we put down."

Standing up straight, Steve looked up to the sky above him.

"Rules? I think I'd like you to tell me the rules," Steve said. "I can't follow them if I don't know them."

"That wouldn't be correct," said the voice.

"Then maybe I'll just kill myself and assume I'll get to see the rules and start over again," Steve said. "I wouldn't know I was doing wrong unless I did it, which means it's easier to assume I could just start over."

"That… that's not logical," said the voice.

"Logical or not, that doesn't matter. All that matters is I don't understand. And if I don't understand, I could do something truly stupid and not realize it was against the rules," Steve said. "So… maybe tell me the rules?"

"No," said the voice. "You're welcome to take your own life as you see fit, but that would be your own choice.

"This entire examination was your own choice. You sacrificing your memories was part of that choice. I'll respect what you chose previously and abide by your decision."

"How am I supposed to succeed if I don't even know what I'm supposed to do?" Steve complained.

"I would argue that your results indicate that concern is irrelevant at this time," said the voice. "You're doing better than you did previously. It's very likely you'll achieve your second goal by the end of this upcoming month. At that point you'll have surpassed yourself previously."

What'd I do?

I took all those prisoners.

I more or less finished up the fort.

I cornered Geneva into getting into my bed.

I bedded Lucia and put a kid in her.

I can't imagine having children would be part of my goal. Which means that's just… secondary. That really only leaves taking prisoners and building the fort.

Or… or that I killed all those murderers.

I gained a title doing it.

If I go on this trip with Geneva, it's quite likely I'll find more people to kill and increase my title.

Is that it? Is this all just… how high can I go?

Wait, let's ask him about the brainwashing.

"I ask for a favor in exchange for having passed my first task," Steve said.

"No," said the voice.

"No, I think you need to give me this favor because it's starting to make it difficult to function," Steve said. "The brainwashing. The fact that everyone has this insane drive to produce children. Is that Lamals, or something else?"

There was no response.

"I really do need to know. I'm not sure if I should be fighting against that or not," Steve said.

Staring up into the sky, Steve received no response.

Damnit. I really don't know what to do about that one.

"That is a function of this world," said the voice suddenly. "They're required to give birth, and so they must. It isn't unique to Lamals."

"Okay. And the way they treat men? Sending them to the front after they have children?" Steve asked.

"Lamals only," said the voice. "As your wife has indicated, Lamals would be flattened to the ground for their treatment of men alone. Many other nations treat men as citizens rather than resources."

Which means it really is just the government here doing that.

But... wouldn't other nations frown on me holding all those murderers as prisoners?

Very likely.

Maybe I'm bound to be in Lamals as much as I dislike the nation.

"Goodbye," said the voice.

"Wait, I need more answers," Steve said quickly.

There was no response.

"Please?" Steve tried.

Silence.

Sixteen

Gwendolin had chosen to remain behind. She'd stated she had fears for losing her unborn child along with her wish to watch over Nia.

Steve didn't blame her. It was more or less what he'd been expecting. To be fair, it was most likely the same exact thing he'd do if he was in her place.

Ferrah, Jaina, Lucia, Xivin, and Geneva all accompanied him on his mission, however.

To say Steve was surprised that Ferrah wanted to come was an understatement.

She'd apparently taught a few of the farm girls how to make iron and bronze bars. Except there wasn't really any material to work with to make anything.

She could sit at the farm and wait for someone to show up with ore to sell, or she could go traveling with Steve. She'd surprisingly chosen the latter.

Everyone was on the march except Xivin. Despite regaining most of her motor control and even getting to the point where she could walk at a normal speed, she didn't have the endurance she used to.

In the end, Steve had managed to talk her into riding in a wagon he'd fashioned. It could seat four people and several chests or barrels.

The whole thing was lashed to a Centaur Steve had hired from Filch specifically to this end.

Although there'd been no Creep sightings, there was no reason to chance it. Two barrels of can water had been loaded up for emergency use. Another two wagons filled with watering-can water had been added to the baggage train for general Creep purposes, just in case. Then Lucia and Xivin had sat in the wagon at the front with the rest of the group as the "drivers."

Lucia due to her pregnancy and Xivin because of the obvious issue.

Ferrah, Geneva, Jaina, and Steve all marched to one side of the wagon.

Steve hadn't wanted any part of being behind the wagon. Staring into a Centaur's personal bits didn't seem interesting to him.

They were all heading north into the lands above Filch after having loaded up the supply wagons with food and water from the farm. Along with half of Geneva's forces. The other half had been left behind in Filch to hold and build a garrison there.

Stomping heavily along next to Steve was Ferrah.

What she lacked in speed and height, she made up for in endurance and stamina. As far as he could tell, she worked her forge all day and night with little break. The only thing that had stopped her was the lack of materials.

"I hope they have ore," Ferrah said for perhaps the tenth time.

"Whether they do or don't, it's more or less pointless to worry over," Steve chided. "Won't change from now till the point we arrive."

"I know that," Ferrah said. "I just... I feel useless without ore. I know how to..."

Ferrah paused, glancing past Steve to Geneva.

The Lionan was busy chatting at Jaina. The former was trying to cautiously develop the start of a friendship with the latter.

Geneva had apparently sensed some form of possible kinship with the Kobold and was going after it.

Maybe Chessa's death affected Jaina more than I realized. She seems very unwilling to let Geneva close, despite her attempts.

"I can make your steel," Ferrah said in a low voice. She apparently didn't trust Geneva despite Steve's assurances. "I feel like I should be making as much of it as I can, too.

"Whether swords or plowshares, doesn't matter who's in charge."

"And what does that mean, exactly?" Steve asked.

"Uh... well," Ferrah said. "It kinda feels like there's two groups in our marriage right now. One group thinks we need to just... keep going. Take more land, put more people under us, and expand.

"The other thinks we should just keep what we have and settle in. Get comfortable. Defensive."

"Oh," Steve said. It wasn't that surprising. Glancing over to Nancy on the other side of Ferrah, he caught her eyes. He'd mentioned his concern about such a thing to her previously. This feeling, like there was a split forming, seemed to be confirmed with Ferrah's remarks.

I'll have to tell Nancy to work on fixing it. She doesn't care about it one way or the other, so long as she continues where she is right now.

"And where do you fall in all of that?" Steve asked.

"With Kassandra. I don't care," Ferrah said. "I'll just stand where you tell me to. Till then, I'll keep beatin' iron, bronze, and steel to shape. Doesn't bother me none at all."

That... makes sense.

Dwarves will be Dwarves.

Though it's good to know Kassandra is in the same boat.

"First I've heard of it," Steve lied.

"Really?" Ferrah asked.

"Yep. I'm afraid I've just been busy trying to get our family and fortune squared away, you know?" Steve said. "So, help me out. Who's thinking we should just settle down?"

"Pfft, as if you couldn't guess it all on your own," Ferrah said. "The Faun, of course. Even though she's the one who wanted you to build the outpost. Now she's all frettin' about how much land you're taking.

"Then there's Misty, Xivin, and Ina. They all support Nikki in that."

Just the mention of Nikki gave Steve an odd stomach-lurching sensation. When he'd gone to track her down before leaving, he couldn't find her. In fact, he'd had the distinct impression she'd been avoiding him.

"Ah, I take it Lucia, Jaina, Shelly, and Gwendolin don't support that view then?" Steve asked.

"Hah, no. They all want to push, push, push. Take more and keep more," Ferrah said. "The Fae leads that group. Seconded by the Siren. Was surprising to me. She changed sides not long after you got to her insides."

Not to me.

Gwendolin would do anything for her daughter. If she thinks taking control would protect her daughter, then she'd push for that.

Likely more so for an unborn.

"Kass leans more toward the Fae at times," Ferrah said.

"And which way do you lean?" Steve asked.

"Towards you," Ferrah said with a shrug. "I'm... enjoying... this weird fluttery feeling I get when I look at you. I like how you treat me. I don't really care about anything else, so long as I know which way you're going.

"Which makes me have ta' ask. Which way are you leaning?"

Steve didn't know how to answer that.

Because he truthfully didn't think he knew the answer. There were times he felt like he should bring his foot down and crush Lamals until it was the country of Bril.

And other times, he wanted to just go back to his farm and think nothing of anyone.

"What if I wanted to burn Lamals to the ground?" Steve asked.

Ferrah grunted at that, wiping her hands against her hips.

"Would need some time to make swords and spears, but I'll do what I can," Ferrah said.

Grinning at the support, Steve laid an arm around Ferrah's shoulders.

"You're a sweet little lady, you know that?" Steve asked.

Ferrah looked up at him through her brows and didn't respond.

***

"I begin to believe," Geneva mused, then paused. "That the capital has gravely underestimated how much devastation has been wrought on the nation."

Bexis stood before them, her gates torn asunder and bodies everywhere. Lots and lots of bodies, in various stages of decomposition. From the road leading into town to the gates and beyond.

Everything in Bexis looked to be dead.

"I mean... what exactly does the capital think?" Steve asked. "We've kinda been out here doing our best to survive. It was honestly lookin' pretty grim for a while."

"They're firmly of the opinion that the lower classes were devastated, much in the way a plague would go," Geneva said.

"To be honest, I wasn't sure myself of the extent of the damage. I may very well be a military governor of a ghost district."

"Perhaps," Lucia said. "Perhaps not. I think what we saw with the villages was more likely to be the truth. Raiding one another, killing, living, dying. The city had one major problem.

"Very few ways in, very few ways out. I mean… look at those doors. Someone must have ordered the gates closed at night. Except the Creep was maybe already inside."

We've seen the Creep just vanish rather than pull back. It's possible it was already inside the city. Polluting its residents.

"If we really look at those doors," Ferrah said, "I'd bet my hiney they were broken down from the inside, not the outside. Whoever remained, escaped."

We didn't really see any of these types of problems with Filch.

The mayor had the gates closed before night fell. That was a long-standing order.

After I killed the mayor and bedded the daughters, they kept most of the same rules in place. Didn't they?

Or maybe… maybe the fact that we had the watering can was far more beneficial than we ever understood. Once I connected the trench to Filch, did that pretty much remove any type of long-term rot the Creep was causing?

"Let's go inside and look," Geneva said, then turned and made a hand signal to a group of guards. "It would be good to know what state the city is in. Perhaps I can organize a colonization and have people moved in."

"I mean, I doubt that," Steve said, his grip on his axe shifting. "But why not? Let's take a look."

"I'll remain with the wagon," Lucia said. "My bow and I would be more useful out here anyways."

"I'll go," Jaina said.

"I'll remain here," Nancy said as she clambered up into the back of the wagon.

"Me too," Ferrah said, following after the Wight.

"I shall… stay and keep the princess company," Xivin said, bowing her head slightly to Steve when he sought out her dark eyes.

Her bright blond hair was starting to grow out now that she wasn't in the guard. Her pointed ears held some of it back.

All around, the squad Geneva had called forward was getting ready. It was a patrol through what was likely enemy territory, which would be dangerous at best.

She thinks she's failing me, the silly Elf.

Coming over to the Elf, Steve took her hand in his and gave it a squeeze.

"Don't even think it," he said, locking her eyes down with his own.

"I… what?" Xivin asked.

"Don't," Steve said, smiling at her. She'd paid a price for him, and he wasn't going to forsake her.

Xivin stared at him and then snorted, putting one hand on her hip. She gave him a wide smile, revealing perfectly straight white teeth and elongated canines. Though she was no longer a swordswoman, she kept herself in shape as best as she could.

She wasn't as slim, but she was still athletic and beautiful. Her change in exercise routine had her filling out in fun ways, however.

"Steven Bril, husband, are you trying to tell me what my role is?" Xivin said.

"No, I'm trying to tell you not to get that stupid Elf brain all twisted up over the fact that you're not going on this little patrol with me," Steve said. "Got it?"

"Stop it," Lucia said, swatting at Steve's hand. "Xivin will be fine. I'll make sure of it. Don't worry for her."

Raising his eyebrows at that, Steve looked at the Fae.

As far as he knew, these two hadn't really seen eye to eye on most things.

"Go on," Lucia said. "Shoo, away with you. Unless you're giving out goodbye kisses, in which case you may kiss me briefly."

Unable to help it, Steve chuckled at that. Then he deliberately kissed the back of Xivin's hand and walked away.

"Hmph. You'll regret that later when I don't give you my full attention in bed," Lucia threatened.

Uh… okay, yeah.

He turned around and immediately went back to kiss Lucia's hand as well.

He wasn't about to endanger his time with her. She was special on a whole new level when it came to the bedroom. She took care of him in a way he'd never known he needed.

Ten minutes later and Geneva, Steve, Jaina, and her squad were moving into Bexis.

"Much, much death," Jaina said. "But no Creep. I sense nothing."

"Then it's the same as we've seen so far," Steve said as they walked past the first set of buildings. "Creep's gone; the aftermath remains."

"So it would seem," Geneva said.

"See? You were foolish," Jaina said. "Steve is the alpha for a reason. He brings strength. You should receive him when we get back to camp. I'll let you be my beta."

Geneva grunted at that, her helmeted head swinging one direction and then the other.

"Captain, you... turned down the homesteader?" asked one of the soldiers around them.

"Enough chatter," Geneva said. "Keep your damn eyes moving and your mouths shut. Enemy territory."

Steve felt like an odd man out here.

He was carrying his axe as he always did, though without a shield, and dressed in little better than his farm clothes.

"Before we stop talking, could someone tell me where the fuck we're going?" Steve asked. "Because I'd really like a plan rather than just 'wander through the graveyard of Bexis,' ya know?"

Calling it a graveyard might have actually been a compliment, truth be told.

Most people would probably call it a butcher's shop, given all the bodies, parts of bodies, and rotting flesh all around.

The stench of death was a near physical thing. Like a hand wrapping around your nose and mouth, preventing you from not tasting it with every breath.

"Keep," Geneva said. "We'll go to the keep. That'd be the last bastion of defense, and the most likely place we'll find someone alive. It's also the first place I would have to fix. An installed mayor would go there."

"Right," Steve said. "Lead on then, cause I have no idea what's what here."

Slowly, walking in a tight group, they moved onward.

Step by step, street by street, they made their way toward the keep.

Nothing moved.

There was no life left in Bexis.

I should probably see about moving a force of prisoners up here. I bet we could capture more murderers. Add more prisoners to my work pool. Could always use more.

Resources are meant to be collected, after all.

Just send them all back with a collar after we capture them.

Finally, turning another corner, they found the keep up ahead of them.

It was obvious there wouldn't be anyone alive in there.

The gates were chained shut. And in front of them, on the citizen side, was a mountain of blackened furniture. Beyond that, the keep itself looked like a burned-out blackened hulk.

"Killed their leader," Jaina proclaimed. "Good. Bad leaders should be removed. They'll hurt the pack worse than any disobedient pack member would."

"I think… this is more than just killing their leader," Steve muttered, staring into the wreck.

"Yes. Yes, I would agree," Geneva said. "This looks like a whole lot more than that. It looks like a traitorous revolt. It would seem we'll have to do some rebel hunting while we're up here."

"Oh? Wonderful. Is that a death sentence?" Steve asked.

"What? How is that wonderful? That's the very opposite of wonderful," Geneva said. "And yes, it's a death sentence. Why?"

"Perfect. And it's wonderful because I want them as prisoners. I'll put them to work and use them on the farm, and at the outpost. If there's nothing left to do there, they can work to fix up Filch, or maybe Bexis," Steve said. "Much better than just killing them. I can kill them later if they prove to be a problem."

"You have no way to control them," Geneva said as they began their exit. There was nothing else to see here now that they'd confirmed the state of the keep. "I can't give them to you without assigning soldiers."

"Oh, I didn't show you, did I?" Steve said, realizing the mistake for what it was. "I have a special control method. Anyone I capture and force into this method has no way to do anything but what I want them to.

"If they disobey, they die. If they run, they die. If they do anything I ordered them not to, they die. Then I collect the bounty for it and go on my merry way."

"That seems… rather far-fetched," Geneva murmured. "I'll need to see how it works."

"Yes, yes, that's fine," Jaina said. "I'll make a witch-stone necklace once we leave here. That isn't an issue. You can wear it to try it out."

Steve briefly considered letting Geneva actually put it on. He was beginning to understand Jaina better, and she had a crafty way of thinking at times.

The way she constantly approached him where he wasn't expecting it, trying to push her boundaries with him.

She was still the loving and generous Kobold she had always been with him, but she was rapidly figuring out how far she could push things.

And if he didn't miss his guess, this was her trying to get Geneva to wear a collar and then give her over to Steve like a present.

"Better she didn't," Steve said, deciding. "We could have one of her soldiers put it on briefly, then remove it."

"Or a prisoner. I'm sure we'll catch one soon enough," Geneva said. "It isn't like they have many places to go, and I have the tax map and census for the area. I know where all the settlements are and how many people should be around. Not that population numbers will be much use anymore, but I can at least validate some things."

A tax map? Huh.

I suppose that makes sense. You do need to tax everyone, and the best way to do that is have a map and a census.

Taxation is big business. The biggest business.

Jaina gave him a sidelong look, but her lips curled up in a cunning smile. She was well aware that he'd broken her away from her course of action. And she didn't find fault or flaw with it. If anything, she seemed rather amused.

Steve grinned back at her.

Between you, Lucia, and Nancy, I'll need to be on my guard.

Opening her mouth, she gave him a tongue-lolling grin, then moved into his side and physically rubbed up against him.

"I love you, husband," Jaina said warmly. "Please mount me when we get back. Right next to the wagon in that patch of dark green grass."

Several women coughed around them, and Geneva gave Steve and Jaina an almost pained look.

It was obvious such a display would make the soldiers rather uncomfortable. Which made Steve have to really think about what it meant to be a soldier.

Very much need to be on my guard with Jaina, Lucia, and Nancy

Seventeen

Geneva growled and flicked a hand at the map in front of her.

"Filch is little better than a debtor to you, Bexis a flaming ruin, and bandit camps all around Faraday," said the Lionan. "I wager I could hardly get close enough to figure out what's going on with the city before getting drowned in cutthroats."

"That does seem likely," Xivin murmured, staring at the map. "There are quite a few of them, too. Far more than I would ever expect."

"Yes, it does seem like there are far more than one would think there should be," Geneva said. "Creep or not. This is more akin to a country being consumed in a civil war."

Well, it was more like an apocalypse. Given that the interior of the country didn't feel the lash of the Creep as strongly, it only makes sense that she doesn't get it.

Out here, it was truly fight to live – or die and be eaten.

Though… I'm really starting to feel leery about the Creep.

I don't feel like it's over. Not really, at least.

"I think you greatly underestimate how terrible the Creep was out here," Xivin said. "If not for Steve, Filch would have fallen. It'd be much more like Faraday or Bexis, I imagine. They have defenses, food, and clean water, all things that were in quite short supply."

"Yes… you're likely right," Geneva muttered. "It's just very hard to wrap my mind around it. The reports we received were nothing like this. Mentioned nothing of it, in fact."

"Did you get any reports from around here?" Xivin asked. "I certainly didn't get word back that my reports made it. Nor did Shelly, for that matter."

"No. No, we didn't. To be honest, it's one of the reasons I was formally dispatched out here. There'd been no word at all. There was suspected treason, but that was about it," Geneva said.

Steve leaned back in the grass and lifted his face up to the sun. He really didn't care one way or the other about any of this.

He wasn't good at military-type decisions. So far, he'd done much better with bigger-picture ideas and plans.

Right now, he just wanted to add more people to his prisoner army and build them up. The bigger and better they were, the more he'd have to work with later.

The stronger he'd be as a leader. The better off everyone would be who was part of his family.

"We should send a scout to see what's going on, if you haven't already," Xivin said.

"Already sent, yes," Geneva confirmed. "They've yet to report back, but they're not due for another several hours so that's not unexpected. Once they get back, we'll have a better idea of what we're dealing with. Though... to be frank, I already fear the worst. I get the impression these camps are all the remaining population of Bexis, and Faraday paid them off or joined them.

"This whole place is likely swarming with treasonous scum. My domain will be that of a graveyard, I think."

Opening his eyes, Steve looked off toward his tent. The last he'd seen of Nancy, she'd been sitting in his tent, working at mending some of his and her clothes. Some of the seams had started to come loose.

Let's have Nancy. That sounds like a lot more fun than sitting here.

And she's always willing and eager for it.

Getting to his feet, he walked over to his tent.

When he lifted the flap and looked inside, he didn't find Nancy. Wherever she'd gone off to, she wasn't there.

Looking around, he spotted Ferrah working at getting a nick out of a blade. As a blacksmith, she'd taken it on herself to assist with the maintenance of arms and armor.

Steve move over to the Dwarf and cleared his throat.

"Husband," Ferrah said, glancing up at him. "Can I do something for ya?"

"Seen Nancy?" Steve asked.

"She left in a bit of a hurry with Lucia," Ferrah reported. "Something about you, but I'm not sure what."

Great. Probably planning something for me tonight.

Lucia takes her job of pleasing me quite seriously. Sometimes even if I don't want it.

"Something I can do?" Ferrah asked, looking up at him.

"I mean... yeah, you could. Not sure how willing you are, though," Steve said with a grin. "Get in my tent, take off all your clothes, and get on your back. I was hoping for a quick romp and would be really excited for you to be my willing partner."

Ferrah blinked once at that, and her cheeks slowly colored.

"Okay," she said, getting to her feet. "I think… I think it's about time I got my Humanist accolade anyways."

Walking by him, Ferrah pushed the flap to his tent aside and went inside.

Oh? Huh.

Fun.

Following the Dwarf inside, Steve turned and tied the flaps closed to make sure they were well and truly shut. He didn't want anyone bothering him during his first go-round with Ferrah.

"I kind of know what goes where. My mom tried to tell me what she could, but I was pretty young," Ferrah said, untying the bindings on the front of her tunic. With her bust as impressive as it was, as most Dwarves' tended to be, her clothing options were limited given the size of the rest of her.

And since most Dwarven girls were made to look like very well put-together but short Humans, he imagined it was doubly difficult for Ferrah to find clothes.

"I think I can take care of your needs," Ferrah said, getting her tunic off and tossing it to one side.

Steve had seriously underestimated her figure. She didn't have Gwendolin's waist or hips, but Ferrah could easily compete with her otherwise. And likely win.

She was also rather thick and had a bit of weight to her. It was a pleasant surprise for Steve.

He liked different things.

Shimmying out of her pants, Ferrah looked at Steve and held up her hands.

"I am as you see me," said the Dwarf. "Sure you want this? There's a whole lot of prettier Dwarves out there. Especially in Hilast. Lot of blacksmith Dwarves there."

"Maybe so, but you're my Ferrah. I don't want just any Dwarf. I want Ferrah. My Ferrah," Steve said with a grin, undoing his pants. "Aren't you my Ferrah?"

"I—yeah. Yes. I'm yours, Steve," Ferrah said, and her hands came down to hang at her sides. "I'm your Ferrah."

"Then that's all I want," Steve said as he stepped out of his pants and pulled at his shirt.

"Okay," Ferrah said.

Before Steve could say anything, she went over to his bedroll and got down on her back. She got her feet down on the ground, then spread her legs wide apart and looked at him.

"Uhm, gently, please," Ferrah said. "Gently and slow."

More like Lucia then.

But I really want to see that cute face of hers with me lodged between her lips.

Nodding his head at that, Steve went over to Ferrah's face instead. He got down on his knees in front of her, laid a hand against her cheek, and then moved his member forward toward her mouth.

"Steve, I don't know what I'm..." Ferrah said as his tip dangled in front of her mouth.

"Well... guess I should learn," she said, then parted her lips and took his head into her mouth.

Pushing forward, he filled her mouth halfway and then drew back.

He gazed down at her as he began to thrust in and out, watching himself slide through her lips.

Much like when he watched Lucia perform, something in Steve's head really ticked over when he watched a beautiful woman taking him into her mouth.

Ferrah's freckled nose and cheeks blushed prettily, her eyes staring up at him, watching him as he had her mouth.

Taking a better hold of her jaw and head, Steve pushed himself up to the hilt. His tip glided down Ferrah's throat.

Ferrah's eyes opened a bit wider as she gagged on him, but she didn't pull away.

"You alright with that?" Steve asked, drawing back to the halfway point.

"Do it again," Ferrah said around him, seemingly unperturbed. "I'll get used to it."

Obliging her, Steve pushed until he was in her throat again.

Ferrah gagged once more, and then her throat contracted as she literally swallowed at him. She didn't pull away, even then, and seemed determined to take it.

Steve began to pump back and forth slowly, filling her mouth and throat.

After around thirty seconds, Ferrah let out a whoosh of air as she gagged on him again.

Then she shook her head, pulling back from him.

"Can't," she said, taking a breath as he came free. "I want to. I can't. Not yet at least. I'm sorry."

"Don't worry about it. It was enough to watch that lovely face of yours taking it," Steve said, moving over the top of her.

"What? My face? I didn't even—"

Ferrah's voice trailed off as Steve got himself up and into her entry. Then he pushed forward, his slickened shaft penetrating her easily.

Ferrah groaned, and her hands came up and grabbed Steve's biceps.

"Uuun, that almost hurts," she groaned. "Jaina was right."

When he reached the hilt, Steve pulled back without waiting and then went forward again. In seconds, he'd built up a steady, deep, methodical rhythm. It wasn't fast, but he was certainly pushing into Ferrah firmly.

Panting as she stared up at him with wide eyes, Ferrah seemed quite lost in what was happening.

Putting his wrists to her hips, Steve began to try and push Ferrah through the bedroll with his hips, grinding against her clit as best he could, but still without speed.

"Faster," Ferrah got out in a pant.

Steve increased his speed as he thrust in and out of the Dwarf, then leaned down next to her ear.

"Tell me when to stop going faster," he whispered, and then he sank his teeth into her neck. He bit down for all he was worth, wanting to mark her visibly.

Ferrah squeaked as Steve began to pick up speed with every thrust.

"There—no faster," she said after twenty seconds had passed, her voice shuddering as he worked himself through her, curling up around her much smaller body with almost every thrust.

Releasing her neck, and admiring the teeth marks he could see in her skin, Steve looked down into her lovely face.

"I feel dizzy," Ferrah murmured. It looked like her eyes were going to roll back into her head as well.

Taking it as her getting close to having her first full-blown orgasm, Steve shifted himself higher and ground down into her pubic mound. He pushed down into her hooded clit much more forcefully.

Ferrah moaned, and her thighs squeezed up against his hips even as he continued to mount her. Spiking her into a full climax.

Slowly, Ferrah became a quivering, shivering, shuddering mess under him, panting hard and fast.

It was obvious she was now in the middle of an orgasm, despite it having started a minute ago.

Pushing down harder on her hips to keep her stationary, Steve began to pound at her, thrusting hard and fast at her. Trying to spear his way up through her and finish at the same time.

Ferrah did little more than grunt and moan as he blasted her into his bedroll.

Then he came up to his peak rapidly. Pushing himself deep into her, Steve came hard.

Impregnate Ferrah Bril?

No. Jaina or Nikki next.

Steve has gained notoriety for breaking the laws of the Lamals.

Steve has gained the Mining a Miner accolade.

Letting out a slow breath as he continued to pump seed into Ferrah, pushing up against her, Steve lowered his head to her shoulder.

Ferrah was, as of yet, unresponsive. Other than her continual shuddering and the occasional moan.

When he finished, Ferrah was still going.

Grinning to himself, Steve ground down into her and caused her to moan again.

Let's see how long she can keep that going. Rather impressive so far and damn fun.

Settling in for this opportunity, Steve reached down with a hand to press his fingers to her clit and begin teasing and caressing it. Then he got comfortable atop the Dwarf.

***

Lying there in the bedroll next to an unconscious Ferrah, Steve felt rather pleased with himself.

He'd kept Ferrah going on her orgasm till she'd actually passed out ten minutes later.

It was flattering that he could do such a thing to her. He knew he was a bit gifted in his endowment, but this was something altogether different.

That's... how many now?

Nikki, Misty, Ina, Jaina, Shelly, Kassandra, Xivin, Gwendolin, Nancy, Lucia, and now Ferrah. Then we have Geneva waiting for a go.

I wonder if there's a limit to how many I can have. Didn't they say ten?

Kinda enjoying this. Having a harem.

Lucia keeps telling me I'll need to develop more women of nobility and class, too.

Could I talk Nikki into letting me have thirty? I bet I could find thirty lovely women with skills.

Or like Lucia said, women of nobility with a few modest skills. I bet I could.

Wouldn't be that hard, would it?

Probably not.

And once I get the citadel commander title from Linne, it'll be even easier. I bet I could simply pick whoever I want.

Steve let out a slow breath and grinned to himself. Despite anything else, whatever his goals were here, he really was having a great time.

"Steve?" Nancy asked from outside the tent.

"Oh, come on in," Steve said, turning toward the tent. He knew Nancy could untie it without help. He also suspected she could get in without even touching the ties.

Sure enough, Nancy lifted a section of the tent to one side and just rolled in over the grass, coming in under the fabric. Not disturbing the ties at all.

She brushed herself off as she got to her feet.

"Come on over and clean me up, Mistress," Steve said, gesturing to his sticky and soft manhood. "Otherwise, what'd you need?"

Nancy looked pained at the command and, of course, excited at the same time.

She hurried over to him, then got down on her knees and inhaled him, a soft moan escaping her lips as she hungrily sucked on him.

Then she whimpered, closing her eyes.

Always so strange. She hates it, and she loves that she hates it and wants to do it, just to hate it.

Reaching down, he set his hand behind Nancy's head, which she energetically responded to. Her fingers tightened on his hips as he pulled her head down into his crotch.

Till her nose was jammed up against his abdomen.

Nancy's tongue came out and began sliding all over the tops of his balls as his shaft grew in her mouth.

After forcing her up and down several times, Steve released her and pushed on her forehead with a finger, getting her to back up.

"What's up?" he asked. He didn't want to be distracted if she actually had something he needed to know.

Nancy quivered, her face looking disgusted and pained. Then beyond excited and obviously wanting to go back down on him.

"I can't believe you made me do that. I'm such a whore," she whispered. "Call me a whore? Call me your whore."

"You're my whore, Nancy," Steve said mildly. "Now what was it you wanted?"

"The scout came back," she said, staring at Steve's hardening member. "They're going to debrief Geneva in a few minutes. She sent me to find you and ask you to come back. She was hoping you'd be there for it."

"Nah, don't want to," Steve said. "Get on your hands and knees above Ferrah. I think I'm ready to go again, and you're going to receive me. Maybe you can catch that pregnancy this time."

Nancy whimpered. Then she did as instructed, getting atop Ferrah without touching the Dwarf.

"I'm a filthy disgusting woman. I'm such a disgrace to my friends and family," Nancy said. "Tell me?"

"You're my filthy disgusting whore," Steve said, grabbing Nancy by the hips. Then he gave her a gentle pat as his hands caressed her flesh. "And I love you for it, Nancy. Love you for that twisted brain of yours."

Nancy made a soft cry, then shifted her hips back and ground her bottom into his lap.

"Give it to me. Give it to your mistress, Steve," she whispered. "I'm all yours."

Steve grinned, excited to do just that.

Reaching between them, he took his hilt in hand and guided his tip into Nancy's willing and waiting entry.

"Yes," Nancy purred as her head dipped down.

Maybe Ferrah will wake up, and we can have a fun three-way.

Twenty minutes of enjoying Nancy later, Steve wandered up to the table Geneva was sitting at.

Ferrah hadn't woken up, and Steve had left Nancy nearly passed out next to her in his bedroll.

"Done with your toy?" Geneva asked, looking up at him with a partial glare.

"Don't you worry," Steve said, sitting down next to her. "When it's your turn, I'm going to pin you to the ground in such a way you can't even move.

"Then I'm going to grab you by the base of the tail with one hand, the back of your neck with the other, and ride you till you beg me for a litter. Beg me in a scream so loud all your soldiers hear it.

"Then I'll come for you every single night until you understand you're mine."

Steve was feeling oddly confident nowadays. Confident and prideful.

Like he could almost do no wrong and he was destined for more. Like he should take more and expect more.

Lucia agreed and told him so, reinforcing his thoughts on the matter.

Geneva stared at him, her eyes slightly unfocused.

"You may address me as Husband, Master, Steve, or Mate." Steve reached across the table and patted Geneva's cheek. "Now, my pretty Lionan, what is it you wanted?"

Breaking herself free from her trance, the soldier gave her head a shake and then gestured a hand out toward the west.

"Faraday isn't surrounded by bandits. It's a city of bandits that's employed all those people we can see around it," Geneva said.

"Good. I can add them all to my collection," Steve said. Then he turned and looked around. "Jaina?"

"Here, husband," said the Kobold, sliding out from the shadow of a tent nearby.

"Start circling up those encampments and bring them over. If they're innocent, we'll let them go. If they're a death sentence, we'll collar them.

"For minor offenses… we'll just let them loose and tell them to leave on pain of death. We can start clearing the whole area," Steve said. "You can do it on your own, yes?"

"Yes, yes. Not a problem, husband. I'm much stronger than I was," Jaina said. "I can easily take care of it by myself."

"Good. Make it happen," Steve said. "Do it really well, capturing as many as possible, and I guarantee you a litter before the end of the year. Even if I have to eat every single herb on the planet to make it so."

"I understand!" Jaina said excitedly and then ran off, spraying grass out behind her.

"There we go," Steve said, turning back to Geneva. "Now it's just a question of how you want to handle Faraday."

"I… want them to respect my authority and submit to me," Geneva said.

"Okay. I'll leave that to you," Steve said. "In the meantime, I'll go play with my 'toys,' as you called them. Not much else to do."

Steve got to his feet and left. He wanted to go find Lucia and Xivin. If he got lucky, he could talk one of them into their tent, or his.

Xivin was rather gifted with her mouth and seemed to focus on that, rather than having sex.

Not that he could blame her. Her hips and legs made it difficult for her.

Eighteen

"In Steve's name," Jaina said, then snapped her hand in a circular motion. In the next moment, the woman's chest simply imploded. Collapsing in on itself.

Crushing her heart and lungs instantly.

"You, get the body and strip it. You may keep one item," Jaina said to the woman she'd just collared. Then she turned to the glowing purple enclosure. "Next, next."

Steve scratched at his stomach, watching the work being done.

He was bored.

There wasn't much for him to do right now.

Jaina was handling all the new prisoners, Nancy was organizing them while turning a number of them to her purposes, and Lucia was overseeing the resources, wagons, and water.

Xivin and Ferrah were doing what they could to keep busy. Xivin often exercised, training with the troops or just supervising training.

Ferrah worked with the camp blacksmiths as often as possible. Otherwise, they were certainly more productive and useful than Steve felt. As of late, he'd been feeling pretty useless.

His life had become mostly sex, waiting around, and watching prisoners get collared.

Not that he was complaining. He was getting used to it. Accustomed to it. It was rather nice to simply do nothing at all.

I wonder if this is what Linne's life is like.

It did seem as if she had almost no worries at all.

That'd be nice.

"I'll wear it," said the woman who stepped up to Jaina.

Nodding her head, Jaina fashioned a collar and held it out to the woman.

The woman snapped it into place around her throat, looking rather eager to get out of the purple box.

Sighing, Steve got up and wandered over to where Geneva was sitting at her table. Her armor no longer glowed with a silly parade polish. The shiny armor she'd been wearing when she'd appeared before him was long gone.

And it wasn't from a lack of cleaning.

She'd replaced the entire set with a different set she'd had in her baggage.

Steve was getting the impression that Geneva had not only known what she'd looked like, but that she'd embraced it until she'd met him.

"Betrothed," Geneva said after glancing up at him from her map for a second. "Can I assist you in some way?"

"I mean, sure," Steve said with a grin. "Want me to push you down over your map, or would you prefer to go back to your tent?"

Clicking her tongue, Geneva shook her head.

"Can't," Geneva said. "Soon though."

"Husband, do you ever get enough?" Lucia asked from her seat. She was sitting at a small table nearby, delicately eating a plate of fruit with a fork and knife. "I swear… I take care of you every night, and I make sure the Mistress tends to you during the day at least once. Are you that insatiable?"

"Apparently," Steve said. "Besides, you tell me often enough that I deserve it."

"And you do, and so much more," Lucia said, turning her head to give him a beautiful smile. "You'll get everything and then some, don't you worry. For now, though, I'll speak with Jaina, Ferrah, and Xivin. They can start assisting during the day. I know for a fact Jaina is eager to do so. Geneva is unfortunately off limits for a little longer.

"And don't bite Ferrah so firmly next time. The poor girl is absolutely mortified. It looks like a zombie got her."

"What if I wanted more Fae?" Steve asked, holding Lucia's gaze with his own. "What if I wanted it all day every day, right up to the point that you went to sleep?"

"Then I'm afraid I'd be of very little use for anything else. Spreading out your… energy… helps keep us all able to assist," Lucia said with a wide smile, the wings on her back fluttering gently. He knew that was a sign she was happy. He assumed she enjoyed the attention. "But if that's what you really want, I think I could handle it. That or we need to go back to my home and find a few of my cousins. You could just fight for the right to claim them against their betrothed. Actually, that's not a bad idea. We should plan a trip."

"Rider," called a soldier coming in at a trot. "Rider with a dispatch."

"Bout damn time," Geneva grumbled, standing up. She put her hands on her hips and stood there waiting.

A minute later, a woman wearing armor and colors Steve didn't recognize walked up to Geneva. Her helmet was in her left hand, a rolled-up paper in her right. She looked like any number of the "noble soldiers" Steve had met lately in Geneva's army. Though this one was clearly a cut above the rest and came from money and heritage.

She was far too pretty, looking slightly bored, and very muscular.

"I'm to give this dispatch to the leader of this... force," said the woman.

"That'd be me. I'm Commander Gosti, appointed by the queen to take this area into hand as the military governor," Geneva said, holding out a gauntleted hand. "I'll take the dispatch."

The soldier immediately went pale at those words. Slowly, she handed the parchment to Geneva.

"Remain a moment," Geneva commanded as the soldier started to turn around. "I'll have a return message, I imagine."

Unrolling the missive, the Lionan began to quickly read over it.

"I see," she said, looking up at the messenger.

"I... I don't know the contents," said the soldier. "I was merely told to deliver it. I'm just doing my duty."

"So it would seem," Geneva said in a cold voice. "The mayor of Faraday has asserted that she's the queen of this area. Which means... you're all traitors."

"I'm just... I didn't—"

"You didn't what? Know that she addresses herself as the queen?" Geneva asked, her eyebrows raising up. "Are you deaf?"

"No, that is... no, I'm not deaf, and of course I knew she— I didn't..." The soldier's voice trailed off. All around her, Geneva's troopers were giving this newcomer very nasty looks.

"Hmm," Geneva hummed, tapping the letter into the palm of her left hand. "I'll make this very simple then. I'll write you a response to the mayor of Faraday. You'll take it to her.

"You'll also deliver a message from me to your fellow soldiers."

The messenger nodded her head quickly, looking rather distraught now.

"Anyone in the city after tomorrow—citizen, soldier, dog, or otherwise—will be classified a traitor. Everyone who doesn't want to be so deemed can join me out here or head back to Bexis to begin re-population efforts there," Geneva said between clenched teeth. "And if I have to burn Faraday to the ground so that it's full of loyal living citizens, then I'll do that."

"If you burn it to the ground... there won't be anyone alive," murmured the messenger.

"That's exactly my point," Geneva said, smiling.

Maybe I'll get to collect an entire city. That'd be helpful. And if there are soldiers and militia, that'd help strengthen my forces for the eventual fight with Linne.

Because let's be honest, there's no way she'll go down without a fight.

Though... I do worry about what Nikki will think of all this. She didn't seem too pleased previously.

She didn't say she was upset, though. I'm not exactly a mind reader.

Geneva slapped a note against the breastplate of the messenger.

"Take my messages and deliver them," she said in a voice heavy with anger. "Run along now."

Immediately, the messenger backed away from Geneva and then began to sprint away. Heading straight back to Faraday.

"Queen, huh?" Steve asked.

"The audacity," Geneva said, shaking her head. "The gall. The nerve. What foolishness. She'll have doomed her entire family with this, and her city if they don't see reason."

"It's not that bad," Steve said.

"Not that bad?" Geneva asked, looking at Steve. "Filch is secure, yes. Bexis no longer exists. Faraday is under revolt. That leaves Hilast and Rennis. If they're in as poor shape as Bexis and Faraday, I'll have precious little under my domain."

Steve waved a hand at that.

"This entire part of Lamals was strangled by the Creep," he said. "It's a wonder Faraday even stands. It really isn't that bad."

Turning in his seat, Steve looked over at Jaina.

"Jaina!" he called.

Looking over at him, Jaina closed her hand to crush the chest of a woman.

"Keep one item, clear her of everything else," Jaina said absently to the woman who'd been collared last. "Quick, quick, before she ruins her pants."

Leaving the purple death cube, Jaina came over to him.

"Yes, husband?" she asked.

"I want that city surrounded in one of your cubes, and then to begin converting everyone to be collared," Steve said. "Can you do that?"

Jaina raised her eyebrows at that.

She looked toward the distant city and seemed to be considering it.

"Too big. Much, much too big," she said, grinning at him. He briefly had a memory of the last time she'd told him such a thing. "I can handle part of it at a time, but that means the other parts can act."

"Could you hold the barracks?" Geneva asked.

"Of that I have no doubt," Jaina said. "Easy, easy."

"There we are then," Geneva crooned, grinning and spreading her hands apart. "My soldiers block the exits, the Creep Witch locks down the barracks, and we begin our bloody harvest."

Steve shrugged at that, then leaned back in his chair.

"I'd rather you didn't, Geneva," Steve said. "Just keep them from leaving. I want them all if possible."

"You… you what?" Geneva asked.

"I want them all," Steve repeated. "Consider it your wedding present to me. I told you I wanted them all."

"I… I don't think—"

Geneva stopped speaking, matching Steve's gaze. Then she sighed and shook her head.

"Fine. As my wedding present to you," Geneva said.

"Don't spoil him," Lucia said, sounding slightly cross. "He deserves much, but we can't let him be spoiled."

Turning in her chair, Lucia stared hard at him.

"You can have the barracks, and half the citizenry," she said. "Geneva needs to make an example of some of them."

"Fine, fine, got it," Steve said, relenting. "Sorry, Geneva. Thank you for giving in to me. I appreciate it."

He had a hard time not doing what Lucia told him. She had a firm grasp on his heart and didn't seem to be letting go.

Geneva nodded her head to him, then turned and nodded it to Lucia.

Makes sense, I guess.

This is an open rebellion.

Need to have examples made, or no one will believe there's any teeth to Geneva's bite.

I think I'd rather be at home with Nikki.

Building a cabin.

***

"Man, look at all those camps," Steve said, gazing at all the bandit camps that'd moved to the other side of Faraday. Away from Steve and Jaina's purple square of captivity. "After we take Faraday, they'll all take off running."

Geneva gave him an odd look, her brows drawing together.

"And why do you want them so badly?" Geneva asked. She was dressed out in her full suit of armor. Her weapons ready and hanging at her sides.

"He's building an army to fight the citadel commander, remember?" Lucia said, as if it were nothing out of the ordinary. "And to that aim, the more prisoners he captures, the better off he is. He can either recruit them to fight for him or execute them for coin.

"Speaking of, we really should send you off to go collect all that. It's starting to get rather high, if I don't miss my guess."

"You really are, then? Going for the citadel commander?" Geneva asked.

"Yes," Steve said. "I see no reason to leave her alive. I think she'll be a problem one way or another."

"You're a very convenient, if lovely and intelligent, chess piece that fell into our hands, Geneva," Lucia said. "Your timing was quite fortuitous."

"I never had a choice, did I?" Geneva asked, her tone becoming curious. He'd partly expected her to be annoyed. "One way or another, I was going to end up yours or... dead."

"Probably," Steve said. "I would have hit you in the head with my axe. Would have been quick and painless."

Geneva's helmeted head turned back toward the city out in front of them.

"Hmm," she said, sounding far more receptive to it all. "Better than what my family had planned for me, I suppose. Far better."

"And what was that?" Jaina asked, building a small purple sphere between her hands. "Your family, that is. What they had planned."

"Oh, I had the distinct impression they were going to give me to my sister's husband as a concubine," Geneva said. "He's been asking for more women for a while, but he's at the legal limit of wives. So they've been collecting consorts and concubines for him. I managed to avoid that fate by joining the officer corps, which doesn't require the same oaths as the army. Which meant I was free to marry later on. Most of my girls are officer corps or noble family soldiers as well.

"Then I just acted like an idiotic armor polishing fool with no sense in her head. I was sent out this way more as a disposable token of force to quiet the nobles who collect taxes from out this way. But now that I'm here... I plan on taking this whole area as mine."

"I think you and I will just... continue to get along famously, Geneva," Lucia said with a soft laugh. "My sweet Steve over there is a giant hammer just waiting to drop. He's going to change the world. Change everything.

"I bet the pig-pen soldiers will cease to exist, men will be given equal rights, and no longer will they be shipped off to the front like useless cargo after breeding."

"Huh," Geneva grunted. "There are several groups that would like to see that happen. Quite a few nobles support equal rights for men and allowing them to decline service.

"Their argument being that if children are so precious, men shouldn't be allowed to leave the home. They should stay home, tend the children, and keep the home in order."

"I'd like that," Steve said, putting his hands on the top of his head. "I bet I'd be a great dad. Probably a better cook than Ina, too."

"You already are one, my beloved consort," Lucia countered. "Nia sees you as her father. And I think anyone can cook better than Ina, poor thing. She's one of my closest friends, but even I can say that she's a truly awful cook."

Jaina laughed at that and nodded.

"Awful, awful," Jaina said. "I'm not much better. Kassandra and husband did the cooking for us when we were raiding farms because of that."

Everyone fell quiet at that. Alone with their thoughts.

When I get back, I'm going to apologize to Nikki. She just… worries. It's fair to say that she probably wouldn't know what to do with herself if I died.

"That's full sunrise," Geneva said with a sigh.

"Goodie," Steve said. "I formally title every fool in that city who remained after Geneva's generous timeline as a traitor and condemned criminal. Or at least, those who didn't renounce the mayor but would have fled if they could have. No sense in condemning innocents.

"Secondly, I name the mayor as a usurper, bandit, traitor, and criminal."

"So be it," Geneva said.

Jaina made a laughing, hissing noise and then flicked out her right hand.

A purple sphere zipped out from her hand and zoomed away toward the city.

"You're sure you'll hit the barracks?" Steve asked.

In situations like this, Ina would have gotten in close to see the layout and plan. As far as he knew, Jaina had done no such thing. She simply looked at a few maps, asked questions, and said she could do it.

"Barracks, yes, and whatever else is nearby, too," Jaina said with a chuckle. "Barracks is at that gate, so we take the gate. No sense being perfect about it."

With a muted thump, a purple dome rose up from where the sphere struck the wall.

Then a massive section of the wall, the gate, and towers began to shift around in a strange, almost comical way.

Everything began to fall in every direction, stonework and bricks shattering and crashing.

Reaching up with one hand, Jaina idly scratched at her throat with her fingertips.

"See, see? All done," she said. "Barracks is all caught up in my spell."

"I… ah… and the walls?" Steve asked.

"The spell cut them loose. No foundation or connections. All loose," Jaina said. "No loss. I can just rebuild with witch-stone. I'm getting very good at it.

"Very, very good."

"Speaking of, I've been meaning to thank you, Jaina," Lucia said, looking at the Kobold. "The witch-stone arrow heads you gave me work wonderfully. They have just the right weight and size to them."

"Course, course," Jaina said with another chuckle. "Happy to help. I'm very good with this kind of work. Ina is more suited towards the building. I do better with… all of this."

"She's a siege weapon," Geneva said. "And a weapon that could win almost any fight."

Turning completely toward Jaina, the larger Lionan pulled off her helmet.

"Jaina, if you were to collapse that dome, what would happen?" Geneva asked.

"They'd be squished," Jaina said with a shrug. "The spell doesn't allow anything out, unless I pull them out. They'd be crushed up to one another and die. Splat, squish."

Oh.

Oh!

She's right. That's quite a weapon, actually.

You could repeat the spell over and over and just… pulp… your enemy to nothing.

If I could get all the other Creep Witches to do the same, no one could stand up to me. I could crush Linne like little better than a tin can.

Wait… a what?

Never mind. Never mind!

More Creep Witches.

Frowning, Steve turned to Nancy who was at his side.

She was near him as ever. Waiting for orders and doing what she felt best for him.

"After this is all said and done," Steve said in a whisper, leaning into Nancy. "We're taking volunteers and heading to the wall. I want to make more Creep Witches. We'll need to figure out a way to find out who'd be willing to take on such a burden for a sentence reduction. It'd involve them dying and coming back to life, after all."

"I understand, Steve. I'll make sure of it," Nancy said, moving in close and pressing her face into his neck. "Can we go back to the tent now?"

"Sure," Steve said. Then he slid his arm around Nancy and began walking her back. They didn't need him here.

Nineteen

Groaning, Steve pushed down on Jaina's hips as he angled himself up against her. He tried to grind himself against her clit as he continued to finish inside of her.

Jaina moaned and held tight to him, her fingers digging into his back as she pulled at him.

Letting out a slow breath, Steve laid his head down on Jaina's shoulder.

"Ooooh. Yes, yes," Jaina growled as she nuzzled and pulled at him. "That was really good. Pups or not, sex is amazing with you, husband."

Always great for the ego. I never feel lacking in any way with Jaina.

"Still too big. Much, much too big. But I like it, too. It's a good ache now that I'm used to it," Jaina said, then started to bite down along his neck and to his shoulder.

She continued to bite at him, in a way he knew had to do with her species and falling deeply in love with him.

Sliding to the side, Steve let out a breath.

One day soon, we'll need to let her get that pregnancy she wants.

Jaina moved with him, then pushed him onto his back, sliding atop him and then cuddling into him.

It was midday after they'd taken the entire barracks of Faraday. Jaina had spent the entirety of the day systematically working through all the soldiers who'd been there.

Today they were recovering and figuring out their next course of action. They hadn't managed to capture every soldier with the attack on the barracks.

In truth, they'd only caught maybe ten percent. After that, the mayor of Faraday had done everything she could to keep her soldiers spread out. Preventing them from repeating the same attack.

Instead, Steve had taken to rewarding Jaina heavily today. This was at least the third time he'd coupled with her today, by her request. Today was about taking care of Jaina's needs.

She'd done too well for him not to make sure he did all he could to make her happy.

Other than her pups.

He really didn't like the idea of having too many pregnancies at the same time.

Truth be told, he'd still rather not have children at all, but that didn't seem to be an option available to him.

"Ooooh, so nice. Nice, nice," Jaina said with a partially muffled voice. She was still gnawing at his shoulder very gently.

"I'd hope so," Steve said. "It takes a little more work, but it's worth trying to make sure you get off too."

"Yes, yes," Jaina said, biting harder for a second before licking at his skin.

"Steve?" Geneva asked from outside his tent. "Someone's coming this way with a white flag. As my betrothed, I'd like you there.

"As an unmarried noblewoman in command, I can sometimes be viewed as... well, depending on the local culture, I might not be viewed as a woman, but a young girl."

Looking at Jaina, Steve asked her permission without asking. Today was her day.

If she told him to stay, he'd stay.

Jaina grunted softly, her arms and legs tightening on Steve. Her teeth sank in a bit deeper. Her eyes locked on his.

Then she sighed and roughly pushed her face up under his jaw against his neck.

"He's coming," Jaina said, looking like she wanted to bite and hold on to him again.

Kinda like it. Easy to understand.

"Much appreciated, Jaina," Geneva said without moving away. Her shadow was quite visible just outside the tent flap.

Then again, Lucia's become very direct and easy to understand as well.

Steve got up out of the bedroll and into his clothes. In perhaps a minute, he was exiting the tent, leaving a sweaty and well-tousled Kobold behind.

As he stepped outside, he found himself practically staring into Geneva's face from a foot away.

He couldn't look at her without feeling a strange pang for Chessa. Which was odd, given that he hadn't felt anything for her loss during the initial stages.

That or he'd simply blocked all of it out and hadn't wanted to deal with it.

If that's true, did I care more than I realized?

Sighing, Steve imagined he could misplace his lost feelings for his Tigan with the Lionan.

Emotions were hard for him. He didn't understand them, they didn't make sense, and quite a few things he thought he should probably feel, he didn't at all.

Then again, does it even matter?

"Is… there a problem?" Geneva asked, looking at him strangely. Her eyes were partially lidded as well.

In a way that was far too similar to Chessa.

"No," Steve said. He didn't want to talk about it or deal with it.

I'll run it by Nikki.

As soon as he thought about the Faun, he remembered that she'd more or less dismissed him.

She'd not wanted to see him off.

Talk to Lucia about it tonight.

"Ah… will you accompany me?" Geneva asked.

"Yes," Steve said, not moving. He stood there, staring at the Lionan.

"I… uhm… alright… then," Geneva said, staring back at him.

Suddenly she broke eye contact, looking down and to the side, and the tail behind her slid down to position itself between her legs. Pointing to the ground.

Then she slowly hunched her shoulders and seemed to lower her posture.

Inexplicably, she partly turned her back toward him.

Reaching out, Steve laid a hand on Geneva's shoulder and grabbed her. Then he began marching forward, holding her out in front of him. Heading for her command pavilion.

The hell was that?

Probably some type of response to me and that I'd been mating with Jaina.

Maybe Chessa's wild behavior wasn't abnormal to her, just something most people work to control?

Geneva slowly seemed to come back out of whatever had gone on inside her head. Her shoulders squared back up, her head lifted, and her tail moved back to its upright position.

She became General Geneva once more, the military governor of the area.

"I'm sorry," Geneva said as they got closer to her tent. "It's… it's very hard to completely submerge it."

"Submerge what?" Steve asked. He assumed she was talking about what had just happened, but he still wasn't quite sure what that'd been.

"My… instincts? Heritage?" Geneva asked. "Just as your Kobold can't seem to stop biting you, I have my own… heritage."

"And it was that?" Steve asked.

"Yes. You reek of sex. It's… almost overwhelming," Geneva explained. "You stink of sexual abandon and power. There's a part of me that wants to get down on the grass and see if you can actually do what you said."

"What, mount you by force? Easily," Steve said.

As an example, he slid his hand over behind her neck and curled his fingers around her. Then he pushed down a little, forcing her to squat just a bit.

"I… I can't… stand up," Geneva said with a grunt, coming to a complete standstill.

"Mm. Wait till I pin you to the grass. You won't be able to move at all," Steve said. "As I said before, I had a Tigan. I'm going to treat you like her until you say otherwise."

Geneva put her hands to her knees and looked like she was struggling with all her might to stand up.

Finally, she gave up. She was panting hard, her mouth partly open.

Realizing she was done, Steve let go.

Geneva turned around and pushed her face into his neck, then took in several deep breaths.

When she leaned away from him, her mouth hung open, her upper lip was curled back, and her eyes were partly closed as she seemed to be inhaling his scent.

Geneva's eyes slowly turned to Steve as she stood there, looking quite strange.

What the fuck is she doing?

Licking her lips suddenly, Geneva turned and headed into her command pavilion without a word.

Right. Okay.

Asking Lucia about that, too.

Fucking strange.

"...demands that her subjects be returned," said a young human woman to one of Geneva's aides.

"No," Geneva said, walking right up to the messenger. The persona she was putting out now was very different from the one Steve had seen moments previously.

Right now, she seemed like a blooded veteran who was tired of letting the person in front of her steal oxygen.

"Those are women who were all guilty of crimes against the crown. They've all been sentenced accordingly," Geneva said. "If she wants them, she can have them back after I remove their heads from their shoulders."

What?

"You wouldn't dare. Her Highness of Faraday would see your entire army on a spit for such an offense," said the messenger.

"Really. You know what? That's exactly what I'm going to do," Geneva said. Then she turned to one of her aides.

"Ah, aren't they mostly mine?" Steve asked.

All heads turned his way.

"And who are you?" the messenger asked.

"I'm Steve. You should probably be quiet before I decide to smoosh your pretty head," he said, glaring at the Human woman. She looked like any other Human woman he'd seen anymore. Eerily pretty, with over-the-top assets. She also had short-cut black hair and piercing green eyes.

Steve couldn't help but admire her for that alone.

"Steve," Geneva said, looking frustrated.

"We talked about it, remember?" Steve said, shaking his head while holding Geneva's eyes with his own. "They work for me now. You can go chop the heads off the corpses who declined my offer.

"They're mine now. They get to live and work for me."

"Steve," Geneva said again, looking like she didn't know how to tell him no. "I'm afraid I need to take them from you to make a point to the mayor."

"No. They're mine, Geneva," Steve said.

"They're neither of yours. They're the subjects of the rightful queen of—"

Steve walked over to the messenger, grabbed her by the throat, and closed his hand partway.

The woman's face started to turn red immediately.

Forcing her to her knees in front of him, Steve leaned in toward her. Practically getting nose-to-nose with her.

She was gripping his wrist with both hands, her wrists and forearms flexing wildly as she tried to break his literal stranglehold on her.

Letting go of her neck just enough that she didn't pass out or die, Steve inspected her.

He even asked for insight into her from Shitty Steve.

Hiren Mess
Human
Knight/Champion
Father: deceased
Mother: living
Traitor- betrayed her nation
Condemned Criminal- has been condemned as a criminal
Royal Lieutenant-lieutenant of the royal guard
Ambassador- speaks on behalf of the queen of Faraday
Envoy- designated to treat with other nations for the queen of Faraday
Champion- one and true champion of Faraday
Noble Line(minor)- part of the nobility of Faraday and Lamals

"Traitor and Condemned Criminal. That's what you are, Hiren," Steve said. "You're a fool for thinking you could come negotiate on behalf of a much larger criminal. Did you really think Geneva would let you leave? Or that you could get anything from this?"

Hiren was wheezing hard, her cheeks bright red, her entire face flushed. It was obvious she could breathe, but only barely.

Steve wasn't sure how he wanted to deal with her. He was half tempted to break her neck or strangle her, then toss her corpse at the wall.

As he tilted Hiren's face to one side, Steve couldn't help but admire her beauty. It wasn't what he'd expected, now that he was really looking at her.

She was stunning and quite different from the women of Filch he was used to.

"You're pretty and likely useful," Steve said, forcing Hiren to lift her chin up. Her hands still grasped at his wrist. "You can serve me, or die right here in accordance with the laws of Lamals."

Turning his head, Steve looked at those around him.

He didn't see who he needed.

"Everyone but Geneva can fuck off," Steve growled. Immediately, the command pavilion cleared of Geneva's aides and lieutenants.

"Nancy!" Steve called out.

Standing up from where she was sitting on the wall, where Steve had honestly overlooked her, Nancy immediately came over.

"Yes, Steve?" she asked, smiling at him.

"Might need you," Steve said, then looked back at Hiren. The woman's eyes were starting to roll up into her head and it looked like she was losing strength in her arms.

Loosening his hold on her, he pulled his thumb back.

Hiren took in a deep breath, then started coughing.

"You get one chance to answer," Steve said. "Be my property or die right here. I'm feeling merciful because you're a brave and pretty little fool. The brave part is what saved you."

Taking in deep, gulping breaths, Hiren continued to gasp, her hands closing on Steve's wrist again.

"Married?" Steve asked. He was fairly certain she wasn't, but he wanted to be sure.

Hiren shook her head.

"No children? No boyfriend or betrothed or anything like that?" Steve asked.

Once more, Hiren shook her head and finally got her breathing under control, her incredibly bright green eyes looking up at Steve this entire time.

"I'll do it," Hiren croaked, coughing once again.

"Hmph," Steve grunted, flexing his fingers against Hiren's neck. "If you refuse to serve, you die, as is right and lawful per your status. If you accept, you live. Then you help us figure out how to take care of the false queen."

Hiren nodded her head slightly.

"I'll do it. I'll serve," she rasped.

"Goodie," Steve said, then turned to Geneva.

The Lionan had been watching Steve this entire time, her tail swishing back and forth behind her.

"They're yours... of course," Geneva said, her tail growing still and moving down between her legs again. "As you said once before... a wedding present from me to you. You may have anyone we capture that is willing to serve. I don't think I'll need an example after all."

"Thanks," Steve said, smiling at her. He didn't need to put any thought behind the change in her words. In fact, he even understood it. "I'll make sure my return gift is equally generous."

"Ah... thank you," Geneva said, nodding her head lightly.

"Geneva, I'm done with Faraday. Send them a message — not a messenger, a message — that they need to send out their next champion since this one is mine now. We'll send out ours.

"Whoever wins, wins. The other army will be forfeit. Got it?"

"I... I... yes, Steve. I've got it," Geneva said. "Who's our champion?"

"I am. Go. Send the message — I want this to be over with."

Geneva nodded rapidly and then ran off to take care of the message.

Turning his head back to Nancy, Steve caught his henchwoman's eyes.

"Do it. Give her a contract," he said.

"Yes, Steve," Nancy said, holding up her hands.

Steve watched as Nancy formed a black ball of magic in her left hand and then touched it to Hiren's head.

It simply enveloped the woman. Oozing over her from the top of her head, it sank down to her boots.

You've been given a black-magic contract.
The contract binds Steven Bril to Hiren Mess for all time.

The majority contract holder is Steven Bril.

The lesser contract holder is Hiren Mess.

The lesser contract holder shall obey, abide, and adhere to all rules given by the majority contract holder.

The penalties of the contract are based on the perception of the majority contract holder.

All penalties will be judged and assessed accordingly by the majority contract holder, Steven Bril, though in accordance with the law.

Major sub-clauses exist:

Should Hiren Mess betray Steven Bril, she will instantly cease to live.

Hiren Mess is under a death sentence and is working to repay her debt.

Please confirm that you wish to accept this black-magic contract.

Of course. But like last time, I don't want anyone to know of this contract.

Nor for it to have a physical manifestation.

Contract accepted under condition of anonymity.

Contract is now active.

"Oh, goddess," Hiren said as the black magic fled her.

"Could be worse—could be a collar," Steve said. "Collar magic would kill you if it misinterpreted your actions. This is better."

"I'll need you to get her situated, Nancy," Steve said, releasing Hiren completely.

"Of course, Steve," Nancy said, smiling at him.

"The queen won't surrender just for losing me, or even losing the next champion," Hiren got out in a scratchy voice.

"That's fine," Steve said. "I'll keep killing her champions till she gives up. Eventually, her soldiers will get tired of being sent to their deaths, or they'll lose belief that the false queen can win."

Hiren got to her feet with one hand on her neck. There was a very distinct handprint there that would match Steve's hand perfectly.

Now that Steve really looked at her, Hiren wasn't just a dazzling beauty, she was quite tall as well. And built like she could fight while having a great figure.

"The armor for show?" Steve asked, reaching out and tapping her bronze breastplate with his knuckles.

"No," Hiren croaked. "I'm a knight. I served the army, and the nobility of the capital. Earned my champion title through combat."

"Hmph. We'll see about that," Steve said. "You belong to me. If I'm not around, Nancy is your keeper. Listen to her completely. I'm going to go wait for their champion."

Geneva came back into the pavilion.

"It's done," she said.

"Great. I'm going to go wait for their champion," Steve repeated for her.

Need the axe.

***

Lucia sighed and rubbed her fingertips along Steve's shoulder.

"Well, I don't think this will work," she said. "But I do think it's the right thing to do. It'll be good to start breaking down their morale."

"Yes, yes," Jaina said, stretching herself out on all fours.

"Hmm, well, one can't expect the common folk to truly understand until they see it," Xivin said. "I imagine there will be people lining the walls. Even if they're not supposed to be there.

"You. Hiren, right? What's the morale of the city?"

"Quite bad," Hiren said. Her voice had just barely started to return to normal. The bruise on her throat in the shape of a hand was still very visible, however. "If… if Steve is able to do what he said he would, it's going to be a very terrible blow for the false queen."

"Delightful," Lucia said with a soft laugh. "Ooooh, you're such a fun and entertaining man, Steve."

The Fae leaned up and kissed the corner of Steve's mouth.

"I love you, my big, tough, beloved consort," Lucia said. "If you do it quick, and with maximum dramatic effect, I'll make sure your evening is extremely entertaining.

"We'll start with a back rub for you, and I'll comb your hair out. Then give you a haircut and a shave. I'll groom you personally until you're feeling warm and fuzzy, and then I'll use my—"

"They're coming," Geneva said, interrupting Lucia before she could continue to what was likely the best part.

Steve didn't need to hear any more from Lucia, though. He was well beyond properly motivated now.

Lucia took care of him. She never shied away from anything he needed from her. Anything he asked of her. Even if he was sure she'd refuse it.

On top of that, she constantly offered to groom, clean, and care for him. He was feeling incredibly pampered right now.

Hefting his axe up on to his shoulder, Steve started toward the broken gate of Faraday.

The camps that'd been out and around the city were gone, all of them now congregated on the far side of Faraday.

A woman in full armor with a long sword held with both hands was heading for Steve.

Sighing, Steve hefted the rock in his left hand.

He could make this look quite dramatic and stupid. Like it was nothing but a slaughter.

Or he could just chuck the rock at the woman and kill her from here.

Cocking his arm back, he hurled the stone with maximum force.

With a whistling crack, the stone flicked by over the woman's head and hit the only standing tower that remained on this side of the city.

A small section of the tower's exterior crumpled inward, and a puff of dust and dirt seemed to rain out of the top of the tower.

That'll do to get my point across.

Snorting, Steve kept moving, heading for the now very nervous-looking woman.

"Sorry," Steve said once she was close enough. "I have to kill you in an ugly way. Not my choice, but... I really want what Lucia offered."

"What?" asked the woman.

Not answering, Steve came at her. It really wasn't personal.

Her sword slid out quicker than Steve had been expecting.

Except it really didn't matter. He only needed to get close enough to get his hands on her.

Swinging his axe at her sword rather than at her, he caught the edge with the head of his weapon.

With a loud ping, her blade snapped in half, right where the two weapons connected.

Stepping in close to the woman, Steve grabbed her around the throat with his left hand.

"Actually, I'll just choke you out real quick so you don't feel this," he said as his hand rapidly cut off the blood and oxygen to the champion's brain.

He was getting a feel for this sort of thing. After having hung onto Hiren, he had a good idea of how hard to squeeze.

In seconds, the face in the mask turned a deep red, and her arms dropped down to her sides.

As soon as the woman stopped struggling, Steve tried to close his hand outright. There was a strange crunching noise as he did so.

Steve held tight to her neck to make sure she was quite dead before he continued.

He didn't want her to suffer for his desire to be cared for by Lucia.

Dropping his axe, Steve grabbed the dead woman's armored right arm and tore it from her torso. He pulled his arm back and flung it toward the city of Faraday.

Grabbing the woman's left arm, he repeated the process. He tore it, armor and all, clear from her torso with a wet squelch.

He lifted the armless dead woman up, then had to reach into her armor to find her hip.

Grabbing hold of her thigh, he started yanking on her leg. A couple quick tugs and it simply detached from her torso.

Leaning back, he chucked it. Without bothering to see where it landed, he reached in and plucked off her last leg, then flung it as well.

Grabbing her by the breastplate, Steve pulled her head away from her torso.

With a sigh, he looked into her pretty face. Her helmet was still strapped into place under her chin.

Strange barely began to describe the view.

"Sorry," Steve said.

He dropped the torso into the grass and held up the woman's head.

"Send out your next champion!" he shouted at the city.

Setting the woman's head to one side, he decided to wait right there. With any luck, they'd send out the next champion soon.

"Or your false queen!" Steve shouted after a second. Then he sat down on the dead woman's torso and looked at her head.

"Shame. She was pretty, like Hiren," Steve lamented.

Twenty

Steve looked up from the grass he was staring at. Turning his head, he directed his gaze toward the city.

Someone was calling out to him even as they came over.

It was a woman, armed and armored very similarly to the last one he'd killed, and to Hiren.

Standing up. Steve swung his axe up onto his shoulder.

"…n't want to…" shouted the woman, the rest of her words not quite understandable.

Steve shrugged his shoulders, deciding to wait. He didn't need to do anything else for the moment.

Holding a shield up in front of her, the woman walked cautiously toward Steve.

"I don't want to fight," she called out to him. "I'm the champion now, but I don't want to fight."

"I mean, that's nice," Steve yelled back. "But unless you've got the false queen's head on you, then I'm gonna have to kill you until she shows up. Or her head does."

"I don't want to fight you," said the woman, her shield still up. She was close enough that they didn't have to shout at one another anymore.

Like the first woman he'd killed, she was wearing an open-faced helmet.

Her mother had apparently been slightly more well to do, since she was prettier than the last champion.

Though she had the same slightly alien beauty as Hiren.

"I mean, I heard you the first time," Steve said. "But that doesn't really matter. Your options are die or turn the queen over."

"I have no choice. I'm the champion — I'm forced to come here," said the woman. "But I don't want to fight."

"Yeah, you mentioned that part. Unless you have an alternative, I kinda have to kill you," Steve said. "I can make it as quick as the last champion, though."

"I… I don't… want to fight," said the woman.

"Like I said. Head or death," Steve said.

"I don't want to die. I don't want to be here," said the champion of Faraday.

"Yeah, well, me too," Steve said. "I'd rather be home having a grand time of Spin the Steve with my wives. Here I am, though.

"You could always just get down on your knees and let this happen."

"On my... knees? I... I... okay," said the woman. "I'd... If you let me live, I'll get on my knees for you. Right here."

Uh...? Did she just offer me head in front of everyone? It wasn't my intention, but I think that'd work.

She'll give me a blow job so that I don't kill her.

Right?

In fact, that'd be better.

"Okay, maybe we can make a deal," Steve said. He figured that'd be pretty demoralizing for Faraday. Their champion made to give head and then captured, in full view of everyone.

Sex is what binds someone in marriage, not a BJ. We can do this without a concern.

Lucia would reward me for this.

"Take your helmet off, drop your weapon, and get on your knees," Steve said.

The champion pulled her helmet off and then dropped her weapon and shield to her side, unable to meet Steve's eyes.

She had slightly animalistic features that reminded Steve of several other Beastkin races. Her nose was very narrow and almost seemed to have a point to it. Her ears weren't catlike, though, or even wolfish. They had a gray edge to them with a black interior.

Her ashen blond hair, almost gray, was finger length and stuck out wildly around her head in sweaty strands. Even her eyelashes were that color. Her blue eyes had a sparkle to them and watched him keenly.

Behind her, a bushy gray-and-black striped tail stuck out behind her and hung low.

"I'm now unarmed," said the woman, doing a small turn, her hands lifted up beside her head. "You'll let me live if I do this?"

"Yep. Having you polish my knob in front of your entire city is probably worse for their morale than killing you, so... yeah," Steve said. "Suck it, become my property, live."

"Okay. Then... okay," said the champion. "I'll do it."

"Great—get to work then," Steve said. Deliberately, he moved a bit to one side, making sure both the city and Geneva's army would see what was happening.

Nodding her head, the champion moved over to Steve. Then she got down on her knees in front of him with a clank of her gear.

She adjusted her armor momentarily, then slowly lifted her eyes to look up at him. It was obvious she didn't know how to proceed.

Deciding to take the initiative, Steve dropped his pants down to his ankles. Exposing himself to her. The champion stared at his privates.

Taking hold of his semi-erect self, he held it in his left hand.

The champion didn't move. She just stared at his crotch, then up at his face.

Not waiting any longer, Steve simply pushed the tip between her lips and then kept going till he was entirely inside her mouth. She was willing to do it, this would destroy the morale of Faraday, and he didn't mind receiving.

It was all perfect.

The champion took him into her mouth without pulling away, though she did make a soft grunt that sounded like surprise when he pushed into her mouth.

Laying his right hand down on her shoulder, Steve looked toward the city of Faraday.

With a soft breath out through her nose, the champion began to reluctantly bob her head back and forth, her mouth and lips tightening around his shaft.

A collective moan went up from Faraday.

"Mm, that's rather good. Your lips are really soft," Steve said as the champion laid her hands on his hips to steady herself.

The champion huffed through her nose at his comment, but kept pumping her head forward and backward.

"What's your name?" Steve asked. If he was going to keep her around to handle some of his needs, he should probably learn her name.

Pulling back far enough that only his tip was in her mouth, the champion looked up at him.

"Beati Tesi," said the champion in an odd tone. It didn't help that her words were just partially muffled.

Steve nodded and then pulled on Beati's shoulder, guiding himself fully back into her mouth.

"Do your best, Beati Tesi. You'll serve under Nancy with Hiren. This'll be your job now," Steve said as Beati got back to work on him. "If you refuse the contract, I'll kill you. Accept it, and live. You're not getting up till I cum, by the way, so work hard."

Beati nodded her head in apparent acceptance of all that, rolling her tongue along the underside of his tip.

Everything felt pretty lacking compared to every single one of his wives and Nancy, but Beati was definitely trying.

He could teach her the rest. And he had a little time right now to get her going in the right direction.

Steve looked back to the city of Faraday.

"Get your next champion ready, or send out your queen!" Steve called to the city. "I'll finish with your current champion soon enough! Maybe the next one could be a redhead?!"

The once-champion of Faraday kept working diligently at him with her lips, tongue, and mouth.

I wonder if she can taste Jaina on me.

Looking back down at Beati, Steve watched her as she worked. He always enjoyed watching.

I bet she can.

***

Three more women came to challenge Steve.

One more ended up on her knees and took it in the mouth rather than fight him. She was given over to Nancy just as Beati had been after she'd finished with Steve.

The other two fought him and died. Having their arms and legs pulled off, just as the first, and being thrown at the city.

Darkness was coming on, and the land was cast in a deep shade of purple.

"I don't think they're going to send anyone else," said Lucia from behind him.

Looking over his shoulder, he found her, Jaina, Geneva, and Nancy.

"No?" Steve asked Lucia.

"I don't think so. You made two service you, and you killed three," Lucia said with a laugh. "It's been hours since the last girl came out, and she ended up taking you in the mouth. What was her name?"

Lucia asked the question to Nancy.

"Felisa," Nancy said. "She's with Hiren and Beati now. They're helping Ferrah with her forge work for the time being."

Nancy had also given a contract matching Hiren's to Beati and Felisa.

"Yes, her. I spoke with her briefly," Lucia said. "It seems the false queen is only sending people she believes are loyal, rather than the most proficient at combat. Felisa was an exception, as she volunteered to fight you.

"I think it may have shaken the false queen that she decided to take the same exit as Beati. I can't imagine it'd be ideal to watching two champions giving blow jobs instead of fighting."

"I can taste their despair," Nancy said, her eyes sliding toward Faraday. "It's delicious."

"I don't think her soldiers will follow her tomorrow," Geneva said. "We'll find her corpse tomorrow. Or her head. Since you called for that repeatedly."

Laughing to herself, Jaina grinned.

"He got head. Twice," she said with a laugh.

Rolling his eyes, Steve walked over to the Kobold with a grin.

Jaina flopped down on her back and lifted her shirt up. She grinned at him, displaying her teeth, her eyes glittering.

"Rub me, pack leader. I'm a good huntress for you," she demanded, laying her hands against her hips. "Rub me lots. Lots, lots."

Today was supposed to be for her, so he had no qualms doing as instructed. Especially with how hard she'd been working lately.

Squatting down next to her, he started to run his hand up and down her belly. Caressing and stroking her.

"Alright," Steve said. "Pack it in for the day then?"

"That'd be my recommendation," Geneva said. "I agree with Lucia. This is done for today. Thank you for solving this… so quickly and efficiently."

- 208 -

"Whatever," Steve said. "I just want to get home."

Despite Lucia's urgings, he was starting to rethink his original goal. He still wanted to be able to protect everything he had, and eliminating Linne still seemed the most likely way to make that happen, but he didn't like being this far away.

He was too far from home.

Too far from Nikki.

There was an ache attached to that thought. Of how she'd casually dismissed him right before he left.

It'd been too much for him to try and solve at the time, though now he did regret not trying to talk to her again.

A set of long, cool fingers slid through his hair and curled down around his ear.

"I know, my beloved consort," Lucia said softly. "I know. We'll go home for a time and rest. Relax. See Nia, check on Gwen's pregnancy. Do you think Nia will have a brother or a sister? I'm sure Gwen is starting to show a bit and looks lovely by now. Don't you think?"

Steve grinned at the idea of it.

"Yeah." He nodded.

Jaina, who had been wriggling slightly back and forth under his hand, grew absolutely still.

"I sense the Creep," she said in a breathless whisper.

She got to her feet and pulled at her tunic, her head turning one way and then the other.

"You do? Seriously?" Steve asked, getting to his feet as well.

"Yes. It's… coming," Jaina said. "From every direction."

"Back to camp," Lucia said. "Quickly."

"I thought you said you sealed it away," Geneva said to Steve.

"I did. Apparently it wasn't enough," Steve replied hotly.

"Let's be honest—we never thought it was actually gone," Lucia said as the group continued back to the camp. "Oh, running just isn't for me. I hate running."

"Jaina, can you put up a spell around the camp?" Steve asked.

"Yes, yes. Not a problem," Jaina said as she moved on all fours. It looked like she was going significantly slower than he knew she could. "Can't help the city, though."

"Right... city," Steve said, looking toward Faraday.

"They can suffer and die," Geneva said, moving along easily even in full armor. "Traitors, the lot of them. Let the Creep have them."

Steve considered that idea briefly and then dismissed it.

His recent dealings with the villages and bandit camps had given him some perspective. Even in a camp full of people who had murdered, killed, raped, and thieved their way through the last year, there were those who'd done nothing wrong. Who were truly innocent.

And Steve wasn't going to leave them to their fate.

Because in the back of his head, all he could think of was Gwendolin, Nia, Lucia, and Ferrah. They would have all been in Filch and, if he hadn't fixed the wall, likely overrun by the Creep.

Most likely dead, too.

"Jaina, once you get the spell up around the camp, can it function without you?" Steve asked.

"Yes, yes," Jaina said. "Why?"

"Because I want to go cover that big hole we made in Faraday," Steve said. "I refuse to seal their fate because of their queen. For all we know, they want nothing to do with her. Go put up the spell, grab several canteens of can water, and come back."

"Right. Okay, right, right," Jaina said. Then she took off at a flying sprint toward the camp.

Steve slowed down and eventually came to a stop. Turning around, he faced Faraday.

It was obvious even from this distance they had no idea what was going on. Soldiers weren't massing in the gap, there was no one moving, and it seemed as if everyone had simply "gone home" for the night.

"Goodness, well, I suppose if we must," Lucia said with a sigh. She walked up to his right and laid a hand on his lower back. "It's a good thing I actually desperately love you, my dashing consort.

"I'll follow you into hell itself, even if I complain at you the entire way. At least I don't have to run anymore."

Nancy fell in next to Steve on his left, Geneva a step beyond her.

His henchwoman was doing well with learning how to read and write, but she wasn't made for combat. It was probably the furthest thing from her wheelhouse he could think of.

Which was why he was flattered she'd stuck around.

"Don't need to be here," Steve said, catching Nancy's eyes.

"I know," said the Wight. "I want to be here. Need to show I can earn my keep in whatever way needed."

With a shrug of his shoulders, Steve turned back to the military camp.

Jaina had just made it there a short minute ago and was probably building her spell even now.

In the middle of the camp, a large purple dome began expanding upward. Soon enough, he saw it coming toward him. Growing faster and faster, it almost seemed to be out of control.

Noiselessly and without warning, the dome slammed to a halt.

Five seconds after that, a blast of wind more akin to something out of a hurricane smashed through Steve and his companions. Then it passed over them just as quickly as it'd come on.

Did her dome just expel all the air inside it? Is the Creep more pervasive than I thought?

I mean, I never really thought about it.

Could that be the reason why everything beyond the wall was dead? After a certain point, it just permeates the air itself?

That'd be… I'm going to need to dig my trench out all the way to Bexis, Faraday, Hilast, and Rennis.

If I want any hope of saving these people.

Wait, why would I save them?

Frowning, Steve stared at the purple dome, unsure himself at why he'd been thinking he needed to save everyone.

The answer that came to him was slow, but unfortunately real.

Because Nikki would want me to. Because it's in my power to do so, and it wouldn't impact their way of life.

And… Nia would want me to do that, too.

Grimacing at the idea of disappointing Nikki and Nia, Steve wondered how long it would take him to dig a trench all the way down to the outpost, Filch, or the farm.

Then to drag it all the way around to the other towns and villages.

Long time.

Could use all the prisoners, though... have them running out from the outpost, and me heading toward them.

Probably do it pretty quick.

"Nancy," Steve said.

"Yes... Steve?" she asked in response.

"Gonna need to dig a trench around all Gennie's cities," Steve said. "Work crews and shovels."

"I understand," Nancy said.

"Gennie?" Geneva asked.

"Yeah, you. Gennie," Steve said. Heading his way was Jaina at a dead-on sprint.

"Oooh? Maybe I should be jealous. I don't have a nickname," Lucia said teasingly. "You're going to make me try to turn Gennie into one of mine."

"If you like. We could go with Lucy. Or if you're looking for something more sappy, we could do my butterfly," Steve said.

He wasn't beyond doing what she was asking, since it cost him nothing and he didn't actually feel any embarrassment for the nickname.

I call Kassandra Kass and little snake, after all.

It was a bit odd at times for Steve. Lucia clearly knew how to lead him around and get what she wanted from him.

But all she wanted was his attention, time, and some spoiling. He was more than willing to give her all of those in spades.

He did care about her.

"Oh? Alright," Lucia said, a smile clear in her voice. "I'll take both and enjoy them. Though I'll be cross if you address anyone else by them. A nickname is meant to be unique and befitting one person. As your wife and a Fae princess, I do like them, dearest."

Steve didn't need to be told that if she wasn't happy, he wouldn't get what he'd been getting every night since leaving home.

And what he craved.

It filled a hole he'd felt after Nikki had turned him out.

"That's... the Creep?" Geneva asked.

Turning away from the camp, Steve looked out at the plains beyond.

A black fog was creeping across the land as the sun fell further into the west.

"Yes, that's the Creep," Lucia said with a sigh. "And the last time we saw it as thick as that, I became little better than a chew toy.

"I still... have... dreams about that day."

Lucia shook her head and shivered lightly.

Steve wouldn't forget that day either. Lucia had nearly died protecting him.

Reaching out, he slipped an arm underneath Lucia's rear end, lifted her up, and started running for the city.

"Oh! Oh my," Lucia said with a soft laugh. She leaned into Steve and gave him a kiss on his temple. "Well, far be it from me to complain about being swept off my feet, my sweet and sexy consort."

"Jaina will catch up long before we get there," Steve said, trying to ignore Lucia. It was difficult with how cuddly she could get in public lately. "Let's get going."

"Aren't they going to attack us?" Nancy asked.

"If they try, we'll just go off to the side where the wall stands. At that point, we'll let them deal with the Creep," Steve said.

"You think Jaina can cover us?" Geneva asked.

"Yeah, I do. Creep Witches are very strong," Steve said, then sighed.

Up ahead, he could see peasants and commoners all shouting and pointing at Steve and his people.

Welcoming committee.

Twenty-One

By the time Steve and his people stopped in the massive gap in the wall that Jaina had created, she'd long since caught up to them.

"Alright," Steve said, looking around. There was quite a bit of rubble all over from the collapsed wall. "Let's see what we can do."

Setting Lucia down to one side, Steve pulled his pickaxe out from the loop on his left hip. There were only two items he always carried with him. His axe and his pickaxe.

His shovel was with his tent more often than not. The rest of his tools were all back at the farm.

"You, citizen," Lucia said, addressing someone else. "Alert the city that the Creep is coming. You'll need to bring your army up to this point."

Walking to the rubble, Steve cocked back his pickaxe.

Come on, you fucking glorified nose-picking asshat Shitty Steve. I really need this to work to build things, too.

It'd worked to fix the wall back at Filch, but that gap had been considerably smaller. This was a much more massive and terrible mess.

"...already on their way, your ladyship," someone said.

"Good. As soon as whoever's in charge shows up, point them out to me," Lucia said. "We'll need to organize your defenses."

"Uh, of course, your ladyship," said the same person.

Steve brought his pickaxe down with the intent to have all the rubble nearby slammed up into the wall.

With a clank, his pickaxe hit the nearest mess of stones. Then, with a strange thud, the mass of broken bricks and mortar around him vanished.

They reappeared where the wall was broken in an odd-looking wall-like structure.

It'd clearly taken significantly more material to make the wall than it would have originally. But it looked stable enough for the time being. It also covered some of the massive gap that'd been there.

Grunting, Steve pulled his pickaxe up to his shoulder and looked at the area around him. There was nothing left to utilize for rebuilding.

Turning around, he bounced off an armored breastplate.

"I'm so sorry, my lord," said Hiren. "I was just awestruck and... I'm sorry."

Gritting his teeth, Steve looked up at Hiren. Standing on either side of her were Beati and Felisa.

The three of them were dressed in their full armor, though they weren't wearing tabards anymore.

"Whatever, move," Steve said, pushing lightly on Hiren's hip. The big, heavily armed woman took two steps to one side.

"How can we serve, my lord?" asked Felisa.

Of the three of them, she'd been the most subservient. She'd practically run up to Steve and gotten down on her knees without a word.

"Well, you sure as hell can't blow me right now," Steve said, walking over to the rubble pile on the other side. "We'll be fighting to keep the Creep out of Faraday. Not letting the Creep in, if I can help it."

In his mind, all he could see were people who would be innocent. People who couldn't leave the city but didn't want anything to do with the false queen.

People who would have been exactly like Gwendolin and Nia, with nowhere to go.

"I understand, my lord," Felisa said. "I'll service your needs as per my duties as soon as we're done here."

Glancing over his shoulder at that, Steve raised his eyebrows.

Felisa was standing where he'd seen her last. Just as tall as Hiren and Beati, and just as fierce, the brunette had dark brown eyes. Her looks ran similar to the other two knights with that alien beauty, though she was prettier than either of them. There was something very different about her.

He couldn't put his finger on it, but he knew she wasn't Human.

"Sure, why not?" Steve said, turning back to the rubble. He couldn't deny that taking the three knights had fed his ego considerably. "Certainly not going to say no if that's what you want to do."

Bringing his pickaxe up behind his head, Steve envisioned what he wanted done again.

"Of course, my lord," Felisa said. "It's... it's why I'm here, now."

"Yes, my lord," Beati agreed.

Bringing his pickaxe down again, Steve watched as the broken wall disappeared and then reappeared once more.

"Good enough," he said, thankful the pickaxe was capable of doing more than he'd expected.

Turning his head, he started looking for Jaina.

Who was right next to him.

"What d'ya have the power for?" he asked, getting straight to the point.

"Not much, not much," Jaina said, shaking her head with a frown. "I'm sorry. I can start absorbing Creep when it gets here. Until then, I'm spent."

"Right, makes sense," Steve said. "Did you get an idea of what we're looking at?"

"All Creep creeps," Jaina said. "Nothing turned. All Creep formed."

"Okay. A lot of them?" Steve asked, looking out toward the plain. He could see the purple dome of Jaina's magic around their camp.

"Lots, lots. More than... more than we've ever seen before," Jaina said.

"Okay then. Answer is simple, I guess," Steve said. "Kill as many as you can, try to funnel them into a narrow area for us, and stock up on power."

"Your ladyship, that's... that's the current champion," said a voice from behind Steve.

Craning his neck around, he looked toward the voice. It was a shabbily dressed citizen.

Heading her way down the street was a woman in full armor, just like Hiren, Beati, and Felisa. Wielding a sword and shield just as they had been.

Another one? Is she a champion?

Shall I add to my collection?

Lucia clicked her tongue and then moved several steps to one side, apparently to intercept the woman.

Grunting, Steve looked out in front of him.

It ain't the shovel, but... would it work?

Hefting his pickaxe again, Steve walked out to the grass and dirt that was in front of the walls. He gave himself more than enough, as he contemplated what he wanted to happen.

For the grass, dirt, and any stone beneath to form into a sheer cliff face.

Then he brought the pickaxe down with force.

A strange shattering noise dominated the area, and the world itself shifted. Faster than he could figure out what'd happened, Steve found himself several feet lower than he'd been previously. He was now standing in a shallow channel.

Not far away, a low mound of stone had appeared.

Right. It's not the shovel, so it can't move dirt, but it can peel out any stone like it's nothing. Whether it's specks, chunks, rocks, or otherwise. Got it.

Sighing, Steve shook his head and walked back over to Hiren, Beati, Felisa, and Jaina.

"Suddenly I wish I had my shovel," he grumbled. "I'm a fortifications expert when I have all my tools. I should have brought it with me."

"Couldn't have known," Jaina said, shaking her head. "No way to have—There they are."

Following the line of Jaina's eyes, Steve could see a black shadow moving toward them at the same speed as the sky grew darker.

Damn.

"If you've got any juice left, I'd say your first spell should be a big ol' fireball that hangs in the sky like a flare," Steve said.

"A what?" Hiren asked.

"We need light," Steve said, not wanting to answer that. "Fighting in the dark against the Creep is a great way to get bit."

"I can do that, yes, yes," Jaina said, then held a hand up above her head.

A purple fireball no bigger than her head leapt out of her palm and then hung above them in the sky.

In the next second, she moved it behind where everyone was. The light of it was cast forward so it wouldn't blind anyone.

Smarter than I gave her credit for.

That or she's learning as we go and this is all new to her.

I wonder… was she a sheltered little thing who'd never really gone outside of her village?

Pulling his pickaxe out of the loop, he turned to his three knights.

"Which one of you is the strongest?" Steve asked.

"I am," Hiren said immediately. "Beati was the third strongest, Felisa the fifth. You… killed the second, fourth, and sixth."

"Great," Steve said. "And what about that champion over there?"

"Her?" Beati asked, turning her head to look to the newest champion of Faraday. She was still talking with Lucia. "She didn't participate. She would have been at least the third, though. Her name's—"

"Don't care," Steve said, then held his pickaxe out to Hiren. "It'll go right through any Creep you hit. More so than your sword. Just be aware of that, or you'll end up overswinging."

Hiren's face through her helmet looked unsure and doubtful.

"Just don't put it down, or you can't pick it up again," Steve said as Hiren took it.

Steve moved over to Lucia wanting to give her a heads up.

"…fill the gaps. We need it covered," Lucia said.

"I… I understand," said the champion in response.

"Good. Now get me those arrows," Lucia said and turned away from the champion. "Oh! Steve, good timing. Can you make me a little tower to stand on?"

Giving him a wide smile, she laid a hand on his chest.

"Please? I know I earned all my scars protecting you, but I'd really rather not add to them," she said.

Steve thought about declining the request, then shrugged his shoulders.

"Hiren," Steve called out. "Get over here and hit the paving stones with the pickaxe. In your head, I need you to keep thinking 'tower' as you do it. Got it?"

"Yes, my lord," Hiren said as she came over.

"Thank you, my beloved consort," Lucia said, then gave him a quick kiss.

Sighing, and feeling like he was ever getting deeper with Lucia, Steve went back to the front line.

The Creep itself looked like it was a minute out, the zombies a few seconds beyond that.

Steve hefted his axe. He really didn't like this. It was going to be an ugly and stupid fight.

Then a wave of soldiers with shields and armor moved past him and set their shields down on the ground.

Uh, what?

Beati and Felisa each took one of Steve's sides.

"You didn't think you'd be fighting, did you?" Nancy asked from directly behind him. "They have soldiers specifically for this. You rebuilt part of the wall and brought your own forces to bear. Now you get to sit here and watch it all happen."

Frowning, Steve watched as seven more rows of soldiers showed up and settled in behind the first.

Slowly, he was pushed further and further into the back of the area with each row that joined.

I guess… I guess she's right.

This isn't my job.

Need to make sure I always have my tools on me going forward.

How do I… Oh! I'll just make Hiren, Beati, and Felisa carry my things. They can just strap them to their backs until I need them.

Perfect.

Then the zombies hit the line of soldiers, and the battle began.

***

Steve brought his axe down on a zombie's neck, severing the head from its body.

At some point, a hole had been made in the line of soldiers and a wave of zombies had gotten through. It hadn't been many, and the hole had been closed rather quickly, but it'd still happened.

Following the head as it rolled to one side, he saw that its jaw and eyes were still moving.

And that's why we remove the jaw.

He grabbed the head with one hand and used his axe to cut the jaw away. Then he stood up and looked around.

Geneva, Hiren, Beati, and Felisa were executing zombies as well. Jaina and Nancy were nowhere to be seen.

Glancing over his shoulder, he found them with Lucia on top of the pillar Hiren had made.

Steve turned back to the line, surprised. There wasn't any fighting going on anymore. It looked like the soldiers were sending back their wounded and reorganizing themselves.

We'll need that can water. But not before I get their queen's head.

Steve started searching through the crowd to find one person in particular. He needed to make a statement, get this done, and have it all buttoned up immediately.

When he found who he was looking for, Steve stuck his bloody axe into the loop at his side. The champion of Faraday was next to the pillar that Lucia, Jaina, and Nancy were standing on. Somehow that spot had become the center for the defense of Faraday.

Blowing out a quick breath, Steve marched himself over that way. People got out of his way as they would if he were digging a trench. No one stood before him as soon as they realized who he was.

When he got in front of the champion, he finally got a good look at her since her helmet was at her feet.

She was a redhead with light brown eyes. Her hair was just as short as the other knights he'd collected.

Once again, he found she shared the odd and alien beauty everyone from Faraday seemed to have. Much like the other champions, she was also extremely well endowed.

Though, she was considerably more muscular than he'd previously thought. He could see the muscles in her neck and shoulders even from here.

He asked for insight into her; he needed to know if he could pull this off.

Siena Atil
Knight/Champion
Ogre Hybrid
Father: living
Mother: deceased
Traitor- betrayed her nation
Condemned Criminal- has been condemned as a criminal

Royal Captain- captain of the royal guard

Ambassador- speaks on the behalf of the queen of Faraday

Envoy- designated to treat with other nations for the queen of Faraday

Champion- one and true champion of Faraday

Noble Line- part of the nobility of Faraday and Lamals

Perfect. Unmarried, untied.

Though, I wonder what an Ogre hybrid means as far as her race goes.

She looks Human. Just rather big for a Human.

Maybe this is more of what Nikki meant. The more a race breeds with Humans, the further they go towards Human.

"You," Steve called out to the champion.

That got the woman's attention, and her eyes turned to Steve.

"I'm the champion of Filch, Geneva, and the forces that just assisted Faraday," Steve said. "I challenge you to combat. Or you can choose to let me use you, just like the other champions have.

"You've got about ten seconds to decide how this turns out."

Looking shocked, frightened, and unable to process it all, the redhead stared at Steve as he walked right up to her.

Then down at him when he was standing in front of her. She was taller than him.

They breed 'em big, pretty, and different here, huh?

"Well?" Steve asked. "You got about five seconds to drop to your knees before I pop your head off. I'm taking Faraday. Today. I'm done with this."

Letting out a slow breath, Siena got down to her knees in front of Steve.

"I do this and I live?" she asked.

"That's right," Steve said. "You become mine and you live."

"Fine," Siena said. "But my family gets their charges cleared."

Nodding his head, Steve undid his pants and then flipped his not very erect self out. He wasn't in the mood and he didn't really want this, but he needed Faraday done.

"That's fine. Get to work then," Steve said.

Easing herself forward, the champion set her lips to his tip. Slowly, she took him into her mouth and began to suck on him.

"Perfect," Steve said, laying his left hand on Siena's head as his right hand took hold of her armored shoulder.

"Now, who's the next champion after her?" Steve asked, as Siena suckled on his rapidly hardening length.

"I am," said a woman who was nearly a clone to the other four knights he'd taken.

"Great, you get a different option," Steve said as Siena slowly started to work her head back and forth along his now rock-hard length. "You can get down on your knees behind Siena here, die, or go knock your false queen out and bring her back here.

"Your pick. Though I'll be honest—after Siena's done with me, it'll take a bit for me to be ready to pop off again. So you'll be working it for a while."

Hesitating for only a few seconds, the knight contemplated her options.

"I'll get the queen," she said, then started jogging off.

"Great," Steve said.

Letting out a slow breath, he closed his eyes and simply enjoyed Siena's mouth.

"My lord, I'm sorry to interrupt," said Beati on his left. "But I must report I was bitten. You… should dispatch me before I turn."

Steve briefly considered simply letting her die. It'd be a quick way to pick up a new Creep Witch, but he also didn't want to scare off his own people.

Letting her die like this would definitely make it harder for him in the future.

That and it was a little hard to think right now with Siena's mouth wrapped around him.

"Fuck that," Steve said, not opening his eyes. Siena was just like the others. Inexperienced, but willing and trying. "You're mine, Beati. Someone go get one of my canteens."

Opening his eyes, Steve looked around.

Lucia, Jaina, Geneva, and Nancy were all talking off to one side. Hiren and Felisa were nearby, and Felisa was coming back with one of his canteens.

All around him, though, were soldiers of Faraday and citizens, watching their current champion servicing him.

He looked down at Siena for a moment to watch her pretty face as it moved to and fro, her red hair shifting as she did so. Her eyes were closed, apparently not wanting to watch him. Felisa and Beati had both stared up at him, which was curious now that he thought about it.

"Here you are, my lord," Beati said, coming back and handing him the canteen.

"Good, where were you bit?" Steve asked, lifting his hand from Siena's shoulder and taking it.

"My forearm," said the knight, then held up her arm.

Sure enough, there was a bleeding and ugly bite there.

"Hmph," Steve said. He opened the stopper on the canteen with one hand, then tipped it to the side over the wound for a single second.

As soon as the water hit her skin, it lit up in small flames.

"There we go," Steve said as the flames died away. Looking up at Beati's face, he could see a faint sheen of sweat on her brow. "Take a drink of this and put it back. Don't be so careless next time. You can't serve me if you're dead."

"I... yes, my lord," Beati said, taking the canteen from Steve. She immediately took a drink, capped it, and hung it on her hip.

Closing his eyes, Steve put both hands on Siena's head and started guiding her with the speed he wanted.

With any luck, he could unload in her mouth before the queen arrived.

"Just like that, Siena," Steve said, his fingers curling into her hair.

Twenty-Two

The clatter and clank of armor and boots drew Steve's attention away from Jaina. She was busily draining Creep out of the wounded and then cleansing wounds with water.

They'd originally just tried it to conserve water, but it seemed to be working.

And empowering Jaina at the same time.

"It's the queen," Siena said and then coughed.

Again.

She'd been coughing since Steve had finished in her mouth a few minutes ago. Apparently, it'd shot straight into the back of her throat.

Even though he'd warned her it was coming, she still hadn't been ready.

Nancy had been merciless, however. No sooner had Steve gotten done with her, she'd taken Siena away from prying eyes and put her into the same black-magic contract that Hiren, Beati, and Felisa were under.

Coughing and sputtering the entire time.

"Good," Steve said. He patted Jaina on the back and looked at his Kobold. "You got this?"

"Of course, of course," Jaina said with a grin. "This is far too easy now. All of it is. I'm your alpha Creep Witch."

So the more I use her, the stronger she gets. I need to take the Creep Witches with me to the wall. Drown them in battle and soak them in combat.

I could conquer Lamals with them.

I wonder how frightening Nancy would be as a Creep Witch.

Standing up straight, Steve walked over to where the street wound up to the gate that used to stand. Right where the battle had occurred.

Heading his way were six women, forcing a seventh between them ever onward. He imagined the seventh was the queen. She didn't look quite human, though. Her ears were odd, her eyes canted in a way that didn't look normal, and her cheeks and jaws seemed wider.

By the time they reached Steve, Geneva and Lucia had joined him.

"Steve, would you please execute her for me?" Geneva asked.

"Course," Steve said. "I'll even do it in your name as the rightful military governor of… uh… what the fuck is this all called?"

"Eastern Lamals," Geneva said.

"Uh, kay. Whatever. Military Governor Gennie of Eastern Lamals," Steve said.

"Thank you, Steve," Geneva said.

The knights, because that was clearly what they were, reached Steve and tossed the false queen down to the ground in front of him.

"Now see here," said the woman, glaring up at Steve. "I'm of the nobility of Lamals and the rightful —"

Steve's hands whipped out in front of him and clapped together on either side of the woman's head. Directly atop her ears.

With a sickening crunch and clicking noises from her skull, the false queen fell limp to the ground. She hit the stones with a pop as her skull bounced off it. Her eyes rolled up into her head and her breathing was strange.

She was clearly already unconscious and probably dying.

"I sentence you to death, in the name of Geneva Gosti, the rightful military governor of Eastern Lamals!" Steve yelled even as he moved to stand over the top of the one-time mayor of Faraday.

Sitting down on her expansive chest, Steve began to punch her face repeatedly. Alternating left and right hands, he didn't stop.

He was making a point. Had been making a point.

Any and all resistance would be met with overwhelming violence from here on out. The only possibility of non-violence was absolute submission.

When the false queen's head was little better than a mess of meat, broken bones, and blood, Steve finally stopped.

"Cut what's left of her head off, then impale her corpse and stick it outside. From her crotch to her neck," Steve said. "City's yours, Gennie. Do as you like. I'm going back to camp now. I'm tired."

Getting to his feet, Steve bent down and wiped his bloody hands on the queen's beautiful dress.

"No bandits outside," Geneva said as the column of soldiers, wagons, and supplies came to a stop outside of Hilast.

"As I said," Xivin said with a nod. She was sitting in the wagon with Lucia. She did all she could to assist whenever she could, but the simple reality was she was very limited. It was obvious to Steve her mindset was changing further and further from where she'd once been as well.

In fact, he'd bet on this excursion having sealed away whatever had remained of the Elven sword master.

"While Filch was the smallest and we had no knights, we were well trained, fortified, and knew our business. Bexis and Faraday were never as well trained as we were, despite being larger," Xivin said with no lack of pride. "Hilast and Rennis should be free of banditry due to their distance from the citadel and the wall."

"Grass seems better, too," Steve said, kicking a foot against the bright green leaves under his boots. "Gets pretty brown the closer you get to the citadel. Or that's what it looked like when I saw it last."

"Hmm. I'm afraid that with the return of the Creep, my plans are now in disarray," Geneva said. "After seeing Filch and Bexis, and what Faraday did to protect themselves… no, my plans won't work."

"We could just have Steve conquer all their champions again, one blow job or kill at a time," Lucia said with a soft laugh. "Though I'm afraid it did annoy me watching them service my husband. And here I thought I was beyond jealousy."

"I mean, I guess," Steve said. He didn't quite like that idea, but he wouldn't be against it if it got the job done.

"Let's treat with the mayor first," Xivin said. "Perhaps she'll have been more prudent up to this point. We should send a messenger out."

Steve nodded at that. It'd only been a few days since they left Faraday. The Creep had come back every single night. The only thing that kept the column safe was Jaina's nightly watch.

Though it did mean the Kobold spent most of the day sleeping in the wagon. The Creep was determined to break through her shielding each night.

Jaina had said the first night had been the worst; every night after that had gotten easier.

I need more Creep Witches. And now.

"You handle that," Steve said, then turned and started walking toward the back of the column.

He'd brought a number of water barrels with him.

We'll offer the knights the chance to die for me and be reborn as Creep Witches. In exchange, I'll remove their statuses and modify their deals a bit. So they aren't as absolute.

Nancy, too. Though that might be a bit different.

She likes it the way it is right now.

The crunch and thump of the four champions behind him was all the proof he needed that his knights were there.

"Nancy," Steve said.

"I'm here, Steve," Nancy said, coming to walk next to him. She'd apparently been right behind him with his knights.

"I want to offer you and your knights something," Steve said. "This is an offer, which means it's completely volunteer only. You can say no."

Looking back over his shoulder, he found the four knights watching him. They were dressed in their full armor, but their helmets were all under their armpits.

Wouldn't figure them to have surrendered and given me head with how they look.

Even Hiren goes down on me on command.

Turning back to the front, Steve continued.

"I want you to die for me. I want you to let a Creep bite you, die, get dunked in a large pool of water, and come back as a Creep Witch," Steve said. "You'd be just like Jaina. Which is what happened to her. Then I—"

"Of course," Nancy said immediately. "But only if you strangle me to death, right before I turn. Then I'll agree. And after I turn and come back, I guarantee your bedroom knights will agree."

The fuck?

And what does she mean bedroom knights? Is that what she's calling them?

"If Nancy comes back… alive and fine… I'll… agree as well," Hiren said.

"I'll die with Nancy," Felisa said, once more the overeager one.

"I'll wait to see what happens," said Beati.

"Yes," Siena agreed.

Steve gritted his teeth, realizing Nancy would finally get what she wanted to a degree.

"This is the one and only time something like this will happen," he said, glaring at her.

"You'll do it?" she asked, sounding beyond excited.

"Yeah. This one time." Steve felt somewhat sick with himself. He really didn't like the idea of actually harming Nancy.

She was different. Crazy in her own way.

But he did have a strange bit of care for her. He didn't like the idea of hurting her, even if it was what she wanted.

The closest he got was the light and rough stuff he did with Kassandra and Ina.

"Could you maybe ra—"

"No," Steve said before she could even finish. He knew exactly what she was going to ask, and he had no intention of fulfilling that.

"Okay," Nancy said. "Make sure you kinda run me on the edge for a while, though. Like what you did with Hiren."

Steve closed his eyes, suddenly regretting this. But he needed more Creep Witches, immediately. He'd have to wait till tonight for them to get bitten, but he could at least prepare everything else until then.

Two hours later and one head-deep pit, a messenger arrived from Hilast. The mayor would be willing to meet and discuss things. She'd prefer it to be a location between the encampment and the city.

Out in the open.

She was going to bring three people with her. So Geneva could bring three as well.

Which meant Geneva, Steve, Lucia and Nancy would be accompanying her to the meeting.

"I wonder how this'll go," Lucia murmured, moving with the ethereal grace she always seemed to have.

"Dunno, don't care," Steve said. "We have other shit we need to work on. This is a distraction we need to stomp out."

"Indeed," Geneva said with a nod of her head. "We should be focusing on our battle with Linne.

"I'm sure she's heard I've arrived by now. Which means she's probably building her forces."

"Oh, we definitely have other things to do, but this isn't so bad," Lucia said, waving a hand dismissively. "We got a commitment of soldiers from the new mayor of Faraday, and they had quite a few knights left. Even some knights from Bexis.

"If we can line Hilast and Rennis up, and receive troops, this'll be significantly easier. Don't get me wrong, Linne will have some very well-trained soldiers, but she has no food or clean water. We have both."

"There they are," Nancy said.

Up ahead, Steve could see four people. One was dressed rather richly, and three were in knight's armor.

Steve couldn't tell what their races were from here, but they seemed to be more on the "bestial" side of things. The woman in the flashy garb was actually sprouting antlers from her head at the temples.

Now that he looked, all the knights also had antlers coming up from their helmets. Steve had taken them as decorative.

There was a rectangular table set out with eight chairs as well, four to a side.

"Another queen?" Steve asked.

"Yes," Geneva said with a sigh. "Maybe you really will have to do a repeat performance. Her species tends to fight anyone and anything."

Explains the antlers, I guess. Still kinda weird, though.

"Huh," Steve said, then sighed as well. "Whatever. I don't mind collecting knights, I guess. It's just… not very quick. Might be fun to hold onto their antlers."

"I want to say I'm the bigger woman and I can handle that, but I'd really rather not watch a bunch of strangers go down on you, beloved consort," Lucia said. Her words had none of the teasing mischievousness he'd come to expect from her.

Apparently it genuinely bothered her.

"Do what I can to prevent that," Steve said. "Can't promise it, though. Sorry, my butterfly."

As if in response to his words, Lucia's hair fluttered as her gossamer-like wings flicked out from behind her and beat several times before lying back down on her back.

"I find I actually like that nickname. Considerably more than I thought I would," she murmured. "Do what you must. Just… try to spare me if possible."

"Ho there," called one of the female knights, waving a hand above her head.

"Greetings," Geneva called back. "I'm Her Majesty's military governor, Geneva Gosti, deployed to handle and administer her rule to Eastern Lamals."

"So I see," said the richly dressed woman. "I'm Queen Valist, first of my line, ruler of Hilast and Rennis."

"Oh? That'll make this easier, then," Geneva said, walking straight to the table. She held a hand out toward the other woman.

"I don't think for an instant this'll be easy," Valist said, though she did take Geneva's hand and shake it.

"It really will be. I've been sent to do exactly what I said. Bring everything back to order," Geneva said. "In addition, I have tools and the ability to fight the Creep. I can even stop someone from dying of Creep disease. Beyond even that, I can actually bring someone back to life who's died to the Creep. Providing their body hasn't been completely destroyed."

Geneva pulled a seat out and sat down at the table. Everything she'd said was what they'd all agreed previously that she'd tell them.

If it was possible to bring them into the fold without fighting, all the better.

"I… see," said Valist. "And what would you have me do? Give up my crown?"

"Yes," Geneva said as Steve, Lucia, and Nancy all took seats as well. "Because your crown is false. I speak for her majesty in this, and she'd be willing to forgive your transgression. You weren't aware that the capital and the queen were fine."

Fat chance of that. She probably just thought she could get away with it.

Valist and her knights all took their own seats, the false queen looking like she was deep in thought.

"In other words, I'd become mayor of Hilast once again," she said. "I don't find that very… beneficial to me."

"The alternative is the same thing that happened to Faraday," Geneva said. "My champion defeats eight or nine in a row of your champions, then you get your head cut off and your body impaled, then put out front like a decoration.

"No, that isn't a threat—that's really what happened. This is my champion right here, by the way."

Geneva lifted a hand and laid it on Steve's shoulder.

"Hmph," Valist said. "I'm dealing with an unwed, without-child noble with nothing between her ears, it seems. Why would I ever agree to a champions' duel with you?"

"Unwed," Steve said. "If she was wed, you'd agree to the battle? A champion's duel for your crown?"

"Of course," Valist said with an exaggerated sigh. "It's a shame, though, isn't it? She's not wed, and you're just a human."

Steve looked at Geneva, wondering how she'd like to proceed. She had mentioned that this could be an issue.

"So be it," Geneva said. "I'd hoped to not have my first time until after all this, but it seems that's for naught."

"I beg your—no," Valist said, looking at Steve, her mind clearly jumping tracks.

"Betrothed, I'd ask you to please wed me here and now," Geneva said, standing up. She began working at the armor around her hips. "She already stated that'd satisfy her needs to a champions' duel for her crown."

Shrugging, Steve stood up as well and started unfastening his belt.

"Goodness, it seems this entire trip is just me being forced to watch my husband in almost every sexual act possible," Lucia said with a growl to her voice. "I'm not a cuck-queen—this isn't something I enjoy. It's different if I've prepared the entertainment myself."

Feeling bad about it but unsure how to really move forward other than with what Geneva had suggested, Steve couldn't really look at Lucia.

"Oh, I know, I know. It's what must be done," Lucia said, her tone cooling off somewhat. "I just really don't like it. At all."

Geneva laid her armor down on the table with a clatter.

"It isn't as if I'd choose my consummation to be witnessed by strangers," muttered the Lionan.

Nancy was kneeling in front of Steve before he realized it. She eagerly scooped up his member with her lips and began to suck on him, her hands coming up to rest on his thighs.

To be honest, he needed the help. With Lucia and Geneva clearly non-enthused about the situation, he wasn't quite into it.

Laying her torso down on the table, her tail going straight into the air, Geneva made herself as comfortable as she could.

"I'm ready for you, husband," she said. She clearly hadn't noticed what Nancy was doing behind her.

Releasing Steve's now rather firmed-up length, Nancy gave it a look and then smiled up at Steve. Then she winked at him and moved away.

Not wanting to wait, because he wasn't sure he could keep it up, Steve pivoted toward Geneva.

Laying his left hand down against the back of her shoulders, he grabbed her at the base of her tail with his right.

Casually, with little effort, he pinned Geneva to the table and then sank himself into her. His head and shaft pushing into and past her entry.

Grunting, Geneva seemed to push at him for a moment before she lay still against the table. By the time he was hilt deep in her, she didn't struggle at all.

It was as if she'd conceded to him completely.

"You're a monster," Valist said with a sneer. "And wed or not, you're still no mother. I'll agree to nothing. You'll have to burn down my city, and I think you'll run out of food or die to the Creep before that happens."

"Shut your mouth," Steve growled out, releasing Geneva's tail and then laying his hand on her hip. She was pushing her rear end up against him now. Her need to be dominated had apparently been met already.

Or his previous display of strength had already flicked her instincts into position.

Seems like Tigans and Lionans are rather similar after all.

"For all you know…" Steve said, drawing his hips back. There was a wet swish noise as his shaft glided free of Geneva's tight depths. "She'll be pregnant when I'm done. So shut your mouth and sit down. When I'm done, I'm going to kill your champion."

No one said anything else after that.

Holding Geneva's shoulder with his left hand, he moved his right hand around to her front and her privates. It forced him to bend over slightly to get his hand around her, but he knew it'd be worth it.

With all the practice he'd been getting with Lucia and Jaina lately, he'd been trying to up his game with them.

Laying his fingertips on each side of Geneva's clit, Steve pushed into her again.

Geneva took in a sudden and slow deep breath as he did it. It was obvious to everyone that she was suddenly much more into this.

Using a third fingertip, Steve lightly brushed it back and forth over the Lionan's hooded clit as he started to push in and out of her.

Geneva squirmed slightly to one side, and Steve immediately pushed down a bit harder on her back, pinning her to the table.

"No," Geneva whimpered. "Flip me… flip me over. On my back."

Oh? Maybe Lionans aren't that similar to Tigans after all.

Pulling out of Geneva, Steve flipped her over onto her back with a thump.

Then he moved forward and thrust right back into her, even as her knees came up and her eyes found his.

Reaching down with his left hand, he laid his hand flat against Geneva's armor, and then he pushed down. Pinning her to the table again.

"Yes. I really like that," she purred at him.

Taking hold of her hip with his right hand, Steve began to thrust in and out of her. Her armor clicked and rattled each time he bottomed out against her, his hilt wedged tight in her lips.

Angling himself higher, he worked to rub the top of his shaft and groin against her clit. Of his wives, only Xivin could get off from pure penetration. Everyone else needed more work. And he was always willing to give it.

Squeaking, Geneva's thighs pressed in tighter around Steve's hips. Clearly, he was doing the right thing.

He panted as he worked himself back and forth against Geneva, the Lionan receiving him eagerly and clearly in what looked like the early stages of her very first orgasm. Steve was enjoying himself.

Geneva was also loud.

Very loud.

"Yes," she said, her hands coming up to clutch at his forearms. "Oh, yes."

Her actions and words called out to his ego and inflated it.

Finding himself rapidly climbing to orgasm, he tried to push harder at Geneva's hood with each thrust. He really wanted her to hit her peak before he finished.

Steve felt her tail curl partially around his hips, and her entire body began to shudder under him with each thrust.

Impregnate Geneva Bril?

No.

Yes. Yes!

Impregnate… impregnate Geneva.

Grunting, Steve pulled at the Lionan as he started to climax. He crammed himself as deep into her as he could while his shaft flexed.

Emptying into her.

Geneva's hands clamped down tight on his forearms as her walls did the same, her face turning a faint red. Her eyes were wide open, watching him.

Conception achieved.

Steve has gained notoriety for breaking the laws of the Lamals.

Steve has gained prestige for wedding a noble of the Lamals queendom.

Steve has gained prestige for impregnating a noble of the Lamals queendom.

Steve has gained prestige for impregnating a royal of the Lamals queendom.

Steve has gained the King of the Queen of the Jungle accolade.

Steve has gained the Noble Consort accolade.

With a soft exhalation, Steve pushed into Geneva one more time as his climax ended.

"I'm pregnant," Geneva said in a whisper. She looked shocked, excited, and terrified all at the same time.

Even though she was spread-eagled with a man between her thighs, Geneva turned and looked at Valist. She had all the pride and presence she'd always had about her. "I'm wedded, bedded, and pregnant. Time for your champion to die."

Pulling out of Geneva, Steve took in a slow breath.

She was pretty great, actually.

"Hey, if possible, send out whoever your second-best champion is," Steve said. "That way when you send out your best one after I kill the second, I can make the first blow me so I can keep her."

Queen Valist turned a deep dark red at that.

"You dare—"

"Actually," Steve said, interrupting Valist. He grabbed Geneva by her hands and helped her sit upright. "Send both out at the same time. I'll kill one, and the other can suck me clean. Then we can be done with this. Or maybe I just beat them both black and blue till they surrender and tag-team me."

Lucia sighed audibly, putting her chin in her hands. She'd sat at the table the entire time. Watching Geneva be had.

"I'll never get used to this, I think," she muttered.

Twenty-Three

Valist hadn't left the field, but one of the women she'd brought with her returned to the city.

She was apparently getting the second champion along with their gear.

Lucia had gone back to the camp, and Nancy had accompanied her.

Apparently, the idea of possibly watching more women go down on Steve was too much for the Fae. She'd apologized to Steve and left.

Not that he blamed her.

He didn't for a second believe he could have been as stoic as she'd been.

Though he'd been surprised that Nancy had gone with her. It seemed somewhat out of character for her.

Standing not far from Steve and Geneva were the queen and her two knights.

"I'm pregnant," Geneva murmured, staring off into the distance.

"Yup," Steve said. "I mean… that was the goal, wasn't it?"

"I… yes. It was. It's just so unexpected," Geneva said. "I thought… well, it doesn't matter what I thought. Does it? I'm a wedded expectant mother. Though… at least you're married to a princess… that'll make it easier to explain to her highness when we return to the capital."

"Yeah, no thanks," Steve muttered. "No reason for me to go."

Turning his head, Steve looked at the knight standing next to Valist.

He couldn't see much of her, since her helmet covered up her head, but she looked tall. Really tall. Taller than Hiren, Beati, Felisa, and even Siena.

Hey, Shitty Steve, how about you tell me about her?

Kimor Barra
Knight/Champion
Reindeerkin
Father: deceased

Mother: deceased

Royal Captain- captain of the royal guard.

Champion- one and true champion of the queendom of Hilanis

Noble Line- part of the nobility of the queendom of Hilanis

"I forgot to name them all traitors and condemned criminals," Steve said, turning back to Geneva. "Should I do that now or later?"

"Oh, yes. Ah... her champion, royal guards, and herself for now. If they had given in without forcing me to have my first time on a table, I wouldn't ask you to do that," Geneva said with a small head shake, turning her eyes to Steve. "Thank you, by the way. That... was unexpectedly pleasant."

"I mean, I try?" Steve asked. Clearing his throat, he got the attention of the queen and her champion. "Hey, I formally name you as a false queen, traitor to Lamals, and a condemned criminal. I name your champion all the same, as well as your royal guard and knights."

Both the queen and her knights stood stock still.

"You... how did you—you're the Blade of the Law?!" the false queen Valist asked, her voice going up an octave.

"Yup," Steve said. "And a zookeeper, bringer of justice, and whole bunch of other stuff. I also can murder knights with one hand while tearing their arms and legs off.

"So when I kill Kimor over there, or whoever else you send out with her, I imagine the other remaining champions will beg me to let them suck my dick in exchange for their lives.

"You don't get that option, Valist. Sorry. Gennie wants the pretenders to die if they don't bend the knee immediately."

The knight named Kimor was facing Steve head on now, her helmet turned completely toward him.

"Seriously," Steve said, thinking that maybe she was doubting him. "I broke four champions of Faraday down, and they all serve in my bedroom now. I killed three others. I think it was three."

"It was three," Geneva said.

"Tell you what, Kimor," Steve said. "If you want to come over here and give me a kiss, I'll let you earn your place in my bedroom later and spare you today.

"Or if you want, pull Valist's head off and I'll let you go completely."

The second knight with the queen eased herself between Kimor and Valist before Kimor could do anything.

By the time the champion had looked at the queen, as if to contemplate it, the knight had eased the queen away from Kimor.

"Seriously," Steve said. "We've got bigger issues to deal with, like the Creep. We should—"

A horn blasted, and several knights came storming out of the keep of Hilast. Numbering at least six, they immediately started heading for the meeting point.

"Huh, that's certainly more than one champion," Steve said. "Whatever. If that's what it'll take to get this done with.

"Go on back to camp, Gennie. I'll bring back the leftovers with me when I'm done."

Wasting no time, Steve began jogging to the far side of Valist, Kimor, and her knight. He watched the trio as he pulled his axe from its loop.

Geneva was already heading back toward the camp without question.

"Alright, you're not going anywhere Valist," Steve said. "I'm going to kill or use your champions, and I'm going to pop your head off when I'm done."

"Arrogant little man," hissed the false queen. "I'll have you begging me for mercy, which I'll only grant after you rescind your title adjudication upon me."

"Will I? Huh. Maybe I'll have Kimor use you as a pillow as she takes care of my needs," Steve said. "Then I'll let her spit up my seed on your face so you can dream of the taste of it before I cut your head off."

Giving his axe a light swish, Steve felt ready.

He wasn't trained in combat and he had no idea what he was really doing, but he felt ready.

With his strength and speed alone, he was confident he could easily overpower eight knights.

Before he realized it, though, all eight of Valist's knights had surrounded him in a circle. Even if he'd tried to do something about it, the end result would have been the same. Eight versus one meant a guarantee of being surrounded.

"Alright, could you all remove your helmets?" Steve asked. "I really don't want to kill the prettiest ones. If you could do that, and agree that I can claim any of you as a victory prize if I haven't killed you, I'll agree to this champion duel, eight versus one."

"Do nothing," Valist commanded before any of the knights could say anything. "And what do we get for the prize agreement?"

"Geneva will let you execute her," Steve said. "And if she fails to do so, she'll be named an oathbreaker, traitor, and condemned criminal. Which I think would effectively kill her anyways, wouldn't it?"

Valist laughed at that and flicked a hand at Steve.

"Fine, we agree," Valist said. "Remove your helmets."

All around him, the knights began pulling off their helmets.

It required them to remove a latch at the back so they could open up a plate and then slide it off their head. Mostly because of their antlers, he imagined.

Kimor turned out to be a golden-colored blond with dark blue eyes. She was, of course, far too pretty. It seemed to be a very common theme with knights.

The rest of the knights were all variations of that.

There was only one other woman who mildly interested Steve. She had dark brown hair, blue eyes, and a lovely face.

"Okay. Kimor and you," Steve said, pointing at the other woman. "I'm going to claim you two as prizes. The rest of you I'm just going to murder. You two try and stay out of my way till the end. I'd hate to harm you."

"Just kill him," Valist said. "Go."

Darting forward, Steve brought his axe around.

With an explosive pinging sound, it slammed through the raised sword of the knight in front of him. Bits of bronze shattered in every direction.

Unfortunately, the attempted block redirected Steve's axe.

Rather than connect at the neck of the knight, it hit the brow of her helmet.

And sheared right through it.

With a spray of blood and bone, the bronze-armored woman spun and went down in a heap.

Moving with the swing of his axe that threatened to keep him unbalanced, Steve went toward the closest knight.

He got a hand around her wrist that held her sword and pulled hard.

The knight shrieked as her arm was torn from its socket, and she took several steps away.

Falling back and out of the circle, Steve grinned. He wasn't afraid of combat anymore. Wasn't afraid of people getting the better of him.

There was little anyone could do to him if he got up close to them.

"Hey, this is yours," Steve said, cocking the severed arm and then throwing it forward.

The arm caught its one-time owner low at the thighs. Suddenly, the woman did a maximum-force face plant as the arm smashed into her, her knees bending the wrong way. Her wail cut off as her helmeted head slammed into the ground.

Looking at the remaining six knights, Steve picked out Kimor and the other one he wanted.

"Kimor, and you, stay back now," he said. "I really don't want to hurt my victory prizes."

All six of the remaining knights looked spooked, unsure how to proceed.

"Kill him!" Valist said. "Rush him at the same time!"

The knights leapt forward at Steve.

Reaching down, Steve picked up the sword that had been dropped by the severed arm. Unfortunately, he picked it up from the blade side as the hilt had been facing away from him.

Kimor was the closest, her blade whipping around towards him.

Dodging to one side, to her side in fact, he put a foot to her rear end and kicked. The big knight went tumbling away from him.

Whipping the hilt of the sword around like a club at the next knight, Steve caught her just under the jaw.

The guard of the sword blasted into the soft flesh and lodged itself against the inside of her cheek, the sword bending terribly with the force of it.

Gurgling, the knight fell to one side even as the next one came at Steve.

It was the other knight he wanted to keep.

She swung at him from one side to the other, not giving Steve much room to do anything.

Not wanting to damage her, Steve swung his axe at her blade and caught it at the midpoint.

Bronze fragments of the weapon blew out and peppered the knight who was coming on next.

Screaming in pain, the woman immediately went down to her knees, her hands pressed to her breastplate as if she could get to her torso through it.

"I told you to stay back." Steve grabbed the wrist of the knight he was going to keep. "Listen to me or I'll just end you."

Pulling lightly, he yanked her off her feet and down to her knees. She dropped the shattered blade she'd been holding.

As gently as he could, he slapped the knight with an open palm.

Her head whipped to one side, the smack of his hand on her cheek sounding like a whip crack.

When he checked Kimor, he found she was just barely getting to her feet not far away.

Steve refocused on the last two knights and moved forward at them.

"I-I-I surrender!" said one of them, dropping her sword and holding up her hands.

"Fine, shut up and stay there," Steve growled, closing in on the last one.

Holding her sword up, the knight looked like she wasn't going to surrender or back down.

Steve stopped next to the woman who was trying to pull her breastplate off to get to her chest. The bronze fragments from the sword must have really messed her up. Blood was flowing down the front of her chest.

Reaching over, he wrapped a hand around her throat.

"Surrender," croaked the woman before he could fully close his hand. "I surrender. Help me."

Frowning, Steve sighed and then lightly tossed the woman toward the other who'd surrendered.

"If she lives, you live," Steve said. "She dies, you die. And you—"

Steve paused to look at the last knight standing.

"Give me a second to finish off your comrades. They're suffering," Steve said.

Turning his head down and to the side, Steve looked into the face of the woman with the hilt of a sword lodged in her throat and jaw. She was gurgling, likely drowning in her own blood.

There wouldn't be a way to save her.

He lifted his axe up and smashed the back of it down into the top of her head.

It crunched grotesquely as her skull caved in. She was instantly killed.

Moving over to the woman with only one arm, Steve was rather pleased to see she was dead.

He didn't want them to suffer; he just wanted them dead or out of the way.

"Alright, we can move on to you now," Steve said to the last knight.

Who promptly dropped her sword, fell to her knees, and held her hands up.

"Oh? Done? Alright," Steve said, then turned to look for Kimor and the other knight.

The one he'd slapped was kneeling not far, one hand to her cheek, looking very subdued.

Kimor was glaring at him, her sword held in her hands.

"I guess it's time for you to choose. Submit and become a prize, or get your head pulled off," Steve said. "Think on that for a second."

Looking to the one he'd slapped, Steve walked over and tapped her with the toe of his boot.

"Hey, submit or die," Steve said.

"Submit," murmured the woman.

Steve nodded at that, then turned to the two who had surrendered willingly.

"Submit or die," Steve stated.

"Submit," they both said, though both of them were now working to save the life of the one who'd been shotgunned by the bronze sword fragments.

"Okay, Kimor?" Steve asked, looking back at the big champion.

Panting softly, red faced, and looking extremely angry, Kimor was clearly considering her options.

"Right. You keep thinking on that, I'm going to go pull Valist's head off," Steve said.

The false queen hadn't been idle during all of this. She'd grabbed a sword from one of the women who had surrendered and was holding it in front of herself.

"Stay back, you filthy pigpen monster," hissed the queen. "Lamals would do well to—"

Steve closed the distance to the queen and casually batted the sword out of her hands. With a squeak, the false queen partially spun to one side from the force of the hit.

Grabbing her by an antler, Steve pulled upward and bodily lifted her into the air. Screaming at the top of her lungs. Valist flailed at Steve and his wrist.

He brought his axe around and neatly separated her head from her shoulders.

Holding on to her by the antler, Steve nodded.

"Alright, Kimor, time to decide," he said, looking back at the champion. Then he held up Valist's head. "Or you can join her."

Kimor shivered once with what looked like rage, then threw her sword down to the grass. Then she dropped to her knees.

"I submit," she said.

"Perfect. I claim all five of you as prizes for the time being," Steve said. He didn't plan on keeping all of them, but it was easier this way for the moment.

He didn't want to leave his prizes alone, which meant he had to get Geneva over here. At least until he figured out who to keep and had Nancy bind them.

Moving to an unobstructed view of Geneva's camp, Steve waved his axe at them to get their attention.

"She's dying—I'm sorry," said a woman from behind him. "I'm doing everything I can! I swear! I'm sorry!"

Looking back, Steve found the two knights kneeling next to a woman who was clearly fading fast.

"Fine," Steve commanded. "Keep working on her. Your life depends on it."

Steve pulled the canteen at his hip off and threw it over.

"Make her drink that, too," Steve said. "Might help, might not."

If she dies, she dies. I'm sure I can give her gear to someone else. Hopefully she'll have a chance to submit, though.

***

Geneva's soldiers were rapidly moving through the city. It wasn't going to take long to have it under wraps as there was no reason to support a dead monarch.

This was mostly to root out anyone who didn't belong.

Somewhat of a shame.

In the end, there weren't that many of the citizenry for me to take from Faraday. The soldiers are hers, too. I really only got the royal guard and the knights.

I'm getting ripped off, aren't I?

"With this done, it means we have to turn our attention back to the real problem," Lucia murmured. "The Creep."

"Indeed," Geneva said. "Though I'm uncertain how to handle that. My plans are moot, as I've mentioned before."

"Creep Witches," Steve said. He was watching Hiren question his new knights. He'd kept all of them in the end. "I just need to make more Creep Witches. I'll have that taken care of tonight.

"That'll keep the cities relatively safe. Doesn't solve the problem of the Creep itself, though."

"If… if you really can keep the cities safe," Geneva said, putting her hands behind her back. "That'd mean all we really need to do for the area is put together a fortification at the leading edge, garrison it, and have it ready to defend from threats. Internal and external. A wall behind the citadel wall, so to speak."

"Yep, I can have the cities kept safe. I'll parcel out three of my new knights to handle the city work after I have them converted," Steve said. Steve had added becoming a Creep Witch as part of the agreement Nancy had put on the knights.

He needed Creep Witches. Not knights.

"Then that's what we'll do," Geneva said. "I'll have all the mayors from Faraday, Hilast, and Rennis send their forces to the new location. They can start building it."

"Can use Creep Witches for that, too," Steve said. He was starting to just want an army of Creep Witches. His current plan was to take the entire royal guard he'd condemned from Hilast and Rennis and force them to become Creep Witches.

He wasn't going to take no as an answer, or let Geneva convince him otherwise.

Creep Witches were needed.

And he had a force of condemned criminals he could put under a contract with Nancy and use to his benefit.

"Do what you need to do," Steve said, glancing at the horizon. He had an hour or two before sunset. "I'm going to get my Creep Witches. Keep everyone away from my part of the camp, except the royal guard and knights from Hilast and Rennis. Those are all mine. Send them all my way. Tonight."

He walked away from where Lucia and Geneva would likely plan where to put down the fortress. It didn't concern him, and he really didn't have anything to offer.

Walking over to Hiren, he knew what he had to do.

All eight of his knights turned toward him as he approached.

"I want all eight of you to become Creep Witches tonight," Steve said. "If you volunteer for it, you stay with me. If you don't, I'm going to give you to Nancy to deal with as she sees fit."

All eight knights looked at the Wight who'd been standing there quietly.

She gave them a wide smile.

"I'm sure I can think of interesting ways to make use of you," she said.

Steve immediately got eight knights all volunteering to become Creep Witches at the same time.

"Great," Steve said, interrupting them. "Thank you for volunteering."

"I'm going to go get our tent set up next to the pit, since you'll be taking care of me tonight, Steve," Nancy said, then started to skip off. Looking far too excited for someone who was about to die.

By being choked to death. Something she desperately wanted to happen.

Crazy.

But... she's my crazy.

Twenty-Four

"Tomorrow?" Steve asked with a yawn.

"Tomorrow morning," Geneva said.

"Alright. Fine," Steve said with a bit of annoyance. He was tired of marching around. They'd been on the move all day, and he was spent. It'd only been two days since they'd put Hilast and Rennis back to order.

Not a soldier. Barely a farmer. This sucks. I want to just... go home.

"This is the best location," Geneva said, not for the first time. "It'll be the best place to set up our fortifications. All it'll take is some work here and there in the surrounding areas, close up some paths, and we'll be guiding any type of problem from the east right through here."

"Yeah, yeah, heard you the last time." Steve waved a hand at her. "Fight off bandits, Creeps, and whatever the hell else."

"My beloved consort, you're being a bit short," Lucia murmured softly, turning her head to catch him with her eyes. She was still sitting in the wagon with Xivin, even though they were stopped for the night. For whatever reason, she'd taken it upon herself to remain with the Elf if at all possible.

Checking a sigh, Steve glanced down at the grass beneath his boots.

"Sorry, tired of being away from home," Steve muttered. "Your home too, ya know, Gennie."

"I... I suppose that's true," Geneva said. "Well, after this fortification goes up, we can head back home. Most of the troops to be stationed here will be from Faraday, Hilast, and Rennis. I'd rather not spend any of the soldiers I brought with me here."

"Uh huh," Steve said. "If the witches are up for it, can they start building tonight?"

"I... don't see why not," Geneva said.

Steve nodded his head, then turned and found Hiren not far off. She'd become the nominal leader of his knights, which included everyone in the converted royal guard.

In the end he'd kept Hiren, Beati, Felisa, Siena, and Kimor of the converted knights and champions. The other three he'd left to protect Faraday, Hilast, and Rennis.

"Nancy," Steve said, looking toward his Creep Witch, mistress, and henchwoman.

"Yes?" she said, giving him a grand smile. Ever since he'd done what he'd promised and strangled her to death, she'd become unable to contain herself around others. It was very obvious she was completely his creature.

"I want all the Creep Witches spun up. Have them build a fort or something and—"

"I can guide them," Geneva said quickly.

"Fine, have Gennie guide them and get this done. I'm not just over this, I'm done with it," Steve said. "In fact... maybe I should just take my wagon and go home. This is stupid. I don't need to be here anymore."

"That's—" Lucia paused almost as soon as she started talking. "Actually, we really don't need to be here now. Do we?"

Lucia toward Geneva and looked to be considering the whole thing.

Geneva's face blanked out as if she'd been struck.

"No," she said after several seconds. "I guess... no. No, you're not needed here."

"Great. Leave the royal guard with an overseer, Gennie," Steve said. "Let's go home."

Geneva sighed at that and shook her head. "I can't. I must remain. I simply can't abandon my troopers here."

Closing his eyes, Steve turned his face to the sky.

"Okay, fine. Fine. Leave the royal guard here with Gennie," Steve said.

"And the bedroom knights?" Nancy asked.

"Coming with me. They're going to help me train up more Creep-Witch knights. Witch-knights," Steve said. "Huh. Knights who are made into Creep Witches. Witch-knights. Done, I like that."

"Still... bothers me that you can do that," Xivin said, shaking her head. "Though I'm quite glad to be married to you. It's wonderful to have such a strong husband."

Steve grunted at that.

"Whatever," he said. "So... that's it then? We're... done?"

"You're done," Geneva said. "I'll head home once we have this up and ready. In the meanwhile, I'll wish you safe journey, husband."

Huh… that's… unexpected.
Alright. Home… home to Nikki, then.

***

"This is much bigger than I expected," Hiren said softly from Steve's right.

When he looked over, he found the four other knights in line with her. They were all wearing their bronze armor, with their shields at their hips.

Bronze is really heavy, isn't it?
And let's be honest, they call themselves knights but they're not. Not really.
Breastplate, shoulder guards, forearm guards, waist protectors, and leg guards.
More like something from ancient Greek warfare. I wonder how they got to the term knight from that.
Wait… what was that? Ugh. Whatever. I don't care anymore.

"Won't be big enough, I'm afraid," Lucia said with a sigh. "We'll need to expand the house again to house your bedroom knights."

"They're not wives," Nancy said. "They can live separately. A garrison bunkhouse next door. I'll live there as well."

"Oh. Oh! Yes, that'd actually be preferable, wouldn't it?" Lucia commented and then laughed softly.

"Can't wait to get back to my forge," Ferrah said. Sitting atop the wagon and guiding it, she'd taken the place of Xivin, who had been dropped off at Filch on the way by. "Never leaving again. Not meant for travel."

Steve chuckled at that. Ferrah had truly been uncomfortable almost the entirety of the trip.

"Hated it completely, huh?" Steve asked.

"Well… not… not completely." Ferrah's cheeks turned a deep dark red.

"Such a soft-hearted Dwarf you are," Lucia said, looping an arm around Ferrah's shoulders. "Though I really do appreciate you. You're a wonderful conversationalist."

Really? Huh.
I can't get her to talk to me about anything.
Or maybe she's still figuring 'us' out. That'd make sense, wouldn't it?

I think it would.

"…easy to talk to," Ferrah said, still looking down at the oxen in front of them. The Centaur who'd carted them this far had gone back home in Filch, and the oxen had moved in to replace her.

It'd ended up being convenient since the oxen were due to be sent over to the farm anyways.

Steve heard it as soon as the bridge came down.

Nia singing her Steve song.

Before it'd even hit the grass, the small Siren was sprinting toward him. Her dress and hair flew out behind her as she pumped her little arms and legs.

Grinning, he could feel her song's power. It grew stronger and more powerful with every step she took toward him.

Of strength.

Indomitable strength that couldn't be brought down by anything. A pebble stuck in the way of a boulder but refused to move.

And wouldn't be moved.

"Steve!" Nia shouted. She flung her arms up even as she came at him.

Getting down to one knee, Steve opened his arms up to her. When she slammed into him at full speed, he stood up, slid his left arm under her butt, and planted her onto his hip.

"Welcome home!" the little girl shouted, then kissed his cheek. Her arms wrapped up around his neck and began squeezing the life from him. "I missed you, Daddy."

Without him wishing it, an entire slew of memories threatened him. Of a little girl hugging him in the same way, telling him she'd missed him. Growing up into a young woman, an adult, and then a mother herself.

Steve hadn't just had a daughter, but grandchildren.

And then corpses all around him. Blood pooling and filling the cracks between the paving stones. A soldier wearing a bright green surcoat and holding two bronze swords.

Before he could latch on to any of it, it was all gone in the blink of an eye.

Missing a step, Steve almost lost his footing and went tumbling. Only Hiren's hand catching his elbow kept him from doing so.

"Whooooa!" Nia said, and then she laughed, leaning back to look him square in the face. "You're silly."

"I... I guess I am at that," Steve said, not understanding why he felt completely unhinged at the moment. He was angry and despairing at the same time.

Though the feelings were fading quickly.

"I'm going to be an older sister," Nia said.

"I know," Steve said with a chuckle.

"Will you be an older sister for my child as well?" Lucia asked, leaning over the side of the wagon and running her fingers through Nia's hair.

"Aun' Lusa? You're having a baby?" Nia turned toward Lucia, her voice going up in volume excitedly.

"I am. Will you be their older sister?" Lucia asked, grinning at the girl.

"Yes! I will be older sister to everyone!" Nia said, holding her arms out above her head.

"Good!" Lucia said with a laugh even as the wagon moved ahead to cross the bridge.

Steve and everyone on foot waited behind, giving it the space it needed to get over.

"You're staying home?" Nia asked.

"Yep! For as long as I can," Steve said. Then he pointed at Hiren and the others. "I need to build some houses. One for Nancy and my knights."

"Oooh," Nia said, looking at the women. "You're all really pretty. You can be my auns."

One and all, Nancy and the knights smiled at that.

Then Nia looked at Steve and put both her hands to his face.

"They're my auns," Nia said. "They're pretty. And big."

"Yes. They're pretty and big," Steve said. "But they can't be your aun—"

"They're my auns," Nia repeated, interrupting him. "My auns."

Sighing, and grinning at the Siren, Steve nodded.

"I'll make sure they're your aunts," Steve said.

"I'm already your aunt. I'm Aunt Nancy," Nancy said, then held her arms open to the little girl. "Can I hold you?"

"Yes! Hold me!" Nia practically dove out of Steve's arms and into Nancy's. The little girl immediately grabbed hold of Nancy's face and stared into her eyes. "You're pretty, Aun' Nanshe. Really pretty."

"Thank you. My mother tried very hard for me with what we had," Nancy said, grinning at the little girl.

Looking ahead, Steve practically forgot about everyone else.

Standing there were Nikki and Gwendolin.

Smiling at him, Gwendolin barely waited for him to cross the bridge before she intercepted him. Her arms were tight around him, her lips pressed hard to his.

Pulling him bodily to one side, the Siren began to hum as she kissed him. Her hands pressed against his back and held him close.

It was, of course, her Steve song.

And it made him almost dizzy. It all did. This was so far out of character for her that he didn't know what to do.

Her song had changed as well. Last time he'd heard it, there'd been a need for intimacy in it.

This time, however, it was overwhelming sexual need, lust, and screaming, shrieking, quivering desire all blown out with absolute dedication and love.

The feeling that if he didn't throw her down into the grass and maul her right here, she'd do it to him instead.

Breaking the kiss, Gwendolin stopped humming and laid her lips to his ear. Then she kissed it.

"Welcome home, my husband," she whispered. "I'm coming for you tonight and taking you away. Before Nikki, after Nikki, and maybe a third time."

Kissing his ear again, Gwendolin turned to the side, slipped her arm through his, and began leading him over to Nikki.

The Faun was watching him with a smile.

It was in her eyes that he saw she wasn't happy, however. As well as in the way she was holding herself.

She looked unsure of how to proceed, but trying to push on.

"Welcome home, my dearest," Nikki said, reaching out and laying her hands on Steve's face after a momentary hesitation.

Gently pulling on him, she guided his head down and kissed him tenderly.

She broke away some several seconds later and laid her brow to his.

"Please… come with me?" she pleaded.

"Of course," Steve said.

Nikki took his hand in hers and led him into the house.

"I wanted to apologize," Nikki said almost before she'd closed the door to their room.

"Uh? Okay. What for?" Steve asked. "Did something happen while I was gone?"

Moving over to the bed, he sat down on the edge of it.

"Hmm? No, no. Nothing happened," Nikki said as she laced and unlaced her fingers together. "I'm apologizing because I didn't… didn't really say goodbye to you. I was mad and… and I didn't handle it very well."

"Oh, yeah, well… I could have probably gone about the whole thing in a better way," Steve said.

"Maybe?" Nikki said in a voice that lacked confidence. "Probably not. It wasn't that you didn't approach it well. It was just… the whole thing.

"I didn't like any of it. Geneva's going to pull you away from the farm far more often, I think. To the point that you won't really… be… here."

"Well, now that I took care of what she needed, I can probably lie low for a while. It's not like I have to go back out there for a while," Steve said.

Nikki shrugged her shoulders, her arms folded atop one another in front of her.

"Did it go well?" she asked.

"Very," Steve said. "Every city that was supposed to be hers is hers. They're up north building a fortification and garrison."

"Oh," Nikki said, walking slowly over to Steve. "That's good then. That'll help control the area. Especially with the Creep having come back."

"Yeah," Steve said. "We had an entire wave of them to fight off at one point. We were trying to save a city. It been alright down here?"

Sitting down on the bed next to him, Nikki nodded.

"Well enough," she said. "There's been a fairly constant and steady stream of zombies at night. Nothing too terrible. They just… stand there unless we pull them into the moat.

"Some of the guards take it as a game. They use long poles and pull them into the water. They make little bets on how long they'll burn and — well, anyways. Yes, everything is going really well.

"Ina's up at the outpost. She's been working hard to get it into a manageable location. Farm and outpost both.

"Misty and Shelly are still both at Filch. They've been tied up there for a little while. Linne's been sending messengers back and forth. Demanding food and other things."

Raising his eyebrows at that, Steve waited. It sounded like there was more to it.

"And?" he asked after several seconds.

"And…" Nikki said and then paused. Leaning over, she laid her head down on Steve's shoulder. "And you were right. We sent them a little bit of food with their first demand. We claimed it was all we could spare. I figured they'd take it and go elsewhere."

My poor little optimist.

Steve lifted his arm and gently laid it around Nikki's shoulders.

"They came back again, demanding we give them all the food we had, regardless of what we could or couldn't spare," Nikki said.

"Uh huh," Steve said. That didn't sound very surprising to him. In fact, it seemed like a guarantee given Linne's personality the last time he'd seen her.

"We couldn't really give her anything at that point," Nikki said. "All of our excess has been spent trying to keep everyone in Filch fed."

Of course it has.

Because the moment I left, you took it up as your personal crusade to care for everyone.

"I'm sorry, I know. I know," Nikki said, taking Steve's arm in her hands. "Shelly sent a note that she had a large number of people who were about to go without food.

"And with the Creep having vanished, everything returning to normal, I thought we could spare it. Have them come work some fields in return for their meals."

Mm, at least that's better than just giving it to them.

"I'm not sure you saw, but I expanded all the fields. We still have a lot of room left to grow, but I used all the workers to get more planted. They'll come back when it's time to harvest and collect their pay. In food," Nikki said. "We have more than enough food now, and everyone's fed."

"But our personal trade fell out the bottom, didn't it?" Steve said.

"I... yes," Nikki said, shaking her head and looking at her hooves. "No one wants to trade for food; they'd rather come work for it. So many that the outpost has to be used to assist in providing work for them.

"I'm sorry. I thought it was just... you being the brute, my brute... I never... never thought it would turn out like this.

"Now we can't really go back and... yeah."

"Well." Steve leaned over and kissed Nikki's brow. "Thankfully, with the inclusion of Faraday, Hilast, and Rennis, we'll probably start getting trade up and going again. It'll take longer for villages and smaller things to get back into motion, but... should be moving."

"Oh, yes. Good," Nikki said, then sighed. "I'm sorry. I didn't think doing good things like feeding people would just... sink everything like that."

"That bad?" Steve asked.

"They wouldn't even sell me anything for food," she said. "There's no value in food when everyone has enough to eat and it's readily available."

"I... yeah. Yeah. Well, that'll end quickly enough," Steve muttered. "We'll just have to... well, I dunno. We'll figure out something. I certainly don't have an answer to it, though."

"I hired a bunch of craftswomen onto the farm instead," Nikki said. "And a... a leatherworker. I mentioned it to you?"

"Oh? Good," Steve said. "That's at least a good answer for the meantime."

"Exactly!" Nikki said. "I'm so glad you feel that way. So glad!"

"I mean, it makes sense. We need leather, you don't really like working with it, so... leatherworker," Steve said. Then he thought about his "bedroom knights." "Speaking of... additions."

"Yes, I noticed them. Witch-knights." Nikki leaned to one side and looked up at him with a grin. "Something new?"

"Kinda," Steve said. "They were all champions. I made them, uh… service me… or die. It was mostly to humiliate their cities into surrendering and—why are you laughing?"

Nikki laughed for a short while longer, then patted his arm.

"My brute, you sweet, silly man. Only you would be able to force a champion, on her home turf, to do that," Nikki said.

"Well, whatever. They're mine now. I made them get bitten, let them die, then ran them through a pit filled with watering-can water. I also did it to the entire royal guard of Hilast and Rennis. They were traitors," Steve said. "So now I have a good-sized force of Creep Witches."

"Previously, I think I would have bristled at the idea of making more… soldiers… so to speak. But it seems you were right about Linne. She wasn't going to back down, nor was she going to take no for an answer," Nikki said. "Anything else I need to know?"

"Not that I can think of?" Steve said, then shrugged. "Geneva is up north building her fort. Xivin is at Filch. Jaina went to the outpost."

"Okay," Nikki said. Then she leaned up and kissed his cheek. "How about… how about you show your lonely Faun that you love her?

"She made a mistake… and she's been lonely with only her regret for company. She's very sorry for how she acted, and she shouldn't have sent you away as she did."

Grinning, Steve laid a hand on her shoulder and eased her into the bed, immediately beginning to kiss up along her neck and jawline.

"Ooooh, yes," Nikki said with a soft laugh. "Show your Faun lots of energy and attention. She feels terrible and really needs some reassurance."

Steve was going to do just that.

Twenty-Five

Groaning, Steve slowly drifted out of a deep sleep.
His head felt heavy.

He was also sweaty, the sheet was sticking to him, and he felt like his night shirt and shorts were twisted around him.

The fact that Gwendolin was sprawled over him, her hair partially draped over his face, didn't help any of that at all.

Ugh. Sleeping next to Gwen isn't so fun.

Like sleeping with a heater.

The very naked and lovely Siren shifted around, then pulled her hair back behind her head. Turning his head slightly, he found Gwendolin staring up at him. Her green eyes watched him like a dog at point.

"You okay?" Steve asked, reaching up with his hand to run his fingertips through her hair.

"Yes," Gwendolin said, then smiled at him. "Just… enjoying my new life. You were very… eager… for me. In a way I didn't expect."

Steve grinned at the memory and shrugged his shoulders. Gwendolin had done exactly what she'd told him she would. She'd collected him before Nikki took him to bed, then again after Nikki. Except after the second time, he'd just stayed with Gwendolin in her bed and did his best to keep her awake for most of the night.

"What can I say? I'm a big fan apparently," Steve said. Then he leaned down and kissed her.

The equally sweaty and sticky Siren snuggled up to his side and kissed him back. A few seconds passed before she eased his head back.

"Oooh, so I'm discovering," Gwendolin said, and then she sighed. "I have to go take care of Nia, though. She's probably running around with Ryker and hasn't even bothered to eat anything."

"You sleep a bit longer," Steve said, his hand running along Gwendolin's side. He really was a fan of hers. From her looks to her song, to her being a caring mother, she fit something Steve needed. "I'll go get her fed. She need a bath or anything today?"

"No. She doesn't. You will? Really?" Gwendolin asked, smiling at him.

"Yeah. Sleep in, Mama. Daddy's got it," Steve said, then patted her hip. "You get some rest. You're making us a baby, aren't you?"

"Yes… yes, I am," Gwendolin said with a wide smile. Then she took the sheet and pulled it up to her chin. "Okay… I'll… sleep a bit longer. I'm… making a baby, after all."

"Good," Steve said. Then he kissed her quickly and slid out of bed.

His goal was simple.

Get a quick bath in Misty's inside pool, get dressed, and get Nia fed.

By the time he got out of the house freshly cleaned and dressed, Gwendolin the beautiful and womanly Siren was snoring like it was her job.

No sooner had he got the door closed behind him, Steve was searching his farm and its fields. Walking out into the morning sun while stretching his arms above his head, Steve realized it was just past dawn by a minuscule amount.

Nia wasn't far away, running through the grass with Ryker chasing after her, the dog ever doing as it was told. Giggling the entire time, the small girl seemed to have no cares in the world.

Feed Nia, start working on a place for the knights to sleep.

That thought popped into his head when his eyes fell on the massive lean-to that held all five knights and Nancy. Five of those six people were sleeping.

Felisa was apparently on duty, as she was sitting on a stump not far away, watching everything. Her head turned his way, and her eyes leapt to him.

Raising a hand toward her, Steve kept moving towards Nia. He had a job to do, and he wanted to take care of it correctly.

"My lord," Felisa said, coming up next to him. "Do you have any needs I can attend to?"

In other words, can I service you?

She's… the oddest one of the bunch. She always volunteers, always wants it, and volunteered to fight me only to immediately surrender herself to me.

What… what is she again?

Felisa Cana
Witch-Knight
Banshee
Property of Steven Bril
Father: deceased
Mother: deceased
Traitor- betrayed her nation
Condemned Criminal- has been condemned as a criminal
Depraved Predator- lives on the suffering of others
Reborn- living dead
Sellout- willingly became the property of another
Prostitute- willingly sold herself for gains
Knight- one of the five knights of Steven Bril
Black-magic contractor*- vile magic enthusiast *This title is hidden.

The hell is a Banshee?

"What's a Banshee?" Steve asked, not responding to her previous question.

"I... I'm a Banshee. We, or I, ah... we're a type of Undead, I guess? We survive on the... the deaths of others," Felisa said. He wasn't even looking at her, and he could tell she was staring at him. That her cold, dark brown eyes were boring down hard on Steve.

"Oh, so you're like Nancy," Steve said. "Is that why you wanted to die?"

"My death was amazingly beautiful, and... it was delicious," Felisa said, her tone becoming rather strange.

"Uh huh. So you're crazy like her, but you feed on death. Right," Steve said. "How often do I need to feed you?"

"Once or twice every six months, if it's sentient," Felisa murmured, her voice becoming much softer. "Animals work, but that's more of a monthly thing."

"Fine," Steve said. "You can slaughter one of the rabbits when you're hungry. They're breeding far faster than Jaina seems to have expected them to."

"Okay," Felisa said. "Thank you, my lor—"

"Yeah, no more of that," Steve said. "I'm Steve. Call me anything else at your own risk."

"I... okay, Steve," Felisa mumbled.

"Daddy!" Nia shouted, apparently just having noticed Steve was headed her way.

She turned and began to run straight at him.

When she was close enough, he reached down and grabbed her, picking her up and settling her on his hip.

"Hey there," Steve said with a grin. He couldn't begin to explain how being called Daddy made him feel like the world was better. "Mama said you need to eat something. What do you want?"

"Uhm… can… can I have apples?" Nia asked.

"Apples? We have apples?" Steve asked. He hadn't remembered there being apples on his farm.

"Ena planted them," Nia replied with a laugh. Then she pointed to one side. "See?"

"Ena…? Oh! Enart? She's alive?" Steve asked, looking where Nia had pointed.

"Yes! Ena came. Said she won't be my aun' but she'll help out," Nia said.

In other words, she wants to stay and utilize the farm, and provide for it, but not officially be wed to me.

That's fine. I've got more than enough to keep me busy anyway.

As he walked over to the apple trees that were suspiciously large and overflowing with apples, Steve didn't really know what to say.

"They got big fast," Nia said, and then she pointed to an apple. "That one!"

The apple she wanted was higher than Steve could reach.

Felisa jumped up and snatched it off the branch. Landing with a thump and a light clatter as her armor resettled, she held the apple out to Nia.

"Thank you me, Aun'!" Nia said and took the apple, immediately biting into it.

"That's it? That's all you want for your breakfast?" Steve asked.

Nia nodded and then started wriggling every which way in his arms.

"Down please," she said.

Getting the hint, Steve put her down. As soon as her feet hit the grass, Nia was off and running, giggling and holding her apple above her head like it was a victory prize.

"Cute little girl," Felisa said softly. "Reminds me of my nieces."

"Uh huh," Steve said. "How long you been up?"

"Only a few hours," Felisa said. "Siena had the early morning watch. I'm to wake everyone once the sun is a palm's width from the horizon."

"Great," Steve said. "You can help me with your cabin then. Can't have you sleeping in that lean-to."

Steve walked toward where he stored his logs, wanting to see what he had to work with.

Camden better have kept it stocked, or I'm going to get pissy. I told him to keep it stocked for me.

When he turned the corner around the back of his cabin, Steve found someone he didn't know.

A woman was standing behind a table, diligently working at shoving a rather large wooden-handled spike through a thick piece of leather.

She looked up from her work, and Steve found himself staring at an extremely delicate and pretty woman with shining blue eyes and platinum-blond hair that came down to her elbows.

A single long white horn came up from the middle of her forehead and angled itself toward the sky.

In every way, she looked fragile. Made of beautifully spun glass that needed to be put upon a shelf and taken care of.

"Oh, hello," said the woman with a gentle smile. "You must be Steve."

Even her voice was light and gentle.

She set her work down on the table and held her hand out across it.

"Yeah, that's me," Steve said, taking her hand and shaking it once.

Ah, the leatherworker Nikki brought on. I wonder what kind of race she is to have a horn.

"Delighted to meet you," said the woman with a wide, sweet smile. "I'm Airlea Korinna. I look forward to our wedding night, though I think it would be best if we got to know each other first."

Ah! I get it now!

That's why Nikki brought it up the way she did. She was happy with how accepting of the situation I was. Okay, I get it now.

I probably should have asked more questions when she mentioned it. I just... didn't think about it.

Whatever. At least she's pretty and has a useful skill.

Steve smiled and nodded at that.

"I'd prefer it that way," he agreed. "I wouldn't want to rush into it, not really understanding each other."

"Oh, good. I'm so glad to hear that," Airlea said. "You're such an understanding and kind man. I never thought I'd be so lucky."

Airlea stood up, and Steve found he was breathless.

Airlea wasn't human.

From the waist down and backward, she was a horse.

The... fuck?

She's a unicorn.

A unicorn. Wasn't there a... Shit. Shit, shit.

She's from Filch!

Airlea was rather small, however. Her height was only a little better than Jaina's. Her hind quarters weren't that large either.

He'd assumed she was a human because she'd been sitting behind a table and seemed normal sized. She'd just been lying down with her belly flat on the ground.

Walking up to Steve, the Unicorn wrapped her arms around him and gave him a tight hug.

"Thank you so much, Steve," Airlea said. "You have no idea how many of my kind end up old and very much alone. Thank you for being so open-minded and willing to take me in. Nikki sang your praises up and down, but I still didn't quite believe her."

He looked across Airlea's back and ended up staring down at her other "back," which was that of a very tiny horse. She had short, soft-looking white fur that ran all the way down to her platinum-blond tail.

"Yup," Steve said, settling his arms around Airlea in return. He didn't have it in him to reject her or send her back. "Yup. Not a problem. We'll make it work one way or another."

Airlea's tail swished back and forth at that, and she gave him a little bit tighter of a hug for a second. Then she released him and went back behind the table. Lying down on the grass, she continued to smile at him even as she picked up her tools.

"You're a very kind man, Steve, my future husband," Airlea said. "I'm truly grateful to you. It's also rather nice to be out on a farm such as this. It's lovely to be outside. Filch was truly starting to weigh on my heart."

Even as she spoke, Airlea rapidly stitched the leather pieces together with only occasional glances downward. She seemed determined to keep her eyes on Steve.

"I definitely feel ya there," Steve said, scratching at his shoulder. He felt really awkward right now, and like a scumbag. He didn't want to have anything to do with Airlea, but he didn't want to hurt the poor thing either. She seemed incredibly kind and pure hearted. "Cities and me don't seem to get along."

"Yes," Airlea said, nodding her head at that and smiling all the while. "Oh! I made a set of leather armor for you. I stitched in a number of those little... plates... Ferrah had lying around. As well as those scales I found in a bag for the smaller areas, and to link it together. It took quite a bit to punch through the scales.

"Both the plates and scales seemed quite strong. I felt like it would give you good freedom of movement but much more protection than just leather. It's in the chest at the foot of your bed."

She... made me Lamia-scale and steel leather armor.
I... okay.
I'm... going to be banging a Unicorn. Okay.
I can do this. It's just like Jaina, just... a bit more. Okay. Okay. Yes. I can do this.
Easy.
I'm going to bed her and make her feel like the most well-loved Unicorn there ever was.
Sex her so hard she can't even stand up.
I bet I can really pull at her, too.

Steve smiled at that, genuinely moved by her concern for him. Leaning across the table, he kissed her on the cheek.

"Thanks, Airlea. I'm going to get to work," Steve said. "I'll see you later."

"Of course," Airlea said, watching him as he walked away.

When he made it to his log pile, Steve had nearly forgotten why he'd come over here to begin with.

"You're a very open-minded man," Felisa said from beside him.

"Yep, that's... that's me," Steve said. Apparently, he hadn't been acting too strange. Which was a blessing in and of itself. He'd been almost positive he was probably acting like a nut-ball.

That or they don't know me well enough yet.

Sighing, Steve grabbed a log off his stack and began dragging it off.

***

As he stared out at his fields, Steve felt far better than he had in a long while. Being able to work on his home, his farm, was considerably more enjoyable than wandering around.

He wasn't made for that lifestyle, it would seem.

"You look like you're feeling better."

Smiling, Steve turned his head to find Nikki taking her small, hopping steps toward him.

"And then some," Steve said. "There's just something about our farm. Our home. It... makes me feel better just being here. More so being able to work on it. To build something for us."

"I could certainly see that having an appeal for you, my brute." Nikki came to a stop next to him.

They were in nearly the furthest corner of the fields. From here he could see almost the entire layout of his land.

While many more fields were planted and being worked since he'd last looked, there was still a considerable amount of open grass.

"Going to build that water tower tomorrow," Steve said. "With the amount of water we're using, we really should have a reservoir available for emergencies. That and I want my shower back. Cold or not."

"Yes. That'd be a good goal to accomplish," Nikki said. "Though I'm not so sure about the shower. The last one we took was long and cold."

Laughing at that, Steve reached out to wrap an arm around Nikki's hips and drew her in close.

"Yes, but it was the same night a young Faun tempted me into her bed." Steve leaned down to nuzzle the side of her face. "Haven't left it since."

Nikki laughed softly at that and then sighed, leaning into him.

"Truly? You haven't left it?" Nikki asked.

"I was in it last night, wasn't I?" Steve asked with a laugh. "I mean, admittedly Gwen came and stole me away, but you get my point."

"Yeah," Nikki said. "I guess... maybe I'm just being silly. Insecure, I suppose. We separated in such a poor way and... and you're back now, and it feels right. But... Lucia is pregnant and I'm not, and... I feel like I made a mess of all this. Like my little temper tantrum put some distance between us. Like now you're going to go to Lucia and not me."

Truth be told, he'd almost gone to Lucia's bed last night. He'd gotten so used to simply being with the Fae every night that he'd almost gone on autopilot alone.

In fact, he couldn't even deny he'd had a moment of regret that he wasn't going to Lucia's bed. She always treated him to an evening of delights, no matter what had happened in the day.

She'd never send me away, would she?

Frowning, Steve realized a conflict would be coming from this. One he probably couldn't stop unless he deliberately forced himself to push Lucia back a step.

Except he wasn't sure he wanted to push Lucia a step back.

She spoiled me.

Figured out me and my wants. Then brought me close, lured me into her bed, and spoiled me rotten. Spoiled me rotten while bending Gennie, Ferrah, Xivin, Jaina, and Nancy into her game. They all happily did whatever she asked, especially if it came to me and the bedroom.

How often did she bring 'entertainment,' as she called it, for me and our bed? Jaina never complained. Nor did Gennie or Nancy.

Or even Ferrah.

And... do I even care that she did that to me? Or am I flattered that she worked out how to bring me in?

I liked everything she did.

Enjoyed all of it.

Want more of it.

The more he thought about it, the more it felt like his relationship with Nikki was far more traditional, or perhaps slightly in her favor.

When he didn't get his way, he'd just let it go and get on with it.

Except the one time he'd disagreed with Nikki about their direction, she'd pushed away from him and sent him out into the wilds of the world with little more than a pat on the back.

What he had with Lucia was her working him over for her own gains and ends. Though the whole thing felt extremely in his favor and weighted towards his personal needs.

With that in mind, he unsurprisingly actually preferred Lucia.

She wound him up, put him on the path she wanted, and rewarded him for everything he did.

And when he didn't do what she wanted, when he didn't do as she asked, she'd simply let it go and start drowning him in attention again.

It'd only happened a few times that he hadn't wanted to do what she'd wished, but every time it happened, she'd simply moved right past it as if it didn't bother her at all.

And when I didn't do what Nikki wanted me to, she ran off, avoided me.

Steve couldn't help but feel like perhaps he was being petty. But he couldn't change the fact that he did feel some hurt over the way Nikki had dismissed him previously.

Or at least, how he felt like she had.

"I really am sorry for avoiding you before you left," Nikki murmured softly. "I just... I really didn't like what you were doing. I disagreed with it, and I felt like I couldn't support it.

"So I didn't want to see you."

Ah... so... she did avoid me.

She did distance me, to a degree.

Steve didn't know how to respond to that. Realistically, he knew it wasn't that big a deal. That there would likely be much larger hurdles to overcome in the future.

That this was nothing.

Yet, he still couldn't quite get his mind past it.

He felt hurt.

And he wanted to see Lucia, if only to let her soothe it for him. Because he knew she'd be able to peel him apart, figure out what he needed, and give it to him.

Except that would just make everything so much worse.

"Don't know what to say to that," Steve murmured, coming to a semblance of a decision. "I can't deny that it hurt me. That there's a part of me that's still hurt, even if I feel like I probably shouldn't be. Like it's nothing.

"But I do feel it.

"As far as Lucia goes… well, I went to your bed last night, you'll remember, not hers."

"I… okay," Nikki said. "Okay. I can work with that. I guess it doesn't help that she's pregnant. And I'm… well, I'm not."

Steve nodded at that. He'd wanted to impregnate her a while back, but he'd not felt the desire to do so since their last encounter.

"Geneva's pregnant, too," Steve said. He didn't want that surprise to hit her later.

"I heard," Nikki said, her tone growing flat. "Lucia, Gwendolin, and Geneva are all pregnant. It would seem everyone in Lucia's sphere of influence is getting what they want, and no one from my circle is."

"Really shouldn't think of it like that," Steve said. "There are no factions. We're all part of the farm."

Nikki didn't respond to that, but she did push in closer to Steve.

"Let's go have dinner. Privately," Nikki said. "Maybe I can help to ease some of that hurt you're feeling afterward."

"Sure," Steve said, all the while contemplating how he could get over to see Lucia tonight.

Twenty-Six

Steve tilted his head to the side. He couldn't really figure out what he was looking at.

It looked a lot like a boat to him, but it didn't really fit with anything his mind registered as a boat.

"I guess it's more like... a boat that's been merged with a raft," he muttered, then sighed. "A raft with walls."

"Or something of that nature," Lucia said, standing next to him along the riverbank. "Clearly it was built for the purpose of running the river against the current. It's no wonder it doesn't exactly look like a boat."

One of their hunting parties had spotted the vessel and immediately reported back, going straight to Lucia to let her know about it.

The Fae had found Steve, and the two had gone looking to find it.

From here, he could see a number of women all working on tasks and projects on the shore, and on the raft itself. They looked to be dressed as commoners, but there was a sharpness to their work.

Almost as if they'd at one point served in the military.

I wonder how the southeastern Lamals territories are doing. They probably got it just as bad as we did. Right? Or did my little river experiment change their fortunes that drastically?

"Obviously, it came from downriver," Lucia said. "That should still be Lamals territory, but it'll come up against our southern neighbors. Odistran."

Steve nodded at that. He didn't really know who their neighbors were.

He didn't know much of anything.

"Oh! That'd actually be something worth checking," Lucia said. "If they're in contact with Odistran, they might be able to pass along a letter to the Fae courts. Odistran borders on the summer court's spring lands. I really do have to report back on my current status."

"Uh huh," Steve said.

"Consort? Make it happen for me?" Lucia asked, her left hand sliding up along his waist toward the middle of his back. Her fingers lightly tickled over him.

He was about to agree out of hand and make it happen for her.

But then, he had a strange thought. This was something Lucia really wanted to happen. It was something she'd talked about repeatedly.

Getting in touch with the courts.

His conversation with Nikki came back to him. How she'd handled it when he'd disagreed with her.

What would happen if I said no to Lucia?
Would she react the same way Nikki did?

"No," Steve declared. "I don't want you to report in to the courts."

"Oh? Hmm," Lucia said, her tone clearly moving in a disappointed direction. "Consort, I really would like to do that, though. I can't even begin to express how important this is."

"I don't want you to," Steve said, deciding to push. "Sorry, butterfly."

Lucia sighed, then leaned over into him and kissed his cheek. This was followed by her hand continuing to stroke and pet his back.

"As you wish, my beloved consort," Lucia said. "Though I do hope to change your mind in the future. It's very important to me. Very, really, extremely important to me. I really do need to check in. And—"

"No," Steve said, simply cutting her off. He really wanted to press her into a corner on this one.

"I understand," Lucia said, sidling in closer to him and pressing her hip to his. "Well, shall we find their camp and figure out what they want with us? I'm not exactly keen on the idea of them wandering around in an area that could easily be described as our territory."

And... that's it?
She just lets it go and continues on? That's... that's it?

"Is it really that important to you?" Steve asked.

"Yes, Steve, my consort, it really is," Lucia said. "I won't deny I'm rather angry and frustrated with you right now. I can't even begin to understand why you'd forbid such a thing... In fact, I'd almost say you're doing it to spite me."

There was no hiding the fact that she was angry with him. Upset, even.

But that hadn't impacted the way she treated him at all.

"Okay, I'm sorry," Steve said. He wanted to back up and immediately fix things. "If we have the possibility of reaching out, we will."

"Wait, really?" Lucia said, turning her head to peer up at him.

"Yes, really."

"Hmm," Lucia said, then smiled at him, her nose wrinkling. "Maybe I should tell you more often when you annoy me."

"I'd prefer it. I'm not a mind reader," Steve said. He suddenly felt a whole lot better about Lucia. Even if she was angry at him. Frustrated with him. Even when she couldn't understand him and thought he was just goading her.

She still showed her love for him and didn't just ice him out.

"A good point," Lucia said, then smacked Steve on the rear end. "I'll be sure to voice my grievances as well as my desires. Now, how shall we do this? We can't let them remain in our lands like this without reaching out to them."

"Use the witch-knights," Nancy said off to Steve's left side. "It's their job."

"Good thought," Lucia mused, nodding her head. "I'd think... Felisa, Siena, and Kimor?"

"Yes," Nancy said. "Hiren and Beati can remain here to protect Steve with me."

Since becoming a Creep Witch, Nancy had been practicing her craft every evening. With Jaina, the Creep Witches on the farm, or the witch-knights. Every night for her was practice if it wasn't sleeping with Steve.

"Hell with that," Steve said. "Go get the witch-knights. We'll all go together. Between the eight of us, we should be able to handle anything."

Steve pulled his axe from its loop and let the head of it rest on the ground.

Nancy turned and vanished in a second, disappearing into the vegetation.

"For a while," Lucia said, pulling the unstrung bow off her back. "I truly believed I'd made her my own creature."

Reaching out, she looped her bowstring into the nock on the lower limb of her bow. Then she put it down against the grass on the side of her ankle. Pulling the string taught, she sighed.

"She really is completely yours, though," Lucia said. "I'm thankful she never pretended otherwise. Did she relay anything truly embarrassing back to you about me?"

Stepping forward with her left foot, Lucia pulled the belly of the bow up against the back of her left thigh. Then she pulled on the back of it, the belly flexing around her leg.

Working expertly, she bent the bow into the correct shape while pulling with her hands and easily flicked the bow string into its position.

"Apparently you really want me to mark you," Steve said. "She told me you wanted me to p—"

"That's enough of that," Lucia said, interrupting him. Then she coughed lightly into her hand before pulling her bow up. "Yes, I remember that conversation. And I'd like you to forget that—"

"I'll do it to you," Steve said. "Tonight."

Lucia took in a slow breath, then let it out.

"Okay," she said softly. "By the lake?"

"That'd be best, wouldn't it? You could wash off after I'm done," Steve said.

"Yes. That'd be... yes," Lucia said.

After that, their conversation fell off. There wasn't anything else to be said. It wasn't an uncomfortable silence, thankfully.

Nancy returned within minutes along with the witch-knights.

Who were all fully armed and armored, prepared for anything and everything.

"I'll lead the way," Hiren said from behind her helmet. "Beati, Felisa, you take my flanks. Siena, Kimor, Steve."

Giving his axe a spin, Steve and company moved off down the river. But the moment they got moving, a flurry of activity happened down near the boat.

Women began running in from the brush nearby. Those who had been working on the shore immediately took flight and started to load the raft up with everything they could.

Then an entire party of women in leathers stormed out from one side of the tree line and simply boarded the boat.

In a minute flat, everyone and everything was on the boat. Long before Steve and his party ever made it there.

"They were watching us," Lucia said. "Though they weren't close enough for me to see them or hear them."

Really sucks being a Human.

"That's fine," Siena said. "Better that they run from us in fear than stand and fight."

Says the woman who ended up on her knees for me rather than fight me.

"Agreed," Hiren said. "We're stronger as a question mark than a definitive answer."

Oh. That makes more sense.

When he reached the point where the women had been working on the shore, Steve was mildly surprised. The entire time as they got closer, the raft hadn't left. It had shoved out to the middle of the river, dropped something that was likely an anchor, and waited there.

"I think they'd like to chat," Lucia said, an arrow resting in her fingers. "I hope they're civil. It'd be a problem to send their corpses back downriver. I'm not looking forward to trying to fly after a boat as it sails downriver."

A number of women were staring at Steve and his group on the bank. No one said anything, however.

Wish Misty was here.

"Hello, the boat," Steve called, standing amongst his witch-knights.

There was no response from those on the boat, though a number of people looked around. Apparently trying to find someone but not.

"I'm the farm owner from upriver, and you're pretty close to what we consider our territory. We came to see what you were about. We've had problems with bandits, so you'll have to forgive our paranoia," Steve called.

Again, there was no response at all.

"Hello?" Steve asked, trying one more time.

Many of the women on the boat walked away. Moving to other parts of the boat and to work on things there.

"Fine. Give me a pier of witch-stone to them," Steve muttered. "And a wall behind them so they can't move."

"I'll do the pier," Nancy said. Then she lifted up her left hand, and a purple ball of writhing magic immediately sprang to life there. It was interspersed with black flecks.

She's mixing magics.

The witch-knights held their hands up almost at the same time, their magic looking far more singular in color.

A wall of witch-stone slammed up out of the water behind the craft as a pier of witch-stone oozed up from the slimy shallow bank of the river. It ran straight to the boat.

There was even a small lip of stone that ran up over the side of the boat and locked it in place.

Three of his knights moved ahead, their shields raised. Steve and Lucia followed them as they walked down the pier.

"Move," growled Siena to someone.

Kimor hopped up over the side of the boat and into it. There was a bang as something collided with her shield, followed by a single thud.

Siena and Hiren bounced up and over the side of the boat as well.

When Steve reached the jump point, he looked down into the boat.

A single woman was on her rear end with a lump forming on her brow, a club next to her on the ground. No one else was harmed, and everyone was staring at Steve's knights.

"So, anyone going to talk to me?" Steve asked, looking around. "Or do I take you all prisoner and sacrifice you to the Creep?"

No one responded again.

"Fine, bind everyone up. We'll take 'em all back home," Steve said. "Maybe they'll send another group after this and we can capture them too. Always need more hands working."

"Stop," said a woman near a large number of crates piled to one side of the boat. "We can talk."

"Oh? Only now?" Steve said. "I don't care anymore. Start tying them up. If they resist, kill 'em."

"Stop! We're… we're here under the orders of our military governor," said the same woman. "That's why we're here. We're here to find out why the water repels the Creep and secure it."

As one, his knights turned to look at him. Clearly asking if they should go through with his orders.

"Well," Steve said. "I can answer that for you here and now and make this whole thing very easy.

"I'm the reason the water can defeat the Creep. Without me, it doesn't happen. As for securing it… no thanks. You're not the prettiest thing I've ever seen, and honestly, I'm kinda deep in my harem at this point."

Sighing, Steve realized this would be more problematic than he wanted it to be. The more he thought about it, the less likely it seemed that this military governor would leave him alone. If she was anything like Geneva, she'd be looking to turn herself into a local power.

And Steve and his farm were power they needed.

"What were your orders if you ended up having to deal with another city, village, or town?" Steve asked.

"Leave, and return with force to take it," said the same woman.

"Uh huh," Steve said. He'd expected that answer, but he wasn't at all happy to hear it. "I'm going to let you all leave after I search your ship for anything or anyone I want to keep.

"After that, you can go on your way. But I'm sending a message with you as well for your military governor. Do you understand?"

"I understand," said the woman, lifting her chin up.

"Great," Steve said, starting to inspect every woman he found.

He wasn't about to let someone go who could be useful. Especially anyone who had the potential to be an enemy.

He was confident in his people and Geneva's soldiers. If it came down to it, he doubted whoever was south of them could mount a defense against him.

"Tell your military governor that Military Governor Geneva Gosti's husband welcomes his wife's peer to the area," Steve said, closing another information window on yet another sailor. "I'd be delighted to host her for an evening meal to discuss the situation as a whole and figure out what we can do for one another. Perhaps we can even form an alliance to ensure the entire area is stable."

Shaking his head, Steve closed yet another information window. So far, every single person he'd checked was a sailor or a woman without skills, which meant a soldier. Neither of which he was willing to abduct for their skills.

"You... you're married to the military governor," said the woman.

"Uh huh," Steve said. "A princess, a few nobles, a mayoress, as well as the military governor.

"Is this everyone? Is there anyone else hidden around here?"

He'd checked everyone visible, and it felt like that had been everyone he'd seen running on board the boat.

But he wanted to be sure.

"Yes," said the woman he was treating as the leader. "This is everyone. Though there's... there's a few left out there who couldn't get back in time."

"Ah, yes, that's another line of questioning I wanted to ask you about," Steve said. "Did you know we were there? And how long did you know?"

"We knew. A scout saw your group and came back to warn us. They'd only just arrived a minute before you started moving," said the woman.

"Hmm. Alright," Steve said. "Do tell the military governor she's welcome to bring a force of no more than fifty with her if she likes, or she can come alone. Either is up to her.

"I do look forward to seeing her, though."

Steve turned his head toward Lucia.

"I don't see anything I want. How about you?" he asked.

"No," Lucia said. "Nothing."

Nodding his head, he flicked his eyes to Nancy.

His mistress gave him a smile as her brows went up slightly. Then she gave him the barest shakes of her head.

"Alright, everyone back to shore," Steve said. Stepping back over the side of the boat, he began walking down the pier without a concern.

This could be fruitful.

If I can bring the other military governor under my thumb, that'd give us a better area of control.

Or at the least, we can open trade with them. We could easily use the river to facilitate that.

Definitely a good idea on how to sidestep the little problem Nikki made for us.

Just thinking of the Faun gave him conflicted emotions.

He loved her. Truly. And he was determined to work his way through what they were dealing with.

But he couldn't deny that he'd rather snuggle up with Lucia and be pampered to death.

Grunting, Steve turned back to the boat.

His knights were clearing the pier and settling into formation around him.

"Get rid of it all and cut their anchor," Steve said.

Nancy flicked her right hand out and all the witch-stone instantly crumbled down into the water. There was an audible *pang* noise, and the boat started to drift free.

"Tell the governor I look forward to seeing her, one week from today," Steve called to the boat as it slid away with the current.

Watching the vessel vanish, Steve wasn't quite sure what to think of the whole encounter. It was quite likely this would end up as just another enemy to add to the pile.

"Think she'll show up?" Beati asked.

"No," Kimor said.

"Maybe," Siena offered.

"She won't," Hiren said firmly. "Steve is too strong. She'll not bother to face him at all."

"I'm not so sure," Lucia said, leaning into Steve's side. Her hand immediately went to his back, and she began to touch and stroke him once again. "Steve really is too strong, but I'd say the allure of a strong man is somewhat hard to resist. She'll show up if only to see him. From there, it's a question of whether she'll decide he's so strong he can't be allowed to remain, or so strong she can't even try to fight him."

"Will you make her join us?" Felisa asked.

Join us…?

Oh! Oh.

"Unless she's a knight, no," Steve said. "Besides, Gennie might not want me to turn a military governor into a witch-knight.

"If she's a knight, and Gennie doesn't care, maybe? She'd need to be strong enough to keep up with you five."

"Makes sense," Hiren said.

Kimor snorted at that, turning her antlered head toward Steve.

"Is that why you got rid of Moora?" she asked. "She wasn't strong enough?"

"Moora?" Steve echoed back. He didn't know the name.

"Never mind," Kimor said with a laugh. "That answers my question."

"Moora was the name of the other champion you picked out as a 'prize,'" Lucia said into his ear, disguising the whole thing as a kiss to his cheek. "Now, shall we go? I tire of this and would very much like to be back home. I'm all for adventuring, my beloved consort, but I am a woman with child after all."

"Yeah, back we go," Steve said. He needed to have a conversation with Nikki.

It wouldn't do anyone any good to let his feelings dwell, and it certainly wasn't an adult thing to do either.

Twenty-Seven

Steve found Nikki relatively quickly. She was sitting in one of the warehouses, working at a loom.

To Steve, the whole machine had a strange quality to it. It reminded him of far too many things at once that instantly vanished from his mind.

Every time he looked at it, he had a strange feeling of déjà vu that never left.

The Faun was busily working, the strange wooden contraption buzzing away in front of her. It hummed as she worked, lost in her own world.

Not wanting to surprise her, Steve walked past her and leaned up against a nearby wall. That way she could see him and acknowledge him when she was ready.

Nikki started to smile, her slotted eyes having only flicked to him for an instant before she got back to work. It was obvious she was glad to see him.

A minute passed before Nikki's loom slowed down and came to a stop.

"Well hello, my love. To what do I owe the pleasure?" she questioned.

"Couple things," Steve replied, moving over to stand in front of her. Leaning down, he kissed her for a moment, then promptly sat down on the ground in front of her. "First and foremost, we made contact with our southern neighbors. Lucia said some name, but I already forgot it."

"Odristan," Nikki supplied with a grin.

"Burpfartistan," Steve remarked and shook his head. "Anyways. They showed up. Apparently, a military governor is down there as well."

"Oh? Goodness," Nikki murmured and then sighed. "It seems I really underestimated the state of affairs."

"Actually, it's backwards. The capital doesn't realize how bad it is out here. They had no clue. Geneva was completely unprepared for all of this," Steve explained, holding his hands up in an "I don't know" gesture. "Apparently communication was far more broken down than we realized. That and the Creep wasn't reaching that far past where we were."

"Hmmmm? I wonder. Do you think maybe we're the reason for that?" Nikki mused aloud. "Maybe we became an accidental second barrier to the Creep. The water we sent south through the river probably went all the way to the border. Our reach is all of the east and some of the north, after all. And nothing got past us unless it avoided us entirely."

"Which… doesn't seem like a normal Creep response," Steve muttered. "In other words, the Creep didn't want to move beyond us until we were cleared?"

"I mean, it's a thought. I have no way to prove that, of course. Anyways, our southern neighbors have their own Geneva," Nikki said, then smirked with half her mouth. "Should I be expecting a new wife?"

"Hope not," Steve immediately replied with a shake of his head. "Got enough lady problems. Don't need two military governors battling for my attention. And that kinda leads into my next subject."

Nikki raised her eyebrows but didn't respond.

"I feel like a man torn," Steve said, deciding to get straight to it. "I love you, Nikki. But it really felt like you just… tossed me aside when I left.

"It may sound petty, or stupid, or small minded, but I'm not… I'm not over that. Maybe it's no big deal to others, but for whatever reason it's sticking with me. I can't shake it."

Nikki's face flickered from confusion to panic, then to a forced neutral state. She was clearly trying to work through whatever she was feeling while also listening to him.

"Okay," Nikki said slowly. "Could you explain more of that to me?"

"I… it just felt like you were mad that I didn't agree with you," Steve offered, trying to put into words how he felt. "That rather than talk more about it, or figure it out, you just got mad, told me to leave, and left me there."

Taking in a short breath and then letting it out quickly, Nikki nodded her head.

"You're right. I did do that," she agreed. "And we talked about it briefly not long ago."

"Yeah, I know. You apologized and I accepted and all that, and… yeah, we talked about it," Steve admitted. "But that doesn't mean I don't still feel it."

"That's… okay. That's fair, actually," Nikki said. "I'm sure that'll fade with time. We're in this for a long time, my love. This won't be the last time we bicker."

Steve nodded his head with a grin at that. "Yeah. Next fight will probably be that you're not allowed to eat barley before bed. You smell like a rotten den of Creeps and it sounds like someone playing a broken trumpet."

"I do not!" Nikki denied, turning a deep, dark red.

"Yeah, you do. It's so damned awful," Steve said. "I mean, wow, Nikki, I had no idea something that thick and nasty could come from a tiny pretty thing like you."

Nikki opened and closed her mouth several times, turning ever redder.

"Hmph," she concluded, smiling at him. "I suppose it's a good thing you love me, then."

Grinning at that, Steve let out a breath. "Yep. It's a good thing I love you. Though there's another part to this. And I'm not sure if it's me missing something, or maybe I'm just dumb."

"Okay. I'm listening," Nikki said, sliding one leg over the other and folding her hands in her lap.

Reaching out, Steve took hold of one of her hooves and began to toy with it.

"I feel like Lucia is trying to become… I don't know… first wife? Leading wife? Head wife?" Steve probed.

"Any of those would work, but… yes. You've seen how everyone else defers to me and asks me for… time… with you," Nikki said. "And you feel like Lucia is trying to move into that role?"

"I mean… maybe? I don't know," Steve said, suddenly feeling strange. "Is she?"

"I haven't noticed anything, no. At first I was afraid she might be, but… she didn't. In fact, after the day she got back, she began deferring to me rather heavily," Nikki murmured, her hands coming out to lightly slide through Steve's hair. "She's been very deferential to me. Truth of the matter is, I knew someone had come up from the south before you even came in. Lucia sent someone to tell me about it."

"Really?" Steve asked, lifting his eyes up to Nikki's face.

"Mm-hmm. She did. Though, I'm rather grateful at your concern," Nikki purred as she curled her fingers into his hair.

Pulling him closer to her. "Very grateful. You were worried someone was trying to supplant me? Even though you were hurt and angry at me?"

"I mean… yeah?" Steve responded. He wasn't quite sure what to say. He felt somewhat guilty at the idea that he'd rather spend time with Lucia, but if she wasn't pushing in on Nikki, that definitely alleviated some of the guilt.

"Well, Lucia isn't doing anything wrong. I'm well aware she spoils you rotten and treats you far different than any of the rest of us do," Nikki said, drawing Steve's head onto her bosom. "And while that does annoy me a little, it doesn't threaten my position at all."

"Got it," Steve said, laying his hands on Nikki's hips.

"I do have to admit I'm rather annoyed that there are three pregnancies and I'm not one of them," Nikki admitted. "But that's just how it goes. I can't deny I'm still a little… a little afraid you might suddenly decide to start living out of Lucia's bed. That'd make her first wife.

"But she hasn't asked you to do that, has she?"

"No," Steve said. She hadn't, either. Lucia hadn't mentioned the fact that he hadn't gone to her bed. Nor had she even seemed frustrated by it.

She'd definitely pulled him into her own bed twice during the day, but she'd said nothing of the fact that he hadn't gone with her to bed at night.

"Then there you are," Nikki said. "Now. As for me and my… my silliness… I'm sorry. I'll not send you away like that again. I'll explain how I'm feeling to you and if I need some time, I'll tell you that rather than run away."

"That'd be… good," Steve said cautiously. That actually sounded like a really good way to prevent it from happening again.

"Good. I expect the same courtesy from you, of course," Nikki said with a chuckle, tapping a thumb against his temple. "Does any of that feel better now that we've talked about it?"

Nikki's fingers were trailing through his hair with one hand, and up and down his back with the other.

"Yeah," Steve said. He meant it, too. He did feel better for talking about it. Having an actionable plan for the next time they had a fight.

Doubly so now that Nikki had reassured him Lucia wasn't doing anything wrong.

So long as I don't stay in her bed at night, everything is fine, I guess.

"Great," Nikki whispered against his ear. Then she nuzzled him. He could feel the tips of her horns lightly grazing his hair. "I heard you met Airlea. She said you were rather nice. What'd you think of her?"

"Honestly? I didn't realize you meant you were hiring her," Steve confessed. "And that I'd have to go hump a horse."

"Steven," Nikki said with a laugh, but she didn't push him away. If anything, she held tighter to him. "That's just not very nice. She's such a sweet girl."

"Sweet girl with a horse vagina," Steve said bitterly. "You're asking me to go rock a horse."

"Well, it isn't as if I'm Human. Or Jaina, or Kassandra," Nikki said.

"Yeah, well, her lady bits are going to be horse bits, aren't they?" Steve asked.

"Not that I know of," Nikki said, kissing along his temple and into his hair. "It'll be in the wrong place, but a Unicorn is a very special kind of creature. Did the matchmaker explain her at all?"

"A little. Centaur with another who has too much Human genetic material," Steve said.

"Gen-gen-uh-tick?" Nikki repeated.

Steve shook his head. The memory had already failed him. "One of those lost-memory things."

"Ah, well, Unicorns are a strange race. They didn't originally exist. They came about from overbreeding with Humans from Centaurs," Nikki explained. "They're Human all the way through, and they can actually produce Human offspring. They just have the hind-quarters of a horse."

"Yeah, so her privates are a horse's," Steve said, stuck on that point.

"If a Centaur tried to have Airlea, she'd almost certainly die," Nikki replied, her square teeth nibbling at the top of his ear. "She's far too small to take anything but a Human."

Sighing, Steve realized it wasn't that Nikki wasn't hearing him. It was just that unless he said he wasn't going to do it, the expectation was he'd bed the Unicorn.

"Fine," Steve said. "Got it. Should I go bed her now or what?"

"No, you're going to bed me," Nikki whispered in his ear. "Here and now. I'm going to ravage you with my mouth, mount you, and then ride you into the ground."

Before Steve could reply, Nikki had eased him down to the ground and was quickly working at his belt and pants.

Okay. Alright.

Sounds fun.

Pulling his pants down to his ankles, Nikki leaned over the top of him and took in a deep breath through her nose.

She moved her head down and began to sniff at him directly, her nose practically pressed against his shaft.

I... that's kinda different.

Nikki kept sniffing at him, working her way down. Pressing her nose practically into his jewels, she took another hard whiff of him.

Her long tongue slid out of her mouth and then rolled over his balls from one side to the other.

"Steve," Nikki murmured as she continued to lick at him, his extremely rock-hard shaft resting on her cheek now. "I want a child. And I'm telling you this because I want it soon. I'm feeling very insecure about it. If you could give me a child, you'd give me one, right?"

The fuck. Does she know?

Or suspect?

Uh, shit.

Shifting around at the warm, wet feeling of her tongue moving over him, Steve nodded his head. "Yeah, giving you a child is on my to-do list."

"Good," Nikki whispered, then rolled her tongue up along his length from the underside. Her eyes flicked up to his, and then she opened her mouth and laid her lips on his head.

Her pink lips tightened around him and began to work down his shaft. He could feel her long, firm tongue practically wrapping around him as she took him.

Down to the hilt she went, until she had her lips pressed to his abdomen. His tip was throat deep, and he could feel her swallowing at him. Her throat contracting at him and pulling on him.

"Damn, Nikki," Steve said, unable to help himself. His hands came down and wrapped around her horns.

Nikki moaned softly as soon as his hands got a hold of her. He knew for a fact she loved her horns being gripped.

Unless she told him to "guide her," though, he'd only hold her horns.

Nikki moved her head back and left a very wet and messy trail behind. When she reached the tip, she clearly swallowed, still watching Steve, then went back down on him.

Smoothly, she bobbed her head back and forth, sucking and pulling at him with her lips as she did so.

She came off him far sooner than he wanted, after only a minute or so. Kissing his tip and then licking once at the precum oozing free, she smiled up at him.

"I've changed my mind," Nikki purred at him. "I'd like you to put me face down into my loom, hang onto my horns, and put a child in me. Use me up and treat me like the farm. Force that seed in me. That's what you do, isn't it? Conquer, take, and disrupt? So do that."

Taking his tip between her lips, she sucked on him and rolled her tongue over it for a few more seconds. Then she turned, hiked her dress up to her hips, and bent down over her loom. Looking back at him, she grabbed hold of her seat and gave him a lovely view.

"Come take it, brute," Nikki crooned at him as she wiggled her small fluffy tail back and forth.

Getting up in a hurry, Steve grabbed at Nikki and stuffed himself into her as fast as he could.

Groaning, Nikki straightened herself out and then tilted her head back so her horns pointed toward him.

It reminded him of what she'd asked for.

Steve let go of her hips once he'd pushed all the way into her, then reached up and grabbed her by the horns.

"Yes," Nikki said in a whisper as he began to bend her backward. "Take it, brute. Take it all and leave a child behind. Conquer me completely."

Swallowing, Steve felt like she'd hit the right points in his head. She'd not just ticked his boxes, she'd filled them in and smashed them.

Pulling at her horns, Steve kept bending her, forcing her head back and her stomach down.

"No more, my brute. Conquer me now," Nikki pleaded. "Take the last vestiges of me you don't own."

Pulling his hips back, his member sliding out of the Faun with a wet swish, Steve could barely think.

He drove forward and crashed himself into her, the force of it driving her forward. His hold on her horns kept her from going far, though.

Nikki cried out softly but pushed herself back into him.

"Conquer me," she moaned. "Don't worry about me, just conquer me."

Thoroughly lost in that idea now, Steve began to thrust in and out of Nikki. Normally he'd spend the time to make sure she got off as well, but she'd told him what she wanted. He was going to do just that.

Nikki squirmed, moaned, pushed back at him, and generally seemed to be enjoying herself.

Breathing hard as he pummeled Nikki's depths with his member, he didn't want to climax. He wanted to just ride the Faun till she gave out and collapsed.

Right now, he really did want to conquer her until she was spent. Just like she'd said.

Grunting now at the force of his thrusts, Nikki had to almost fling herself back at him to get back in position as he withdrew from her.

Then he felt her hands down between his legs. Every time he thrust deep into her, her fingers played with his jewels. Squeezing at him each and every time.

"Conquer—your—Faun," Nikki got out between thrusts. Apparently she'd stopped holding herself up and was letting Steve keep her upright. Because he could feel all ten fingers squeeze at him.

Impregnate Nikkolet Bril?
Yeah.
Impregnate Nikki.

She'll be a really good mom, and she clearly wants it. More than even Jaina does.

Jaina's more of a sex addict now.

Letting out a sudden exhalation, Steve held tight to Nikki's horns as he started to empty out his seed into her.

"Yes," Nikki groaned even as he continued to fill her up. Thrusting into her over and over as he came, Steve could feel it as her fingers squeezed and gripped his jewels.

Conception failed.

Available ovum not viable.

New ovum available in nine days.

The fuck? Apparently it isn't a guarantee after all?

Shit.

Maybe... maybe I need to start trying more often with Nikki and Jaina both.

Sighing, Steve held to Nikki's horns even as his climax came to a close.

Nikki, however, was a quivering mess as she hung there. Her arms were dangling now toward the ground.

"That was amazing," Nikki whispered. "And I saw it. I saw it that time. It worked."

"Huh?" Steve asked, pushing himself into Nikki again. Even though he was spent, and he was rapidly going soft, he could enjoy a few more thrusts into her.

"Took a bunch of herbs while you were gone. Spoke to a lot of midwives," Nikki panted out trembling in his grasp. "So many herbs I took, I thought I'd die. I was sick for a week.

"It worked, though. I saw the message. We can try again really soon. I can get pregnant."

Hmm. At least the timing kinda works out.

She did go into this thinking it might not be possible. So... whatever.

I'll take my luck where I can get it.

Odd that she saw the message, though.

"Everything hurts," Nikki groaned. "But it feels good, too. We've never done it like that, have we?"

"No," Steve said, finally pulling himself free of Nikki. "Usually we do it with me on top and I make sure I get you off, but you kinda dictate the pace."

"Oh," Nikki said. "I got off, don't you worry about that. Don't think I can handle that every time, though."

Steve grinned at that and gave Nikki's left butt-cheek a light slap with his left hand, eliciting a squeal from her. He held her up with his right hand.

"I dunno, I liked conquering you," Steve said. "Maybe I want it like that every time."

The light smack left a very faint red hand print on the Faun's rear end.

Nikki took in a deep breath and then pushed her rear end into his lap.

"Aaaah… well… maybe I can handle it. We could try again tonight. I'm sure I can handle it, actually. Didn't think I'd like it as much as I did," Nikki said, still dangling in his grasp. It sounded like she was a little fuzzy headed right now. "But I think I really liked it. I can see what Kass was talking about now."

Twenty-Eight

Walking up to the gate guard, Steve waved a hand at her.

"Hey," he said, not bothering to stop.

Both of the women at the gate nodded their heads at him. Steve was probably the single most well-known man in all of Filch. No one tended to bother him, stop him, or even question him.

It didn't hurt that given all his accolades, anyone who didn't know who he was would still likely leave him alone.

"The meeting should have already started. They're all out at the front gate," said one of the guards.

"Meeting?" Steve asked, looking at the speaker.

"Yeah. Commander Linne wanted to speak to the mayor. She and a few others went to go speak with her out in front of the gate," explained the guard.

Linne.

I'll need to remain out of sight. I can't imagine she'd be very happy to see me if I showed up.

Let's just hope she's forgotten my name. That'd be ideal.

"Thanks." And with that said, Steve was off at a jog. He wanted to be there to watch even if he didn't participate. He imagined he could probably peek on them from one of the towers.

The towers have arrow slits, don't they?

Moving through Filch quickly, Steve found he was able to get to his destination with almost no difficulties at all.

Everyone just seemed to melt away from him.

Steve stormed past a guard on the exterior door of the tower, then went inside and started up the staircase.

He could faintly hear people talking, but he couldn't make anything out.

When he reached a mid-level platform, Steve paused and went straight to the arrow slit. Looking out, he found Xivin, Shelly, Misty, and Kassandra all standing on the drawbridge. They looked ready but also on guard. Steve didn't need to be on top of the wall to know they were under heavy security.

Standing across from his wives was Linne Lynn.

Her dark brown hair was slicked back and parted around the cat ears perched atop her head. She looked to be in her thirties, and she was extremely pretty with a well-maintained look.

She was wearing full armor, had a sword belted on each hip, and looked ready for war.

Gennie's arrival must have spooked her. Far more than any of us expected.

"...food. Whether you can spare it or not, and that's the end of the discussion," Linne said.

"I'm afraid Military Governor Geneva Gosti has requisitioned all we have," Shelly said, holding her hands out to her sides. "There is literally nothing to give you."

Linne's chin lifted up, and her ears slowly swiveled around toward the rear.

Steve got the impression she was looking from one person to the other, but he couldn't tell from this angle.

"Geneva Gosti, is it?" Linne asked.

"Yes," Shelly said. "She's recently subjugated Bexis, Faraday, Hilast, and Rennis. I've received word that the military governor to our south has also reached out to Filch to discuss the situation with us.

"Perhaps the citadel commander has not received her orders from Her Majesty as of yet? I imagine they might perchance assume you've fallen in combat. I'm sure that as soon as either of the military commanders report back, your orders will arrive."

I'm suddenly very thankful Shelly is here. She's much better at saying it subtly without making it a threat.

'Get in line, you nasty bitch, before the queen comes and smacks you. You're a citadel commander, but you report to the queen.'

Heh.

I'd probably just end up —

Linne moved then. Moved in a way Steve didn't expect.

Her sword whipped out and simply removed Shelly's head from her shoulders. Then it swung to the right, cleaving Xivin from her shoulder down to her hip. Bringing it to the left, she stabbed forward and caught Misty in the chest.

Linne flung her left hand forward, and a dagger flew free of it to embed itself into Kassandra's throat.

And right out of the back of it, turning her entire neck into a bloody ruin. Her head nearly fell off with how much of her throat had been torn away.

Linne ripped her sword out of Misty and to the side. She nearly cut the Nereid in half as neatly as she had Xivin.

Steve has gained a second Widower accolade.

Arrows began to immediately rain down on Linne from the top of the walls.

Standing there, Steve didn't understand what'd just happened.

"You'll all surrender to me and—"

Steve roared at the top of his lungs. It felt like something had bubbled up from the darkest, ugliest part of him.

He slammed his fist into the tower, and the stone exploded outward.

Not waiting, Steve leapt out of the tower straight for Linne.

"I'll fucking kill you!" he shrieked, his voice breaking and cracking.

Linne's blue eyes looked at him, recognized him, tracked him through the air.

Taking a step to the side, she brought her sword back, covered in the blood of his wives, and waited.

When he landed next to her, he didn't bother trying to dodge. He just punched with all the force he had in him at her weapon.

Which was now whistling toward him.

His fist connected with the tip, and Linne was sent tumbling away. Her sword exploded into fragments and made the grass and dirt crater.

"I'll kill you!" Steve shrieked again.

Linne got to her feet and looked at her right hand. Two of her fingers seemed to be broken and twisted from the impact of having her sword detonated.

Her eyes flicked back to Steve, and he saw fear there. Absolute and uninhibited dread.

Getting his feet under him, Steve began running as fast as he could at Linne.

Who promptly turned around and ran away from him.

"I'm going to cut a hole open in your head and fuck your brain until you die!" Steve screamed at her. Or tried to.

He wasn't sure he wasn't just yelling incoherent nonsense.

Linne was fast. Very fast. She was turning up the earth with just how hard she was running.

Steve wasn't as fast. His feet slammed into the ground and practically knocked him off balance with each impact.

But he was quickly figuring out how to run with his full strength.

Keeping the strength from piling on until after his boots made contact, he began to practically leap through the air towards Linne.

"Gonna kill you, Linne!" screamed Steve as he began gaining ground on her.

Linne glanced over her shoulder and spotted him, her blue eyes wide and terrified.

Up ahead, Steve could see Linne's camp forming up. It looked like they were trying to get themselves organized.

The miserable cunt must have left orders behind.

"I name you liar! Betrayer! Prostitute! Whore! Slaver! War profiteer! Murderer! Extortionist! Dishonest! Oathbreaker! Criminal! Felon! Condemned! Wanted dead!

"I put a thousand-gold bounty on your head! I name you the most wanted criminal in all of Lamals, if not the world!" yelled Steve. "I name you my personal property, and I'm going to fuck you in the goddamn eye socket!"

Then Steve and Linne were in her camp. The commander didn't stop. In fact, she tried to run straight past her own soldiers.

Losing her in the press of bodies, Steve was only marginally able to keep an eye on her.

Then hands and weapons tried to stop him. Her soldiers had apparently decided they wanted to die before she did.

Swinging out with his fist, Steve punched the soldier in front of him. A massive woman wearing even more armor than his own witch-knights.

The breastplate buckled inward, and blood and meat splashed out through the holes her arms went through.

Grabbing her helmet, he yanked it from her head and whipped it around to bludgeon another knight with it.

When the bronze armor smashed into the head of the knight next to the first, Steve realized he'd torn the woman's head off when he'd snatched her helmet.

Steve grabbed at the second knight's large axe on a pole-looking weapon and whipped it around.

There was a massive cracking sound as the haft shattered and the head of the weapon lodged itself in someone's guts.

Steve pulled back with the broken wooden handle and then rammed it through the helmet of another woman who was close enough.

Around him was a sea of armed and armored soldiers.

Shouting wordlessly, Steve threw a round house punch that exploded a woman's helmet and her head, then went into the shoulder of the woman next to her. Her torso made a sickening crunching noise as her shoulder was jammed into her ribcage.

Literally.

Snatching at someone's arm, he tore it from them bodily and swung it like a club at the women in front of him. He needed to keep after Linne.

He needed to murder her by removing her skull and fucking her brain.

The armored arm exploded with the force of the impact, sending another woman's head zipping away into the crowd.

Steve kicked out with a foot, launching a knight like a bowling ball through her comrades. Arms, legs, and armor went flying in every direction.

Chasing after Linne like a human battering ram, Steve caught sight of her.

She was standing near the rear of the army and watching everything happen.

"Linne! You're mine!" Steve shrieked, grabbing the breastplate of a soldier nearby and bodily throwing her at the cat-girl commander. "I'm going to use you as a goddamn outhouse!"

Apparently, that was too much for Linne. Or it was the knight that had just been thrown at her like a rock.

The fallen citadel commander turned and ran away. Most of her command went with her. Retreating.

More soldiers got in front of Steve, blocking his path.

As his target got away, so far that he couldn't even catch her if he wanted to, Steve howled and laid into everyone around him.

He lost himself entirely in his work.

***

Gasping for breath, Steve crushed the woman's head between his hands even as she begged for her life.

Bits of skull, brain, and a lot of blood welled up between his fingers.

Taking in a heaving breath, he looked around. Up ahead, a soldier was running away as fast as she could.

Grabbing at the leg of the woman he'd just murdered, Steve tore it from her hip and then hurled it at the runner.

It smashed into the back of breastplate with a bang accompanied by a sickening explosion of blood and meat. Both from the runner and the leg.

Panting, Steve checked his surroundings again. No one was standing or moving.

There was finally no one left to kill.

Checking the ground, he found there were a large number of women with their hands behind their heads. At some point they'd taken to surrendering, and he hadn't noticed.

Stomping over to the closest one, he grabbed the soldier by the helmet.

"Please gods no!" she shrieked. "No! No! Please, I—"

Steve smashed his hands together, and her head vanished into a pulpy mess.

Growling, Steve started over to the next closest soldier. She was praying endlessly, her gauntleted hands resting behind her head as if to protect it.

"Steve, I think you should stop," offered a soft voice. It didn't put any ownership on him. A suggestion, really.

Looking toward the speaker, Steve found Nancy there. She and his witch-knights had likely followed him as soon as they'd realized he'd left the farm to go visit Filch.

"They're not all dead," rasped Steve.

"I know," Nancy agreed. "But I think you should take them as prisoners and use them as resources. There's no need to execute them, is there?"

"They live. They should die," Steve countered.

"Okay," Nancy said, shrugging her shoulders. "I just thought you'd want to use them against Linne."

Linne.

The name made Steve's head swim.

"She killed them," he whispered. "Killed Shelly, Xivin, Kassandra, and Misty. She killed them."

"She… did," Nancy said, looking uncomfortable. "She did kill them. I pushed Misty into the moat. Nereids are said to be part spirit. It seemed right.

"The others I've loaded into a wagon. I felt you'd want to bury them at the farm."

Steve swallowed at that, looking away.

"They were all dead?" he asked.

"Yes," Nancy said. "Even before we got down to them, it was… They were very dead. I don't think any of them even realized what was happening, it was that quick."

"I'm going to crush Linne," Steve growled. "I'm going to fuck her in the eye socket until she dies from it. Cum inside her damn brain."

"I'll do all I can to support you," Nancy promised.

"This is because I didn't just… declare war on Linne. I should have just gone back and murdered her," Steve said, staring off at nothing now. "I could have prevented all of this. Everything. But I didn't."

"I don't think anyone could have predicted this outcome," Nancy said. "Linne didn't seem like the type to do such a thing."

Yes… she was.

She was likely responsible for the entire Creep invasion.

"I name Linne the reason why the Creep invaded Lamals," Steve said. "I name her the bane of the alliance."

"She… what?" Nancy asked.

"Pretty sure she killed a fellow citadel commander, and their city," Steve answered. "She's the reason we're all in this mess. Her and her hatred of Humans. It's obvious she only did it because the commander was a human."

"Commander Tahvo? He was a Human, yes, but he was also a great warrior. There was no one who could best him," Nancy said, sounding confused. "Why would anyone damage the walls?"

"Because she hates Humans," Steve said. "She breeds them in her 'pig pens,' after all. To her, Humanity is little more than a weapon. Well. We'll see about that.

"We'll see. I'm going to kill her. Then hunt down whatever family she has and kill them, too. I'll kill everyone. Everything."

The guards of Filch were slowly making their way towards Steve. In his maddened craze, he'd been chasing everyone who tried to retreat or flee from the carnage.

A trail of corpses would lead to where he was now.

"I believe it, Steve," Nancy murmured, right next to him now. "I believe you. Come. Let me give you a bath and wash you clean.

"You look like a mess."

"This is nothing compared to what I'll do to Linne. Nothing," Steve promised.

"I know… come… follow your mistress," Nancy said, taking his hand in her own.

Falling into somewhat of a trance, Steve did as he was told. He allowed Nancy to walk him off the field and back to Filch.

Hours later, Steve felt like he was waking up.

Looking around, he realized he was sitting in a bed. He didn't really know where he was, but he knew Nancy wasn't far.

He could hear her talking in the other room.

"…leave them in the field," she said. "There's no reason to bother with them. Just strip them of anything of value."

"I understand," said someone Steve didn't recognize. The sound of booted feet clacking against the wood told him that whoever they were, they were leaving.

A door opened, then closed.

"Did you get a messenger off to Lucia?" Nancy asked.

"Yes," Hiren said. "I sent Kimor. She has the most stamina and can probably get it there by tonight."

"Good. Good thinking," Nancy followed up with.

"I should go take care of him," Felisa said with annoyance clear in her tone.

"No, leave him for now," disagreed Beati. "When he wants one of us, he'll ask for one of us. Let's let him rest until then."

"Yes," Siena agreed with the Ogre. "Let him rest. If he wants comfort, he'll ask."

"I'm going to go take care of him," Felisa said.

"Stop," Nancy commanded. "Leave. Him. -Be. He'll ask for it, if he wants it. For now, we let him rest. Let him come back to himself and find his own thoughts. I really think this… I think this isn't something he can just be serviced out of."

"Won't know till I try," Felisa countered. "So let me try. It's not like I'm telling any of you to join me."

The door to the bedroom he was in opened, and Felisa stepped inside.

"Steve?" she asked, walking into his view. She was dressed in what he'd call house clothes.

"Hey," Steve said, meeting her eyes.

"I was wondering if I could perform my duties for you?" Felisa asked. "Would that help?"

Steve blinked and thought on what she'd just offered.

If I'd been more aggressive.

If I'd just killed Linne. They'd all be alive.

All I had to do was be aggressive. To push, kill, and conquer. To take and hold rather than let others dictate terms to me.

Lucia told me to push and take it all.

That I deserved it all.

I didn't listen. And now I'm paying the price for that.

No more.

No more of that. I'll not let anyone push me around or take anything from me ever again. From now on, I'm going to take from everyone else. I'm going to crush everyone and everything.

It'll bow to me or be broken in half, and that's all there is to it.

"Sure," Steve said and started to work at his belt buckle. "That'd be great, Felisa. Go close the door and then come back over here."

He wasn't going to say no anymore. He was going to take what he wanted and make sure no one else could ever hurt him or his loved ones again.

Starting with the military governor from Odristan.

She'll face the iron hand of my rule and bend low to me.

Or die.

Felisa came back and got down on her knees in front of Steve. She leaned forward and opened her mouth, inviting him to take control as he always did with her.

Putting a hand behind the Banshee's head, he guided her down while angling his limp self into her mouth.

With a soft swishing sound, she took him and slid down to his hilt. Her eyes moved up toward his as she began to carefully work him back and forth through her mouth.

Never again.

Watching his witch-knight, Steve thought on all the things he'd do to protect what was his.

Twenty-Nine

Steve buried Kassandra, Xivin, and Shelly outside the palisade walls. He'd put together a location for a cemetery and set them to rest there.

He didn't want to see their tombstones too often, but he wanted them close enough that he could visit them when he wished.

It'd been exactly a week since he'd sent the boat back downriver to Odristan.

Standing at the exact point where they'd landed last time, Steve stared into the water as it flowed by.

I wonder if Misty ended up being taken in by the water after all. Couldn't find her corpse despite going to where Nancy said she'd pushed her in.

That'd be nice… if maybe Misty is still alive in some way.

Moving forward to the edge of the river, Steve stuck his fingers into it. He hadn't actually been near the lake, river, or trench since he got back. He'd simply had too much to do.

"You in there, Misty?" Steve whispered to no one.

The only ones with him were Nancy and his knights, but they were backed up considerably. Steve wanted to be the first one to hopefully invite the military governor ashore.

Nancy and the five knights were now his personal bodyguards, despite him saying he didn't need it. Everyone else was on "farm arrest" and not really allowed to leave.

He wasn't going to risk anyone else.

Ever again.

The river water pooled in an odd way that wasn't normal. It then made a small wave and crashed lightly on his fingers.

"Misty?" Steve asked, his voice cracking.

The water withdrew itself around his hand, leaving a strange circle with no water. At the center of that point, under his hand, was a small green stone.

Steve picked it up and held it in his palm.

Instantly, the water rushed in to fill the spot that'd been vacant, and the river did nothing more.

Looking at the stone, Steve wasn't quite sure what it was. But he was rather glad to know that at least Misty wasn't completely lost to him.

"I'll come visit you tonight for a good, long soak," Steve said, reaching out to trail his fingers in the water for a moment.

Then he stood up, holding the green stone tightly in his hand. He wasn't about to risk losing it.

Another hour passed before the same raft-like boat started creeping up the river.

Steve put his empty hands together in front of him. Only a small slice through the skin along his knuckles remained of his battle, and it was healing well. It'd been from punching Linne's enchanted and blessed sword barehanded.

Everything else had faded quickly under Gwendolin's ministrations. Supposedly, it was all done without magic, but he was beginning to doubt that. She seemed to have a power over him all her own.

"Ho the craft," Steve called, watching the vessel without a concern. If they decided to be stupid, he'd just pick up a rock and chuck it right through their hull.

He was done playing games. Done dealing with idiots. Steve was just done.

"Ho the shore!" called a voice back. A woman came up to the side of the boat. Steve assumed it was the owner. She was a young woman that looked to be in her twenties. She had a very similar bearing to Geneva, but she belonged to some type of reptilian race.

Or so Steve guessed from the green-scaled skin, yellow eyes, and complete lack of hair. She had small ridges coming out the top of her head that reminded him of an iguana.

"Would you be the owner of the farm, and husband to Military Governor Gosti?" asked the woman.

"That I am," Steve said. Then he looked back at Nancy and gestured to the water. Before he could look back at the water, witch-stone was already rising up from the riverbed.

Faster than last time, a pier formed that stretched right out to where the boat was heading.

The woman watched what happened closely. Her head tilted curiously to one side as the stone formed into place and stopped.

"Drop the anchor," said the woman, turning to address someone else. "Hurry up, you little fool."

Sounds like I'll be pulling off a lizard's head today.

I doubt she'd be willing to serve under Geneva and me.

Well, so be it. I'm done.

Standing there, Steve waited. He wasn't about to do anything problematic at the moment. Not till he could get his hands on the military governor in a far easier fashion.

If she was anything like Linne, she was probably underestimating him.

With a shudder, the boat bounced up against the pier and then came to a stop. The splash of something going over the edge likely meant they'd dropped the anchor.

"Idiot!" said the lizard. "Are you trying to sink us?"

There was a response that Steve didn't hear.

Then the military governor hopped up over the side of the boat and onto the pier. She was dressed in a full-on military uniform.

Isn't a shining doll in armor like Geneva, at least.

"I'm the military governor," said the woman, walking up to him. "My name is Ssisik. You have the honor of meeting me personally."

"I'm Steve," Steve said.

"So I see," said the woman, her eyes moving back and forth. She was likely reading the entirety of Steve's information. "You're a most... interesting man."

Steve shrugged. He really didn't want to be here. He'd rather be running around the citadel city in the east. Figuring out how to knock down the walls and butcher Linne.

"Your people told me you sent them up this way to secure whatever it was that was changing the water. Making it something that kept out the Creep," Steve said, getting right to it. "That's me. I'm the reason it's doing that. And I'm certainly not giving away my ability to treat the water, nor am I leaving my home."

"Yes. So my people told me when they returned," admitted Ssisik. "And that you'd told them I should be here. Today."

Steve nodded at that.

"Thank you for coming," Steve deadpanned. "I'll make it simple so there's no qualms about this.

"I'm bedding a Fae princess, a few nobles and minor nobles, and the military governor herself, Geneva Gosti. I'll not be bullied, pushed, or pressed on. I'm going to respond to anything and everything with violence. Right now my attention is focused on the false-fallen-whore of a commander Linne Lynn."

"The… the citadel commander?" asked Ssisik.

"Uh huh. I'm going to fuck her in the skull. Right through her eye, and into her brain," Steve said with some heat in his voice. "After I bury everything she loves or owns in a mountain of shit.

"Any problems with that?"

"No… no problems from me," Ssisik promised. "I'll just manage my governorship and keep it running as per Her Majesty's orders."

"Hmph. I'll offer you trade then," Steve said, changing the subject. "We have an overabundance of food—clean food, free of the Creep—and would be happy to exchange it for goods."

"Oh? Wonderful," Ssisik replied with a smile, showing off her very sharp teeth. "We have some concerns about long-term food growth. That'll help us offset that."

"Great. We also trade with Filch, Faraday, Hilast, and Rennis," Steve continued. "So if you have anything else you want to trade further into these lands, we could act as a midpoint. Maybe make Filch a trade hub, since you can reach them by river from my farm."

"Ah, does this river go all the way up then?" Ssisik asked.

"No. Dead-ends at my lake. But I can dig it out enough that you can start bringing boats up into a safe harbor. Can move by wagon or such from here to Filch, while others travel to Filch as well," Steve said, planning out what he thought would work. "Beyond that, I have nothing to discuss with you."

"Ah, alright," Ssisik said, looking momentarily bewildered.

"Oh, and before I go," Steve said, staring hard into the lizard's eyes. "I should tell you now. I single-handedly beat Linne in a fight. She ran from me.

"I give you this statement because the next time we meet, I may be done killing Linne. At that point, it's very likely I'm going to tell you to join me and Geneva. Or I'll have to sail south and see what I see."

Ssisik blinked once, her eyes focusing and then unfocusing on Steve.

"I understand," said the governor, then bowed at the waist to Steve. "I'll be ready, and will gladly pledge my allegiance to you when that day arrives."

"Good. You're welcome to travel up to the lake if you wish for dinner and to rest the night," Steve said. "I'll be leaving soon, I think, to murder Linne. Tomorrow possibly."

"I think... we'll simply return home. My sincerest apologies for leaving so quickly, but I feel like I should get my trade goods in order immediately," Ssisik said.

"Right," Steve replied. "Goodbye then."

He said nothing more. Steve stood there waiting for Ssisik to get back on her boat and leave.

Fuck off already. Shit to do.

Cat-girl to fuck through the eye.

Turning, Steve didn't bother to see her off. He really did have other things to work through. The last thing he wanted to do was sit here.

***

"I don't like it," Nikki said.

"I'm pretty sure we're past liking or not liking it," Lucia countered. "Linne killed some of our number. Killed them. They're dead.

"Our direction is clear. We go and kill them all."

"No, it isn't," Nikki disagreed, shaking her head. "We could easily reach out to her and see if she's willing to surrender or face the queen's judgment. We don't have to be the ones to seek her out and carry out her sentence."

"Yes, we do have to be the ones," Steve said in a flat tone. "Because we're the ones who let her remain when we could have easily taken care of her before this. But we didn't. I didn't. I should have stomped over there and kicked in her teeth and buried her face in a pit.

"And because I didn't do that, I've got four more dead wives that... that are my fault. And I'm going to fix it."

"It isn't your fault, and we don't have to be the ones to do it," Nikki continued. "This is all Linne's own doing, and we can let her suffer the consequences without having to be the ones to dole it out."

"No, because if we rely on the queen and her justice now, she'll probably pardon her," Lucia said with a shake of her head. "She killed, at most, a mayor and a once-soldier. A Human mayor. The queen will pardon her with a slap on the wrist and little better.

"No. If we don't drop the axe on her, no one will. No one can."

That's right!

Lamals has always been against Humanity. Let alone men.

The queen won't do shit for us because Shelly was just a Human. A mayor, certainly, but also just a human. If anything, she might even say it's pointless because it should have been handed over to Geneva.

No, the queen won't help us here.

"…can work it out through the queen. I'm sure we can have her imprisoned for the rest of her life," Nikki said. "It isn't like I don't have anger in my heart over this, you know. It isn't as if I don't want justice. I just think for it to be proper justice, we need to seek it from the queen."

"And I truly believe the queen won't have any of it," Lucia stated, tapping two fingers to the table. "Because we don't matter to her. We're on the eastern end of nowhere, and Linne can just claim she's the only thing holding back the Creep. It isn't like the queen knew of anything that was going on out here. She's worthless!"

"That's not true at all. She sent out the military governors, after all, along with soldiers," Nikki said. "And supplies. That was all to bring the population back into a manageable state. Not to grind it into the ground or anything like that."

"That's… amusing, in a way," Steve murmured and then laughed. It caught both Nikki and Lucia off guard. "That Ssisik from the south. She was going to force our farm into her domain. If it wasn't for the fact that I told her I was Gennie's husband and going to kill Linne.

"We'd be fighting on two different fronts if we went your route, Nikki. It's a lovely sentiment. A beautiful one. But it just doesn't fit in our world. This is all… it's all a shit show. It's all just one big battle to the death. And I refuse to be the one on the other end burying more family."

"That isn't what Misty would want. Or Xivin, Shelly, Kassandra, or Chessa!" Nikki declared. "They would all tell you that this'll just become a never-ending circle of violence. We must use this opportunity to be better than them."

Laughing at that, Steve looked up from the table to Nikki's face.

She was as beautiful to him as ever. Her pure and loving heart that'd won him over and brought him ever closer to her.

Now it was pushing him away from her. Faster and faster by the second, he realized Nikki wasn't ever going to see eye to eye with him on this.

"We should talk to the others," Nikki cautioned. "It's their lives too in this, isn't it?"

Steve, Nikki, and Lucia all turned to look at everyone else in the room.

Jaina, Ferrah, Ina, Airlea, Gwendolin, and Nancy were all present. They just hadn't decided to join the conversation.

"I think we should see the queen's justice served," Ina said, shrugging her shoulders. "I think... I think that if we get any further into this, it's just going to get worse.

"What if the queen sends her armies against us for taking up arms in the way we're talking about?

"No one's ever gone after a citadel commander before."

"And if we let them keep going the way they have?" Gwendolin asked, shaking her head. "Then what? They were coming to demand even more from us. That's why Linne killed everyone. Because they said no.

"Only a monster would allow someone like that to remain in power. No, the queen will give us no justice, and she'll see to it that we vanish."

Jaina flipped her hands up in a neutral gesture.

"I don't care," she said. "I'll follow Steve. He's my husband, my pack master, my alpha. I'm his Creep Witch. I'll kill everyone for him, or save everyone. No matter."

"I don' rightly care either," Ferrah drawled, leaning back in her chair. "I just want to work metal and live my life."

"Well, I'm very new here, and I'm not formally a wife yet," Airlea said. "But I think we should go with Nikki's suggestion. If we seek out the queen's justice and it fails, I'd be willing to consider alternatives then."

"I'd say by the time we knew she wouldn't do us any good," Gwendolin countered, folding her arms under her breasts, "it'd be too late for us to do anything about it. You seem to forget that our Steve isn't normal. He isn't going to just be allowed to live freely after we seek out the queen's justice. Not unless we've protected ourselves sufficiently."

"Geneva would agree," Lucia said, nodding her head. "She's not here, but I can reasonably speak for her."

"Yes, yes," Jaina agreed. "Gennie would push for Lucia's statement."

"I'm Steve's," Nancy said, as if that were the only answer that mattered to her.

"So," Steve said, deciding to summarize it. "We're at an impasse as far as opinions go. Three neutral, three to attack, three to hold."

"And five dead," Gwendolin huffed. "Five lost because we seem to believe others will care for us in the same way we might for them.

"No. I'll not wait around for them to come for my children."

Gwendolin laid her hands on her stomach. The implication was clear she was including her unborn child as well as Nia in that statement.

"What... what if we did both?" Nikki inquired, looking both pained and upset.

"Both how?" Steve asked.

"You go capture Linne. Alive," Nikki explained. "Bring her back, and we tie her up and sit on her. We send for the queen's justice after that. If she tries to do anything other than give her that justice, through Geneva, then we... we can reconsider then."

Steve raised his eyebrows at that.

"No, let's not reconsider then," Lucia countered. "Let's consider now. What would you have us do if the queen said to release her and let her go."

"I'd say... I'd... I don't know," Nikki offered lamely. "I wouldn't know until the time came. That'd be more or less committing to going to war against the queen, wouldn't it?"

"Maybe that's what it'll take," Gwendolin said, her hands stroking her stomach. "To protect what's ours, maybe that's what we need to do. I already lost a husband and five wives to little better than the evilness of others. Maybe it's time Lamals fell."

"Maybe it's time indeed," Lucia pondered, leaning back in her chair. One hand went to her stomach, and the other caressed her chin.

"No!" Ina said. "No. That won't solve this. It'll just replace a broken government with a new one no one trusts. If anything, even more people would die and be hurt in such a thing.

"A civil war never results in a hand-off of power that benefits the citizens."

"Why do the citizens matter at all?" Gwendolin said in a hiss. "They didn't care when I was left nearly on the street because they forced my husband to go and die! The only thing that saved Nia and me was Steve. A Human man.

"A Human man that would be little better than a chair in the capital. And you somehow think the queen will give us justice?"

"But, couldn't we all end up losing more by starting a civil war?" Airlea asked. "Isn't it just as likely we could all die doing such a thing?"

Everyone stopped talking at that.

It wasn't as if Airlea was wrong—that was clearly what would happen if they lost such a fight.

They wouldn't be imprisoned or hit with a slap. They'd be executed, one and all.

"We'll capture Linne," Steve said, coming to a decision. "Capture her and bring her back here. If possible. If I can reasonably tie her up and drag her here, I'll do so. But I'm not going to risk letting her live over tying her up."

"I... I can agree to that," Nikki said with a heavy sigh. "May fortune favor us and your capture of her, but I can agree to that plan."

"I don't like it," Ina said. "It leaves far too much room for her to simply die."

"I'd say it leaves far too much room for the queen to butt in and ruin our lives," Gwendolin said. "But I can agree to the plan."

"Right... so who's going with me?" Steve asked.

"I am, obviously," Lucia said.

"Me, me," Jaina said in a hurry, raising an arm above her head.

"I'll stay," Ina added. To Steve it sounded like she wanted to say something else entirely. "I'll go to Filch and keep it safe from the Creep."

"I… I know the area really well," Airlea said. "I've often been on the other side of the Creep wall since it fell. Just to explore. The Creep leaves Unicorns alone. Or more importantly, it stays away from our horns. So I'll go with you."

Well that's frightening.

I wonder if people would kill a Unicorn just for the horn.

"No," Steve said after a second. "You stay here, Airlea. Pretty sure there's going to be a lot of fighting in this. Unless you're going to tell me you're proficient with a weapon?"

"I'm… alright with a lance, but… no. I'm not that good with it," Airlea murmured, looking down. "I just want to help and earn my keep. That's all."

Well, aren't you a darling one?

"Thank you for volunteering. Stay here. Maybe practice with your spear," Steve proposed. "Keep making leather armor."

"Okay," Airlea said.

"I'll stay," Ferrah said. "I'll keep forgin' steel. Arms and armor to make."

"I'll remain behind as well," Nikki said with a sigh. "I would wish to go, but someone must remain here of course to manage the farm. Without… without… ah… I'll be forced to travel between Filch and here, I think."

"I'll stay at the farm," Gwendolin declared with a nod of her head. "Nia will need me."

"There it is then," Steve said, looking down at the table again.

Fuck that cat-girl cunt right in the eye, then bring her corpse back to Nikki.

Promise to bring her back alive or not.

Thirty

Leaving Filch, Steve felt like he was doing the right thing. Taking the right option and direction.

He regretted that he'd been in conflict with Nikki once again, but she hadn't spurned him. There'd been an open dialogue that included everyone.

And it had concluded with Nikki bedding him repeatedly, fervently, and rather demandingly.

Like she was trying to make up for the fact that she sent me off last time with almost nothing.

"Mine, mine," Jaina called out, scampering forward and moving toward a zombie.

Kimor clicked her tongue audibly.

"Didn't see it in time," grumbled the witch-knight.

Jaina, Nancy, and his witch-knights had taken to obliterating zombies they found. It'd become a strange type of game to them.

"Can someone explain to me why you're each so determined to be the one to kill them?" Lucia asked. "I mean… I'm not against it and I think it's a good thing to do — I just don't understand the joy you take in it."

"Every kill generates power," Nancy said. "The more you kill, the more Creep you destroy, the stronger you get as a witch."

"Wait, really?" Steve asked. He'd never heard any of that from anyone.

"Jaina told me," Nancy said. "She was weaker than Ina before the trip, and now she's several times stronger than her. The only difference before and after was a lot of killing."

Huh. That's not wrong, is it?

"We should collect the witch-knight royal guard and bring them to the citadel," Steve said. "Leave a gap in the defenses and just let the witch-knights train up."

"Yes," Hiren stated firmly, her helmeted head turning toward him. "That's a good idea."

"I think I'd rather stay with you," Felisa said, a step behind Steve. "I'm enjoying my other duties far more than being a witch-knight."

"You would," Siena grumbled. "You're a Banshee. Wouldn't be surprised if you had your own song for Steve."

"Song?" Steve asked, taking a moment to glance back at Felisa.

"Banshees are the same species as Sirens," Lucia said before Felisa could respond. "Sirens feed off attention, Banshees feed off attention and death. Haven't you heard those old tales about Sirens drawing men to their deaths? Same species, different goal."

Oh.

Oh! Okay, that's rather interesting.

"Do you have a song for me?" Steve asked bluntly.

Felisa's eyes slid away from Steve. He couldn't see much of her face behind her helmet, other than her eyes, but he got the impression she was embarrassed.

"Yes," she admitted after a few seconds. "It's... I don't think you'd like it, though. It's not like... it's not like Gwendolin's."

Steve raised his eyebrows at that. He had no idea Gwendolin had spoken to Felisa at all. His knights had mostly stayed away from his wives.

"I think I'd still want to hear it," Steve said.

Felisa shook her head.

"Okay," she mumbled, coming to a stop. "No one else should be here."

"Whatever," Kimor rumbled. "Let's move up ahead. Maybe we can find some zombies."

Breaking into a light trot, Kimor started moving away. Hiren, Siena, and Beati immediately followed after her.

"Oh? Hmm, alright," Lucia said. She slipped her arm into Nancy's and continued to walk away. "Where were we?"

"Fae court etiquette regarding second wives," Nancy answered.

"Ah, yes. Second wives. They're to be brought to family meals only when—"

Lucia's voice faded away, leaving Steve alone with Felisa.

Felisa pulled her helmet off and gave him a nervous look. A smile slowly formed on her face.

Reaching up with one hand she smoothed her sweaty hair back across her head.

"Are you sure, Steve?" she asked. "It's… it's not like Gwendolin's at all. And I'm a Banshee, not a Siren. It could—"

"Sing for me, Felisa," Steve said.

He'd heard two different Siren songs for him. One was for a father, the other for a husband. Curiosity wasn't something he normally lived for, but he really did want to hear what a witch-knight in service to him would feel through her song.

Felisa's eyes slowly came up to his and snared him.

Steve couldn't look away.

Felisa began to sing a wordless melody that was low in pitch, slow in the change of notes, and almost haunting.

She sang of a deep and dark void that was exactly that. A void of everything.

Then the void was filled with the promise of sex and violence. Of death.

Sweet, tasty, delicious death. A never-ending life filled with being satiated and tempted by the first blush of romance.

Dark, twisted, and bent over itself, it was a song more like a funeral dirge mixed with a lover's lament.

And for all of that, it pulled at Steve and drew him in close to Felisa. He felt a kinship with the void. He'd felt that void recently in his life and wanted to fill it himself.

He didn't need to be a smart man to know that the void had clearly been Felisa and Steve the promise that filled it.

To Felisa, Steve was clearly something she'd ached to find and had been searching for.

When she leaned down and kissed him, she hummed her song instead. The break in volume and power gave Steve the ability to come back into his own mind.

Breaking the kiss, Felisa leaned away from him and watched him, her eyes still holding his.

"Well," Steve said after taking a breath. "I can certainly see how your song is not a Siren's song. But I didn't dislike it. Though… I do have to ask… there was something in there that was unexpected."

"There was?" Felisa asked, her eyebrows moving upward.

"Mmm. Almost like you were falling in love with me," Steve said. He'd never been one to shy away from telling someone something. He wasn't about to start now with someone he owned.

"Oh," Felisa said, then nodded. "Yes. I'm falling in love with you. My duties may only be to service you and kill on your behalf, but it's not a poor existence. It's better than I was doing previously, and you treat me very well.

"Nancy's no different. She loves you, too. Mostly for the same reasons."

"Huh," Steve said. "Sounds like I need to find all the dark races and bind them together. You're all so desperate for affection that you'd thank me for putting an owner's tag on you."

Felisa nodded slightly at that.

"Probably," she murmured.

Something to consider.

***

"This is the point of no return," Lucia said and then sighed. "I really don't want to be back here. My memories of this road aren't so pleasant."

"No?" Nancy asked, looking at Lucia.

"Not in the least," grumped Lucia. "I was turned into a half-chewed meal and almost died. All for the love of a Human who managed to knock himself out.

"The scars are... they're hideous. My skin is ugly and ruined."

"No, it's very much not," Steve interjected, reaching up to lay a hand on Lucia's back. "It's one of the reasons why I have such a hard time denying you anything, my sweet butterfly. You know that. I tell you it often."

Lucia shook her head, then tossed her hair over her shoulder.

"Hmph. It's good you recognize my beauty for what it was before and after," said the Fae. "Lucky man that you are to have become my consort."

Rolling his eyes at that, Steve couldn't help but grin. He was glad to see Lucia seemed to be over her experience, for the most part. It probably wasn't an incident that anyone could get over.

"Right, well, this definitely is our turning point. I wonder how we should approach it?" Steve asked.

"We march forward, kill them all, and you kill the commander by skull-fucking her," Kimor said, patting her fist into her open hand. "Simple."

"You're as simple as you are stupid," Siena said.

"What? You're stupid. Stupid Ogre," Kimor said, her antlers trembling slightly. "You should service Steve and learn your place tonight."

"I will service Steve tonight, as it's my right to do so," Siena said. "But you're still a stupid and simple idiot, Kimor. We can't just bust in their front door and lay waste to them."

"Why not?" Kimor asked, holding her hands up. "Steve is our lord. We've all seen what he can do. He'll be King of Lamals soon. Better we show how he will rule now, so there are no questions later.

"We go in, kill everyone, hold the commander down, Steve skull-fucks her to death. I bet he'd get prestige for it."

"To be sure, you're right," Beati said. "We should herald our lord in that way. I agree with the stupid Reindeer. Since becoming witch-knights, we've become much stronger. Both martially and as witches."

"I'm not stupid," Kimor groused bitterly.

I mean… you kind of are though, Kimor. That's not a bad thing, but… you really are.

"Yes, you are," Hiren said. "But that's okay. We respect you all the same, Kimor, stupid or not. Just as we respect Felisa for wanting to be our lord's personal bed toy, Beati for being an actual scumbag thief, and Siena for… well… she's an Ogre. That says enough."

The knights glared at one another, then started to laugh.

"Is there a reason we shouldn't just go kick in the door?" Steve asked. He really didn't know why that wasn't the best answer.

"Truthfully? Because the more soldiers you kill, the worse off Lamals will be. Unless you want to breed a whole lot of pig-pen soldiers to replace them," Lucia replied, laying a hand on her cheek. "The losses you've already caused them are more than enough to set them back by at least five years of very heavy recruiting.

"And if Lamals is going to survive after we get through this, we'll need the soldiers. So while I do think it'd be ideal to simply invade and slaughter the lot of them, we probably shouldn't."

Oh. That makes sense.

If we lose too many soldiers, our neighbors could simply try to wipe us out after the fact.

That, and didn't Nikki said the only saving grace we had as a nation was our ability to produce soldiers? That's pig-pen soldiers, I bet.

And I don't plan on letting that continue without their consent, so… damn.

Alright.

"Fine," Steve acceded. "Fine. I prefer Kimor's idea, but we'll do what we must. Let's head to the shattered gap and see what we find there. Maybe we can get up on the wall and travel inward from there. That seemed to be a definite weak point, as Linne herself proved."

"I like that idea," Nancy said, nodding her head. "It'll give us a chance to see how bad it is, and how to contain the Creep."

"Yeah. Alright, let's just call it a night for here then. Last time we found a nice spot up that way, didn't we?" Steve asked, pointing off toward where a small group of trees were set together.

"Indeed," Lucia agreed. "It wasn't bad at all."

Soon after that, Steve and company were safely tucked away from the world. The knights and Jaina would take turns on Creep watch, which apparently wasn't much of a duty to them anymore.

Because whoever was on duty got an increase to their power as they drank in Creep through their dome.

Lying there in his tent, Steve wasn't sure what to make of the most recent changes in his life.

He hadn't really felt what most people would call remorse over the deaths of his wives.

It was more of a boiling rage. Full of anger and the absolute desire for revenge.

But none of the sobbing, teary stuff that people seemed to be expecting from him.

Steve felt like that wasn't normal. He'd felt the same way over Chessa's death, in fact. Nothing felt quite right to Steve when it came to that sort of thing, and he couldn't pinpoint it.

Maybe it's because… I'm not… normal.

I don't have the same brainwashing as everyone else.

I clearly see things differently than others. Things don't affect me in the same way.

I have powers no one else does.

And then there's that voice I hear.

"Steve?" asked a soft voice from outside. He couldn't quite place who it was. They were speaking too softly.

"Yup?"

"May I enter?"

Eh… maybe it's Siena. She said it was her turn, right?

"Sure, come in," Steve said.

The flap slid to one side and Nancy entered.

Smiling at him, the lovely Wight swiftly came over and lay down next to him.

"Siena will take her turn tomorrow," Nancy said, pushing Steve's arm out to one side and then pillowing her head on it. Then she snuggled up to his side. "I pulled rank on her and claimed tonight for myself."

"Decided to take her punishment on yourself?" Steve asked, grinning at her.

"No, she was rather annoyed with me," Nancy said, smiling up at him. "I think you misunderstand how your witch-knights feel about you. They're not mad at you. Not anymore.

"They all want you to bed them. Each of them have different reasons, but… no, they don't view their evening duties as punishments. At least not anymore."

"Hmm. And what about you, my delicious little Wight?" Steve asked. "Ever since… since I did what you wanted… you've been a little different."

"I have?" Nancy asked, frowning.

"Well, you still beg for all the things you normally do," Steve said. Nancy hadn't stopped asking for him to brand, slap, hit, punch, cut, strangle, abuse, or impregnate her. "You just… you don't seem to be as twisted about it."

Nancy sighed and shrugged her shoulders.

"My parents always told me that once I started having regular sex with my husband, I'd understand how a relationship can grow just from that," Nancy said, her words slow and cautious. "I thought it was just them being stupid. But… it seems there's something to that, I guess. At first, it was being forced into sex and taken as I was. It was delicious.

"I know. I know you didn't force me, and it wasn't actually rape. That was in my head. In my own little fantasy, I guess."

Steve had just been about to object to the way she'd phrased that. He remembered things very differently.

"I don't taste as good anymore," Nancy said. "The misery just… isn't there anymore, I guess. That's why I really want you to do the physical stuff.

"But I do understand why you have a hard time doing it."

"You do?" Steve asked. He hadn't expected such a change from Nancy.

"You love me. It's why hurting me seems backward to you," Nancy said, reaching over to pat his bare chest. "But I'm telling you, if you love me, you need to start hurting me. Just enough to make me taste good to myself. I can tell you when I'm at that point, if it helps."

Once more, Steve ran into that absolute wall he had inside himself. He didn't want to harm Nancy in any way.

"Even the fear of getting pregnant doesn't really do it for me anymore," Nancy revealed. "Mostly because I think… I think I want to be pregnant now. Though the idea of being pregnant and not being a formal wife does taste amazing right afterward."

"You're telling me that if I love you, I should slap you," Steve clarified.

"That's exactly right," Nancy said. "Slap me, choke me some, or brand me. I really want you to brand me. Right on my face. So everyone can see it for that day before it heals.

"I want to be branded so badly."

Steve was already shaking his head. He didn't want to do any of that to her.

She was his henchwoman, his mistress. Nancy had already pulled all the darkness out of him with how she let herself be treated and encouraged it.

Doing more to her seemed wrong.

Except that it was what she wanted.

"It was… so… amazing, when you killed me," Nancy said, her voice sounding dreamy. "Everything went black and it felt like my head was going to explode. Your hands were so tight on my neck. I don't think I'll taste anything like it again."

Coming to a decision, Steve realized he could do something for Nancy after all.

"Suck me," Steve said, putting his left hand behind her head. With his right hand, he slipped off his sleep shorts.

"Oh, gladly," Nancy enthused. Before he could pull on her head, she was already moving down toward his lap.

Her lips wrapped around his tip, and she went down on him instantly. Sucking at his hilt, she began to bob her head up and down, her hair fluttering around her head.

Letting out a slow breath, Steve couldn't help but feel really good. Nancy was always generous with him. As much as Lucia, if not more so.

Laying his hand on the back of her head, he pushed down on her.

Wedging his tip in her throat and his hilt to her lips.

Nancy coughed once, her back and shoulders flexing.

Steve didn't let her up. He held her down. Even when Nancy pushed at his hand, he didn't move. He held her there.

After ten seconds, she gently patted his hip with one hand.

Steve let her go, taking that as her signal to stop.

Coming off him, Nancy took in a deep breath, gasping.

Steve grabbed her around the throat with one hand and pushed her down next to him. Squeezing gently, he watched as her already-red face turned redder. Her eyes were wide, staring at him.

With his left hand, he flipped her dress up and then forced her legs apart long enough to wedge his hips up between her thighs.

He could feel Nancy resisting him, her hands holding tight to his wrist even as her legs tried to push him free.

Settling himself down atop her, Steve let go of her throat.

"You're alright?" he asked, wanting to make sure she was fine.

Gasping deeply as soon as he let go, Nancy took several wheezing breaths.

"Oh gods, yes," she croaked. "Taste so good. Take it all from me, Steve."

"That's the plan," Steve said. He'd realized he could probably choke her without actually causing her harm, but it'd still give her what she wanted. Then he closed his hand around her throat again and squeezed. "Pat me like last time when you need air."

Nancy's eyes partially started to roll up into her head, but she did nod in response.

Sliding his left arm across her shoulders, he made sure he could hold her down. Steve shifted around, found her entry with his tip, and thrust into her roughly.

Nancy grunted and let her legs fall to the sides, going completely spread eagle for him.

Holding onto the Wight, Steve tried to gauge how hard to choke her as he started to roll himself back and forth. Gliding through her extremely wet insides.

Steve let go after several pumps and gave Nancy a chance to breathe.

Coughing softly, Nancy lay there as Steve rode her into the ground. Holding her down as he did so.

"Okay," she said, looking back at him. "Ready."

Grinning, Steve closed his hand around Nancy's throat again, slowly increasing the pressure as he mounted her.

Nancy was moaning, grunting, and shivering beneath him. All the while pushing at him ineffectually.

He wasn't sure where her mind was at, but guessing from what she'd said earlier, she was roleplaying this a bit.

Reaching his peak sooner than he expected, Steve contemplated Nancy, then he realized how he should finish.

He slowed himself down and let go of her neck again.

Nancy groaned when he did so.

"I love this," she said, taking in deep breaths. "Oh, I love this. It's so amazing. Every night like this from now on."

Smirking, Steve kept working at her, pushing himself deep into her.

"Okay," Nancy said, her fingers flexing against his arm. "Do it again."

Steve nodded his head, then started to get off her.

"Steve...? What are you—"

Nancy was cut off as he knelt down on her shoulders and grabbed her hair with one hand, his other balancing himself against the ground, then thrust himself into her mouth.

Grunting, Nancy didn't fight him, though her hands opened and closed several times.

Then she moaned hard, her body quivering under him.

Leaning forward, Steve began to thrust wildly and hard against Nancy's face. He pushed down as deeply as he could each time, pausing there to make sure Nancy got what she wanted out of this.

Then he was ready again to finish.

"Ready for it?" he asked, looking down at Nancy's face.

Spit and what was probably precum were trailing down the sides of her mouth, and her face was covered in sweat.

She grunted and nodded her head minutely, looking far too excited.

Letting out a breath, Steve thrust down into Nancy's throat and came.

"Swallow it down then," he said as his member flexed.

Pushing down with his hips, he tried his damnedest to be as deep as he could.

There was a groan from Nancy, which was followed by a rough and hard gulping sound. He could feel it pulling at him when she swallowed.

It only made him push harder, spasming again.

Nancy groaned again, then swallowed once more.

Thrusting against her face as he continued to climax, Steve held on to Nancy's head, keeping her pinned down to the ground.

Moaning, Steve thrust down into her mouth one more time as the last spurt of seed left him.

Another hard gulp from Nancy told him everything was done.

"Phew," Steve said, then rolled off Nancy and back onto his bedroll.

Gasping for breath, Nancy lay there sputtering.

"So good," she said in a gasp. "So good."

Snorting at that, Steve closed his eyes.

"Glad I could please you," he said. He hadn't liked the idea of hurting her, but he'd do what he could to help her with her own needs.

After all, she was his henchwoman. She looked after him, so why couldn't he look after her?

Thirty-One

"This isn't the direction the Creep was coming from," Beati said.

"No. No, it isn't," Hiren agreed, nodding her head. "I don't feel it in the earth either."

"Nope," Kimor said with a grunt. Then she stamped a booted foot. "Not a thing."

"Yes, yes, it's more like the farmland," Jaina said, prowling along on all fours.

"Well, that's where the break is," Lucia said. She lifted a hand and pointed at the large broken chunk of wall that wasn't far off. "That's where I earned my scars to save my beloved consort."

Never going to let that one die, are you?

"Lots of zombies," Siena said as she pulled her helmet off. She began to run a leather-gloved hand through her hair. "We'll have to fight our way to that point if we really want to see it."

"Can't get up the wall?" Kimor asked.

"Can you fly or something we don't know about?" Beati snapped. "Because I can't. Stupid oaf."

Kimor made a gesture with her hand at Beati but didn't verbally respond.

"We had a rope we left up there, didn't we?" Steve asked.

"Can't remember," Lucia said. "Honestly, it's all... a bit jumbled in my memory. I think we did."

"Where?" Felisa asked. "Is it further in or—"

Jaina pointed.

"There. It's still up on the wall," confirmed the Kobold. "We left it there. No reason to pull it down. Because it was made out of Ogre and Troll hair that was braided. Heavy, heavy."

"Okay!" Kimor enthused. "We kill our way there, climb the rope, kill things up there, then go more, Steve skull-fucks Linne."

Kimor started marching forward as soon as she finished talking, pulling out a rather large one-handed double-bladed axe.

"Does your whole world revolve around killing?" Beati asked.

"Of course. That's my job. My duty," Kimor admitted. "Killing and servicing Steve."

"So your whole outlook is a dick and your axe?" Beati asked, clearly intent on badgering Kimor right now.

"Isn't yours? You're just angry because he holds on to my antlers and compliments me on them," Kimor accused. "You just have those little cat ears. You're practically a Human."

"You're such an idiot," Beati growled, pulling her longsword free from her side.

"You're both idiots," Felisa said, drawing two longswords from the sheaths on either side of her. "Arguing in front of our lord and looking like fools."

"Steve doesn't care. He likes me the way I am," Kimor said. "Told me to be myself."

"Shut your traps," Hiren said.

The five knights and Jaina were moving faster than Steve, Nancy, and Lucia. They continued to bicker and quibble as they went.

"They fight quite a bit," Lucia said.

"Yeah," Steve said. "Whatever. As long as they don't actually betray me, I couldn't care less if they like each other."

"I do suppose that's the right answer, isn't it?" Lucia said.

"I'm going to join them," Nancy said. "I want to keep powering myself up. I'm only just a little behind Ina."

"Ah! That's a very good point," Lucia said, pulling an arrow from the quiver on her hip.

Nancy was off at a jog, chasing after the others.

"Steve," Lucia said as soon as Nancy was out of earshot. Up ahead, Kimor had just closed in on a Creep. A purple flame leapt out from her axe and burnt the corpse to a crisp.

"Yup?" Steve answered, not really sure what she wanted.

"Are you going to take Linne back to Nikki like you promised?" Lucia asked.

"No," Steve replied honestly. "I'm going to skull-fuck her to death. Just like Kimor said."

"Oh, hmm. Alright," Lucia said.

"That a problem?" Steve asked with a catch in his voice.

"I don't think so," Lucia admitted. "But I do think it's not very fair of you to promise something like that and then go back on it.

"You can't really expect anyone to take you at your word if it doesn't mean anything."

Grimacing at that, Steve didn't respond. He didn't like it.

"Now, keep in mind, my beloved consort, I'm not telling you what to do," Lucia amended. "I'm just telling you I think it's a bit of a slippery slope. You know I think we should just kill Linne and be done with it. I'll go along with whatever you decide. But that's not what you said you'd do."

The knights were tearing into the zombies now. With weapons glowing purple from enchantments and spells alike, there wasn't much the enemy could do to them.

They were simply too empowered now. Too powerful.

Witch-knights are the answer to the Creep.

I could actually... solve... the Creep. Couldn't I?

I could end it.

Though... maybe that's not the answer, either.

"Would you... lose respect for me if I didn't do as I said?" Steve asked as his mind started to wander.

"Honestly? I would some, yes," Lucia admitted. "You've never been a liar up to this point. It'd be disappointing to watch you become one. But as I said, my beloved consort, I'll support you in whatever your endeavor is. I love you. I'm here for you. Liar, murderer, rapist, or traitor. You're my sweet, beloved, darling consort.

"Consider yourself honored to hold the unwavering affection of a lady such as myself."

"Yeah... I do, actually. I do consider myself lucky," Steve said. "Okay... I'll bring... Linne back. I just don't want to."

"A fair admission," Lucia said.

Then she lifted her bow, fit the arrow into it, and let it fly.

A zombie not far away from them went down in a heap as the arrow smashed into the front part of its skull.

Not the right time for talking.

Focusing in on the situation at hand, Steve and his team made it without injury to the rope, which really was still there. It was considerably easier than last time, given how many of them had powers that fed off the Creep itself.

When your fuel source was the enemy you were fighting, the battle became an exponential increase in power.

"I'll go first," Steve said, grabbing the rope. "Because honestly, you ladies are in some heavy armor I don't think you'll be able to pull yourself up in."

As if realizing the situation, all five knights looked at themselves.

"Jaina will go last; she can hold out the best," Steve said, grabbing the rope and starting to haul himself up. "Just tie the rope around you and I'll pull you all up."

Pulling himself up hand over hand, Steve made it to the top quickly and then looked down. Hiren was staring back up at him, the end of the rope looped around her midsection several times.

Steve grabbed the rope and began to pull her up as fast as he could.

"Aaaaah!" yelped Hiren as she started to soar upward toward him.

Grabbing her by the breastplate when she was close enough, Steve simply pulled her over the top and then flicked the rope back down the wall.

"Steve," Hiren said a little breathlessly. "You are far too strong. Occasionally, I forget what you did to the champions with only your hands. It's just so hard to remember what you're capable of at times."

Shrugging his shoulders, Steve watched Felisa start winding the rope around herself.

"And you didn't even have to fight me," Steve said. He waited until Felisa held a hand up toward him. "You guys give Kimor a lot of shit, but she actually tried to fight me."

"Oh, dear heavens," Felisa whimpered as Steve physically yanked her onto the wall by her breastplate.

Beati, Siena, Kimor, Nancy, and Lucia came next.

"Woooooah!" Jaina cried out as Steve started pulling her up. Considering how light she was in comparison to everyone else, it felt like he could probably fling her around like a yo-yo.

Yanking at the rope when she got to the top, Jaina practically came up over the wall all on that alone.

Steve grabbed Jaina around the waist and pulled her into his side, then looked at everyone else. They were all watching him.

"All done," Steve said, pulling the rope away from Jaina but not putting her down. "Shall we get going?"

Jaina for her part struggled only for a second before she just cuddled into him and laid her head down on his shoulder.

"You're not tired...?" Siena asked.

"No. Would you like me to carry you, too?" Steve asked, grinning at the bigger woman.

Walking over to the big bronze-clad woman, Steve slipped his arm under her rear end, stood up, and then started walking towards the ruined citadel city.

Jaina on his right hip, Siena on his left.

"I… could… you…" Siena fell silent, her gloved hands resting on Steve's shoulder. "Put me down, my lord?

"Fine," Steve said, and he let the Ogre down even as he kept walking.

Jaina took the opportunity and slid herself more towards Steve's middle, getting her legs around his waist. Then she laid her mouth on his neck and bit him gently.

Repeatedly.

Each one followed by several gentle licks.

"Still want pups?" Steve asked.

"Yes," Jaina said, nipping at him over and over. "But not as badly anymore. I like our sex life. Pups will ruin it."

Reaching the side entrance of the city, Steve walked straight in. From his memory, they could move through here into the courtyard and be able to see into the rubble pile he'd made.

After taking a few steps beyond the doors, he came to a stop. He set Jaina down to one side, not sure what he was looking at.

There in front of him was the breach he'd created. It was firm, stable, and looked far sturdier than he thought it'd be.

In fact, there was an ocean of zombies on the other side of it. All milling around, looking for a way through. Even some of the larger and more frightening monsters they'd seen last time.

"Hnng," Kimor grunted. "No breach, no break, no gap."

"No," Beati murmured. "And we didn't feel any Creep the entire way in, either. Are we in the wrong spot?"

"No," Lucia said and pointed off to the side. Down toward the actual ground beyond the wall.

There was a mound of rubble over there, along with a number of long-decomposing bodies.

"That's where Steve and I fell," she said. "This is where we made this mess, and where they should be getting through. Though I — what… what's that?"

Everyone was watching the same thing, though, and no one had an answer.

Previously Steve had wondered what would happen to their neighbors. The way the wall had fallen had almost made it into an odd curve that would lead Creep into their lands.

Rather than Lamals.

There was a garrison there with soldiers, right where the crumbled remains of the citadel wall would end. They were all in uniforms and gear that Steve couldn't recognize. They seemed to be quite bored, all lazing around.

Looking back at the heap of stones blocking the Creep completely, Steve could see that it wasn't the same.

"They filled the hole up," Steve mused. "There was enough for a Creep to get through, right? They came, filled it up, and left it alone after that.

"They could have done that the entire time. Couldn't they?"

"I would say so, yes," Lucia murmured with a sniff. "It was exactly what we thought. They were using it as leverage to bring Lamals to its knees. When it benefited them to fix the problem, they fixed it. Until then, they left it alone."

"I'd do the same," Nancy said, turning to look at Steve.

"You're not wrong," he said, then quickly shook his head. "I mean, really. Wouldn't we do the same? After what's happened to us, all of us, I'd say we've all become much more ruthless. We'd do the same to them.

"So... why don't we? Killing Linne is just the first step, I'm coming to realize."

"It is?" Nancy asked, looking rather curious.

"It is," Steve said, nodding his head. He was starting to figure out what he wanted to do now. How he wanted to conquer everyone.

Everything.

To bring his brand of justice to every doorstep.

"It'll take some planning, some work, but I'm... I'm done," Steve professed. "I'm... so very done. So done. And I know exactly how to make this issue a moot point."

Leaving the ruins of the city, Steve walked back out to the wall and stared off into the distance. Into the Creep lands.

Far in the horizon, Steve swore he could see what looked like towers.

"Tell me, what's out there?" he inquired.

"Out there?" Hiren asked.

"The Creep lands?" Felisa added.

"Nothing. Creeps, poisoned everything, dirt. Not even animals," Kimor grumbled, throwing a hand out in that direction.

"What kingdom was out there, and why were they so blessed that they had someone absolutely destroy them like this?" Steve asked. "Why would they get hit by something so bad that it would literally curse the earth?"

"We did it," Lucia confessed with a sigh. "The Fae, that is. We made the Creep. As for who they were, I'm afraid even I don't know. I just know the Creep is the great shame of the Fae. There's a reason why the alliance keeps an eye on us as a nation."

"See, but that just makes it even more obvious to me," Steve said, gazing out into the Creep lands.

"What?" Kimor asked.

"That I need to take the Creep land back and make it Steve land," Steve said. "That the Creep will be mine. All of it. It'll be the easiest thing in the world to do. At least… for me.

"I'm going to set up a city out there. I've already built one outpost; I can make another. First I'll make a river. One that runs from Filch to Linne's citadel city, to all the way out there. Somewhere I can take over."

"I… what?" Jaina asked.

"Yeah," Steve said. "A river out into the Creep lands. And as I dig, I'm going to have my lovely and talented Creep Witches and witch-knights cover me. And build over my river so that no one sees it. So they don't have any idea of what's happening. A canal that literally runs through the ground as a means of travel no one can see. A simple chain or rope so one can pull themselves along in a small boat.

"And I'm going to build out there. My watering can will go out there. We'll start cleansing the ground and the surrounding areas, and build. My witch-knights and Creep Witches will all go with me and be the shield that holds everything back.

"I'll take everything out there for myself. Everything. I'll build up something that can crush the rest of the world under its heel and bring them all into my hand.

Steve spotted something out in the distance that looked almost like a gray river. After staring at it for several seconds, he figured out what it was.

"Is that a road?" Steve asked, pointing out toward it.

"I dunno," Kimor said, pulling her helmet off to scratch at the base of her antlers. "Maybe?"

"Looks like one," Beati said. "Can't really tell from this distance, though. Could be a dry riverbed."

"It's a road," Lucia stated firmly. "It doesn't seem to be laid with paving stones, though. It looks rather odd."

"Where there's a road, there's a destination," Steve said. "And that destination is where I want to go to see what's going on. Because I'd be willing to bet it's interesting. And a spot I'd really like to see."

"Oh?" Lucia mused. "Hmm. I've never been in the Creep lands themselves. This should be interesting."

"We can do it," Jaina promised, nodding her head rapidly. "Easy, easy. We can use it as a chance to power up, too."

"Yes," Siena said, nodding her head. "I need more power."

"Power... power indeed, Siena," Steve murmured. "Yes... power, then. I'm done. Done with all this and everyone."

Steve lifted his chin when he finished speaking.

It'd been a building thought since Linne had killed his wives. A building thought and a burning ember stoked now into a raging bonfire.

One that would consume the world.

Thirty-Two

Jaina hit the ground with a purple sphere enclosed around her.

All the zombies around her immediately vanished in a puff of black powder and purple smoke.

"Next?" Steve asked, looking at the women around him.

Kimor grunted and slapped a hand to her breastplate as she moved forward.

"Me," said the Reindeerkin.

Steve shrugged his shoulders and then held out the rope to her.

Kimor wrapped it around her middle, got up to the top of the wall, and simply walked off the edge.

Holding tight to the rope, Steve began to lower her down. It was like Kimor was literally walking down the side of the wall.

"Faster!" Kimor called up.

Not feeling like fighting her, Steve started to lower her significantly faster.

When she landed next to Jaina, she started flinging around purple blades of Creep magic.

"I almost feel useless with them around," Lucia said, watching Jaina and Kimor tear into the zombies around them.

"You could become a Creep Fae or something," Steve said, yanking the rope back up. He grabbed the end and looked at his knights.

Beati stepped forward and took the rope from him.

"I suppose I could at that, couldn't I?" Lucia murmured. "Is it hard to die?"

"No," Felisa answered as Beati went over the edge. "It was like falling asleep against my will."

"It was more frightening than anything else," Hiren offered up.

"Hmm," Lucia hummed, tapping a finger against her chin. "Maybe I will at that."

Steve didn't bother to respond to that. He was busy. As soon as Beati made it down, he was lowering Felisa next. Then Hiren, Nancy, and Lucia.

Looking down at the ground far below him, Steve wanted to test something.

He was beginning to think he was practically indestructible at this point.

One didn't punch the tip of an enchanted weapon and only suffer a light cut. But that's exactly what he'd done.

Tossing the rope back down over the side of the wall for their return trip, Steve vaulted the wall and fell.

He hit the ground with a thud. The force of the landing made it so he'd practically hit his ass on the ground, but he was remarkably unhurt.

He stood up and looked at himself.

Everything was where it should be. Nothing was out of place or even sore.

Huh. Well.

Apparently, I'm not... really... Human anymore.

All around the knights, Nancy, Jaina, and Lucia were clearing the area.

From above, it'd looked like a sea of zombies.

Nancy held her hands above her head and made a swirling motion with them.

Instantly, a half-dome of glittering purple magic sprang up and swept outward.

"Goodness," Nancy exclaimed. "It's as if it costs nothing at all. I'm just... drawing it from the ground itself."

"Yeah?" Steve asked, an idea forming in his head.

"Indeed, it's easier than eating," Nancy said, and she began walking forward. Their goal was the road he'd seen. They were going to find out what was at the end of it.

After that, Steve could plan further.

Linne was a secondary goal now.

She'd face justice—Steve would make sure of that. His goal right now was to explore the Creep lands while he could. While he had the time.

He had a theory now. One he couldn't prove, but he was fairly certain it was accurate.

Linne was letting the Creep in herself. To incite fear, provide credibility for her cause, and keep everyone in line.

The Creep wasn't getting in through the gap, which really only left one other point it could be.

Linne.

Steve figured she'd come to the same conclusion he had and why he was moving forward with his plan.

A citadel city commander could hold a country hostage if they held the citadel.

Disagree with me? I let the Creep in.

Try to attack me? I hole up and let the Creep in.

Don't send me food? I let the Creep in.

Don't tell me bless you when I sneeze? Let the Creep in.

All I have to do is hold Linne's citadel and have a base in the Creep lands that sustain it, and... the country is my hostage.

We just need somewhere to work out of now.

Following behind Nancy, Steve smirked as the Wight single-handedly wrecked the Creep. His knights on the perimeter were attacking outward for the sake of attacking.

Jaina was at the front, wielding cones of purple flame that obliterated everything in front of them.

The Creep isn't a problem for me.

It's a resource.

***

"And how much longer can we be out here?" Kimor asked as they walked along the road. They could see their destination now, less than a minute away. It'd taken them several days of walking on the road from where they'd found it.

"Not long," Hiren replied immediately. "A few days. Then we have to turn around, or we won't have enough supplies to get back."

Damn.

I didn't think it'd be this far away.

Have to change the plan a bit, I guess.

"It's a castle and a town. But it's not something I've seen the like of," Lucia said, her eyes moving around as they got closer by the second. "The walls are so high for a castle, and the construction looks like it's made from the same material as this road. I'd be lying to myself if I could claim I knew how it was all made."

"It's concrete," Steve said, watching Nancy and Jaina. They were the two putting in the most effort right now, and he wanted to keep an eye on them. If they were taxing themselves, he'd expect them to lie about it before admitting it.

"Concrete?" Lucia inquired. "I don't think I've ever heard of that."

"You add sand and gravel to cement, then mix that with water and there ya go," Steve replied almost automatically.

"Cement?" Lucia asked, sounding more confused now.

"No idea on cement. I think someone told me it was limestone or something, but I can't remember it very well," Steve said, then realized what he was talking about.

And immediately the memory faded and fled as if it had never existed.

"Well, I'll have to look into that," Lucia said with a curious tone. "Limestone to make cement, then cement, sand, and gravel with water to make concrete. Should I assume you've lost the memory now?"

"I... yeah. It's a weird... place... now," Steve said. "I can remember telling you what it was, but not what it is, except you said it, so... ugh."

Lucia reached over and lightly ran the tips of her fingers through Steve's hair, tickling along the back of his neck.

"It's alright, my beloved consort. I'll always be here to pick up the pieces for you," she promised.

The endless waves of zombies continued to blast themselves apart on Nancy's dome. Or they got picked off by his knights and Jaina.

If ever there was a place to train his Creep Witches and witch-knights, it was here. In the Creep lands themselves.

When they finally reached the castle, Steve realized he didn't want anyone to go exploring.

The zombies they were finding here were clearly long-dead citizens of this country. They were lurking in darkened corners and hallways.

Their supply of watering-can water wasn't in excess, either. They'd been forced to start drinking it as soon as they'd entered the Creep lands.

Standing in the plaza in front of the castle, everyone was looking around.

"And is this what you wanted?" Nancy asked, still holding her dome in place.

"Yeah. This is what I wanted," Steve said, nodding his head.

It really was, too.

Everything of the city remained intact. Whatever the Creep had been originally, it had more or less instantly converted the city into Undead. By and large, most of the city and its infrastructure remained standing.

Although anything made out of wood had rotted away, the stone buildings and the castle itself looked impressively sturdy.

"For now, though, this place won't do," Steve muttered. "Let's head out past the city limits. See if we can't find a field we can turn into a farm with some work."

"Farm?" Kimor asked. "I make the ground catch fire when I piss on it. I'm not so sure you can make anything grow here."

Steve chuckled softly. He found himself enjoying Kimor.

"Uh huh. Maybe it's just you, Kimor," he said, walking toward the exit of the city. "Maybe all those sexy thoughts in your head are making your urine fiery."

"That's not possible," Kimor grumbled, catching up to him. "Is it?"

"No, you idiot, it's not," Beati said with a long-suffering sigh. "We all make the ground burn when we urinate on it. Defecation, too."

"Defe-what?" Kimor asked.

"When you shit," Steve helpfully interpreted for her.

"Oh, yeah. Smells awful when it catches fire," Kimor agreed.

"It's the watering-can water," Jaina said, moving out in front again. Then she began blasting ahead of herself with her two-handed flamethrower technique.

"Is that it?" Felisa asked.

"Yep. Which is why I know for a fact we can bring the ground back to life and use it for a farm," Steve explained. "It'll just take some time, effort, and the watering can."

Maybe that's my goal in all of this?

Was my task to retake the Creep land? Not just to hold it back?

Is that why I've been completing my goal and making progress?

Could be. Probably is.

It's the most likely answer.

It'd fit everything else. I mean, this feels like… the whole thing is set up for me to solve the problem.

"This'd work, wouldn't it?" Lucia asked.

Steve gave his head a shake. He hadn't even been paying attention, and they'd left the courtyard and the city around the castle quickly.

They were just outside the walls in the middle of a giant city. The ruins of a house were nearby, and the road ran quite close to it.

"Yep," Steve said after just a few seconds. "This'd be the place alright. One of you put down a dome. Big as you can make it. I figure the ground, air, and Creeps nearby can feed it even if we're not here.

"Right?"

"Yes, yes," Jaina said, grinning at him. "I'm the strongest—I'll do it!"

Before anyone could disagree, Jaina slapped her paws together and then flung them outward.

A massive, glowing, and crackling purple dome blasted out in every direction.

It grew bigger by the second, sweeping up zombies as it went.

So large was the dome, Steve could only see the parts of it that were in the distant plains. The rest of it had swept right over the city.

Looking back over his shoulder, Steve watched as it zipped right through the castle and beyond it.

Well, that'll clean everyone and everything out.

"Ah!" Jaina barked out. "That's all I can do. That's it, that's it."

Sighing, Jaina let her hands fall down to her sides.

"Whew. Tired, tired," said the Kobold. "Will you carry me, my pack master, my alpha, my husband?"

"Course I will," Steve said, and he immediately scooped up the small woman. Grabbing her by the rear end, he held her against his front. "Should we take a sleep here and head back? No reason to stick around. Found what we needed to find."

"That'd be the best course of action, I'd say," Hiren mused. "If the goal was to find what was at the end, we've found it."

"Yes," Kimor exclaimed loudly. "I want to watch you skull-fuck Linne, my lord. Can I be the one to put a hole in her skull for you to use?"

Grinning, Steve looked at Kimor.

"I dunno, maybe I just want to fuck you instead. Hold you by those antlers and really give you a good bedding," Steve said, feeling odd about the Reindeerkin now. For whatever reason, he'd found himself drawn to her and her fellow witch-knights lately.

Maybe it's because they follow orders and do what I tell them.

"Oh. Okay. I'd like that," Kimor said, shrugging her shoulders. "Should I keep my armor on for it or what?"

"You're such an idiot," Beati said, putting a gloved hand over her eyes.

"What? It's a valid question," Kimor complained.

"No. No, it really… it really isn't. But you're an idiot, so… maybe it's valid for you and you alone," Hiren wondered aloud.

"Hmph. He wants me, not you all. You're just envious," Kimor said defiantly, shaking her head and making her antlers tremble. "I'll let you know what it's like to be a woman when he's done and give you advice. Like the little sisters you are."

"At least she used the right word," Nancy deadpanned.

"Right word? Oh. Wants? Yes. That's the word. He wants me. I mean… he said so. Well, I guess that's not true. He said he wanted to fuck me. So I guess I could have said he wants to fuck me," Kimor said, staring at Nancy. "Right? My lord wants to fuck me?"

"I meant envious versus jeal—never mind. Just… never mind," Nancy said, holding her hands up in front of her.

Laughing to himself, Steve couldn't help it. His witch-knights were becoming more entertaining to him by the day.

***

Keeping low to the ground, Steve and his group watched the citadel city from the Creep lands' side of the fortification.

It was deep night, and they were far enough away that they were very unlikely to be seen.

The only concern and possibility of them being seen was in the small shields his people had put up around themselves. Nancy was providing the one for himself and Lucia.

A massive, oppressive-looking wall spread as far as the eye could see. Holding back the Creep and protecting the land.

Except for the citadel, which had its gates wide open. A flood of Creep and zombies flowed through it into Lamals.

This was exactly what Steve had been expecting to find here.

"They're... letting the Creep in," Lucia hissed. She sounded absolutely floored. As if someone had told her that her wings no longer existed.

"Indeed they are, my butterfly," Steve said. "Indeed they are. I can only guess at the motives, but... it's exactly what I plan to do."

"What?" Nancy asked, looking at Steve.

"If you control the citadel, you control the Creep. If you control the Creep, you control what happens to the country. If you control what happens to the country, you're the leader of the country," Steve explained simply. "And I plan to control Lamals, one way or another. As I said earlier, I'm done. I'm done with everything that Lamals is and is involved in.

"From the fact that I'm apparently not much better than a chair in the capital, to the fact that my race is called a 'breeder' race, and the fact that the 'pig-pen' is allowed. And the most offensive on that list... giving someone like Linne the responsibility of the citadel.

"No. I'm going to crush Lamals as a whole."

"First things first then, my sweet kingly consort," Lucia purred at him. "How are we going to get Linne?"

"I'm going to jump at the citadel, smash into the top of it, break my way in, and ambush her in her bed," Steve said. "Because let's be honest, I know where she lives in there. We were there. She's overconfident that I'd have to go through the front door. So I'm going to go in from the top."

"I... you're..." Nancy hesitated, pausing mid-sentence. "You're going to go in all by yourself?"

"That I am," Steve confirmed. "Because if I don't have to risk any of you, I never will again. And honestly, you're all better at fighting the Creep than you are other living beings.

"Me? Whatever I did to myself, made me a goddamn sexual tyrannosaurus. And I'm going to rain down pain on her like she's never even considered before."

"Alright," Lucia murmured. "Let's say you capture Linne without a problem. What should we do? Where should we go? We can't get back up that wall without you, you realize."

"That's not true at all," Steve said with a laugh. "All you have to do is use witch-stone to lift yourself up to the top of the wall.

"Jaina could probably do it on her own without any help at all."

"Oh. Oh, yes," Lucia said, shaking her head. "Honestly, I'm not used to the fact that we have such power available to us."

"Yeah, well, that's what everyone else is going to feel when I ram my Creep Witch, witch-knight forces down their throats," Steve growled. "Unless, of course... unless, of course, the queen can see reason. If she can do what I want her to and not make me have to crush her skull like a melon.

"As for you, my sweet butterfly—"

Steve paused to turn to his side. Reaching over Nancy, and partially leaning into her on purpose, he laid a hand on Lucia's jaw and pulled at her gently. Meeting her lips with his, he kissed her tenderly for several seconds.

Breaking the kiss, he patted her cheek and then laid his hand on Nancy's rear end.

He had some ideas on how to make Nancy feel miserable going forward. First and foremost was to see if he could get her jealousy engaged.

If he could do that, he had an easy way to keep her happy.

"Go get as many supplies as you can. Wagons of them. Then bring them back to this citadel city," Steve said. "Because regardless of anything else, no matter what happens, my goal will still be to claim the Creep lands."

"Mmm. I'll take care of it," Lucia said with a chuckle. "Suppose that'll make me the queen of the Creep lands, if you'll be its king?"

"And Lamals. You'll be the queen of Lamals," Steve said. Then he squeezed Nancy's rear end, kissed the side of her face, and stood up.

Moving forward at a jog, Steve took only two seconds to get to a full-on run.

Which immediately became leaping strides.

Getting both his feet under him, he kicked off the ground.

And flew away into the night. Straight towards Linne's citadel.

Thirty-Three

Slamming into the top of the citadel fortress with far more force than he'd been expecting, Steve grabbed at it with his whole body.

He needn't have worried about falling off, though. In fact, he should have been far more concerned with the fact that he wasn't Human.

There was a loud crackle as a spiderweb of cracks spread out in a vaguely humanoid shape.

"Oh, fuck," Steve grumbled, laying a hand on the stonework. "I'll have to get that fixed after I stuff Linne's head up her own ass."

Looking down, he could see guards moving around below. They seemed agitated, but they were all looking toward the stream of Creep and zombies going through the open gates of the citadel.

"Yeah, that'd probably make me rather angry, too," Steve mumbled. "I'll need to make sure I use only witch-knights and Creep Witches for the citadel. Loyal to me and no one else."

Frowning, Steve looked at the stonework in front of him.

As far as he could remember, Linne was in this part of the building, though more towards the bottom of the top. He wasn't quite sure what was actually up here.

Steve shrugged. This was as good an entry as any.

Pulling with his fingers, he forcefully dislodged several large stones. He pulled them free one by one and hurled them into the Creep lands.

The last thing he needed was any of this falling on the soldiers below him.

After working a number of stones free, he managed to make a hole large enough to get through.

When he peered into the dark interior, Steve couldn't see or hear anything. Nothing to tell him if this was actually a room that led down toward Linne's bedroom.

Probably a damn sealed-off attic with her "good" twin she's kept locked away since birth.

The evil cunt.

Stepping into the room, Steve scratched at his stomach. Then he looked down at himself when it felt like he couldn't really reach it.

He was wearing the armor Airlea had made him.

Patting the plates over his stomach, Steve knew he needed to thank her. He didn't need armor, but the effort and craftsmanship she'd put into it was at a master's level.

More so than that, it'd been made out of Kassandra's scales.

Walking deeper into the room, Steve kept his eyes moving. He needed to find a way out or down from here, but so far he hadn't seen anything at all. It was starting to look like this really was just a sealed-off room.

Steve bumped into a pillar he hadn't seen, then took a few steps back.

Shit. Okay, yeah. I'm in some type of... load... bearing... ceiling... place.

Whatever.

Off to one side, Steve could see a faint bit of light filtering up from the ground.

Moving that way quickly, he found it wasn't anything he'd been looking for, but it might do.

The mortar that was holding the bricks together here seemed to have partially crumbled away.

Frowning, he looked down at the light that was allowing him to see his boots.

Okay. Ah... I guess I could break into whatever room that is from he – AHH!

Steve was caught off guard as the floor fell out from under him, the stones giving way under his weight.

Steve crashed into a table and ended up splayed out on top of it.

He didn't hurt at all, but the wind had been knocked out of him.

Wheezing softly, he rolled to one side and fell off the table.

"...was that!?" said a voice from not far off.

Groaning, Steve scurried forward and slid behind a counter. Pushing his back up against it, he had to grab his pickaxe and shovel as they partially came out of their loops. Their handles wedged into the ground.

"What...?" asked a second voice.

"The ceiling?" replied the first voice. "Yeah, the ceiling. Do you think—"

There was a soft yelp, followed by a clatter. It sounded like more stones were falling.

"Mortar's little better than sand," said the second voice. "Look at this. I can just touch it and—"

There was another bang as what sounded like a stone fell and slammed into the coffee table.

"Stop it—are you trying to make it worse? You're as dumb as the pen soldiers sometimes," lectured the first.

"I mean, the masons are going to have to pull it all down anyways. Don't be such a bitch," complained the second. "Look at this. It's just crumbling apart."

"Stop it. Whatever. Let's just... go report this and get it cleaned up," said the first with a sigh.

Steve heard the click and tap of boots leaving after that.

Well. I'm inside... now... so... now what?

I should have brought Lucia or Nancy with me.

Standing up, Steve pulled his axe out.

There was no one in the room with him. The two soldiers really had left.

Looking around, he got the impression he was in a rarely used guest suite. Bathroom, bedroom, and study included.

Chewing at his lip, Steve skulked over to the doorway. He needed someone to tell him where Linne was.

The two soldiers who'd just been in the room were nowhere to be seen when he peeked around the corner.

Guh. For fuck's sake.

When he moved into the hallway, Steve only found a set of stairs. He went down them and eventually came to a small common room with multiple doorways and stairs. A few led up, but many more led down.

Fortunately, Steve actually recognized this place. He'd been on a never-ending climb upward last time, but he remembered walking through here.

One of the staircases here led straight to Linne's private rooms.

Oh, this isn't so bad after all.

Moving up the stairs, Steve nearly ran over two soldiers who were coming down.

He smashed one with his axe in the chest and grabbed the other around the throat.

Groaning, the woman who no longer really had a chest went down in a heap and a clatter. Blood and gore splashed all over the stairs as her corpse started to slide down them.

"Well, fuck," Steve said, looking to the soldier he had around the throat. Giving her a light squeeze, he smiled at her. "Now… I'm looking for Linne. Is she at the top of these stairs?"

Nodding her head rapidly, the soldier — who was holding on to Steve's wrist with both hands — was already starting to turn bright red.

"Mm, well, alright then," Steve muttered.

Holding onto the soldier, he walked down the stairs to find the corpse at the bottom. He grabbed her by a limp arm and started dragging her up the stairs. In his other hand, he held on to the other soldier by the throat. He was being careful not to kill her, though. He might need her, for all he knew.

"Any other guards up here?" Steve asked, looking at the soldier.

She shook her head, holding on to his wrist and looking more like a tomato.

"Huh. Any reason I need to keep you alive?" Steve asked.

Wincing, the soldier didn't seem to know how to respond to that. She forced her watering eyes open and looked at Steve.

Opening her mouth, she tried to say something, but Steve's grip was too tight.

He moved his thumb and released his hold on her.

"Well?" he asked, quirking a brow.

"No," said the woman with a sputter.

Huh.

Shrugging his shoulders, Steve pressed his thumb back down and put pressure back on the soldier's throat. Then he started climbing the stairs again.

He appreciated honesty and blunt responses. He understood them.

When he reached the top stair, Steve knew exactly where he was. Moving quickly, he entered the study he'd found Linne in last.

"What is it?" asked a voice from around the corner.

Steve immediately looked at the soldier still in his hand. Then he motioned with his head toward Linne and let go of her throat.

Taking a gasping breath, the soldier nodded rapidly as she looked up at Steve.

"Well?" called Linne, sounding much angrier now.

"Sorry, Commander, I only came to report that I've taken care of the issue per your orders," said the soldier. Her voice only sounded partially strained. "The chamberlain reports it should be cleaned, cleared, and repaired by tomorrow evening."

"Oh. Alright," Linne replied, sounding much more bored than annoyed now. "Good work. You may go."

"Of course, Commander," said the soldier.

Nodding his head at that, Steve smiled at the soldier. Then he closed his hand on her throat again and began to squeeze. Her face instantly turned red, and her eyes teared up and closed.

After dropping the corpse of the other soldier into a chair nearby, Steve turned and closed the door behind him.

As he walked through the study, he found it was exactly as he remembered it.

He passed through a doorway to find he was now in what was likely Linne's bedroom.

But there was no commander.

Peering around, he found another doorway off to one side. Now that he was closer, he could hear the soft splash of water.

Figuring the commander was taking a bath, Steve walked over to the bed and pressed the soldier down into it.

Slowly, he let go of her. Her strained soft breaths normalized in about a minute. Then her eyes opened.

Reaching down, Steve tapped her leg.

"Put your—"

Before he could finish telling her to put her legs together, the soldier spread her legs wide apart, and her hands moved down to her belt buckle.

"Uh, no," Steve denied in a whisper, already realizing what she was doing. "Put your legs together. Going to tie you up."

The soldier looked absolutely thrilled at that idea, in comparison to what she'd clearly thought he wanted. Nodding her head, she pressed her hands together in front of her, and then her legs.

Reaching down to the soldier's belt, he started to unhitch it.

"I won't... I won't do or say anything," said the soldier, staring up at him with wide green eyes. "I'll just lie here. Promise. I'll just... lie here and... be quiet."

"You'll be quiet?" Steve asked, looking into her face.

She was cute, much in the way so many lower-class soldiers were. Steve would say she wasn't to his personal taste, but she wasn't bad looking.

"Yes," declared the soldier. "Yes. If you mount me, leave me here, beat me, I'll be quiet. Just... ah... just... don't kill me?"

Steve wrinkled his nose at that.

He had no intention of raping the young woman. She wasn't a champion he was supposed to kill, nor was she his opponent in any way.

This woman was little better than what a farmhand would be to Steve.

"Then lie there and be silent," he said.

Licking her lips, the soldier smiled shakily at that. "Yes. Lie here, be silent. Ah... I'm... I'm—"

"Not interesting to me," Steve said, giving her a weird look. "Shut up."

Shaking his head, he moved away from the bed and crept up on the bathroom.

Linne was indeed bathing. She was casually lying there in the water, unmoving. The beautiful cat-girl was soaked, her hair wet and pulled back across the top of her head.

Grinning, Steve walked into the bathroom openly. His heart was hammering in his chest. Just looking at this woman made him shiver uncontrollably with rage. His skin felt cold, and his stomach folded in on itself.

"Weren't you leaving?" asked Linne, not bothering to open her eyes.

Reaching the tub, Steve squatted down in front of it, staring hungrily at Linne.

"Leave. I don't have any needs right no—"

Linne's nose twitched once, and her ears slowly flattened to the top of her head. Suddenly, she let out a slow breath, sinking into the tub, her chin tilting toward her chest.

"Hello, Steven Bril," Linne muttered.

"Evening, dead lady," Steve purred at her.

"I… I didn't know," Linne said, not opening her eyes. Her hands sank into the tub and moved to cover her womanhood. "I had no idea they were your wives. I truly… truly didn't know. I had… I didn't know."

"Awfully sweet of you to say that," Steve said, getting closer to Linne. To the point that his mouth and nose were next to her ear.

Sniffing at her, he pressed his nose into her ear. Then he proceeded to smell down the side of her head.

"I… yes. I mean it. If I had known they were yours, I wouldn't have taken such an ac-ac-action," Linne said, her words catching as Steve leaned back up to her ear and sniffed it once more.

"And how do you plan to make it up to me, Linne? You killed four of them. Four of my wives," Steve whispered, his left hand coming up. "Killing you rather than handing you over to the queen for execution seems ideal to me."

Trembling, shaking, and looking more like a claw, his hand hovered in front of Linne's throat.

Tear out her throat and fuck her right in the eye as she dies. Right through her pretty eye and into her rotten brain.

"I-I-I'll do whatever I must, of course," Linne said. "I'll be your wife, your-your-your everything. I'll bear you as many children as I can. I'll give you so many litters that-that you won't even know what to do with them all.

"I've never been married and my whole—"

Steve rested his hand on Linne's throat, his fingers slowly closing into her soft flesh.

"Do you really think you can take their place?" Steve asked, his lips inside her ear now. He wasn't squeezing the life out of her, wasn't even causing her any harm yet, but he had a very firm grip on her throat. "Can you bed me with the ferocity of four women? Cater to my needs as if you were four women? Can you truly give me everything they could have?"

"Of-of course," Linne said. "I'll make your entire life a blissful one. I-I-I can be anything to you. I'll do anything to you, or for you. You can do anything to-to me."

"And what would be your price for all of this? Mmmm? What would you want for me to let you live, Linne?" Steve asked, his breathing becoming almost irregular. He wanted to sink his teeth into Linne's ear and tear it off her head.

She smelled like flowers and soap. He wanted to defile her, break her, and then murder her.

Leave her broken corpse at the bottom of an outhouse.

He'd rather sleep with a zombie than Linne.

"Oh, j-just my life. That's all," Linne said as if it were the easiest thing in the world. "That's it. Nothing else. I'll give you all of m-me in exchange for you letting me live.

"I'm sure I'm worth more alive than d-dead."

Leaning up, Steve sank his teeth into Linne's ear. Biting down just hard enough that he knew it was probably a slight pain, he pulled at it.

"Ahhhh, p-please," Linne said. "Don't. I can give you so much. I'll do so much."

He pulled harder on her ear, until he got the impression he was just a little way away from breaking the skin.

Sighing, he let go of her ear.

A better man would kill her and spare her humiliation. A better man would let her end her life without suffering.

A better man, Steve was not.

"No," Steve said, and started to squeeze just a little harder. "But if you give everything to me in exchange for absolutely nothing, I might accept that.

"Oh... would you rather drown in the bathtub... or be strangled?"

Wheezing, Linne lifted her chin up. Her hands fluttered in the tub, but she seemed to resist the urge to grab at him.

"Okay," she croaked. "E-e-everything for nothing."

"Accepted," Steve said, pressing his teeth to the side of her head. He scraped his teeth along her flesh, contemplating how much damage he could do to her but still keep his promise to Nikki. "Drowning or strangling?"

"I didn't know, Steve. I didn't know. I didn't, I really didn't, I wouldn't have—" Linne groaned when Steve closed his hand tighter, cutting off her words.

"No more apologies," Steve said. "You're my property. Willingly. Aren't you?'

Linne nodded her head, unable to speak, her face starting to sweat. She still kept her hands in the tub, though.

"Now, drowning or strangling?" Steve asked, moving down to bite her cheek. He did ease up the pressure on her neck, though.

"S-s-s-strangling," Linne whimpered.

"Delightful," Steve said, and then proceeded to do just that. He knew how much pressure to apply now that he'd actually practiced with Nancy.

Ten seconds in, he let her go when her body started to tremble in the tub.

Taking in a massive gulp of air, Linne let out a sob.

"Please, Steve, master, lord, my owner, please," Linne begged in a pant. "Please. Please. Everything of me is yours. There's no need to kill me. I can do so much."

"Hmm," Steve said. Then he turned his head toward the bedroom.

The soldier was lying there, exactly in the position he'd left her in. Her hands over her chest, ankles together, straining to watch him while only moving her head.

"You, get my pet some clothes," Steve said. "We'll be leaving momentarily. I need to take her home and get her settled."

"Yes! Of course! May I move?" asked the soldier.

"Yup, get going," Steve commanded.

Hopping off the bed, the soldier immediately scurried off.

"Thank you—thank you, Steve, thank you," said Linne, sounding extremely relieved. "Thank you. I'll serve you so well. So well. I'll be your everything. As many children as you want, sex in any way, as often as you want. I'll… I'm yours. All yours."

No. You aren't.

You'll be a corpse.

But you don't need to know that right now. Clearly you were smart enough to know your place. To surrender and give your wretched self to me.

Clever enough to sign yourself away for nothing.

- 345 -

But… it won't matter. You'll die, and I'll enjoy it. Until then, though, your absolute humiliation will be more than enough.

More than enough.

There was a vague heat in his pocket. It was steadily growing hotter by the second. To the point that it was actually getting uncomfortable.

Holding tight to Linne's throat and ignoring her constant stream of thanks, promises of sexual heaven, and all the duties she'd commit to, Steve leaned away from her. He reached into his pocket with his right hand and found what was causing him a problem.

Sitting in his palm was the green stone he'd received from the river.

From Misty.

He felt distinctly that it was unhappy with him. Unhappy with how he was behaving.

Guilt immediately welled up from inside him. He knew this was indeed not something Misty would wish.

Except… she wasn't here to tell him that. All that was left of her was maybe, possibly, the stone in his hand.

And there was no proof of that.

None.

The reason Misty wasn't here was because Linne killed her.

Killed her, Xivin, Shelly, and Kassandra.

Holding Linne by the neck, Steve stood up, frowning. Not struggling, not even bothering to hold on to his arm, Linne gurgled softly, dangling in his grasp. Water ran off her and into the tub, her pristine skin glistening.

Her reaction to everything, that she was so complacent, so willing, and so absolutely defeated, made it harder for him to simply bash her head in.

Contemplating the stone in his hand, Steve was conflicted.

No… we'll… no.

Setting Linne down on her feet, Steve moved his hand around to the back of her neck. She wasn't going to be let go for any reason until they were much further away.

Then Steve tucked the stone back into his pocket. The uncomfortable heat didn't fade or go away.

Instead, it served as a reminder for him.

To keep moving and complete his promise to Nikki.

"I name myself the citadel commander," Steve muttered as he stewed on his anger for Linne.

Thirty-Four

Steve began to slowly walk Linne down the stairs from her personal rooms.

The soldier, whose name he'd refused to learn, remained in Linne's bedroom. Only after having gone and fetched Steve an iron collar and a good length of heavy iron chain.

Linne was wearing that collar now, and the heavy iron chain was linked to her collar and clutched firmly in Steve's left hand.

"If you misbehave at all, my pet, I'm going to yank on this chain," Steve growled. "I imagine it'd break your neck, or simply remove your head. Do you understand?"

"Of course. I understand completely," Linne promised. "I'm all yours, Steve. All yours. Do with me as you please. Just give me direction."

"Tell everyone who asks that you're my pet, you're doing what you wish, and you're leaving with me. Instruct everyone else to stay here. Just like I told the soldier back there to tell everyone," Steve commanded. "Oh, and get the gates closed on the Creep."

"Certainly. That's not a problem at all. I'm your pet, after all," Linne said easily.

Steve grunted, really not liking that answer.

Her complete subservience really was keeping him from turning her head into paste. But it also set his nerves on edge. To say Steve was leery and distrustful of her was an understatement.

Rattling as they went down step by step, the chain felt like a firm, reassuring presence in his hand. As if it didn't weigh anything at all and was actually holding Steve up.

When they reached the disgusting bloody mess that had been a soldier earlier in the day, Steve found a group of soldiers waiting there for him.

Each one had a spear and was wearing full armor.

"Good evening," Steve said, giving Linne's chain a very light pull.

"Good evening," Linne said. "I'm going for a walk with my master. I'm very excited for this opportunity to be with him. I'm not sure when I'll return, but I don't think it'll be anytime soon.

"Please pass my command to my champion and instruct everyone to remain at the citadel, while closing the gates to the Creep."

"C… Commander Linne?" asked one of the soldiers. They all were pointing their spears toward Steve.

"Yes?" Linne asked.

"Are you… alright?" asked a second soldier.

"I'm very well. As I said, I'm going to go for a walk with my master. I'm extremely excited to be able to do this," Linne said. "Now, if you don't have any other questions, please get out of the way. My master is a busy man."

"I… alright… Commander," murmured the first soldier who had spoken. One of their number left at a jog, more than likely to go inform the champion who was receiving command.

All the spears were lowered.

Steve and Linne passed by them without incident. Though Steve did stare at them as they walked by, as if daring them to do something.

When they reached the bottom of the stairs, Steve realized just now how stupid this was going to be. They'd need to walk across a whole lot of real estate to get to the front gates.

Staring at the two guards on either side of the door, Steve had a brief trip down memory lane.

Last time he'd been through here, he'd nearly been assaulted and kidnapped by the soldiers.

"I'm going on a walk with my master," Linne said, as if that explained everything.

"I… what?" asked the guard Linne had addressed.

"Please open the door. I'm going on a walk with my master," Linne said.

The guard blinked, then opened the door, saying nothing else at all.

Moving out into the fresh air, Steve briefly considered grabbing Linne and just leaping out of here. He wasn't sure if Linne would survive the jump, though.

Then again, does it matter?

Deciding he wanted to just jump his way to safety, Steve pulled on Linne's leash.

"You! I challenge you!" came a shout.

Looking toward the owner of the voice, Steve found a rather large, muscular, and beautiful version of Linne. Same species, same coloring, same features. Though a bit more angular in the cheekbones and jaw. Even the color of her eyes was the same as Linne's.

Though this woman was taller than Kimor and Siena both.

"Uh huh," Steve drawled.

Hey, Shitty Steve, tell me about big and muscular over there.

Aubrey Ainne
Beastkin
Family- none
Champion- champion of a citadel city
Temporary Citadel City Leader- leader of a citadel city

"You related to my pet here?" Steve asked, holding up Linne's chain.

"Your… what?!" asked Aubrey, her blue eyes going wide.

"She's my pet. Now, are you related to her?" Steve asked again.

"She's… much removed from my family, though we are of a relation," Linne said mildly. She turned to look at Steve. "I technically have no family, however."

"Huh," Steve grumped, looking back at the rather large and impressive cat-girl champion. "If I win, I'm keeping you as a prize. You'll be made to pleasure me with your mouth on command, and I may eventually bed you.

"And yes, I require a bet. Otherwise there's no reason to fight you."

"Hmph, stupid. You don't stand a chance. I agree," Aubrey said, folding her arms across her breastplate. "If I win, you'll be my personal sex-slave. I'll rent you out by the hour and feed you Harden until your heart gives out."

"Oh? Alright," Steve said. "Though before we begin, we'll need another iron collar and chain. I'll hold both of you with the left hand, and you can start earning your keep tonight, Aubrey."

Growling, Aubrey flicked a hand at someone else nearby. Then she picked up a very large two-handed mace that was nearby.

"Going to have to try not to kill you with this. You can still hump a bunk with only one arm, right?" Aubrey said, sneering at him. "Might turn your bones to powder."

"Hah, yeah. Don't worry, though—I won't hurt you at all. I'm going to slap you down till you surrender," Steve said, thinking back to how he'd won Kimor.

"Slap me? I'm going to take your arm, after all!" Aubrey roared and then charged him.

Not releasing Linne's leash, Steve stood there and waited.

Aubrey swung her weapon across at him, far outside of his range and reach.

Not even trying to step away from it, Steve stepped into it and punched out at the head of the mace.

A massive clang sounded, and the sharp crack of her handle breaking in half was like a thunderclap.

The head of Aubrey's mace shot away and smashed through a soldier standing nearby.

Pulling on Linne's leash, Steve moved forward toward Aubrey, who had been spun around with the force of his punch. So much so that she'd ended up falling to her knees, facing away from him.

"Huh," Steve said, walking up behind her. Reaching down, he wrapped his right hand around her throat and then pulled her up to her feet. "Well, that was rather brave of you. Very brave considering you've likely seen me fight before."

Steve peered into Aubrey's face as she scrabbled at his wrist with her hands. Trying to find some way to break his hold on her throat.

Somehow, she squirmed out of his grasp and took several steps away from him. Her hands came up in some sort of defensive pose.

"Very brave," Steve said with some admiration. "You're probably as stupid as Kimor, though. Maybe more so. At least she'll have someone to talk to about dumb things."

Aubrey sniffed at that and then launched forward, her fists moving faster at him than he could actually register.

Steve's head cracked to one side and then the other. Aubrey went low and put two punches into his stomach, then threw an uppercut that actually snapped Steve's head straight up.

Feeling like she'd actually rung his bell, though it didn't really hurt, Steve looked back at Aubrey. She was a few steps away now, looking pleased with herself.

"Wow," Steve said, actually wondering if he had to take her seriously to a degree. She was simply faster than him. Using a weapon had slowed her down.

"You like that?" Aubrey said. "You're welcome to admire me. Maybe I'll let you mount me once rather than having you on your back, if you do."

"I mean… they were good. But… you did notice it didn't do anything to me, right?" Steve asked. "Or… I guess… you really are dumber than Kimor."

"I'm not dumb," Aubrey said, her face pulling down into a frown.

"Yeah, you're dumb," Steve said. "But so very, very brave. I like it. I like it a lot. I'm going to try to be gentle now, okay?"

Aubrey wrinkled her nose and actually hissed at him, baring sharp fangs.

In a flash, she was moving toward him again.

Steve didn't bother to try to doge, block, or move away.

Instead, he just focused on slapping Aubrey as gently as he could.

There was a whipcrack-like sound, and the massive cat-girl went sprawling to the ground in a heap.

"Shit. Are you okay?" Steve asked, immediately moving over to Aubrey.

Slowly, shakily, Aubrey got to her feet.

"I'm gonna… gonna beat you down," she slurred. "You stupid… stupid stupid."

"Did… you just call me a stupid stupid?" Steve asked, grinning.

"Stupid stupid," Aubrey repeated, her eyes almost unable to track him.

Sighing, though still grinning, Steve walked up to the cat-girl and grabbed her around the throat with his free hand.

Aubrey futilely grabbed at his wrist. This time, she wasn't able to slip away from him.

Ignoring her attempts since she couldn't do anything to him, Steve began to gently squeeze down on her neck. Pulling her in close, he began to inspect her face.

He couldn't see any harm that he'd caused.

Okay. She looks okay. I probably just... nearly gave her a concussion? I'll make her drink some of my canteen. Maybe make her finish it off.

Pity it's the last of my watering-can water. Need to get to Filch.

"Your kin here is rather pretty, my pet," Steve said, looking deeply at Aubrey. Her cheeks were starting to turn red, and he could hear her breathing, though clearly it was a bit of a struggle.

"Aubrey was always the pretty one in her family," Linne said.

"Alright. You done, Aubrey? Or do you need another slap?" Steve inquired. He really hoped she was done.

Such a brave little thing. I want to keep her and take her home.

Hiren, Beati, and Felisa didn't even try.

You'll be a lot of fun to train as a witch-knight, I bet.

Even if you are stupid.

"Beat-you-down," Aubrey gurgled.

"Right. I'm going to slap you again, okay? I need you to hold your teeth together so you don't lose any or bite your tongue," Steve instructed. "Do you understand?"

"Ride-you-after-I-beat-you-down," Aubrey got out.

Laughing at that, Steve sighed and set Aubrey down on her feet again.

"Clench your teeth, love," Steve said. He really didn't want to hit her again, but she was leaving him with no choice.

Aubrey leered at him, her lips spreading into a smile. A trickle of blood was seeping down from the corner of her mouth.

Must have bit her cheek. Damn, I wish —

The massive cat-girl promptly fell flat on her face, unmoving on the ground.

"Oh. Good," Steve said. Reaching down, he flipped Aubrey over on her back to check her over.

Snoring hard and heavy, the champion was completely out.

"Eh... she's fine," Steve said, prying at her jaw to look into her mouth. He could see exactly where her teeth had cut into her cheek. It didn't look too bad.

"Who's got that collar and chain for me?" Steve asked, looking up to the surrounding soldiers.

They were standing there in absolute shock.

"No one? Do I need to start handing out beat-downs?" Steve asked. "Someone go get me an iron collar and a chain. I have to take my pets on a walk."

Several soldiers in heavy bronze armor, veterans of the citadel, the endless war with the Creep, and having lived a life of never-ending combat, went scurrying in every direction. Clearly intent on doing what he'd told them to.

"Good," Steve said. Then he looked back at Aubrey. "Ah, my poor love. I do hope you'll wake up soon. Carrying you on my shoulder will be rather awkward when I'm holding Linne's leash."

For whatever odd reason, Steve felt a strange affinity for the hulking idiot known as Aubrey.

He could truly appreciate someone charging forward, despite what anyone else would think, and just fighting. In truth, it felt a lot like his entire life up to this point, regardless of how short it had been.

Grabbing Aubrey by her breastplate, he heaved her up onto his left shoulder. He curled his left arm around her thighs and gave Linne's leash a tug.

"Stay where I can see you, my pet," Steve commanded.

"Of course, Master," Linne said, moving quickly to stand in front of him.

Standing there, Steve decided to wait for Aubrey's collar and leash.

***

Snoring away, Aubrey was quite asleep. Sprawled out like someone trying to make a snow angel, the big woman took up a lot of space.

When Steve had removed her armor, he'd found she was put together in a lovely way that he was quite appreciative of.

A lot of money had been sunk into Aubrey. A lot of money.

So much that Steve had briefly lamented for the poor girl's mother when she had inevitably found out Aubrey had joined the military.

Linne wasn't far away, sleeping as well. Her leash was tied to Aubrey's, and both of them were wrapped around a large tree, then staked to the ground with a log Steve had found.

Yawning, Steve put his hands on the top of his head and decided to go for a short walk.

With the gates of the citadel shut, there wouldn't be any Creep moving over the land tonight. Though any existing zombies would still be out and about.

He was also feeling rather thirsty.

Aubrey had woken up for a brief period, and Steve had forced her to drink the contents of his canteen.

As soon as that was done, she'd passed out again. There wasn't much else he could do for the poor girl until he got Gwendolin to look at her. It'd have to wait till then.

Or I just… have a Creep bite her, then dunk her in the water. Probably would be easier for her while she's kinda out of it.

I'll ask Lucia about it.

"You've completed all of your tasks but one," said a voice out of nowhere. "While it's pointless to tell you, as you won't understand, I must abide by the rules we put down."

Growling, Steve glanced at the sky above him.

"You know," Steve said. "I'd almost prefer it if you didn't talk to me."

"What?" asked the voice.

"I'd almost prefer it if you didn't talk to me," Steve repeated.

"What?" asked the voice in the same exact tone.

Deciding to be an ass, Steve grinned.

"I'd almost prefer it if you didn't talk to me," Steve repeated for the third time.

There was no response from the voice above.

Nodding his head, Steve started walking again.

"You do not wish to speak with me," said the voice after what was perhaps a minute.

"I don't see a point in talking to you," Steve admitted with a shrug. "You won't tell me what's going on, and you offer no information. It'd be easier if you didn't talk to me."

"I understand," said the voice. "Last time, you weren't as abrasive."

"That's nice," Steve said nonchalantly. "We both agree I'm not the same person I was before."

"You are not," said the voice. "Which lends itself to your success."

"So I'd assume. So I'd… assume. Well, if that's all you had, you can go now," Steve said, excusing the voice.

"I am not yours to dictate commands to," said the voice. The tone hadn't changed, but Steve definitely felt something there.

"Oh? And how would I know? I don't know who you are, I don't know your relation to me, and I don't even know what you are," Steve said. "As far as I'm concerned… you're a figment of my imagination. Maybe I'm crazy?

"I should just stop listening to you, in fact. Go away, figment. You may leave and not come back again."

A strange sensation was growing in the back of Steve's head. A headache that made everything feel heavy.

Heavy and like the world around him was starting to grow blurry.

Fuzzy, almost.

Like static.

"You will know me then," said the voice. "I'm your lord and master. I'm the only thing responsible for you being alive. You may not know it, but your death would have already occurred without my interference."

Unable to keep himself upright, Steve slowly sank to his knees. He felt absolutely sick.

"You are here by my wish. If it pleases me, I shall wish you into nonexistence as quickly as you would flush a toilet. You will not speak to me as such, ever again, or I will make you and yours suffer for all eternity," said the voice. It was the same neutral tone throughout, despite what was being said. "Do you understand, Steven Bril?"

"Yup," Steve rasped. "Got it. Got it."

Instantly the pressure and sickness vanished, as if it had never been there and was only a dream.

"Your life is to complete the task I've set forth for you. You've made choices on how to accomplish that, and now you must follow through with it. Whether you remember doing it or not," said the voice. "This conversation is over."

Panting, Steve rolled over onto his back and stared up into the night sky above him.

My life isn't my own... I am to the voice as my witch-knights and Nancy are to me.

Ah.

Irony.

It tastes awful.

Now... I just need to figure out a way I can slip out of their grasp. While protecting everyone.

Hmm.

Thirty-Five

"This it?" Aubrey asked, walking with her hands on top of her head. She seemed rather well at ease. Especially for someone who'd had the silly slapped out of them and then fallen unconscious for a day.

"It's the farm," Steve said.

"Farm my ass. Could put a carrot in my asshole and call me a farm, too," Aubrey swore.

"I… what?" Steve asked, looking at the massive cat-girl. Her leash dangled between her and Linne as if it were nothing at all.

Aubrey was far stronger than Steve had expected.

"I said you might as well shove a carrot up my ass and call me a farm, if that's a farm," Aubrey said, gesturing at the farm.

The palisade wall stood tall and strong, the moat in front of it quite wide. Between the moat and the wall were barricades made out of sharpened logs.

Behind all that were the witch-stone towers. Those reinforced defensive points were spread throughout. Each tower was clearly manned with people utilizing bows.

"Guess I'm putting a carrot up your ass and trying to farm you then, cause that really is a farm," Steve said.

Smirking at that, Steve shrugged his shoulders. They'd been walking since first light when Steve had realized Aubrey was actually awake.

All morning long, she'd been rather amusing.

And she was truly as dumb as Kimor.

"Bullshit. Farms are supposed to be… uh… open fields with pigs, goats, cows, and stuff," Aubrey said. "Aren't they?"

"I'll be sure to check on that while I stuff that carrot up you and see if I can't plant some seed in you at the same time," Steve replied calmly.

"I'm not a farm. You can't grow seeds in me. Are you as stupid as you are good looking?" Aubrey asked, smirking at him. "That's okay. I'll still take your carrot."

Okay… dumber than Kimor after all.

That's fine, though. It's alright. Dumb and brave is great. Fight everyone, never give up until you can't fight anymore.

All the inspiration I need for my own struggle.

Since Steve had realized he was on a leash himself, almost all his attention and brain power had been turned toward that problem. He didn't want to remain under someone else's power any longer than he had to.

"Likewise, Aubrey. You're as stupid as you are beautiful," he said, smiling back at Aubrey. "That's okay, though. I'll give you my carrot as often as you can handle it."

Aubrey laughed at that, turning to look back at the farm.

"Hey, let's fight later," Aubrey said. "Or make Linne fight me. Or some other people. I wanna fight. I like fighting."

"Insufferable buffoon," Linne said under her breath.

Walking as far away from Aubrey as possible, Linne had been moving as if she didn't have a care in the world. In the last few hours, though, her demeanor had shifted slightly.

The complete surrender and absolute devotion to him was cracking. She was getting snippy and was clearly annoyed.

Though it was all directed at Aubrey, not Steve.

It was becoming quite clear that Linne couldn't stand the larger woman.

Lying flat on the ground, the drawbridge was empty and clear. Obviously someone had seen Steve coming long before he'd seen the farm.

Nancy came out from the interior of the farm, moving at a light jog.

"Hold up, we'll wait for her here," Steve murmured.

Aubrey let her hands fall to her sides and then sighed, sticking a finger into her mouth and picking at something in her teeth.

Linne crossed her arms and looked quite bored with everything. Though there was no sign of any defiance in her.

Nancy was moving quickly toward him, so they wouldn't have that long to wait. She rapidly closed the distance and walked in close to his side.

"Steve," Nancy said, pulling his head down.

Expecting a kiss, Steve was surprised when Nancy pressed her mouth to his ear instead.

"I just arrived this morning," she whispered. "Everyone else is at the outpost, getting ready. Geneva and the royal guard witch-knights are all heading for the citadel city already."

Oh? Good, that makes everything easier and —

"Nikki sent for the queen's justice the same day you left," Nancy continued. "They're due to arrive tomorrow. They sent a messenger ahead.

"I only found out because I spoke to Gwen about it."

Blinking slowly, Steve didn't know how to react to that. If true, it meant Nikki had planned ahead for him. So that he wouldn't have to tolerate Linne after bringing her back home.

Part of him regretted that they'd be arriving so soon. He'd been hoping to learn more about Linne and see what was going on in her head.

Over the morning's march, he'd begun to suspect she hadn't surrendered as completely as she'd let on.

Steve wanted to pick her apart.

"Thank you, my darling mistress," Steve said, then tipped Nancy's head to one side and kissed her. Pulling away quickly as he didn't want to cause a scene, he put his lips to her ear. "Take the big one—her name is Aubrey—and make her a contract. Get her bit by a Creep and transfer her into a witch-knight contract. Fast as you can. Then take her to the outpost to start training with the others."

"Okay," Nancy said, her hands resting on his shoulders. "Darling, hmm?"

Steve didn't respond. Instead he grinned and gave her hip a pat.

Turning away from him, Nancy walked over to Aubrey.

"Hello," she said, waving a hand at Aubrey. "I'm Nancy. I'm going to walk you through your introduction to service. Your duties will be—"

"Am I going to get to fight?" Aubrey interrupted Nancy.

"Uhm, yes," Nancy said. "It's one of the primary duties you'll be handling. As well as devoting yourself sexually to Steve and servicing him with your mouth and—"

"Do I get to fuck him?" Aubrey asked, breaking into Nancy's spiel again. "No marriage, just fucking. Never gotten laid, but if I'm going to be devoted to him, I wanna fuck him."

"I… that is—"

"Yes," Steve said, trying to step in and save Nancy from the brutal onslaught that was Aubrey. At the same time, he smiled at the big champion.

If she wants to do that, who am I to argue?

"More often than not, you'll end up just sucking me, but we'll definitely fuck too," Steve said crassly, trying to speak to Aubrey's point of view. "You good with that?"

"Huh. Yeah, whatever. Don't know how to do any type of fucking, though," Aubrey said with a shrug of her shoulders.

"I'm sure we can get you all trained up," Nancy said. Then she reached up and took hold of Aubrey's leash.

Getting the picture, Steve separated Aubrey's from Linne's and then let it drop.

With a grunt, Nancy picked up the chain and started to roll it up.

Aubrey reached over and took it from Nancy, flicking it over her shoulder.

"Get movin' short stuff," Aubrey said. "Sooner we finish this, the sooner I can fight someone. Or fuck Steve. Whichever."

"Yes, we'll—yes," Nancy said, turning away from the farm.

Steve knew they were going to wander off into the distance, form the black-magic contract, and go to the outpost. They didn't need to be here.

"Shall we continue, my master?" Linne asked, smiling at Steve.

Apparently, the fact that Aubrey was leaving had put Linne in a much better mood all of a sudden.

"Yep," Steve said, starting forward again.

"Centaurs with riders!" called a voice from one of the towers as Steve put his first foot on the bridge.

What?

Looking into the farm, Steve saw Nikki, Gwendolin, and Ferrah. Nia was already sprinting back for the home, Gwendolin urging her on.

Shit.

Pulling his axe out of its loop, he let out a short breath.

He was confident in himself now. Confident and felt like he could handle anything anyone threw at him.

Looking out toward the west, Steve could see the Centaurs now. They were riding hard and fast for the drawbridge. On each of the Centaurs rode another person.

"Mages," Nikki said in a whisper, and he glanced at the Faun. He hadn't noticed it, but she must have hopped her way over.

Gwendolin and Ferrah were both also heading for the homestead now.

"Mages?" Steve asked, looking back at the Centaurs.

"Mages," Nikki repeated. "Those who can cast and utilize mana. As soon as a Mage or Wizard is discovered, they're immediately sent to the capital for training.

"There's… maybe twenty in the whole of Lamals."

Linne was watching Nikki and Steve, her brow furrowed. Clearly their exchange had left her with a few questions he'd have to explain later.

Actually. Probably not. If those are Mages, that means it's the queen's justice. Right?

She's as good as dead.

Maybe the fact that the citadel commander is going rogue panicked the queen.

As they slowed down to a trot, it was clear the Centaurs had spotted Steve. They were also smart enough to not come up at a dead run. That'd be likely to get them fired on by the towers.

No sooner had the lead Centaur stopped in front of Steve than their rider hopped off. They wore a full helmet, mask, and garments that covered them from head to toe. Steve was almost positive it was a woman, given that men were so rare, but there was no way to tell.

"Greetings on behalf of the queen," said the mage. Their voice sounded oddly hollow and high pitched.

"Allo," Steve said, not putting down his axe. "I'm Steve. This is my farm."

Pulling back with his left hand, he forced Linne to come up to his side.

"This is my prisoner, the one-time commander of the citadel," Steve said, his voice quite cold. "You may check her accolades and titles to confirm her status and just what she's done."

Linne sidled up to Steve casually and looked at the Mage.

"I see," the Mage said. "She's… your property."

"That she is," Steve confirmed. "By her own will. Aren't you, my pet?"

"I'm indeed the possession of my master," Linne said.

"The queen received your missive," said a second mage, getting down from their Centaur mount as well. "We were dispatched as soon as we received it. Would you be Nikkolet?"

"I am indeed," Nikki said. "This is my husband, Steven Bril. Owner of this farm and the enchanted tools that keep it maintained. He's also wedded to Geneva Gosti, the military commander of the area, as well as a princess of the Fae courts."

"So I noticed," said the second mage, putting their hands behind their back. "Very accomplished. I understand your reasoning for pointing that out, however. At this time, the priestess and her believers are in... a delicate position with the queen. Laws involving the crown and the church have been suspended. Such as marrying outside your race."

"Good," Nikki said.

Everyone fell silent at that. More and more Mages dismounted, spreading out in a line in front of Steve.

"You... subdued the commander by yourself?" asked one of the Mages.

"I did," Steve said. "And her champion as well."

He was getting a strange feeling about these Mages. Like they weren't here for his benefit. Like he wasn't going to like this at all.

"Well," Steve said, not willing to sit in this silence any longer. "I've captured my prey. I'll be going home now to decide what to do with her. I'll decline the bounty on her head for the time being as well."

"We can't let you leave," said the Mage who'd spoken first. "At least... we can't let you leave with the commander."

"The one-time commander. She's not the commander anymore," Steve said. "I am. And why can't you let me leave with what's mine? What's mine by her own choice?

"You chose this, didn't you, my pet?"

"I chose this," Linne said, nodding her head. "I'm with my master."

There was a strange tension building in all the Mages now. It made Steve want to start killing them.

Now.

"By royal decree of the queen, Linne Lynn is pardoned of all crimes, negative accolades, and restored to citizenship status," said the second Mage.

"Oh, thank heavens," Linne said, reaching up to start pulling at her collar. "Could any of you please get me out of this before this pig decides to do something stupid?

"I'm lucky he didn't try to bed me on the way here. I thought for sure I'd end up having to nearly kill myself with herbs to end a pregnancy."

I... I... what?

Steve pulled on Linne's leash, drawing her up to his chest.

"I beg your pardon?" Steve asked, glaring at the Mage. In his right hand, his axe felt ready.

This was more than a simple impasse now.

"The queen requires Linne Lynn be returned to her. In recompense for your losses, the queen awards you the title of citadel commander," said one of the Mages.

"She offers me nothing I didn't already have," Steve said. "And is trying to take something from me that's mine.

"Are you telling me she views my wives' lives as little more than... nothing? That murder is excusable depending on who it is?"

"I cannot speak for Her Majesty. I can only carry out her orders. Please hand over Miss Lynn," said the Mage who'd dismounted first.

"Maybe... maybe we should just let this happen," Nikki murmured from beside him.

Steve was thunderstruck in that moment.

As if someone had sucker punched him and left him in the desert for a day.

His mind couldn't process what he'd just heard. Nor could he handle it at this moment. Steve felt as if he'd just lost everything and everyone important to him.

Slowly, his fingers loosened their grip of Linne's leash, the chain slipping from his hand.

Linne scurried away from Steve and dodged into the ranks of the Mages.

"Her Majesty appreciates your compliance," said the Mage. "And... for what it's worth, I'm sorry."

Standing there, shocked and unable to comprehend anything, Steve watched as Linne was pushed up onto a Centaur.

In less than seconds, Linne, the Mages, and the Centaurs were gone.

Leaving behind Steve, who felt like he was dead.

"I'm so glad you listened," Nikki said, patting his back. "Thank you, my brute. I really thought—"

Steve jerked away from her touch, not wanting to even look at her.

"Traitor," he hissed.

Moving away from Nikki, Steve headed off toward the house.

He needed to get going, and he had no time.

Need to plan. Need to get things ready.

Need to… need to… need to fucking wreck the queen and take Linne back, and kill her.

She's mine to kill. Mine. No one else's.

"I… Steve, wait," Nikki called, hurrying after him. "I'm not a tr-traitor! It wasn't worth fighting Mages for. We have so much to live for and—"

Steve pulled away the moment he felt Nikki's hand on him again.

"She killed Misty, Xivin, Kassandra, and Shelly. Maybe you don't care, but I do," Steve said. "They were my wives, and I loved them. I may not be the best at expressing grief or even having emotions most of the time, but I knew I loved them. And I miss them.

"And that… that monster… killed them. And you seem to think that's okay."

"Of course, it's not okay," Nikki said, still trailing after him. "But we can't fight the queen. She's the queen! We should… we should just… live our lives. Do our best to move on and live for those we lost.

"We have so much now. We can do whatever we want."

"What I want? What I want is to pull Linne's head off her shoulders, put it on a spike, and leave it overlooking the cemetery she caused," Steve said. "That's what I want. And you… you think… you believe… that you can just… live in harmony with these bastards.

"With the queen. Like you can bury your head in the sand and it'll all just pass over without a concern?"

"She made you the citadel commander," Nikki said. "That's practically the second-highest position in the whole country. Of course she had to pardon Linne."

"No. She didn't have to. She could have realized Linne was a murderer, what she'd done and was doing, and given her to me, or executed her," Steve growled. "I cannot accept she had to pardon Linne. Not even for a millisecond."

Steve had kept moving the entire time, reaching his tool shed. Where he kept the tools he didn't normally travel with.

Grabbing all of them, he bound them up with two cords and put the bundle over his shoulder.

"What... what are you doing?" Nikki asked.

"I'm leaving," Steve stated. "There's nothing here for me now that you've decided our marriage doesn't matter. That we don't stand as one. That you would rather duck your head and bow it than fight for justice for your wives."

"No! Steve... no, you... no. There's no reason to leave," Nikki said, her hands immediately latching on his arm. "We can talk about this and work through it."

"I don't want to!" Steve shouted, finally looking at Nikki. It made him sick to his stomach. "I don't want to talk about it at all because there isn't anything more to say. You didn't want to fight for the justice Misty, Xivin, Kassandra, and Shelly deserved. You wanted to just... roll over... and let it happen.

"Well, I'm not going to do that. I'm going to go get justice. And if that means murdering the queen on her own throne, then fucking so be it."

"No, Steve, no. That's... no. Your place is here, with me," Nikki pleaded. "Remember? I'm your Faun, and your Faun needs you. I need you here with me. Everyone here needs you. The living need you."

Steve snorted at that and gestured with his hand at his farm.

"I haven't been home in a long time," he disagreed. "It grows quite well on its own without me. All it needs is a feed from the watering-can. And I'll make sure that happens, regardless of whatever I do.

"It'll be just like it is when I'm not here. I just won't be coming back, that's all."

"What?" Ferrah asked.

Looking over, Steve found there was literally a crowd standing there.

Ferrah, Lucia, Jaina, Geneva, Ina, Gwendolin, and Airlea.

"The queen just pardoned Linne for murdering Misty, Xivin, Shelly, and Kassandra," Steve said. "I'm going to get justice for them. If that means a civil war or killing the queen, so be it."

"Oh," Lucia said. "Okay. Are we leaving today?"

"No, we're not leaving at all," Nikki said. "We're going…we're going to stay here and live on. We're going to live for the living, and let the dead rest."

"That's certainly not a position I can adopt," Geneva said mildly. "I'm not so sure about killing the queen, but I'm all for seeking justice on Linne. She's been a problem for my family in the past."

"No, no. No, this isn't something we can do," Ina said. "We need to stop. This is anger talking. We need to just settle down and really talk this out."

"Yes! We could petition the queen to reconsider," Airlea said.

"That and this is home," Ferrah said, nodding her head. "This is where we should stay."

Gwendolin scoffed at that, folding her arms across her midsection.

"This is exactly what I'd expect from the queen," Gwendolin hissed. "She'll send husbands and sons to die for no reason other than to die.

"Then care not at all for those left behind as families are shattered and broken. We should get justice for our fallen and put the queen where her ass should be."

Suddenly, everyone began arguing with one another. Voices raised, and then became shouts.

Shouts became outright yelling.

"I don't care what we do," Jaina said, not far from Steve. "I love you. I just want to be with you and have lots and lots of sex."

Snorting at that, Steve smiled at the Kobold.

At least I have one in my corner no matter what I choose.

"Alright!" Steve shouted, getting everyone's attention. "If you want to stay here, stay here. If you want to come, come. My goal is to get justice, and I know where that starts."

"Nia!" Gwendolin called, moving toward the house. "We need to pack up! We're going on a trip!"

Lucia nodded at that and followed Gwendolin into the house.

"Where should I station my forces?" Geneva asked.

"Citadel city," Steve answered.

Nodding at that, Geneva left at a very quick jog. Her armor rattled as she went.

"Steve…" Nikki said in a soft voice. "Please… stay. We can… work this out. Come… come to bed with me. Let's make time for one another and then talk after you get some of that anger out. Okay? Please?"

Turning to Nikki, Steve smiled sadly at her.

You're still a traitor.

Leaning down, Steve kissed her cheek and patted her shoulder.

"Be safe," he said, then turned away from her. He had to fetch the watering can and get back to the Creep lands.

Moving over to Ferrah, he grabbed her up in a hug and held tight to her.

"I love you," Steve said in her ear. "I'll come back eventually."

Ferrah hugged him back, though it was obvious she was rather upset.

Shuffling away from the Dwarf as she started to look like she was going to cry, Steve moved to Ina.

"Steve, just… stay with me," Ina said, smiling at him. "Stay with us. I know I can… I can do a lot to take your mind off things. And we could start trying for kids.

"Besides, you know you'll miss what I've got if you leave."

Grinning at that, Steve couldn't deny it.

"I will miss you, Ina, and I love you. I'll come back, and we can try then if you like," Steve said.

Grumpily, Ina hugged him, leaving a rather ferocious bite mark on his neck.

Last was Airlea. He hadn't known her long, but she'd done well by him.

"So soon?" asked the Unicorn.

"Yeah. But I'll be back. Just you wait and see. Then we can pick things up from there. If you want," Steve said. "I'm willing, if you are."

Airlea sighed, smiling at him.

"I'll wait. You're interesting. Though I do think you're making a mistake," admitted the Unicorn.

"Probably. We'll find out," Steve said. Then he left.

The queen had declared war on him.

Steve was going to respond.

Time was wasting.

Epilogue

Standing at the edge of the farm, Steve felt like he'd made more than enough progress in the last month.

"It was a little close here and there, but... ehhh... we're good now," Steve said, leaning on the hoe.

"It really was, wasn't it?" Gwendolin said with a heavy sigh, putting her hands on her hips. In front of her was a wheelbarrow filled to the brim with vegetables.

It'd taken some doing, but they'd managed to find any and every seed, tree, and vine Steve could ever want. Including fruit trees and nut trees.

He glanced at her belly, not very happy with her right now. Despite starting to show her pregnancy, the Siren refused any and all requests for her to not work the fields.

"Don't," Gwendolin said, smiling as she stared out at the field. "Pregnant or not, I can pitch in, and you need the help."

He couldn't argue that point.

The simple reality was the witch-knights spent most of their days and nights battling the Creep and its inhabitants.

If he hadn't converted the entire royal guard to witch-knights, he wasn't sure he'd be able to hold this land as he was.

A high-pitched keening sound rang out. Loud, shrill, and echoing, it seemed to endlessly travel over the open dead plains of the Creep lands.

"Sunset in an hour," Gwendolin said, grabbing her wheelbarrow. As she lifted it up, Gwendolin's newfound muscles bunched on her arms. Easily, smoothly, she began walking her load toward the warehouse and root cellar.

Nodding his head, Steve looked out toward the massive witch-stone tower Lucia was in. She'd been posted up there during the sunset watch.

The simple reality was that Lucia could see further, hear more, and actually be heard, given her odd vocal talents, better than anyone else.

That very same tower doubled as a water tower, and below it was a massive reservoir. Steve wasn't sure it would do much, but he wanted to see if he could get the water to spread that way as well.

From that water tower, though, water spilled endlessly.

All that water ran into the new river that was life here in the Creep lands. The only reason they were able to grow anything in these barren, forsaken lands was the watering can and its cleansing effects.

Forming a channel, it ran through their farm, plains, and the area they'd claimed for themselves. From here it traveled down to the citadel city, all underground and out of sight.

Then on to Filch and back to its normal channels.

Steve made sure that Nikki and the farm wouldn't notice a difference at all.

Deciding it was time to head in, since being outside during sunset was just asking for trouble, Steve started making his way for the massive farmhouse that he, his family, and his personal witch-knights worked out of.

Reaching the sleeping Kobold who never left his side, Steve bent down and lightly scratched at her stomach.

"Wakey wakey, my pretty Kobold," Steve murmured. "Time to head in."

"Nnnngh," Jaina groaned, rolling onto her side and curling up around Steve's food.

"Come on. We need to get a move on," Steve said with a laugh.

"Carry me, I'm tired," Jaina complained.

Rolling his eyes, Steve reached down and grabbed Jaina's rear end.

"Get moving and I'll make sure to visit you tonight," Steve said.

Sighing, Jaina got to her hands and feet. Then she grabbed Steve's hand and bit it gently, following that with several licks.

Laughing, Steve flicked a finger against Jaina's brow and pulled her to her feet.

All over the farm, those who had been given tasks in the fields were heading home. Most everyone here had been given their own small dwelling. It wasn't luxurious, but everyone had their own.

The wood was all chopped down in Lamals and shipped along the river. Though there was an entire forest being grown as well.

Passing under the tower, Steve spotted Nia. She was diligently using a stone to shape a stick.

Curious, he drifted a bit closer to see what she was doing.

"She's making a bow."

Looking to the speaker, Steve found Nancy.

He grinned and raised his eyebrows at that.

"Lucia's teaching her," Nancy said, walking up on Steve's right. "Jaina."

"Nancy," Jaina replied, grinning at Nancy.

Everyone who'd come with Steve had become complicit in this venture. And grown all the closer for it.

Slipping her arm through Steve's, Nancy walked along with him.

"Few more arrivals showed up today," she said.

"Oh?" Steve asked. A number of unmarried young women had all started moving into the Creep lands. Predominantly, they were coming out of the prisoners Steve had captured.

In exchange for their freedom, they became Creep Witches and took on black-magic contracts with Nancy.

"More little girls barely able to wed," Nancy said. "They'll be earning their bite tonight."

"Hum," Steve mumbled. "Whatever. It's their choice."

"Gennie came as well," Nancy added.

"Oh, guess I'll be visiting her tonight," Steve said.

"Lucia's doing a very good job of managing everyone," Nancy said.

Walking to the back of the manse he lived in, Steve shuffled up to the empty trough there. A quick couple pulls on the handle from the pump nearby got him some water pumped up from the reservoir.

They'd discovered quite a few convenience technologies in the ruins. Ruined and left to rot.

Imitating and repurposing the tech wasn't hard.

"Haha, that's what you get," crowed a voice nearby.

Glancing over as he washed his hands off in the trough, Steve saw Kimor and Aubrey not far off. Kimor was wrestling with getting a tunic over her head.

"You're the idiot who said it'd work," she complained bitterly, the fabric caught up in her antlers. She was giving Steve a rather lovely show at the same time.

"Yeah, I was wrong," Aubrey said. "I could pull on it really hard?"

"No, idiot, you'll rip it," Kimor said.

"They really are… stupid," Hiren said with a sigh, walking up to his side.

"Yeah. But they're fun," Steve said with a grin. He liked Kimor and Aubrey. Both of them constantly wanted to fight. Him, each other, anyone.

Didn't matter the odds, they wanted to fight.

Right now, he really appreciated it.

"I… guess," Hiren replied. "Everything alright?"

"Yeah, just coming in for the evening," Steve said, looking up at the Human witch-knight. She wasn't their leader, but his personal group of knights were looking to her more and more.

And Hiren looked to Nancy for direction.

"I'm going to take 'em out to the castle area just before sunset. Been finding unique and interesting Creeps over there," Hiren said. "Giving us a chance to break into groups of two and train."

"You don't put," Steve said and paused, pointing a finger at the two women who were now both struggling to get the shirt either on or off Kimor, "them together, do you?"

"No. No, no. They'd wind up dead," Hiren said with a laugh. "I take Kimor, and Felisa takes Aubrey. Beati and Siena pair up after that."

"I'll go with you," Jaina said, nodding her head. "I'll maintain the dome. Yes, yes."

"You're welcome, of course, Jaina," Hiren said with a wide grin. "You're always welcome. Your power is a blessing and a great reassurance for us."

Jaina grinned at that, looking quite pleased with herself.

"There you are, Steve," Geneva said from behind him.

Apparently, everyone was looking for him today, or wanted to be nearby.

"I've got a letter for you," Geneva said.

"Oh, thanks, Gennie," Steve said, grabbing the fabric rag nearby and drying his hands off with it. "Can I see you tonight?"

He tried to get ahead of them asking him to bed. For whatever reason, it felt more genuine for him to ask than to make them ask.

"I... I'd be delighted," Geneva accepted with a happy tone. "Uhm, just... before dinner maybe? Feels like my food goes everywhere when we do it after... and the baby gives me some terrible indigestion, too."

"Course. Love you, Gennie," Steve said, then kissed Geneva lightly before going into the home. He never wanted to disguise his feelings again after having lost so many people in his life.

Walking into the manse, Steve headed straight to Lucia's bed. This was where he spent every night now, and it was more or less his room.

Sitting down on the edge of the bed, Steve broke the wax square that held the letter shut and unfolded it.

Dear Steve,

Ina's offered to write this letter for me, so I'm taking her up on it!

Steve's eyes flicked down to the bottom of the letter and noted it was from Nikki. Frowning, he considered tossing the letter aside immediately.

After a few seconds of that thought, he sighed and continued.

First, I love you.
I desperately miss you and am maintaining our farm in readiness for when you come home. Everything is going quite well and normal here.

Although Ina and Ferrah miss you. (Ina: I really, really, really miss you. Come home?) Airlea seems rather forlorn, but Unicorns often like to overdramatize such things.

I swear it's like she's in a romantic tale and her husband's gone off to war.

Steve smirked at both Nikki's comment and Ina breaking into the letter. He could see what Nikki meant about Airlea, though. She'd had an interesting disposition, from what he'd seen of her.

Enart dropped by to hand off some more plants, seeds, and the like. She said she still has no intention of marrying.

Ever. Or anyone.

But that she appreciates your willingness to let her come and go as she pleases.

The mayor Geneva installed defers to me on anything I bring up. On the expressed orders of Geneva herself. Please do be sure to thank her for me, just in case I haven't had a chance to thank her myself yet.

Do remind her as well that she's always welcome to come home, with or without you.

Other than that, I can only reiterate again that I love you. I know you disagree with me and how I wish to treat this, but I cannot help but want to let it pass. Let it pass and live our lives.

I'm sure you think me foolish and optimistic. Naïve, I'm sure.

But that doesn't change that I do strongly feel that our lost would agree with me. I think they'd be rather saddened to see we've separated ourselves from one another.

And beyond that, I know that you'll come home to me eventually. I'll wait for you, and when you do come back, I'm going to be angry at you.

For at least a little while. Until we have sex.

I think you called it anger sex at one point? It really did help alleviate some of it.

You're a stupid brute of a man.

But I desperately love you, and I want you to come home.

Tell you what, if you come home with this letter in your hand, I'll pretend nothing ever happened. Come home and conquer your Faun instead of a queen?

Pausing, Steve was sorely tempted to go straight back to Nikki. He didn't agree with her.

He felt mildly betrayed by her, in truth.

But he did love her. Deeply so.

If not, that's alright as well. I'll just keep mailing you every week until you come home.

I wouldn't mind if you wrote me back? If only to keep up communication?

Honestly, I'd be rather distraught if I thought you were ignoring me outright. I know I upset you, angered you, and possibly hurt you, but

I really am doing only what I think is best for our family. The living members of our family.

Well, I'll close this letter and get it sent. Today's the third day of the second week of the last month of fall.

I hope this reaches you quickly.

With all of my love and more,
Your Faun, Nikki

Sighing, Steve looked at the letter for several more seconds.

"And I'm doing what I feel is best for our family," he said. "Because honestly… I don't for an instant believe the queen would have left it the way she had. Not at all.

"But there's no way you'd see that until it was too late. So I'll protect you, my traitorous Faun. Even as you wound me.

"Because I love you."

Steve took the letter, walked over to the bedside table he'd made, pulled out a drawer, and dropped it in.

He'd write her back later tonight.

Even if he was angry, sore, and hurt by her, he could at least write her back.

"Steve? Are you up there?" called Aubrey.

"I am," Steve called back. "What's up?"

"Can you help me? Everyone just—" There was a thud as it sounded like Aubrey hit something. "Everyone just laughs at me."

Grinning, Steve nodded his head.

"What'd you do?" Steve asked, walking to the doorway. He couldn't see down the stairs from here, but he'd hear her better.

"Kimor told me to put on a helmet and then put my tunic on over it. Now it's stuck," Aubrey said.

Yeah… those two really are stupid.

Good thing I've surrounded myself with a lot of intelligent women to make up for my dear sweet idiot duo.

"Can you make it up the stairs?" Steve asked.

"Yeah, comin'," Aubrey said, her heavy footfalls coming toward him.

"Can't promise I won't get handsy with you, though," Steve said.

- 376 -

"Huh? Oh, that's fine. You always do a little bit of that when I suck you off," Aubrey said, getting closer. "We gonna fuck soon?"

"Probably. Just haven't had the right time for it yet," Steve said. "Come on over here, you big dummy. I'll take care of you."

"Okay, thanks. You're pretty nice, you know that? I thought for sure my life was done for. One way or another. Really thought I wasn't going to wake up after you hit me," Aubrey said, stumbling into Steve's room. "Oh, there you are."

"I try to be, and I really was trying to hit you as gently as I could. Didn't want to hurt you," Steve said, looking at Aubrey. The helmet was on correctly, and even the facemask was down hiding away her features, but the tunic was wedged in tight to it and didn't seem like it was going to be going anywhere.

"You're not gonna rip it, are you?" Aubrey asked, sounding rather sad. "I really like this tunic."

Rolling his eyes, Steve abandoned the idea of tearing it off her.

"No, I won't rip it. Just sit down," Steve said, taking Aubrey by the elbow and guiding her over to the bed.

"Are we officially an army now?" Aubrey asked, the helmet turning partially toward him as she sat down.

"Suppose so," Steve answered as he started to pull at the tunic to get it up and back over Aubrey's head. "An army on the brink of declaring civil war while clearing the Creep and all the lost lands it entails."

"Okay," Aubrey said, her hands sitting in her lap. "Is it okay that I don't care about that? I just wanna fight and fuck. Is that alright?"

"I mean… sure? Did you have someone else in mind you wanted to fuck, or—"

"Oh, no, no. Just you. I just want to fight and fuck you," Aubrey said. "The other girls said you don't fuck your witch-knights, though."

"I don't," Steve said, pulling a corner of wedged fabric away from the helmet. It came loose with a ping and the tunic came free. Exposing Aubrey's bare chest and all its glory to the world.

"Huh," Aubrey said, the metal helmet turning toward him. It was odd having a semi-naked woman wearing a helmet on his bed. "Would you fuck me first? That way I can lord it over Kimor? That'd wipe the smug grin off her stupid face. She keeps telling everyone she'll be first."

Grinning at that, Steve shrugged, laying his hands on Aubrey's extremely muscular and lovely body.

"Sure, why not? You can be first," Steve said. "Just not today, mind you, or right now."

Why not indeed?

He wasn't going to say no anymore. He wasn't going to decline what was rightfully his. He wasn't going to let anyone take anything from him ever again.

"Your hands are warm. Feels good," Aubrey said, not pulling off the helmet or pulling away from him.

I'll start by taking my pet back. And the queen. She can be my pet, too. I'll take their lands from them. And then… maybe the alliance, too.

They'd try to stop me, wouldn't they?

Nothing would ever be taken from Steve again.

Ever.

Thank you, dear reader!

I'm hopeful you enjoyed reading this story. Please consider leaving a review, commentary, or messages. Feedback is imperative to an author's growth.

Oh, and of course, positive reviews never hurt. So do be a friend and go add a review.

Feel free to drop me a line at:
WilliamDArand@gmail.com

Join my mailing list for book updates: William D. Arand Newsletter

Keep up to date — Facebook:
https://www.facebook.com/WilliamDArand

Patreon: https://www.patreon.com/WilliamDArand

Blog: http://williamdarand.blogspot.com/

My Personal Group:
https://www.facebook.com/groups/WilliamDArand

Harem Lit Group:
https://www.facebook.com/groups/haremlit/

If you enjoyed this book, try out the books of some of my close friends. I can heartily recommend them.

Blaise Corvin- A close and dear friend of mine.

He's been there for me since I was nothing but a rookie with a single book to my name. He told me from the start that it was clear I had talent and had to keep writing. His background in European martial arts creates an accurate and detail driven action segments as well as his world building.

https://www.amazon.com/Blaise-Corvin/e/B01LYK8VG5

John Van Stry- John was an author I read, and re-read, and re-read again, before I was an author. In a world of books written for everything except harems, I found that not only did I truly enjoy his writing, but his concepts as well.

In discovering he was an indie author, I realized that there was nothing separating me from being just like him. I attribute him as an influence in my own work. He now has two pen names, and both are great.

https://www.amazon.com/John-Van-Stry/e/B004U7JY8I

Jan Stryvant-

https://www.amazon.com/Jan-Stryvant/e/B06ZY7L62L

Daniel Schinhofen- Daniel was another one of those early adopters of my work who encouraged and pushed me along. He's almost as introverted as I am, so we get along famously. He recently released a

new book, and by all accounts including mine, is a well written author with interesting storylines.

https://www.amazon.com/Daniel-Schinhofen/e/B01LXQWPZA

Printed by Amazon Italia Logistica S.r.l.
Torrazza Piemonte (TO), Italy